"They're not going to blow up the world, Rikki. Not yet. And that's why we've got to make this conference happen so perfectly that the next time any military order to destroy is put out, from the Kremlin *or* the Pentagon . . . they'll be thinking about NEWS. About what NEWS is going to do. Because there are so many of us. Rikki."

And some of us will outsmart them at their own game, thought Sylvia.

Can they pull it off? Can a bunch of women really gain control of the world's most sophisticated computers and create the Action to make the empire-builders and the money-makers stop destroying the people and the Earth? Can the thousands of them together in NEWS truly bring peace and love into the world on a global scale?

D1372557

N·E·W·S

a novel

by

Heather Conrad

Published by Mother Courage Press

Library of Congress catalog card number 86-63765.
ISBN 0-941300-04-8

Mother Courage Press
1533 Illinois Street
Racine, WI 53405

Acknowledgments

I would like to express my love and appreciation to the following people whose creative assistance and moral support contributed so greatly to the completion of this book: Jane Ferguson, Deirdre Gillis, Gemma Grott, Art Rogers, Mindy Spatt, Sandra Treacy, Laurie Wager and deForest Walker; and also for the help and advice given by Robert Bunker, Al Conrad, John Kaman, Diana Rabenold and Beth Youhn.

The author gratefully acknowledges written permission to quote from the following sources:

"Arms Industry—A Sellers' Market" by F. C. Barnaby and "Atomic Colonialism" by T.T. Poulouse, reprinted by permission of *The Bulletin of the Atomic Scientists*, a magazine of science and world affairs. © 1978 and 1981 by the Educational Foundation for Nuclear Science, Chicago, IL 60637.

"Covering the Unthinkable" by R. Pollack and "Why Nonaligned Isn't Neutral" by Michael Manley, reprinted with permission of *The Nation Magazine*/Nation Associates, Inc., 72 Fifth Avenue, New York, NY 10011.

Cry of the People by Penny Lernoux.

"Fate of Nonalignment" by F. Ajami, reprinted by permission of *Foreign Affairs*, Winter 1980/81. Copyright ©1980 by the Council on Foreign Relations, Inc.

Sandino's Daughters, Testimonies of Nicaraguan Women in Struggle by Margaret Randall, New Star Books, Vancouver, B.C., Canada, 1981.

"Strategic Soviet Region" by Drew Middleton, (September 2, 1983) Copyright © 1983. Reprinted with permission of *The New York Times*.

The Third World Speaks Out" September 22, 1973, reprinted with permission of America Press, Inc., 106 West 56th Street, New York, NY, 10019. All rights reserved. © 1973.

For you, the reader

Chapter I

At 5:00 in the morning Sylvia woke, thinking of the conference. It had been in her dream. A small room, then a house, or cathedral, vaulted, huge spaces outlined in stone, neither outside nor inside. So many thousands of people filled the interiors she thought it would burst, then a voice began calling off numbers and a siren wailed in the background. She woke to the siren. Wide awake, she thought of Claire.

But Claire had been in the dream. Standing back, far, in an alcove, waiting, her brown eyes wide. That's when the siren had torn through the dream.

Sylvia turned on her side and waited for her mind to settle.

The conference.

Claire.

The conference. It seemed impossible. So little time and still so much to do, but how else could there be the direct communication needed? It had to be worked through. Though last night's meeting had seemed to make it less possible than ever, four hours of discussion and still the most basic logistics undecided, with 15 weeks left to prepare for 1,200 women from 40 nations and an issue as straightforward as housing still under debate. At that rate how in hell could they hope to bring off an action as outrageous—the shriek of the siren split her thought, the chaos of the dream. She threw herself to her other side.

Claire. For the first time they had seemed to be at odds at a meeting. It was as if the immense task of planning the conference had superimposed itself on the simple daily reality of their lives. Claire had almost seemed to be challenging Sylvia directly when she spoke of the need for interpreters at the conference. Every language must be interpreted by a native speaker. Ridiculous!

Sylvia threw herself on her back and stared into the predawn darkness. Just outside, the ceaseless revving of a car engine hammered at the early morning silence. She had a sinking sensation, yes, that Claire's insistence was arrogance, an obsession with her own language, not a real concern for the needs of the conference. "*Tu le crois!*" she heard Claire's voice. And with it another sinking sensation that in fact her own English-speaking dependence, privilege, had blocked her view of Claire's point.

She looked at the clock. An hour left to sleep. She would be more than busy all day today at work, and then dinner with Linda and Steven at 6:00. Tomorrow, Saturday, would be a succession of meetings, it was her turn to buy food for the house, and the laundry could not possibly wait another minute. Sunday. Sunday morning was free. Maybe then she could have time to think through her problems with Claire. Time to think. It seemed sadly strange to have to schedule the workings of her own mind. But there seemed no choice. She had to sleep, she had to make her living, she had to do her share of keeping house, she couldn't postpone the committee meetings, and she had to attend them to know what it was she needed to think about, at least in regard to the conference. And now she had wasted all this time figuring out that she had no time to think. But the trick had served its purpose, the conference, and Claire, slipped back into her unconscious as she drifted off into a quieter dream.

As Sylvia floated back into the oblivion of sleep, the city itself was just beginning the first stirrings of day. The rising sun splayed its misty light through gaps in the lifting fog, and the mournful cries of foghorns receded farther out to sea. The quiet empty streets were slowly filling with morning traffic, from the Embarcadero to Daly City, from Ocean Beach to China Basin. Streetcars and buses, gorging and disgorging their loads of workers, stumbled along through the rush-hour maze. Newspapers flung onto doorsteps in the last hours of the night, or wrenched from metal boxes on street corners in the first day's light, were opened and closed and discarded. Elevators hummed up and down the towers of offices piled on offices, monuments erected to business on the sandy slopes of downtown San Francisco.

In the Mission, shopkeepers opened their shades, strains of Latin music drifting from open windows as schoolchildren, laughing and scrambling, waited on street corners for their buses. Babies cried as mothers struggled to prepare their food, while police cars cruised the streets, bored, reading license plates, looking for the odd incident or random wino. Lines formed in front of the employment and welfare offices and conversations sprang up and warmed as the sun began to warm the day.

In the Outer Sunset and Richmond, the fog still lay thick as house after house flickered its lights and children and parents began their morning rituals. The paths of Golden Gate Park were lined with joggers squeezing in a morning run before called to their sedentary duties of the day.

In North Beach, the espresso machines noisily ground out their first cappuccinos as cafe workers waited on would-be poets who seemed to live on coffee alone. The bells of Saints Peter and Paul in Washington Square chimed to awake the hungry transients asleep on their benches, drenched in mist and dreading another day of scrapping and scamming for change.

In Chinatown, life had been pulsing since the first crack of dawn as crates were unloaded from trucks blocking traffic, burst open and emptied, stacked into doorways, sewing machines clacked under sidewalks, food was cooked, shops were opened, young and old moved into their daily routines.

On the northeast side of Potrero, the massive warehouses rolled up their aluminum doors as overalled, hard-hatted workers pulled out their equipment, grinding motors, metal on metal, as from the hill's warehouses to the basin's docks trains, trucks, ships were brought to life with the motion of workers.

On the southeast side of Potrero Hill, the early morning motion in the Projects had already been shattered by sirens as police crashed in a young black man's door looking for someone who looked like him. Women and men looked with hate, then looked away as children sick with the noise and lack of breakfast fought their way to the door and off to school and the streets.

In Seacliff, little could be heard in the empty quiet streets save the ocean surf pounding the rocks of the cliffs below. Hardly a sound came from the huge many-roomed homes, mansions really, that stood high on the bluffs overlooking the sea. Just once the purr of a garage door motor broke the silence as a white limousine loomed out of its housing into the road, and across the street, the strained breathing of an older black woman in a white uniform could be heard as she made her way up the hill to her employer's home.

In Noe Valley, young mothers fed their babies while their husbands dressed for work. Young men and women, briefcases in hand, strolled to their cars and bus stops for another day at the office, while the shops and cafes on 24th Street beckoned the day's business.

And not far away, in a third-floor flat on 26th and Noe, a clock-radio burst into the consciousness of its sleeping owner with the 7:00 a.m. news. A hand shot out to silence it, but the damage had been done. The hand stopped in midair, then fell with a plop to the bed. Steven Walden ground his teeth and stared wide-eyed at the ceiling.

The radio went on.

". . . two hours after leaving Anchorage, the Korean airliner and its 244 passengers strayed into Soviet airspace over Sakhalin Island and came to the attention of Soviet radar. Almost immediately Soviet jet fighters were in the air. At 3:26 a.m., a Soviet pilot reported that he fired a missile and the target was destroyed. All passengers and crew aboard the Korean jet were killed."

Steven stirred and muttered, "What the hell?" He looked at Linda. Linda was looking back at him, though her eyes were distant, struggling with the meaning of what she had heard.

The radio rasped on,

". . . the President is cutting short his vacation in California, and will return to the White House immediately."

"So. Ready for World War III, Linda?" Steven asked as he got out of bed.

"That's not funny, Steven," Linda answered as she turned her head to the wall. After a moment, as Steven was going through drawers, she said, "Steven, how do you think this is going to stop?"

He slipped his pens in his shirt pocket and reached for his tie. "The Armageddon. What else?"

Linda heard Justin talking in his crib, soon his calling for her would begin. She got out of bed and walked to the bathroom.

Steven went to the kitchen and turned on the kettle. Distracted, he worked to focus his thoughts on his 9:00 a.m. court appearance before Judge Whitmore. He could hardly endure being in the same room with the old asshole, let alone pleading a case to him. He just hoped it would end quickly. His client didn't have a chance anyway, everyone in the bar had seen her shoot the man. She'd been in and out of mental institutions for years. It exhausted him to think of it.

Linda walked into the kitchen with Justin, and Steven recalled the radio news. His eyes glistened as he looked at his son and for a moment he felt sick with fear. As Linda started Justin's breakfast, Steven poured her a cup of coffee.

"Where's the paper?" Linda asked.

"I'll put it inside when I leave. Are you going to be able to get everything done without the car? I'm sure I won't be home before 4:00."

"Of course, don't worry about it, Steve." She put her arm around his waist and leaned her head on his shoulder. Steven held her for a moment and then got his keys and kissed Justin.

"When is Sylvia coming?" he asked.

"At 6:00. I'll be home in plenty of time. I hope she remembers to bring those books for Aunt Maureen."

"Oh, I think she will. She knows we're leaving early tomorrow."

They kissed and he hurried down the hall and out to his car.

The motor ground slightly as he winced and shifted it into gear. He hoped the car wasn't deciding to fall apart now that they were finally going to get down to L.A. for the weekend. Linda's mother had been waiting for months for this visit. And Sylvia's mother, Maureen. She hadn't seen Justin since he'd been born. Everyone was really counting on this visit.

As he reached the top of the Dolores Street hill, he looked out at the day. It was a clouded sky, great billows of soft grey and white, yet somehow the sun's light cast through to give such a vibrant depth to the multicolored hillscape of houses, with the line of the bare golden hill beyond so sharply defined against the white-grey sky, it was as if a very old but luminous oil painting lay before him. Suddenly the rasping radio news sounded again in his ears. His eyes closed, tight, and then, looking back to the road, he drove on. His stomach growled for lack of breakfast, and he thought of Aunt Maureen, wondering if it would be painful for her to see Justin. It was clear Sylvia would never have children.

Arriving at the Hall of Justice, Steven discovered his hearing had been put over until after Labor Day. He felt the burden of having the case still on his mind, still more days of feeling there should be more he could do. He got back in his car and drove to the office.

As he picked up his morning mail and glanced through it on the way to his desk, a foreign stamp caught his eye. France. He didn't know anyone in France. He sat at his desk. Well, there was Claire, but he was quite sure she was here in the city. She hadn't been in France for years, and of course Sylvia would have told him if Claire were going back.

The postmark was August 18. This was the first week of September. Of course he would have known if Claire had left in August. But as he ripped open the envelope, he discovered only another sealed envelope with the message: "Please give this personally to Claire Duval," written across the front. He held it a moment, wrinkling his forehead. He felt a slight irritation with Claire and yet mildly amused at the same time. He put the envelope in his briefcase and looked at the rest of his mail. But his amused irritation gave way to curiosity as his mind stayed on Claire's letter. Why on earth would she find it necessary to give his office address for her personal mail? It was a liberty to take, whatever her reasons. Sylvia must know what it's about. Why hadn't she mentioned it?

A buzz on his com-line drew his attention back to the office. He realized he should let Linda know he wouldn't be using the car today after all. But he found himself getting up from his desk, ignoring the buzz, and running down the stairs to the first floor of the building. He picked up the last *Chronicle* at the concessions counter and headed back up the stairs.

Spreading the paper on his desk, he lit a cigarette and scanned the front page.

HOW RUSSIAN MISSILE SHOT DOWN AIRLINER
WRECKAGE TRACES SEEN
EXPERTS PONDER THE ATTACK
Soviet sensitivity over foreign radar penetration of
defenses guarding La Perouse Strait south of Sakhalin may
have been the motivation for the reported destruction of a
South Korean airliner by a jet fighter, according to
American officers. In war the strait would be the direct
route for the deployment of the Soviet Pacific fleet into the
northwest Pacific, the officers said . . .

Steven inhaled long on his cigarette and looked at the wall in front
of him. As if there were a movie screen, he saw a fleet of Navy
destroyers bearing through a choppy northern Pacific sea. In black and
white he saw the grey ships, flags snapping with ominous purpose,
Randolph Scott standing at the helm of the lead ship, giving orders to
the seamen. Groups of sailors in uniform taking their stations, looking
proud and sentimental, gripped with fear.

He shook off the image and sat at his desk, glancing quickly
through the front page article, but he could not get those young somber
sailors out of his mind, and for the second time that morning his eyes
glistened with tears.

His com-line buzzed again and this time he jabbed it down as he
picked up the telephone receiver. "Yeah? OK." He pushed another
flashing plastic button. "Hi. How'd you know I was here? My
hearing got canceled."

"Oh, I just thought you might be, Steve, I feel scared by this
missile thing, I really do." Linda's voice was strained.

"Oh, it'll blow over, Lin. They're not going to bring out the
bombs for one lousy little airliner. Of course, if it had been one of
ours . . ."

"Well, South Korean. It may as well be. Steve, I've been
watching the news on TV. Everyone is all hysterical and enraged."

"I know." Steven looked up as his secretary laid a note on his
desk. Judge Whitmore's clerk on five-eleven. "Listen, Lin, I've got to
go, I'll call you back in a few minutes. Maybe I can bring you the car
at noon. I'll call you back."

Linda laid the receiver back in its cradle, her lips still drawn to a
frown as she walked back down the hall to Justin's room. He was
squatting next to a pile of toys, painstakingly constructing a second
pile from the first, his lumpy, padded shorts seeming to ballast the
motion of his little arms as he tottered over his work. Watching him,
Linda found herself going to him, scooping him up in her arms and

holding him close to her as he squirmed in surprise, then settled into her embrace.

At 6:00 p.m. Steven turned the corner of 26th Street. Walking up his front steps, he saw Sylvia ringing the bell at the door. "Hi, Sylvia," he called.

"Hi, Steven. How was work?"

"Oh. Hard to keep my mind on."

"Mmm," Sylvia nodded as he opened the door for her and Linda came into the hallway.

"Hi, Linda," Sylvia said as she embraced her cousin and the three of them walked down the hall.

"Justin's still asleep. We were out all afternoon; he just went down around 5:30," Linda informed them both.

"What time are you leaving tomorrow?" Sylvia asked.

Linda looked at Steven who was on his way to the kitchen. "What do you think, Steve? Around 7:00?"

"If we're lucky," he called back as Sylvia and Linda turned into the living room.

"Well, Sylvia, I assume you've seen the papers," Linda began, an urgency in her voice as she sat on the edge of a rattan chair. Sylvia laid her package on the coffee table and sank back into the couch.

"Steven and I both just felt sick," Linda went on. "I watched the news all morning and, you know, it's hard to tell where this is going to go. It could just pass as another 'incident.' But then all this talk of moral outrage against the Soviet Union, like the people in Congress are outdoing themselves to think up adjectives for how 'deplorable,' how 'inhuman and evil' . . . Though Steven says he doesn't think this is the ultimate incident, World War III, but it is really stirring up anti-Soviet war hysteria. That draftable kind of patriotism, you know?"

"Oh tell me, god I do," Sylvia agreed, rubbing the back of her neck with her hand as she lay back into the sofa cushion. "It's perfect for playing up the need for more defense. And it gives Reagan just the excuse he needs to take a hard line in the arms talks. I almost think the whole thing was planned to cover up his military build-up in the Third World."

Linda looked up at the sound of Steven's laughter. "Sylvia, you don't really think the whole thing was planned by the CIA, do you?" he asked, walking in the room with a bottle of wine and glasses. "Of course, the whole incident is being exaggerated. The military is full of disgusting hypocrites. But I think it's going pretty far to say that they would actually plan to send a commercial airliner and over 200 innocent people to their deaths as a *media ploy*."

"Well, the Soviet Union is saying the plane was on a spy

mission," Linda interjected. "It does seem pretty strange that they were floating around off course for two hours over some major Soviet military outpost. But I really can't see using a regular airline flight for a spy mission."

"I'm not necessarily saying it was a spy mission," Sylvia said, taking the glass of white wine Steven held out to her. "Though god knows, it's happened before. In 1973 Israel shot down a Libyan passenger plane over the Sinai. Over 100 were killed then. And in the '50s an Israeli commercial plane was shot down in Bulgaria, on the same basis, that it was spying."

Sylvia turned to Steven as he sat back in his chair. "I know it seems unfathomably morbid, Steven, to think that a regular airliner and its innocent passengers would be sacrificed to make the Soviets look bad . . ."

"Sylvia." Steven set his own glass on the coffee table. "I know that the Soviets' shooting down this plane plays perfectly into the hands of everyone who's in love with the arms race. But I also do believe in the role of coincidence—chance—in international dealings. Not every single thing that happens is strategically mapped out by some diabolical force."

"Maybe not, Steven," Sylvia replied, sitting forward herself. "But you know that United States military maneuvers all over the world *are* very strategically thought out. And the fact that not 200, but thousands of innocent people are massacred or shoved into refugee camps as a byproduct of . . ."

"But, Sylvia," Linda reminded her, "the Soviet Union doesn't exactly hold human life sacred in Afghanistan."

"I'm not saying they do," Sylvia answered. "I'm saying that our government doesn't either. Not anywhere in the world. Human life is something to be manipulated for more power—and money." She sighed and leaned back, glancing at the clock on the mantel.

"Well, Sylvia. You create a pretty nasty picture," Steven said as he refilled his glass.

Sylvia took a sip of wine. "Really, Steven, don't you think the military mind, the same people who create the neutron bomb, the assassination of foreign presidents, torture chambers and dictators, the cover-up of Love Canal, Three-Mile Island . . ."

"Yeah, yeah," Steven said.

"Do you think they give a flying fuck about a few hundred people in an airplane?" she concluded.

"Well, there was the president of the John Birch Society on board," Linda recalled, and she and Sylvia laughed.

"They really are hypocrites though," Linda went on. "It is disgusting, Sylvia, I guess I know what you mean. Their whole outrage about innocent people dying is such . . . bullshit." She bit at her lower lip a moment, looking at Steven with concern. "But whether it was planned, or an accident, or whatever. I want to know what's going to happen."

Steven looked at his wife. Again he saw the faces of boys, young men in uniforms, fighter planes, video games. The rasp of the radio news sounded back to him,

> ". . . and eight minutes later, the airliner disappeared from radar screens. Target destroyed."

They were all silent a moment as Steven put his hand to his shirt pocket and, finding his cigarettes, put one to his lips, turning to strike a match. There was something he wanted to tell Sylvia, what was it? The sudden blast of jet engines overhead gave them all a start, the deafening roar seeming to take forever to fade off into the twilight.

Sylvia drummed her fingers on the side of her glass, an impatience in the sound. "It's this whole goddamn thing about *national security*. People cling to death to the idea, even if it means killing off the rest of the world."

"Yes, but, Sylvia, what do you expect?" Linda asked. "I mean, I can't really say I want foreign nuclear submarines prowling around off Ocean Beach. There's just something instinctive about wanting to protect your own. Your family, your home. Everyone longs for security. Everyone. Don't you think?"

"Yes, but that's just it." Sylvia looked at her cousin. "Everyone wants security for their own lives and their own ways, sure, and that's why the idea of 'national' security doesn't work. I mean, there's no such thing."

"Oh really?" Steven's laugh was abrupt.

"No, really, Steven," Sylvia said, turning to him, her eyes demanding that he take her seriously. "Look at the United States' idea of 'national security,' dominating and scaring off every other nation in the world. It doesn't work. Because the security of any one nation is impossible when it's threatening the security of others. It seems obvious. The idea of national security has to be replaced by the idea of international security."

Steven sipped at his wine, then looked at her. "Sylvia, I believe you. I believe that's true. And I wish to god those abstractions made an ounce of sense to anyone." He smiled.

"Steven. What is abstract about the survival of the planet?" She stared at him, angry now. "Look, 'national security' is a mythical 19th-century idea that works about as well as a king's mirror for a social perspective. This is an age of satellite communication, planetary

travel—very physical, real facts, wouldn't you say? Which make every
television-watcher around the world know that life today is a global
reality, and every act of any so-called nation is related to the act of any
other. There's no such thing as the security of *one* nation. There's the
security of all nations. International . . ."

"Sylvia, Sylvia," Linda stopped her. "You are being abstract. I
know what you're saying, but the fact is that 'every television-watcher'
is still mainly concerned that nobody else comes and messes with their
television. They might fight to the death for that." Linda stopped and
turned her head.

"MamaMamaMama . . ." Justin's waking chant broke through the
silent hallway, its soft refrain bringing Linda to her feet.

"I'll get him, Lin." Steven waved at her to stay as he rose from his
chair.

Sylvia looked at Steven, the exhaustion in the loosened tie at his
neck, the sweetness in his blue-green eyes as he glanced at Linda and
headed down the hall, his tawny hair rumpled, his shoulders straight and
stiff.

"I'm going to get dinner," Linda said as she got up from the couch
and began gathering glasses, the ashtray, and, glancing at the package
Sylvia had left on the coffee table, she asked, "So you brought those
books for Maureen?"

Sylvia looked at her a moment. "Oh. Yeah." She turned. "What
do you think, Linda?" she asked as she took the plastic shopping bag
from the table and, unfolding it, drew out two black and red ledgers.

Linda walked back to the couch and looked over Sylvia's shoulder
at the frayed books. "Was it hard to get them?"

"Not really. It only took a few hours. But god that lawyer is an
ass."

"And a sleaze," Linda added as she turned back toward the kitchen.

"Do you think Maureen's really committed to this search?" Sylvia
asked as she followed Linda down the hall. "I can't really say that I
understand it."

"Well, I can understand why she might be very interested in
researching her history. Though I know, Sylvia . . .'genealogy.' But I
don't think Maureen is looking at it to find out she's the long lost
daughter of a duke, you know. I honestly think she just wants to know
more about your father's family, the history." She stopped as she saw
Steven quietly shutting the door of Justin's room.

"He's going to sleep awhile longer," Steven whispered as they
walked into the kitchen and closed the door.

"Steve, will you get the salad out of the refrigerator?" Linda asked
as she took a steaming casserole from the oven and placed it on the
table.

"Steven," Sylvia asked, taking the salad from him as he searched for a bottle of dressing. "What were people at your office saying about this thing today?"

Steven sat at the table and reached for the bottle of wine. Somehow he couldn't bring himself to think of his office; he shrugged. "Oh I don't know." He poured wine into their glasses and, setting the bottle on the table, he glanced out the kitchen window, his eyes resting there. "I just can't help but think of that pilot, though," he said. "That Soviet pilot. What a choice to make."

Linda looked at him. "What do you mean?"

"Well, I just keep thinking of the inevitability of it all."

"Like it all started with 'Pong'?" Linda asked, seating herself at the table.

Sylvia laughed, nodding her head. "Yeah, it's frightening," she said as she took the dish Steven passed to her. "This looks delicious, Linda."

"And today I just kept thinking of those men, of the men who find their way into the Navy, the Air Force," Steven continued.

Linda reached for the salad. "How much of a choice do you really think it is though?" she asked. "I mean to shoot the plane. Just sitting up there in one of those fighter jets, some blip screen on the dashboard and orders from base."

"Really. Don't let Justin near 'Space Invaders,'" Sylvia warned her, laughing.

"That's not much of a joke," Linda said, looking at her cousin.

"You know though," Steven said, sitting back in his chair. "I think that human beings—trained, crazed, or computerized—we still have minds of our own. Evil by rote is a pretty horrible . . . "

"No, I don't think that, Steven. Like the pilot's a robot, or just a cog in the war machine," Sylvia said. She thought a second. "I mean, I think he really was faced with a moment of decision, but at the exact moment, he didn't *recognize* it as that. And I'm sure that now he's probably going crazy." Linda nodded as Sylvia added, "Or he's back at base having a party."

"Oh, Sylvia," Linda said, as Steven laughed and, reaching for his glass, he looked at the two women. "So you think the man is sick, or crazed, or doing his duty, or . . ."

"I think he had no idea of the consequence of his act," Linda answered as she got up from her chair and, going to the refrigerator, got a second bottle of wine.

"Yeah, because at this point in time," Sylvia said, taking a piece of bread, "so few people in life are faced with a moment of true judgment. You know?" She looked at Steven. "I mean some kind of deep challenge to our ethics that calls on the most profound . . ."

"What do you mean ethics?" Steven asked. "You mean when it's right and when it's wrong to kill?"

"Or destroy. Yeah," Sylvia answered. "I mean a life-or-death act. A decision that comes out of confrontation with some innermost sense of . . . of our own true power over life."

"Maybe that's true, Sylvia," Linda responded. "In fact most people just go through the motions of life, making an occasional superficial decision of wrong and right . . . " She paused as she refilled their glasses and, glancing at the food barely touched on Steven's plate, she gave him a curious glance.

"But not that soul-searching, wrenching, total act of judgment," Sylvia said. She lifted her glass, then set it back down. "You know this issue, it reminds me of that scene in *Doctor Zhivago*, where Pasha has to decide whether to attack that town. Remember? He has to decide whether to send the Bolshevik troops in to take Yuriatin where his wife is living. Lara. It could mean her death. And he decides to do it."

Sylvia looked at Steven. "In a way I always thought it was just too cold. It wasn't even real. But in war people really are faced with those kinds of decisions. And not just the generals. Everyone in the whole society is making those kinds of decisions, whether they recognize it or not."

"That's what I mean," Steven answered, sitting forward. "There is something about that choice. That choice as a soldier. Or, as you say, Sylvia, any member of a society at war . . . "

"That is manipulated." Linda said as she sat back down at the table. "Steven, don't you like the frittata?"

"Yeah, it *is* manipulated," he nodded, glancing at his plate. "I kept thinking today of every 1940's war movie I'd ever seen, including that one we saw the other night." He looked at Linda. "But then I think of the '60s. I'd thought they'd put an end to that kind of World War II patriotism, but . . . now there's something else going on."

"It isn't the World War II psychology, that's true," Sylvia agreed. "I don't think the noble American flag freeing the world can be played up so much anymore. I mean, like building up the fervor of the boys on their mission against Hitler. That kind of thing doesn't work now."

"But, Sylvia, that *was* a reality," Linda interrupted. "The Nazis were a sick, fascist . . . "

"No, but I know what you mean, Sylvia," Steven acknowledged. "There was some kind of false sentiment, or hypocrisy about it." He took a bite of his dinner.

"But there was the notion of moral purpose," Sylvia said. "Regardless of the economic motives our government had in that war and their own aspirations for empire, they still could claim a moral purpose."

"Yeah, and manipulate it," Steven agreed. "But in the Vietnam War it didn't work at all." He pushed his plate away. "This thing you're talking about, Sylvia . . . I think that Vietnam was a time when people, thousands of people were trying to make those kinds of stark moral choices."

"Maybe that's true, Steven," Linda said. "But I also think a lot of people just didn't want themselves or their sons killed. Morally or immorally. You know?"

"But, Linda," Sylvia gave her cousin a questioning look. "Don't you think there was more than that going on? So many values were challenged, not just in this country. . . "

"That's what's different now!" Steven slapped his hand on his thigh so sharply Sylvia thought he was irritated, fed up with the conversation, and sitting back in her chair she looked at him with widened eyes; but he went on, "The pilot in the helicopter still sees his target. The bridge, the village. He sees the fire, he hears the people scream. But a white dot on a screen . . ."

"Steven, who can hear screaming over the roar of helicopter engines?" Linda asked as she pushed back her chair and got up again.

Sylvia put her hand to her eyes, pressing them closed. "Do you have a cigarette?" she asked Steven.

"Let's go in the living room for coffee," Linda said as she cleared the dishes. "Syl, start the water will you?"

"I can't believe that Justin's still sleeping," Sylvia said as she filled the kettle.

"Oh, he hasn't had a nap for two days. I'm really hoping he'll sleep through until morning." Linda wiped off the table with a sponge. "Tomorrow will really be his first long, but *long*, car ride."

Sylvia laughed and leaned against the refrigerator. "It will be great for Rhonda to see him. And for Mom. She hasn't seen him at all yet."

Steven looked at Sylvia and his wife standing beside her. Both had the same thick wavy black hair of their mothers' family, Linda's gracefully curving at her cheek, Sylvia's tossed impatiently back from her face; but there Sylvia's resemblance to Linda stopped. Her features, though not small and classic like Linda's, were nonetheless attractive. The clean, sure lines of her nose and brow gave her large grey eyes a startling clarity. Though they were shining with a glint of affection as she spoke of her mother now, Steven couldn't help but feel that there was a sense of dejection about Sylvia tonight. Her long, lean body, clad in jeans and a loose dark shirt, seemed propped against the refrigerator, barely able to support itself. He felt a sadness for her, for whatever unknown sorrow was draining her vitality.

He stood up and, walking over to her, rested his hand on her shoulder. "Sylvia, I don't like to see you smoking." He laughed as she turned to glare at him. "OK, don't call me paternalistic. The cigarettes are in the living room, help yourself. I'm just going to check on Justin."

As Linda and Sylvia walked toward the living room with coffee and cups, Linda asked, "How are the conference plans going?"

Sylvia straightened her back as if stunned; and the image of Claire, standing alone in a cold stone alcove, was so vivid she stopped short at the living room doorway.

"That bad?" Linda asked as she moved past her and set the cups on the coffee table.

"No, no. Not bad," Sylvia answered and, after a moment, poured coffee into the cups. "It's just that, I know I shouldn't feel overwhelmed, but . . ."

"Well, not yet, dear," Linda said, putting her arm around Sylvia and kissing her cheek.

Sylvia smiled at her cousin and, with a laugh, said, "But Linda, you know really, somehow I am confusing this conference in my mind with . . . " She sat down. "Actually, Claire has been on my mind more than the conference. And I can't seem to stop that."

"You should stop that?" Linda asked.

Steven walked into the room and shut the door behind him. "I think he's going to sleep through, Lin," he said.

"Yeah, I thought he might. He was exhausted."

Steven sat down and handed a cigarette to Sylvia. "Did I interrupt something?" he asked.

"Oh hardly, Steven," Sylvia answered. "I was just trying to tell Linda that I'm a little confused these days. I'm not sure if it's Claire or the conference. But somehow it seems that the problems of the conference, I mean the logistics, and all the contradictions—they're all getting tangled up in Claire's and my relationship somehow, or in some kind of feeling between us that doesn't even make sense to me."

Steven nodded as Linda asked, "You mean that you're irritated with each other if you vote on opposite sides?"

"No, no," Sylvia answered. "It's more like . . . well, for example, the issue at the meeting last night was about interpreters for the women coming to the conference. Claire kept insisting that every language be interpreted by a native speaker. I feel, sure, that would be nice . . . But it's really a luxury given the hundreds of other things that have to happen, all kinds of position papers written and translated, not to mention just housing and food for everyone. And we're supposed to go running around and find over 20 bilingual women native to 20 different languages? It seems absurd to me.

"And I just can't help but feel it's because she's French," Sylvia added with a quick shake of her head. "That whole French obsession with the purity of their own language. They can't stand any foreigner fucking it up. You know, the French Academy and that whole thing. The French are so incredibly arrogant about their own culture. And of course the 19th-century colonial world fed right into it. There still is that idolatry of French aesthetics in Latin America in the upper class, and even some of the intellectuals . . . Actually, the upper class of almost every country in the world spoke French 100 years ago. I think the whole French population is just jealous that English is now the international second language, and French isn't such a big deal anymore, in *reality*. They just like to think it is. And how Claire can carry on in that tradition of arrogance is beyond me to . . ."

"Sylvia, stop!" Linda looked incredulously at her cousin. "How can you talk about Claire that way? You know she is absolutely dedicated to your politics, to 'internationalism.' She lives in the last decades of the 20th century, dear, this is not 1890! I think I agree with her point about the interpreters. She could be Spanish-speaking and make the same point and then what would you say?" Linda paused, and then, with a sadness that startled Sylvia, asked, "What is happening to you two?"

Sylvia turned her head and, closing her eyes for a moment, she didn't answer.

Steven, who had been lounging back in his chair listening to them both, suddenly sat forward. "Oh, Sylvia. I'd forgotten. I got something in the mail today for Claire. At my office. Do you know what it's about?" He stood up and headed toward the hall.

"What?" Sylvia looked bewildered, tired.

Steven returned with his briefcase and, opening it, took out the letter he'd received and handed it to her.

"How strange," she said, as she turned it over and, finding no more explanation on it than Steven had, shrugged her shoulders.

"It came in another envelope addressed to me, from France. The return address was just a Paris post office box." He looked at her as if he thought she would have an explanation.

"I really don't know what this is about, Steven. I'll have Claire phone you about it. I didn't even know she had your office address, much less planned on using it for her mail!"

She stood up. "I've got to get going. I know you three need to get an early start. Thanks very much for dinner, it was great.

"Give my love to Maureen," she continued as they walked to the door. "Tell her I'll call her next week. And love to Aunt Rhonda and Uncle Nick. I'm glad you're going to see them, Lin."

"Oh, I know," Linda answered. "Mom and Dad have been looking forward to this visit for months. I really can't believe so much time has slipped by."

"Well have a good time and drive carefully." They said their good-byes and Sylvia walked out into the night.

Chapter II

Steven was up before the alarm Saturday morning, making coffee. He would give Linda and Justin a few more minutes to sleep. He was thinking about the holiday, the weekend, Labor Day. The end of summer. He could have felt melancholic, but he shrugged it off. In just a couple of months it would be Halloween, though of course that wasn't really a day off. But right after that was Thanksgiving, and then Christmas, and New Year's—a grim time in the courts—but still, there would be less work.

He remembered that Rhonda and Nick had invited them down for Christmas again. It seemed like Linda was of the mind to go this year. He thought of the plane tickets. How much would they charge for Justin? And the presents. Not just for Rhonda and Nick, but for Linda's younger brother, Jeff, and his wife and their kids and Aunt Maureen . . . It would be fun to be with them all. Last year had seemed almost bleak, just the three of them sitting around that tiny tree. But they really couldn't afford it. Money seemed to be becoming more of a problem than less of one. He began to feel the same old gnawing regrets for having left the steady salary of the Public Defender's Office, even as underpaid and overworked as he had felt there. At least then he hadn't had to bill people himself. The city had paid.

He thought of the list of clients he had made up for the secretary at the office to send second-reminder notices to. He definitely needed to have them sent out well before the Christmas season, a really distasteful time to send out bills. But he couldn't imagine giving them to the secretary now either, or at all. She would think he was grubbing for money, that that's all he had on his mind. They both knew that most of the clients who hadn't paid, just couldn't. But Christ, if some money didn't start coming through there was going to be no childcare for Justin in the fall, much less any traveling at Christmas. In his mind he pictured stopping by the office this morning on the way out of town. He could leave the list of billings with a note on the secretary's desk while she wasn't there.

"Steven," Linda called from the bedroom. "Are you up?"

"Yeah," he answered as he poured coffee for her and himself. "I'd really like to get started, Lin," he said as he brought her cup of coffee to her. "Let's wake up Justin and go. Everything's packed, isn't it?"

"Well, yeah," she answered. "How about if I have a sip of coffee first?"

"Oh, yeah, sure," he answered as he got up from the bed and walked to the kitchen to get a cigarette. He lit it and stood against the sink, sipping his coffee, silently composing the note to his secretary.

Linda looked at him with one dark eyebrow raised, then walked down the hall, first to the bathroom, and then to wake Justin.

Steven sensed she wasn't pleased with the way the morning had started, and, shaking off his thoughts and putting out his cigarette, he began to pour some cereal for Justin.

They sat briefly over breakfast, discussing the drive, and began to warm to the idea of getting out of town, of a long-awaited family visit. Steven thought Linda seemed slightly nervous, or maybe he himself was, to visit "the grandparents." So many possible judgments to be made. It had been almost a year since they had seen Justin. Children change so much in a year. But had they? Rhonda and Nick? Or he and Linda? Not much, really. Well, Rhonda and Nick always seemed the same. And he and Linda? They probably seemed the same. Well, in fact probably they were the same. But Justin was not. He was definitely a different boy. Steven looked at Justin.

"What?" Linda asked as she looked up from adjusting Justin's bib and saw Steven smiling, and then, as he didn't answer, she smiled with him.

They loaded the car, Justin in his car seat, and in the trunk, their bags and a picnic lunch. Steven sat in the driver's seat and waited for Linda to get in and shut the door before starting the ignition.

"You know, I thought we might stop by . . ." he started to say as he turned the key but was silenced by a sharp grinding sound. They both looked at each other, startled. Steven looked back at the ignition and turned the key again. The noise was grotesque.

"God, what is that?" he said as he dropped his hands in his lap, bewildered.

"Try it again, Steven. Maybe it's just cold."

"Linda," Steven said, looking at her, still alarmed, "something's really fucked up. You heard that."

Linda turned her head to the side window and leaned her forehead against the glass. "Shit," she said through her teeth.

"Where we going?" Justin asked from the back seat between the sounds of sucking his fist and slapping his hand on the rail of his car seat.

"I don't know what the hell that is, Linda, but . . ." He turned the key again, and the sound was worse, like ground glass in a liquidizer. He opened the door of the car and got out, shutting it sharply behind him, and yanked open the hood. He glanced over the spark plugs and was taking off the distributor cap when a front door opened across the sidewalk.

"Hi, Steve," a blonde, barefoot man in a T-shirt and jeans greeted as he came out of his apartment toward the car. "That a hell of a grind you got there. What kind of gas you using? Or did you dump a box of nails in there, eh?" He laughed.

"Oh, hi, Franz," Steven said as he stood back from the engine. "I don't know what the goddamn . . . I know the transmission's about to go, but . . ."

"Look, Steve, I don't know what kind of car you got there. A Toyota?" Franz said as he looked at the rear end, and then started to unscrew the gas cap. "But it don't matter. I tell you, you got something in the gas." He put his finger in the gas tank, smelled it, and looked at Steven. "You got a piece of hose or something? I check it."

"Franz, I just filled the tank yesterday afternoon, myself, from the same pump at the same gas station I go to all the time."

"Maybe somebody put something in your gas then, Steve. I think really, somebody maybe put sugar in your gas tank."

"What?" Linda asked, holding Justin in her arms, as she walked around to the back of the car where the two men were standing. "There's *sugar* in the gas tank?"

"That's what Franz says." Steven looked at her, not sure what to think.

"You can't drive this car, Steve. You need have it cleaned out. But you turn that key again, you grind your carburetor to its finish, I tell you," Franz said.

Steven and Linda stood looking at each other, speechless, both incredulous that anyone would want to play such a trick on them and also trying to grasp that the car would absolutely not run.

"What the hell?" Steven looked at Franz. "So do you think all the cars on the street have sugar in them? Some nut went running around putting sugar in people's gas tanks."

"I don't know, Steve. I try my car," Franz offered, as he walked up the block, reaching in his pocket for his keys.

"Oh god, Steve," Linda said, as if she might cry. "I just can't call Mom and Dad and tell them we're not coming. I can't! After all this dealing back and forth, phone calls, postponements . . ."

"I know," Steven said quietly, biting his lower lip and staring at the gas cap lying on the trunk.

"Steven," Linda said, suddenly resolute. "I'm going in the house and call the train. It doesn't leave for an hour. Maybe there are cancellations. If not, I'll call Greyhound." With Justin still in her arms asking, "What doing Mommy?" she turned and strode back to their building and ran up the steps.

"I don't know, Linda," Steven called after her, and then looked up the street as he heard the engine of Franz's car turn over smoothly, as if it had just been tuned up. He walked over to the little Audi as Franz was getting out.

"Mine's OK, Steve," Franz said.

"So I see," Steven answered, shaking his head. "What do you make of it, Franz? Why would anyone put sugar in someone's gas tank? Why would anyone put sugar in *my* gas tank?"

"Well, Steve. Really I don't know your life. You got somebody mad with you?" Steven shook his head, thinking. "Or maybe you know," Franz continued, "maybe some guy works in the factories, making cars, in Daly City, you know? Now he got no job. He walks by, he sees you got this Japanese car. He decides he don't like you. Maybe he a little drunk, you know."

"Oh great, a drunk auto worker." Steven almost smiled. But then, raising his eyebrows, "Who knows, you know?" He paused. "Yeah. Or maybe a Latino youth gang," he began, his voice cynical.

"Hey, yeah, Steve. You know those Mexicans. They can do some mean crazy things. They don't like us white people, that's all. Maybe they come up here from the Mission and . . ."

"Oh, I don't know, I don't know, Franz," Steven interrupted wearily. "I just know I'd like to get the goddamn son of a bitch . . ."

"Steven!" Linda was yelling at him from their front steps. "Get the stuff out of the car. We're taking a cab!"

"A cab? To L.A.?" he yelled back, but she had gone back into the house. He turned to Franz. "Hey, Franz, well thanks—I'm sorry if we woke you up this morning, thanks for coming out and looking at it— I'll talk to you later," he finished quickly and ran off toward his flat.

When he got to the front steps, Linda had reemerged with Justin and was locking the front door. "Steven, I called the train station in Oakland and they said that there are cancellations and that we should just get over there. So let's move it. Here's the cab. Mom and Dad will pick us up in L.A. I just called them."

He looked into the street as a cab pulled up, and, running over to their car, got the bags out of the trunk.

On the train, Linda and Steven, holding Justin, wrestled their way down the aisles, car to car, trailing their baggage behind.

"Christ, it's crowded," Steven muttered.

But Linda's eyes were lit with excitement. "Look, Justin, see the train? Choochoo train," she said, pointing out the window to a lone freight car on a neighboring track.

Steven rolled his eyes. "Hey, up there!" he said as he spotted two empty seats across the aisle from each other in the back of the car they had just entered. "Justin can sit in my lap."

They were just settling into their seats as the train released a massive gush of steam and began to inch its way forward. Justin let out a howl and began a wailing cry that seemed, to Steven, to summarize all the morning's tension. "Hey little man, hey little man," he said softly as he turned Justin around and held him close to him. "It's just a train. We're on a choochoo train."

"Steve, I'll take him," Linda offered. "Maybe you could go see if you could find some cold milk or juice for him."

Steven stood up, putting the still wailing Justin into Linda's arms, and headed down the aisle toward the rear of the car. He heard Justin calming, and then quiet as the sliding doors shut behind him and he moved on into the next car.

As the train's motion threw him from side to side, he saw himself handing three ten dollar bills to the cab driver and reaching out to the station clerk for their tickets as over two-hundred-fifty dollars was rung up on his MasterCharge card. He lurched forward as the train ground to a halt just outside the Oakland station, and the squealing brakes split through his ears just like the grotesque sound of his car engine earlier this morning. What was it going to take to get the car running again? He saw three, four, five hundred-dollar bills. Was this day going to cost him a thousand dollars? Even if every single client paid their bill, he couldn't afford to shell out a cool thousand without the slightest notice. Looking ahead, he saw he was just outside of the bar car and, walking on through, he ordered an apple juice and a beer.

Linda sat quietly in her seat looking through the window beyond the man beside her, letting the passing warehouses, broken panes of glass, graffiti, the scorched yellow grasses and blue sky above fill her mind. Justin too was lulled to a quiet reverie as they sat, motionless, watching the moving scenes before them. The little wooden houses backed up to the track, some rundown, some with a hopeful patch of flowers, seemed to flow one into another as Linda's mind wandered to her mother, Rhonda.

She would be 60 next spring. Dear god, is she ready for that? Linda wondered. But yes, Mom is really up to anything. Her stamina is really something, Linda thought as the corners of her mouth turned to a smile. And she still looked stunning. Her vanity has served her well. She had never lost hold of the motive to look good, and swimming and tennis had kept her amazingly fit, despite smoking at least a pack a day. She really seemed to have a core of steel, though. Even through that horrible time with Dad, she had held it together. How long had that gone on? The separations, the mistrust. It must have been at least five years. Her life had seemed to be falling apart, everything she had lived for. Her marriage. Linda grimaced, remembering the pain her mother had been in those years. I wonder if even now, it's really healed. Dad's been at home, it seems to have been working, for quite awhile now—well since just before Justin was born. The prospect of another grandchild had helped. Dad seemed to finally come around; he seemed to be more accepting of his family now, less distant, less cynical. Maureen had really helped Mom during that time too, she really had.

She's so strange—Maureen—Linda thought, shaking her head. Such a mind of her own. Like Sylvia. Both of them, really, had been great with Mom, talking tough to her, helping her find her own strength, outside of Dad. Well actually, they were sort of models for Mom. Maureen, god she's been alone how long now? When did Uncle Louis die? It must be about ten years. Maureen is a real survivor; she has really held her own. But she always was very different than Mom. Sometimes it's hard to believe they're sisters. Maureen always has something cooking, some project or plan or idea. Some of the oddest things. Where does she come up with them? Like that U.N. Reform group she worked with for years. Maybe she's still doing it. And genealogy! Actually, that one may be a good sign. It's certainly a move toward the personal. All her other schemes and projects were always so . . . sort of wacky idealist. Really abstract, impossible goals, that seemed to have nothing to do with her life, or 'real' life. But still, when Mom's life was caving in at the seams, Maureen was a real inspiration to her. Got her out of herself. Helped her to see what there was to life outside of her husband, her family, her own image of herself as the glamorous wife of Nick Delgatto. The airline executive. God, it had been so awful that first time Dad left, moved out. Mom was devastated. Just crushed. It had been so humiliating to her. She still won't talk about it, or say what really happened. I'll never know if it was some other woman, or women, or Dad's weird moods—those sort of restless, angry, melancholic moods he would get in that went on for weeks, sometimes months. As if he were trapped, or had failed, or felt so dissatisfied with his life he had to break out, run away, or go crazy. Mom was so tied up in Dad's moods, she hardly had her own. Though she had her swimming, her tennis—and her good looks. But they belong to him. Well her kids. But Jeff and I haven't lived at home for what—12, 15 years. Dad and the house are her life. Her marriage is her life.

Justin stirred in Linda's lap and, still mesmerized by the fleeing landscape, continued his wide-eyed gaze out the train windows. Looking down at him, Linda felt a wave of uneasiness suddenly pass through her shoulders, her chest and stomach, almost a shudder. Her marriage is her life. It was as if her mother's pain had suddenly become her own, or the possibility of it was so much closer to her, a part of her. She had always looked at it, looked at Rhonda and Nick's relationship so coolly, objectively. With sympathy yes, but, as if it were a scene in a movie or a book.

She craned her neck around to look to the rear of the train car without disturbing Justin. Where the hell is Steven? The concession car can't be *that* far away. How long is this train anyway? She questioned the man next to her, what? The cafe/bar car was only one car behind their own.

Steven slowly stubbed out his cigarette and stared absently out the window of the bar car. He felt better, yes. The beer had really relaxed him. Maybe he should have just one more and then try to sleep. He hadn't been sleeping well at all lately. He really could use a few good hours of sleep. He picked up his can of beer and, lifting it high to his lips, drained off the last few drops. Nope, he told himself as he set it down. Linda's going to need help with Justin. And she probably already wonders where the hell I am. He got up, picked up the can of apple juice and headed back toward their car.

The train was really clipping along now and he was jostled from seat to seat as he made his way down the aisle. He stepped aside, practically having to sit in an older man's lap, to let four teen-age boys push past him. They were laughing, punching each other, calling out each other's names and telling their odd jokes in their barely deepened, cracked voices. They were excited, plowing through the car as if they were the only ones aboard. Steven scrambled back out into the aisle, past them, and was flooded with a *deja vu*, a sensation that this very moment was the dream he had had last night, but it was not a dream. He was on a train, a train packed, like this one. There were boys . . . all boys. All men and boys. And they were in uniform. Yeah. A troop train. It was a troop train. It was a train full of soldiers on their way to . . . Wait. No. That was a movie. That was the scene in that movie with Humphrey Bogart and Raymond Massey when they were going to Dover. He hadn't been there at all. He had just seen it in the movie. But this sensation, this was a sensation from his own experience, it wasn't just . . . He stood still in the aisle, feeling the recollection. It was a bus. That's right. That bus through Georgia. To boot camp. They had all been about 18. Oh god. He remembered the sick fear in his stomach as they had sped over that pot-holed road to Macon. How he had crouched in his seat, grinding his teeth, furious and afraid. The shouting of the other boys, the crude jokes, the hoarse almost hysterical laughter of boys wanting to be men. Boys on their way to war. He moved forward, slowly down the aisle, swaying with the motion of the train. How in hell had he managed to totally forget about that Korean airliner, the Soviet missile attack? For all he knew World War III had been declared. He hadn't even seen a headline yet, he realized, as he struggled with the sliding door between the train cars.

He lingered a moment in the small passage between the cars, the metal plates of the floor sliding back and forth over their coupling beneath, the noise and motion of the speeding train so tenuous here, as if that connection could so easily, suddenly snap and the cars careen wildly off the track in opposite directions. Somewhere, woven into the squealing wheels and scraping cars, metal on metal, he could hear shrieking, wild screams of children, like one of those crazy carnival rides, high-pitched shrieks breaking through the din of gnashing, flying steel contraptions. He had such an overwhelming desire from deep in his chest to screech out an ear-shattering, piercing cry with all the power of his lungs, that he lost his balance and was flung to one side of the passage just as the sliding door in front of him slid back and an older woman with a cane cautiously made her way through. He quickly righted himself and reached out a strong right arm to hold the door back for her as she passed him and went on through the door behind to the next car.

Steven went on through to the car in front and heard Justin say, "There's Daddy. Daddy. Daddy." He was standing on the arm of the seat in the crook of Linda's arm and leaning over the seatback. Linda turned around and looked back. She smiled at Steven, half-quizzically, half-annoyed.

He quickly walked up to the seat and picked up Justin, lifting him high in the air. "Hey, Jus. Do you like the train? Do you like to ride on the train?" he asked, bouncing him in the air while Justin giggled. "How's it going, Lin?" he asked as he settled himself and Justin in the seat across the aisle.

Linda turned her head from the window to face Steven. "Fine. He's OK now. Where's the juice?" she asked coolly.

"Right here," he said as he pulled off the aluminum tab of the can and poured the juice into a cup for Justin.

Linda nodded and, reclining her seat back its full length, she turned back to the window. The dry still September light seemed to hold the brown hills in a scorched heat just short of flames. Gazing at the great empty blue sky shimmering with the absence of rain, she felt the tension drain from her, and the sounds of the train, the low voices of the couple in front of her, a child talking in the front of the car, blended to a small distant clatter floating just beyond her eyes as she dozed in and out of sleep.

In Santa Barbara, the young man sitting next to Steven got off the train and Linda took his seat. Justin had been napping in Steven's lap, and she gently lifted him and laid him down against her.

"Shall I get us a couple of beers?" Steven asked.

"Sure," Linda answered.

"Try and get them back here before we get to L.A.," she said as he was rising from his seat. He turned back to look at her as she gave him a wry, engaging smile. Grinning, he leaned over to kiss her gently, then headed down the aisle.

Returning to their seats, he handed Linda a beer and asked, "Were you able to get some sleep? Or were you just resting?"

"Oh, I'm sure I slept on and off. It was wonderful, really. Thanks for taking Justin all that time, Steve. How was he?"

"Oh, he was pretty good. It was fun. We read some stories, looked at all the things out the window, took a walk to the back of the train." He paused as both of them were drawn to the sparkling blue of the ocean just beyond their window. The late afternoon light had turned the beach dune grasses to a deep autumn gold, and the sun, lowering in the sky, broke through the spray of the surf in an arc of rainbow colors. Linda caught her breath and looked at Steven. They smiled in amazement and sat quietly watching the diamond-studded waters, the rainbows dancing above the waves.

As the train turned inland leaving the ocean behind them, Steven stirred and turned to Linda. "Justin and I found a newspaper in the concessions car."

"So are we at war?" she asked.

"Not yet," he answered. "Actually I think the whole thing might blow over. I mean there won't be any military confrontations. Nobody's pushed any buttons. Obviously."

"Well, what are they saying?" she asked.

"Oh . . . the Soviets are lying, inhuman, massacring maniacs. But for the most part it's a lot of diagrams and charts about what plane was where when. Trying to figure out exactly what happened."

"But nobody's making any threats?"

"Not really."

"Are you sure of that, Steve?" Linda asked, wanting to be reassured.

"Yeah, I think so, Lin. If they were going to make any moves, we'd know it by now."

Linda looked visibly relieved and, unconsciously pulling Justin closer to her, turned to watch the long low fields slipping by the window, their neat rows of green stretching out to meet at a distant point, point moving into point with each new row.

"But what I'd really like to know is how the hell that sugar or whatever got in my gas tank?" Steven said, anger in his voice.

Linda nodded. "I know, Steve." She turned back to him. "I'd sort of put it out of my mind, but . . . Do you think Franz really knows what he's talking about? Maybe it's just something in the ignition."

"Yeah, I would love to think so," Steven answered, "but Franz was a mechanic for the army in Germany. He told me all about it a month or so ago when I went down there to ask him about the noise in the flat next door, remember?"

"Oh yeah. Thank god they moved out, anyway." She was silent. "So, in other words, he knows what he's talking about."

"Yeah, I really think he does," Steven answered. "I mean I never would believe it, but . . . Who the hell would come along and just dump a box of sugar in somebody's gas tank? It's such a fucked thing to do."

"I really can't begin to imagine . . ."

"Franz thinks it's some Mexican kids from the Mission."

"Steven that's sick!"

"Yeah, well, hey, it's a sick world." He paused. "As Sylvia would say."

"Steven! You aren't honestly going to sit there and pick the nearest oppressed group and say it's their fault because you're pissed off and can't figure out who to blame . . ."

"No, Linda, no. For god's sake, I just said that Franz said that. But the fact is, whoever did it, it's an act of vandalism—just random violent spite. Maybe some white punk kids did it, who knows? But you know, I really don't know of any race that never commits acts of vandalism."

"Steven, I am really confused by your logic here," Linda said, an edge of anger cutting through the concern in her voice.

"Linda, I'm saying yes, Franz is a racist to assume it's Mexicans from the Mission. But because Franz is a racist doesn't mean whoever did it was white, for god's sake!" He looked at her incredulously.

"Steven," Linda said, with a visible effort to be patient, "let's drop it."

He shrugged.

"Steve, I just don't think we need to argue about Franz's half-assed opinions. Of course, we have absolutely no way of knowing how it happened. We're not even 100 percent sure of *what* happened. Let's just try to put it on hold until we get home and can really investigate it, and deal with it concretely." She waited. "OK?"

"Yeah," he answered, after a moment. "Yeah, you're right, Lin." He breathed a slow hissing sigh between his teeth. "It just drives me nuts to pay for somebody else's goddamn bullshit."

Linda put a hand on his arm. "Steve," she said, half imploringly, "wait till we get home."

"OK, yeah," he answered. "I'll get us a couple more beers. We've got about 45 minutes before L.A."

Steven felt in his pocket for change on the way back to the bar car. He found himself to be angrier than he had been all day. He was conscious of that, of something in him that he had held quietly and coolly at bay since the early morning, filling his mind—and he let it. Sure, he thought, Linda can wait to think about it. She doesn't give a fuck how we pay for the car. What does she care? I'm the one who has to drag my ass to the office every morning. I'm the one who has to split my brain over every two-bit junkie and whore in San Francisco, hacking out one hopeless case after another, playing chicken with those pompous D.A.'s, kissing butt to those half-dead pederastic old judges, and still hardly making enough for the rent, food, bills. God, if it weren't for the money from the court-appointed cases, we'd be out in the street. And I put in 50, 60 hours a week for that. For what? For some jackass to destroy my car engine for a kick. It was probably some asshole I defended in court. That would be the irony. Perfectly fitting. He shoved the sliding door between cars, ramming it back into its casing, and stood a long moment at the window of the next car, his eyes fixed ahead of him, not really seeing a thing. His teeth still clenched, he turned and headed on down the aisle. I can't even talk to her about it! She just wants us to look good for her parents, all smiles and happiness. Why not? They're loaded. Only some classless slug would be moaning around about money. Ugh. How mundane. Sure. What the hell? What's 300 bucks for a weekend with Mom and Dad. Oh, let the car rot, honey. Let's hop in a cab. Let's hop on a train. And we better have a grin pasted on our faces the whole goddamn time, no matter what it costs. We don't want to remind Mom and Dad that Justin, their little heir apparent, is also the grandson of an alcoholic Southern sharecropper. Goddamit! And little Linda did happen to marry a penniless college boy who bused dishes and racked up $20,000 worth of student loans.

"Christ," he almost spat the word as he slapped a five dollar bill on the counter of the bar car.

"Sounds like you could use a drink right away, pal," the man next to him at the counter turned and said, a good-natured smile on his slightly bloated, reddened face.

Steven, with an effort, raised his head, drawing his mind out of his funk. "Yeah, I guess so," he half-laughed. "A couple of Buds please," he said to the barman. "And a shot of whiskey," he added.

"Hey, pal," the man next to him, who was probably on his fifth or sixth scotch, said, "Cheer up! It's a holiday! A national holiday! Memorial . . . or, uh . . . Labor Day, whatever the hell." He sputtered with laughter at his own slip.

"Yeah," Steven muttered.

"Ain't no holiday to me," the barman said. "I calls it Slave Day. One day a year they gives all us slaves a day off so we can keep on slavin' all the rest the year."

Steven's dulled gaze sharpened as he took in the black man in the white uniform. "You've got a point, there," he said to him, nodding seriously.

"Oh tell me I got a point," the barman answered. "I been laborin' 50 odd years, son. I started workin' these trains when I was 12 years old. I seen some 50 odd of these 'Labor Days' come and go and I worked most of 'em . . . just like I worked most every other day of my life. Labor Day don't mean shit." And he laughed.

"Hey, now," the man next to Steven interjected as Steven put down his empty shot glass and popped open one of his beers. "I have to disagree with you there, brother," the man continued. Steven winced, but the man went on, "Where do you think we got Labor Day from? We got it the same damn way we got the eight-hour day! The five-day work week! We got it through the blood and sweat of the AFL-CIO. My father walked those picket lines till he had holes in his shoes so every honest hard-working man in this country could say, 'Yes, goddamit! We'll work on our terms. For the pay we say, the hours *we* say. That's what Labor Day's about, brother. It's the day the unions made, and I'm goddamn proud of it!" He set his drink on the counter with an exuberance that sloshed half of it over the rim of the glass.

Steven jerked his elbow back from the counter as scotch and water seeped onto his shirt cuff, and looked at the barman, who was busying himself with the ice machine.

The barman looked up at Steven. "Mmhmm," he said. "Mmhmm. I know the unions. I pays 'em half my salary now. But it took 'em 30, 40 years 'fore they grant me the privilege." He laughed. "Wasn't no unions for black folk when your daddy got those holes in his shoes," he said to Steven's neighbor. "We worked twice as long as your daddy, didn't have no shoes at all." He turned back to the ice machine as another passenger moved up to the counter to order a drink and Steven and his drinking companion were edged over toward the wall. Trapped in the corner, Steven finished off his beer.

After a moment the man confided to Steven in a hoarse whisper, "I don't get these goddamn blacks."

Steven popped open the second beer and reached for his cigarettes. "Hey, he's got a point," he eventually answered. "I mean, the labor unions did a lot of great things in the '30s and '40s, sure, I agree with you. But the fact is the only union that ever took a black worker into their ranks back then was the I.W.W., and they hardly even exist anymore. The AFL-CIO was segregated up until . . . Oh, I don't know, but I was brought up in Kentucky and when I was a kid my uncle—he was a miner—his union was all white. He hated blacks. The unions haven't really done too much for black people; they still have the lowest-paid . . ."

"Oh, Christ! don't give me that," the man retorted and Steven looked startled. "The unions made this goddamn country. If it weren't for the unions . . ." He stopped to give Steven a searing look, pointing his finger very close to Steven's face. "Maybe you'd like to live in Russia! There's no unions there, pal. It's a goddamn dictatorship over there. You ever heard of a totalitarian government, pal? Do you know what that's all about?"

Steven tried to edge back from the man but was still cornered between the bar and the wall. "Well . . ."

"I'll tell you what it's about," the man went on, his voice rising slightly. "It's about shooting down innocent people in airplanes! That's what it's about!" His voice continued to rise. "It's about Communists taking over the goddamn world. They don't care who they kill . . ."

"*Steven!*" He heard his name called sharply and, jerking his head around, he saw Linda standing at the entrance of the car with Justin in her arms. Her eyes were blazing.

"Excuse me. Excuse me." He quickly interrupted the conversation and made his way through the cluster of people at the bar to the car door as he heard the conductor announce over a loudspeaker, "We will be arriving in Los Angeles in five minutes. Five minutes to Los Angeles."

Linda had turned and was striding back through the cars to their seats. Steven walked quickly behind her, his brow creased with concern. How on earth had he just let the time go by like that? It was as if he had completely forgotten where he was. Let's see now . . . he had gone to the bar car to get a couple of beers for himself and . . . Oh, he had been thinking about the car, the sugar in the gas . . . But Christ, it was almost as if he had lost consciousness.

"Steven, can you get the bags," Linda said with a quietness that turned his concern to a deeper pain. He reached above the seats and, pulling down their baggage, said, "Linda. I'm sorry. I just . . . I . . ." He really didn't know what to say.

She looked at him, and now there were tears in her eyes. Justin was squirming in her arms, about to cry himself. She shifted him to her other arm and stepped back into the space between the seats as other passengers crowded by.

"Lin," Steven said, putting his arm around her as passengers jostled him from behind. She grimaced involuntarily as the heavy smell of whiskey and beer seemed to drench her face in the stuffiness of the crowded car. "Oh god, Steven," she said, in exasperation, more than anger.

She sat Justin down in the seat as he began to cry and rummaged through her purse. She took out a package of mints and turning back to Steven, took his hand and, putting the package in his palm, she looked at him with a perplexed concern, both questioning and hurt.

"I'm going to try to understand this," she said, looking down at her hands, and shaking her head. "I know you've been under a lot of pressure, Steve."

"Lin, Lin. Honey. I just lost track of the time . . ."

"But, Steven," now her eyes were brimmed with tears as she looked back up at him, "we were having a conversation! You were just going to go and get two beers and come right back."

He looked at the hurt in her eyes as the tears she struggled to hold back spilled to her cheeks. Justin's whimpering had escalated to a full-scale wail. They were the only people left in the car.

He enfolded her in his arms. "Lin, sweetheart, don't. I just . . . I just have felt so hassled. They were talking about Labor Day. I . . . Lin. You know! I love you so much." Linda buried her face in his shoulder and let the tears flow, sobbing now, as if she were Justin, as Steven held her tight, his head bent to hers. Justin, whose wailing had momentarily subsided while he caught his breath, now launched into a high-pitched screech that tore Linda out of Steven's arms.

As she started to bend over him, Steven said, "No, no, honey, I'll get him," and as he picked Justin up, he looked around the empty car. "God, we'd better get going." He rocked Justin in his arms. "Hey, hey little man, that's OK, it's OK."

Linda followed Steven's glance around the empty car. "Oh, god," she said, as again she rummaged through her handbag, extricating a handkerchief and a mirror.

Steven had just managed to quiet Justin as Linda took a last dab at her eyelids and, taking a deep breath, she said, "Let's go, Steve. Mom and Dad probably think we're dead."

She threw the diaper bag over her shoulder and took Justin by the hand as Steven gathered up the rest of the bags and they headed for the car exit.

The minute Linda stepped down from the train she heard her mother. "Linda! There you are!" she called from 30 feet away, and rushing toward her, Nick strolling behind, she called, "My god, we thought something *else* had happened to you! We've been walking up and down this train . . ."

Linda turned from lifting Justin down from the train door and met her mother's full embrace. "Hi, Mom."

"Justin! My god he's grown!" Rhonda exclaimed as she swooped him up from the platform, a radiant smile illuminating her admittedly unusual good looks. Her hair was still a deep black, flung casually back from her high-boned, taut cheeks, tanned to a dark bronze in striking contrast to her pale sky-blue eyes. Steven was always a little taken aback when he encountered Rhonda.

"Steven!" Rhonda held Justin in one arm and threw out her other arm to Steven, bracelets jangling on her slim tan wrist. Steven took her hand and kissed her on the cheek as Nick gave Linda a quick hug. "Hi, doll," he said and then turned to Steven. "Steve," he nodded, as they shook hands.

They gathered up the baggage and, with Rhonda still holding Justin, cooing to him intermittently, questioning Linda and Steven about the train, and calling to Nick to look at his grandson, they walked through the station to the car.

As Nick guided his Continental up the ramp to the Hollywood Freeway, Steven, sitting in the front seat, studied his profile. Though his features certainly matched Rhonda's for classic European good looks, he definitely lacked her vitality. Steven sensed a brooding in the man that gave him a quick misgiving about the weekend ahead.

"Now you kids are staying until Tuesday, aren't you?" Rhonda was saying, Justin sitting in her lap. She's really loving this, Steven thought as he turned back to look at them.

"Well, Mom," Linda began, and then, leaning forward, "Dad, do you think we can get a flight back to San Francisco? We don't really have any reservations for the train, or . . ."

"Oh, Nick will take care of it. Don't you even think about it," Rhonda answered. Steven raised his eyebrows and looked back to Nick for a response, but Nick's face remained impassive. "Now tomorrow afternoon Jeff and Dana are coming up from Laguna," Rhonda continued, "and of course they'll stay over. Now Maureen is dying to see you kids, but she's going to be at some crazy conference tomorrow. What was that conference Maureen is going to, Nick?"

"Genealogy," Nick answered. So he can talk, Steven thought.

"Oh, that's right. Well apparently it's going on all weekend, but Maureen *did* say she will be over Monday afternoon, and then we can all have dinner together. Linda, what do you think of this genealogy, anyway?" She turned to face her daughter. As Linda became engaged in discussing the questionable merits of genealogy with her mother, Steven sank a little deeper into the plush white car seat and gazed out the window at the darkening twilight.

It was the first time he had been to Los Angeles since their wedding, and only the second time in his life. Linda had always come down here on her own, or Rhonda and Nick had flown up to San Francisco to see them. He'd really just never had the time. He barely had it now.

Although there was little light left in the sky, Steven could still sense the thick greyish-brown smog that lay so heavily over the city. He felt his eyes burn but was sure it was only his imagination. Nick seemed to change lanes frequently, shifting his big black car back and forth between traffic with little effort, but it left Steven totally disoriented. It seemed they had been on at least two or three different freeways at this point, and he had yet to distinguish whether they had left the city itself or not yet entered it. He contented himself with watching the streams of headlights and, as the night sky blackened, the flickering lights of the vast sea of flattened city surrounding them.

Steven must have dozed a bit for when he heard Nick say, "Here we are," he sat up abruptly and found they were in the parking lot of a condominium complex.

"You've got some tired boys on your hands, Linda," Nick said with a warmth that surprised and pleased Steven as they opened their car doors and Rhonda carefully lifted a sleeping Justin out of the car with her.

"Oh, Steve's been working awfully hard," Linda answered. "God, it seems ages since I've been here," she said looking up at the stately complex before them, silhouetted against the evening sky. Tall thin date palms swayed gently, high above the tiled roofs. "Let's take a walk on the beach," she said, suddenly excited, and, with the spontaneity Steven so loved in her, she took her father's hand and started leading him toward the sound of the surf beyond the complex. "Come on, Daddy."

"Let me help Steve with the bags, doll," he said, but he smiled as he withdrew his hand.

"It's funny," Linda went on, still exuberant, "whenever I come here I feel like I really never left Redondo! Hurry up, Steve, let's go for a walk."

"Linda, Linda," Rhonda interrupted, "I think Steven could use a nice tall drink, don't you? He's had a long day." And as she looked down at Justin, who was stirring in her arms, she missed the quick change in Linda's expression.

Chapter III

"Sylviaaa!" Rikki yelled again, pounding her knuckles against the glass pane of the door as suddenly it was flung open.

"Hold it. Hold it, Rikki. I heard you. I'm ready. And I'm sorry. I was on the phone," Sylvia said as she locked the door behind her. "What time is it?"

"Oh. Hi," Rikki answered, lowering her arm. "It's not that late. I just didn't feel like standing out on your porch all night. I hate these goddamn Saturday night meetings. Whose idea was this anyway? Claire's?" She turned a teasing smile to Sylvia as they ran down the steps.

Sylvia sighed. "Rikki. It wasn't Claire's idea. Though it could've been," she added. "But who cares? Saturday, Sunday, Monday . . ."

"Monday's a holiday," Rikki interjected.

"We have so much work to do," Sylvia ignored her. "God, if we meet every minute from now until Christmas, I still don't think we'll be ready. Honestly, Rikki."

Rikki opened the door of her dilapidated Dodge. "Yes, yes, Sylvia," she answered, getting in the car and opening Sylvia's door. "But this is the third meeting I've been to today, and it feels like the hundredth this week," she said as she drove up the street and turned east onto Haight. "I feel like . . ." She cut herself short, and Sylvia, looking at her, was moved out of her own preoccupation by the tired, pained look on Rikki's face as she searched for the end of her sentence, "like . . . how much can it really mean?"

"What do you mean, Rikki?" Sylvia asked quietly.

"I guess I mean that . . . while we're sitting around planning this fucking conference, they're going to blow up the fucking world," Rikki answered.

Sylvia leaned back into her seat. "Yeah. I know. I was just talking to Claire about it." She looked out the window of the car, and then back to her friend. "But they're not going to, Rikki. Not yet. And that's why we've got to make this conference happen so perfectly that the next time any military order to destroy is put out, from the Kremlin *or* the Pentagon . . . they'll be thinking about NEWS. About what NEWS is going to do. Because there are that many of us, Rikki." And some of us will outsmart them at their own game, she thought to herself, her lips suddenly dry and taut as she thought of the key-set sitting now, in the bag on her lap.

Rikki, running a hand through her hair, the shiny black curls caught between her small olive-gold fingers, swung the steering wheel with the open palm of her other hand into a turn onto Market Street. "Yeah, well, you always have so much hope, Sylvia."

Sylvia turned and watched Rikki as she maneuvered the car into a parking space at the corner of Market and Laguna. She really did look tired. More than tired. Afraid? The laugh that usually played about her lips, the teasing glint in her black eyes had given way to . . . to what? Was it fear? Or was it all just too much. Too much for her. She must be only 21, 22? And she'd only just come here from New York; she'd only been in the organization for six months.

"Oh relax, Sylvia," Rikki said, turning off the engine and, as if she'd read Sylvia's mind, added, "I still believe!" She turned a mocking, glum stare to Sylvia that brought a smile of relief to Sylvia's face as she turned her head away and then, back again, laughed and gave Rikki a playful push out of the car.

"What time is it?" Sylvia asked again as they rang a buzzer at the corner apartment building.

"We're early, Syl. Early," Rikki answered as she showed her watch to Sylvia. "It's 7:20."

"Yes?" a voice crackled through the small speaker above the buzzers.

"Sylvia and Rikki," Rikki responded. The front door clicked and, pushing it open, they walked through to the stairs.

"When are we going to get a place with an elevator?" Rikki asked with an exaggerated gasp as they neared the top of the third flight.

"Rikki, Rikki. Sacrifice. Discipline! Get with it, girl!" Sylvia answered and laughed as Rikki rolled her eyes.

They rang another buzzer at the door at the end of the fourth-floor hallway.

"Yeah?" a voice called from behind the door.

"Rikki and Sylvia," Sylvia answered. The door opened and they walked through to a large carpeted room.

Seventy to eighty folding chairs were arranged in tight circular rows, a table with stacks of computer printouts at the center. Along the northern wall, the only windows in the room were cracked open at the bottom, shades drawn full-length to the sills. Sounds of street traffic and diesel buses drifted up from Market Street below.

Across the width of the western wall hung a broad blue banner, at its center a great circular Earth with brown and yellow continents and oceans of black. In a double arc above the earth, deep purple letters spelled:

WOMEN'S INTERNATIONAL/FOR PEOPLE'S SOVEREIGNTY,

and in an inverted arc below the earth:

NORTH EAST WEST SOUTH

The eastern wall was covered with maps: the world, the continents, the Mideast, Central America, the Caribbean, Southeast Asia, Southern Africa, the Philippines, Iran, Western Europe, Mexico, the United States and other regions.

The southern wall framed a collage of posters in a wealth of color and languages telling a story of people's movements for freedom, for liberation from foreign domination. Posters of peasant farmers working their land, the rich earth tones in their faces and hands as they stood strong and resolute against the tanks, helicopters. Posters of women, children and men, peasants and laborers, in Africa, Asia, the Americas, demanding peace and freedom to develop their resources without exploitation. Posters of people's movements for liberation, guns raised high in defiance, the centuries-old history of their struggle against foreign colonizers deep in the determination in their eyes. Posters of women and men throughout the world demanding an end to nuclear weapons, an end to war.

And on the wooden door directly across from the front door of the apartment hung a long narrow poster with big, bright red letters speaking out from the top, NEWS, and just beneath, a paragraph in bold black letters read:

THE WOMEN OF NEWS: THE WOMEN'S INTERNATIONAL FOR PEOPLE'S SOVEREIGNTY / NORTH EAST WEST SOUTH, HAVE JOINED TOGETHER IN A WORLDWIDE MOVEMENT FOR THE TRANSFORMATION OF HUMAN POWER ON EARTH.

WE CHOOSE TO SUMMON ALL THE RESOURCES OF OUR CONSCIOUSNESS AND OF OUR LABOR TO CREATE A GROWING, UNPRECEDENTED, AND INVINCIBLE HUMAN FORCE THAT WILL

END the development of NUCLEAR WEAPONS and eliminate the stockpile of nuclear arms that exists;

END the development and sale of conventional arms and the recruitment and training of military forces used for the DOMINATION AND INTIMIDATION of people throughout the world;

CREATE an INTERNATIONAL ALLIANCE among people's liberation movements, founded in political and economic cooperation, with commitment to the goal of HUMAN DEVELOPMENT;

CREATE from these allied movements societies that are committed to the elimination of racism, sexism and economic exploitation;

CREATE from these societies ONE UNITED WORLD GOVERNMENT;

CREATE a united world government constitution that:
• structures international production and trade to equalize the standard of living and quality of life throughout all world societies, in commitment to the development of human life and consciousness, and with respect for the Earth's ecological system to which we belong;
• eliminates national boundaries while promoting cultural integrity and respect among cultures for diversity, autonomy, and cooperation;
• insures women's political, economic and cultural equality with men, promoting women's full participation in all aspects of the development of international society.

OUR GOALS WILL BE REALIZED. WE KNOW THAT WE ARE THE CREATORS OF TRUTH. OUR MOVEMENT TOWARD LIFE AND JUSTICE IS GREATER AND STRONGER THAN ANY MOVEMENT TOWARD DOMINATION AND DEATH. ALL THAT WE PRODUCE, CONSCIOUSLY AND MATERIALLY, IS DEDICATED TO THIS TRANSFORMATION.

On the wall just to the left of this declaration was another map of the world, this one with various areas colored in and others covered with push pins. Standing next to it, deep in conversation and occasionally pointing to the map, was a tall, thin woman with gentle lines about her eyes and mouth, her short thick brown hair streaked with grey. As Sylvia walked toward her, she was struck by the golden light in Ruth's hazel eyes and the kindness and wisdom in the curve of her smile that seemed far older than her 50 years.

"Sylvia." Ruth reached out a hand to her as she approached and, taking her lightly by the arm, brought her into the conversation. "I'd like you to meet Gwen." Sylvia smiled in greeting. "This is Gwen's first meeting with us. She's a close friend of Ellen's," Ruth told Sylvia, and then turning back to Gwen, asked, "You're both computer programmers, aren't you?"

"Yes, I've worked with Ellen for years," Gwen affirmed.

"Gwen's read quite a bit of our literature," Ruth said to Sylvia, "but Ellen's asked if we could give her some information on our organizational structure. You know, some of the mechanical details," she explained with an imperceptible nod that told Sylvia, yes, Gwen could be trusted.

Ruth asked, "Do you think you could fill her in?" Ruth glanced around the room. A good three-quarters of the chairs were filled, although small clusters of women still stood talking in corners and to the side of the circle of chairs. "I'm still waiting for the representatives from AMES and the BCU. Let me go make a couple phone calls." Smiling at them both, she hurried through the door on her right to another room.

"How long have you been doing programming?" Sylvia asked, her eyes scanning Gwen's mauve linen jacket, matching mid-calf skirt and lavender silk blouse. She must be wearing $500 worth of clothes, Sylvia thought, as her eyes rested on Gwen's lightly made-up blue eyes.

"Ten years. I'm working mainly with a UNIX system now, in C."

Sylvia raised her eyebrows. "Great."

"*Hola*, Sylvia." A woman in black and red, her sienna hair only shades darker than her high-boned, youthful face, smiled as she took Sylvia's outstretched hand.

"Cristina, hi. I think Ruth was just going to call you. How are you?"

"Fine." She turned to a small boy who came up beside her, his hand grasping her sleeve. "*¿Jorge, que tiénes? ¿No puedes ver a Pedrito? Está allí en el 'chilcare.' ¿Tu lo conoces, recuerdas?*"

The boy grinned.

"*Si, si, ándale.*" She bent and kissed him lightly, moving him off in the direction of the childcare rooms behind the door to the right.

"Oh you know that bus took so long to get here. They'll give the kids something to eat, won't they?" Cristina said as she straightened and looked at Sylvia.

"Oh, yeah, I'm sure."

"So I hear there's a big question about interpreters for the conference." Cristina laughed.

Sylvia flushed slightly. What had she heard? "Well there's so many things . . . I'm really glad you could come tonight, Cristina. Maybe we can get it settled." She glanced at Gwen who was studying

Cristina. "Oh, Cristina, this is Gwen. She's working with us now."
"How do you do," Cristina clasped Gwen's hand warmly.
"Cristina is with AMES."
Gwen looked questioningly at Sylvia.
"Asociación de Mujeres de El Salvador," Cristina answered.
"You're from El Salvador?" Gwen asked. "You speak perfect
English."
Sylvia's face stiffened, her eyes focusing on Cristina's left earlobe
and, she'd never noticed, an earring, a tiny globe of the Earth.
"Thank you." Cristina simply smiled. "The family who adopted
me in San Salvador sent me to school in Los Angeles when I was
younger."
"But where does AMES . . ." Gwen paused, unsure.
"We're a mass organization of women in El Salvador. We support
the FDR/FMLN and are working for the same goals, but we work
autonomously, as women, under our own leadership. To make sure
that we don't end up with all the shit work of the revolution." Cristina
laughed. "Or actually to make sure that the rights of women are central
in the new society we are creating."
"So then AMES is not a part of the FDR/FMLN, but they are a
part of NEWS? Because they only want to work with women?" Gwen
questioned.
"No, no." Cristina shook her head quickly. "AMES works with
the FDR/FMLN and the people of El Salvador. We're not *in* NEWS,
but we are in a coalitional relationship with them. NEWS supports the
goals of AMES *and* the FDR/FMLN and has a relationship of solidarity
with us."
"So then, who exactly *is* in NEWS?" Gwen asked.
"You can explain that Sylvia, no? Let me find Ruth. Nice to
meet you." Cristina smiled and disappeared behind the door to the
right.
"Well," Sylvia answered, "mostly NEWS is a network of a lot of
different women's groups that have been around for some time, and
who've decided that they agree with our declaration." She nodded toward
the long narrow banner on the door across from her. "But there are also
many politically independent women. And then, especially more
recently, we've had a lot of women join who've never been politically
involved at all. They've become aware of us partly just because we're
growing so fast and reaching so many women."
Gwen nodded, yes, that, in fact, was what had drawn her.
"We're still pretty loosely knit," Sylvia added, "though our
networking and communications are becoming very efficient. The
conference will be a major step toward unifying us, of course."
She turned to the map. "These areas colored in blue are where

NEWS chapters are operating. There are currently 30,000 members in the U.S. alone, about 3,000 here in the Bay Area. We're the headquarters for North America. Then there are at least another 3,000 in New York, 2,000 in the Northwest, 2,500 in Los Angeles and also Chicago, several hundred each in St. Louis, Minneapolis, New Orleans, Albuquerque." Her hand glided across the map. "We have chapters in every major city in the country, and in smaller cities, like Tucson, Akron."

Sylvia glanced at Gwen who was studying the map now, taking in the significance of the shower of blue dots across it. "And in Canada, there are about 12,000," Sylvia continued. "In Europe, well over 35,000. In fact, there're 4,000 women in Amsterdam alone, which is our European headquarters.

"But in Eastern Europe," Sylvia said, growing more enlivened herself as she reviewed the extent of their growth, "we're just beginning to develop a membership. The largest groups are in Yugoslavia, Poland and Czechoslovakia. And in the Soviet Union we're also growing, mainly in the Ukraine, Moscow and Kiev. There are over 8,000 Russian and Eastern European women involved." She turned back to Gwen.

"In all, we have over 100,000 members in the Northern Hemisphere—the 'North.' I mean the industrialized countries. Our membership is primarily made up of what would be called 'white' women, though we're trying to move away from typical racial terminology. We believe that the 'races,' as they've been defined, are European anthropological constructs that arbitrarily divide the world into about three so-called races, and ignore the vast and varied cultural diversity among the world's . . ."

"Hey, Syl, did somebody ask you to give a speech?" Rikki appeared at Gwen's side. "Hi, Gwen. Nice to see you again."

"Oh hi Rikki." Gwen laughed.

"We met at Ellen's party," Rikki explained to Sylvia who stared blankly at Rikki, not sure whether to laugh or glare.

"But whatever, race or culture," Gwen turned back to Sylvia, "all the members of NEWS are white?" She looked slightly horrified, as if she hadn't realized what she was getting into.

"Well, no, not exactly. Let me explain," Sylvia said. "All these chapters of NEWS," she swept her hand across the blue pins on the top half of the map, "are made up of women in the so-called 'developed' countries. We're organized into an autonomous international mobilization—under our own leadership. I mean, we're not part of any other white leftist group or party." She glanced at Rikki who grinned at her, with affection, and nodded.

Sylvia looked back at Gwen. "The only group we have a

significant relationship to in the North are national minorities—black people, native people, Latin people—who aren't really national 'minorities,' because actually they're the cultural *majorities* of the world: the people of Africa, Latin America, Asia, indigenous peoples. And their populations are concentrated in the South," she moved her hand across the bottom half of the map, "or the so-called 'underdeveloped' countries of the world."

Gwen's eyes narrowed as she studied the map, then she turned to Rikki.

"She's just saying that . . ." Rikki began.

"Well, wait a minute, it's like Cristina was saying about AMES," Sylvia said as she touched Rikki's arm. "There are women affiliated with NEWS from almost every cultural group in the world, but they are not *in* NEWS, or *under* our leadership. Mainly they're part of national liberation forces, whether autonomous like AMES, or directly in the liberation movements. And they work with us in an allied, or coalitional relationship."

"But their main thing is with the liberation movements they're part of," Rikki added, "though they're into what we do too. They're in constant contact with our chapters, and they send representatives to our meetings."

"It's because we believe the liberation movements are leading in creating genuine internationalism," Sylvia added. "Though it may seem paradoxical that their current objectives are nationalist . . ."

"No, I can understand that," Gwen said. "I mean, if individual nations don't have their own independence, then there can't be international relationships based on mutual respect. Or an end to the domination of some nations by others."

"Yeah," Sylvia agreed, nodding her head. Clearly Gwen had read some of their literature. "Well, so given the significance of the national liberation movements, we look to the women who are involved in them internationally for the most advanced information, and guidance, in developing our strategies."

"The fact is," Rikki said, "women from the South, and from the liberation movements here in the North too, are not members of NEWS, they're the *vanguard* of NEWS."

"Well, how many of these representatives, or vanguards, or . . ."

"Allies. They're 'allies' of NEWS, as they themselves choose to be called." Sylvia turned to the map again. "There are NEWS Allies Headquarters where groups of women in the South have set up offices to facilitate communication and interaction with us. The bulk of our resources—money, supplies, etcetera—are sent or taken directly to the NEWS Allies Headquarters." She pointed to the map. "These blue pins mark them: in Nicaragua, Mexico, Cuba, Zimbabwe, Angola,

Lebanon, Sri Lanka, Viet Nam . . ."

"What are the orange pins?" Gwen asked.

"Those are where there are women in communication with NEWS, who act as liaisons between their movements and us, though there are no actual headquarters there as yet . . ."

"Sylvia!" She turned abruptly as she heard her name called, and saw Claire motioning for her to take a seat. Ruth was about to start the meeting. Sylvia stood a moment as Claire turned away, preoccupied now with her notebooks.

"And the pink pins are holding up the map," Rikki whispered to Gwen. Sylvia gave Rikki a look of amused disbelief as they turned and walked quietly around the outer circle of chairs to available seats.

"Tonight's agenda is relatively brief," Ruth began. "We're just going to address some of the logistics for the conference. However, the Goals Committee has finalized a draft proposal for the sessions to be held during the five days of the conference."

She reached to a stack of Xerox copies on the table next to her and handed them to the women seated in front of her to pass around the room. "If everyone could review these," she continued, "we want to begin discussion of them Monday night.

"I know it's going to be difficult for us to meet four or five times a week for the next three and a half months, and I want to congratulate all of us who volunteered to be on the Conference Coordinating Committee." Ruth smiled as a light strain of laughter rippled through the room.

Looking down at her notebook she went on, "Tonight's agenda is on language interpreters, transportation and housing. We will have reports from those three committees, all of whom met today, and comments from the Allies represented here tonight, followed by discussion and votes on final proposals.

"We have an hour for interpreters and thirty minutes each for transportation and housing. We'll start with the interpreter issue. Are there any objections? No?" She looked out over the intent faces of the women, her head turning with the circle and, spotting Claire, she said, "Claire? Do you want to give your report?"

Sylvia watched from across the circle as Claire rose from her seat, her pen in one hand and notebook in the other. Her almost frizzy yellow-gold hair was tied loosely at the neck, a few strands straying at her temples. Her large brown eyes, that always seemed to Sylvia slightly liquid, bore an intent, intelligent expression and her thin lips, sometimes so graceful, were compressed in a stern determination that made Sylvia suddenly decide that she would not participate in this discussion.

"*Bon.* Tonight we begin to discuss translation of all materials,"

Claire began. "And also interpreters for the sessions of the conference. Our committee 'as decided to express to you three proposals . . ."

Sylvia sat watching Claire explain each proposal with the careful precision that so characterized all of her work. She really was admirably dedicated. But for some reason Sylvia did not feel the warm flow of pride and affection that usually filled her heart when she watched Claire work; or rather it was held down, stifled by a sharp thin pane of irritation, an antagonism that she could not quite justify or explain to herself but, nonetheless, was there. It isn't just about this interpreters issue; after all, she thought, Linda had made a point last night. Claire has obviously rejected the French tradition of chauvinism in politics and aesthetics. She's as committed to internationalism as it is possible to be, there's no question.

Sylvia thought of that first night she had met Claire, more than three years ago now. Sylvia had been working with the Committee to End Colonial Oppression at that time and had been deeply involved with CECO for at least four years up to then. She was working at the literature table for an event on Zimbabwe. It must have been just before the liberation; the newspapers were still referring to "Rhodesia." It was shortly before the event was going to start. The speaker from ZANU had arrived and Sylvia had just finished a quick consultation about security with JoAnn, who also worked with CECO then, when she heard a low, almost sultry voice saying, *"Tiens. Regarde! Cet article de Sartre!"* Sylvia had turned around and saw Claire, her rich brown eyes wide and amazed, her blonde hair much shorter and curlier then.

"Pardon me?" Sylvia had asked.

"Oh, I . . . I was juss noticing you 'ave zis article by Sartre." She had picked it up and turned it to show Sylvia *"French Intellectuals and Democrats and the Algerian Revolution."* Her face was slightly flushed, she seemed embarrassed for having been caught talking to herself, and she smiled with a shy, amused intelligence that so thoroughly charmed Sylvia she felt a pinkish glow warm her own cheeks.

"Oh, mmm, yeah . . . have you read that?" she asked Claire.

"Well, yes, some time ago. But it 'ad a very profound effect for me. I sink 'ee said so much zat is true about ze French nationalism zat make even ze mos opress French worker so raciss. In fact zis worker, 'ee prefer to give 'is loyalty to 'is own ruling class. 'ee doesn't join wiss ze opress people of Africa to *fight* zat ruling class, to make a justice for all people, 'imself also . . . I mean . . ." She had faltered, as if unsure that her English could carry her through her idea.

"I think I understand you," Sylvia had replied. As she heard that conversation again in her mind, Sylvia realized how greatly Claire's

English had improved in just these last three years. Although her grammar and her vocabulary had always been surprisingly excellent, her accent had been so thick that sometimes she had really been more or less unintelligible. God, she did have guts though, Sylvia thought. Always taking the chance, struggling to express herself, forcing her lips to shape the strange words no matter how frustrating, or sometimes impossible, it must have felt to her.

" . . . and with that, we can ask, which is our greater priority 'ere?" she heard Claire's clear, modulated voice speaking out to the NEWS meeting, and looking up, saw the sincere concern on Claire's face, her words so much crisper and sharper than that night some three years ago, but her passion for her ideas of just the same intensity. Sylvia's eyes lingered on Claire's face a moment, and then, as if she knew that that gnawing, filmy antagonism would slip back over her heart again, she looked down at her hands and drifted back into the memory of that night.

"Yes, I understand you," Sylvia had said, and smiled warmly. Claire had looked relieved and, relaxing a little, stood looking intently at Sylvia's eyes.

"Well," Claire went on, "zis article was so interesting for me too because it speak about ze leff in France, and how ze leff too allow zis nationalism . . ." She paused. *"Bon, regarde,"* she said, 'and flipping through the pages of the article, she laid it on the table and pointed out a passage for Sylvia to read. Sylvia leaned over the table and followed the thin line of Claire's finger to a paragraph.

> *"The passion-charged chauvinism of French public opinion on the Algerian question exerts pressure on this Left, inclines it to excessive caution, shakes its principles, and places it in a paradoxical and increasingly sterile situation.*
>
> *The Algerian people considers that the French Left has not done everything it should within the framework of the Algerian war . . . "*

"Mmhm, really," Sylvia had said as she looked up. "It's that exact point that we, in the left in this country, also need to examine for ourselves. I know this article was written . . . when?"

"Oh, 1957, I sink," Claire had answered.

"Yeah," Sylvia went on, "and 25 years later the very same points are true in the United States. I mean about the white people in the United States, including the white left. An important point I think he makes here is that colonialism, and neo-colonialism, are really just euphemisms for what is really military occupation. That's what's going on in Zimbabwe, Jamaica, Puerto Rico. Practically every country that the U.S. government refers to as 'undeveloped' is actually occupied by foreign military forces, from either the United States or NATO."

"Yes, yes, 'ee make a good point about zat in regard to ze liberal mentality 'ere." She pointed out another passage to Sylvia.

> *"French democrats, in deciding to give the name of 'colonialism' to what has never ceased to be military conquest and occupation , have deliberately simplified facts. The term of colonialism created by the oppressor is too affective, too emotional. It is placing a national problem on a psychological level. This is why, as conceived by these democrats, the contrary of colonialism is not the recognition of the right of peoples to self-determination, but the necessity, on an individual level, for less racist, more open, more liberal types of behavior."*

"Yes, yeah," Sylvia nodded with growing enthusiasm as she remembered when she had read the article some months before, and how she had been excited and moved by Sartre's analysis of the French liberal and left response to the Algerian people's demand for solidarity in their war of independence. It had been Sylvia who had brought the article to the attention of CECO, wanting to include it in their literature. Even within CECO there had been controversy about it. A fair number of CECO members still questioned the statement it made for the absolute need of white leftists to let go of their desire to control the movements and strategies of colonized peoples in their fight against foreign domination.

"You know," Claire had continued, "zis article was a big breaksrough for me. I really 'ad to sink again about ze work I was doing at zat time in France."

Sylvia looked at Claire with an unmasked depth of appreciation. For her too, the article had brought a genuine shift in her thinking, and the arguments that it had generated in CECO had moved the whole committee to a much deeper understanding of its role in working against colonialism and military occupation.

The two women had stood across the table looking at each other from the place of joy that those moments of an awakened knowledge and sudden leap of understanding, such as they had both once experienced from this same article by Sartre, can give the human spirit. But Sylvia's pleasure had been cut short as she realized that JoAnn was standing at the microphone about to begin the opening remarks for the event, and she herself should have been at her post for security. She had glanced at the rear door, and then back to Claire. "The event's starting," she said as she made her way from behind the table to take her position at the back of the room. But then, as Claire turned to go take a seat, Sylvia had reached out and gently caught her arm. Claire turned back and Sylvia had asked, "Could you wait a minute after the event? Maybe we could make a time to talk . . ." Claire had smiled, quite happily, Sylvia thought, and nodded, yes.

It was several days before they had been able to meet again. Sylvia had lived alone in an apartment on Harrison Street at the time, and Claire had come over for dinner. They had both still smoked cigarettes then, and Sylvia remembered them sitting for hours and hours over the bottle of wine Claire had brought, talking and talking, smoking Claire's last Gauloise down to its very end. They had discussed everything it had seemed, and yet everything they discussed seemed to open up entire new topics, uncover deeper layers, as if they could never finish their talking.

Claire's political history had differed from Sylvia's considerably. Brought up in a middle-class family in Paris, politics was a frequent topic of conversation at the dinner table. The French, like all Europeans, did not experience the position of United States citizens who, assured of their economic superiority and domination in the world, could ignore the machinations of their government and focus simply on their personal families, careers, comforts, problems. In fact, denigrating the political and cultural ignorance of 'Americans' was a favorite topic for the Duval family, although, being staunch French liberals, their discussions also broached other, more sophisticated political topics: the role of NATO in Europe, France's role in the Common Market, would Mitterand ever win an election, the split between French Socialists and Communists and their disparate relationships to the Soviet Union. Claire had been quite well versed in French liberalism when she began her first year of university at the Sorbonne. But it was there, at the Sorbonne, almost within her first week, that her ideas began to take a sharp swing to the left. It was the fall of 1967 and as part of the erupting student movement in France that year, she was one of the first to take to the streets in the great rebellions of May 1968 in Paris.

In 1968, Sylvia had been naively plodding through her art classes at San Francisco State, only vaguely aware of the slogans she sometimes heard the groups of students chanting outside the walls of her building. She had had to ask a fellow student who 'Ho Chi Minh' was, and it wasn't until the early '70s that she, too, was demonstrating against the Viet Nam War, and only then with a vague understanding that it was an 'unjust war.' For Sylvia, at that time, had been rather thoroughly preoccupied by the growing realization that she was in love with her art professor. Although her art professor was married, that was not what had troubled Sylvia. What had troubled her was that she was a woman. Miriam Blakely, a young, brilliantly creative and strikingly lovely woman. Sylvia was 21 years old. This was not a schoolgirl crush. She had had lunch with Miriam on several occasions, and they had worked closely on Sylvia's final term project. The fact that Sylvia had a boyfriend at that time, who she was sleeping with, only made it more hopelessly clear to her that she had never been in love—before Miriam. Next to her communications with Miriam, David appeared bizarrely arrogant and emotionally sterile. It had astounded her, when she really looked at it, how much of her relationship with David focused on his life, not hers, and a fairly shallow conception of his life at that—his schoolwork, his parents, his need for sex. In fact, she had long before given up, unconsciously, she had realized, given up even any attempt to share with him or bring him into the deeper questions and thoughts in her mind and stirrings of her soul. But with Miriam, her feelings and thoughts flowed to her and were returned in kind, illuminated and nurtured, brought to the full excitement of completion. More and more frequently, as she sat listening to David's endless tales of his doings that day and his plans for the week, her mind was on Miriam. Though she had resisted, what she had felt then was the inevitable; after several months she had gone to a psychiatrist. "I am in love with a woman," she had told him. And then, her head in her hands, she had wept as if her very life were lost.

It hadn't been too long after that, possibly a month, when, still taking the Stelazine and Milltown the psychiatrist had prescribed which, in fact, served to adequately dull her mind and "keep her out of an institution" as the psychiatrist had said, and to bludgeon her feelings for Miriam to an inconsequential pall; she decided to attend a forum on women's liberation at school.

Here Sylvia's political history began to merge more closely with Claire's, as it was also in the early '70s that Claire had attended her first meeting on *'le feminisme'* in Paris. Although for Claire, her motivations in attending the meeting were not personal, but political. Having been intellectually at the forefront of theoretical development in the French student movement of the late '60s, she found herself repeatedly frustrated and infuriated at her relegation, by the male movement leadership, to subservient positions in the organization in which she participated. There had been only 10 or 12 women at that first meeting in Paris, and for the most part, they were all women with very sophisticated understandings of European left politics. They had come together, in anger, to grapple with the realization that despite their very advanced intellectual abilities, they were consistently excluded from positions of authority and leadership in the movement.

For Sylvia, her first experiences with the women's movement had been a great emotional release. For the first time in her life she had felt validated, understood. Years and years of confused, unarticulated self-doubt and self-hatred for her inadequate adjustment to "life," her inability to move confidently and happily in the direction mapped out for her by her parents, teachers, boyfriends, fell away as she embraced the notions of the new feminism of the '70s. She stopped seeing David, and the psychiatrist, almost immediately, threw away her drugs, and dedicated herself to the development of the Women's Center in San Francisco. Within a year, she had fallen in love with a co-worker at the center, and identified herself as a lesbian.

Claire had found her encounter with early French feminism a very valuable experience, helping to articulate her sense of powerlessness in the student left, but she did not abandon her leftist politics. Rather she, with her feminist comrades, raised the issue of sexism again and again at their *Alliance de Rouge* meetings, demanding to be heard and to be given positions of power in the movement. But also at that time, Claire was very much in love with her comrade and lover Jean Marc. Although they had seemingly endless debates over the rights of women, their relationship endured for several years. It wasn't until 1976 or '77, when the sense of imminent revolution that the late '60s and early '70s had seemed to portend had faded to a cynical malaise in the radical French left, or been watered down to a more "mature" social democracy, that she and Jean Marc parted ways. Jean Marc, having been one of the leading radical and more militant voices of that earlier left, had become cynical to the point of almost complete inactivity. His moods, depressions and negative attitudes became an increasing unhappiness for Claire. Most painful was his sarcasm and disparagement of her more and more enthusiastic involvement in developing a synthesis of her left values with her feminist concerns, and her movement toward the forefront of a developing socialist-feminism in France. Although she sincerely believed that she still loved Jean Marc, her respect for him had eroded to a point that threatened her own self-respect. This, together with her growing affection for Katrine with whom she had co-founded the socialist-feminist organization, *Femmes Libres*, led her, one violent, stormy evening, to finally move out of her apartment with Jean Marc and into Katrine's.

In that same period, Sylvia had become deeply politicized by her experience of life as a lesbian and also by her emergence into the real world of a working "single woman" who could not find a job in her field, and instead found herself typing endless bureaucratic reports for the city government in order to survive. She had moved to the left of the women's movement with those sectors concerned by the class and race questions that the movement never seemed to adequately address. A friendship with a Chilean woman in the office where she worked had led her to participation in the international movement to free Chile from the Pinochet dictatorship. Through this work she had met JoAnn, then a member of CECO. Sylvia, who had just recently come out of a long and painful break-up with her first lover over the issue of nonmonogamy, became involved with JoAnn. Although their romantic involvement had only lasted a year, the basis of their attraction having been more genuinely that of friendship than sexual commitment, that year had been one of very significant political development for Sylvia. Under JoAnn's guidance, Sylvia read literally hundreds of books and articles: Marx, Lenin, Trotsky, Engels, Hegel, Mao, all the communist classics, and then articles, newspapers, position papers from nearly every left movement to come out of the '60s: analyses of imperialism, books on colonialism, papers and documents from the national liberation movements in Puerto Rico, Nicaragua, Viet Nam, Angola, Mozambique, Azania, Namibia, Grenada—and in the United States, the American Indian Movement, the Black Liberation Movement, the Mexicano/Chicano forces—voices of a deeply powerful motion of working and peasant people that had given a new life to, what seemed to Sylvia, the endless abstractions of the original 19th-century European communists.

In the writings of the national liberation forces, "international revolution," as it had been heralded in the '20s and '30s by the great success of the Russian Revolution (and then so tragically diffused by the Communist Party's merge with the U.S.-led antifascist front in the '40s, the Stalin revelations in the '50s, and the corruption of trade unions in Europe and the United States) had taken on a new, life-promising meaning. International revolution, that had once been a concept bandied about by white intellectuals and certain white workers in the industrialized countries, now took on a truly international meaning. The other three-fourths of the world's population, the non-white peoples of the world, were now giving truth to the words "international revolution." Since the Algerian victory of independence from France in 1960, peoples' movements in colonized countries all over the world were creating drastic changes in the relations of capital. Capitalism had become more and more desperate in its efforts to maintain its stranglehold on the resources and labor of the "underdeveloped world." Viet Nam had brought them a major defeat. For the first time, Sylvia felt she understood the significance of the Viet Nam War, while seven years before, when she had trailed after David in demonstration after demonstration, the activity had been little more than a social gesture for both of them. And with her deepened understanding came commitment. She joined CECO. One year later, in 1978, she moved into the CECO cadre leadership. Her life, until the night of the Zimbabwe event two years later, had been totally taken up with two activities: the moronic, alienating work of her office typing job, and the empowering, exciting, totally engaging work as a cadre of CECO.

For Claire, after she had moved in with Katrine in 1977, life had taken on a new dimension. For Claire, who had always subjugated her emotional power to her intellect, whose clearest understanding of pleasure was rooted in a moment of insight, the creation of an idea, the completion of a thought (for which Jean Marc had been such a source of joy to her, until he had lost his vitality with the loss of his prowess in the movement); a new world had opened. Katrine was not entirely Claire's intellectual equal, although her originality and spontaneity of mind could sometimes jar Claire's elaborate mental schematics to sudden leaps, beyond analytical process and calculation, to a visionary purity that was an even sheerer joy; however, this did not occur frequently. Such an experience was only the side door to the new world that opened for Claire. The front door that was wide, wide open those first years, was that other aspect of Katrine's originality and spontaneity—emotional and sexual creativity. Claire felt as if she were swimming in a vast dream, so fully realized was her intimate, physical pleasure, a pleasure that had never even been awakened with Jean Marc. Like their endless discussions and debates, sex with Jean Marc had been a job, a deliberate working through, a step by step precise development to the moment of completion, satisfying, efficient. But Katrine. What a phenomenal magician! Claire was constantly caught off her guard until "guard" seemed to slip away from her entirely and only wave after wave of delight remained. How had she ever lived without this, she had asked herself it seemed a thousand times, especially those first months. She felt a smile never left her face and the experience of laughter took on a proportion of significance in her life that, had she not been so happy, would have seriously concerned her. A year had passed before she realized that she had not written a single word, had only read a book or two (and those on lesbianism), had taken an increasingly peripheral role in *Femmes Libres*, and had had, she thought, the best time in her life. The second year, possibly because it immediately followed the first but also, more accurately, because the same effects were still present, seemed to be a less novel repeat of the first and she found herself more frequently turning to her books, jotting notes to herself, taking leadership at the *Femmes Libres* meetings.

At the beginning of the third year, she had felt as if she were slowly awakening from a long sleep. One night, alone in Katrine's apartment, she had looked about her and almost not known where she was. She got up to walk to her desk and, startled, realized she was looking for her old desk, the one she had left at Jean Marc's in L'Odéon. Here she only had a board on top of crates. Though that board was stacked high with papers, they were papers she hardly recognized, had hardly read. She had sat down slowly at the half-broken chair in front of her makeshift desk and realized it was the first time she had been alone in this apartment in . . . *combien de mois?* She was almost trembling as she looked through the clutter on the desk for a pen, and taking some sheets of paper from the stack before her, turned them over and began to scrawl on their blank backs, *"Qu'est-ce que je fais ici . . ."* When Katrine had come in an hour later, Claire was still writing. Katrine had thrown her net bag on the bed on the floor and with a laugh and a cry, *"Eh, Claire! Qu'est-ce que tu fais?"* and running her hand through Claire's curls, she leaned to give her three sweet kisses on the nape of the neck. *"Eh, laisse-moi, Katrine,"* Claire had answered quietly.

Three months later Claire had dropped out of *Femmes Libres* and moved into her parents house in St. Girdoux. She commuted the 40 kilometres each day to her job in the accounting department of R.A.T.P. in Paris. She spent all her evenings and weekends at the library or reading in the attic room in her parents' home. After six months, she had saved 12,000 francs and, on February 25, 1980, boarded a Pan Am jet to San Francisco. Two weeks later, while staying at the Stanyan Street Hotel, she had attended the CECO event on Zimbabwe at the Mission Cultural Center where she had met Sylvia.

Claire and Sylvia had had dinner together often that March of 1980, followed by the long-into-the-night conversations that so fascinated them both, broken by laughter and the direct, blunt statements that take place when the lack of a common first language must be compensated for with honesty. Their politics, their families, their jobs, their relationships had fueled their hours of intricate and vivid conversation. At the fifth dinner, just three weeks after they had met, Sylvia found herself asking Claire, as she had known that day she would, to stay the night with her.

Sylvia turned her head sharply as she recalled that moment and then, with a glance to the podium where Claire stood listening with a calm, inscrutable gaze as Ruth spoke to the interpreter issue, Sylvia looked back at Ruth. Then, back to her hands, she remembered . . . Claire had been carefully moving her hand through the clutter on the coffee table—the papers, an empty wrapper, a handbag, matchbooks—looking for her cigarettes. Sylvia had been saying that it must be close to 4:00 a.m. and that she really did not feel right about giving money to another cab driver, and Claire was welcome to stay the night on the couch as she had last Monday, but this time . . . Claire had found her pack of cigarettes, but stopped, and, her hand still resting on the blue pack, slowly turned her eyes to Sylvia's. Sylvia smiled and Claire, her eyes that liquid dark that Sylvia so loved, drew back her hand and sat back into the couch. Their eyes still met across the table and neither could begin to repress their smile. Claire rose first, but it seemed as if Sylvia had risen with her, and they moved together, standing to the side of the couch, their lips touching through a breath, as cheek, temple, mind caressed, and hands met the full motion of each other, holding . . . it seemed forever to Sylvia, in a moment, when she had moved her head back from Claire's and looked into her eyes. She had felt that nothing had ever moved her more. Claire's eyes then. The dark, now velvet eyes, so quickly giving, yet frightened, sure, yet waiting, asking, asking so deeply that they held Sylvia still, almost helpless with her hope to give Claire the understanding she looked for, and then somehow, as if by miracle, Claire's eyes filled with light and, their arms encircling, they walked slowly to the bed, their lips brushing, kissing, hands gliding to drape each curve of shoulder, spine, hip, lips full into each other, tongues, tips on end, thrust, and then back, back, their faces held in full view of each other, eyes met again. Slowly Claire unbuttoned and slipped off Sylvia's cotton sweater and, unbuttoning her own blouse, drew her back to her, full into her breasts, swaying together, they stood, forever, as Sylvia slowly loosened Claire's drawstring pants and helped them slip softly to the floor . . .

"Sylvia, enh, what do you think?" Sylvia heard as Claire slapped her shoulder. She started and turned around. Claire stood behind her and was speaking to her in a whisper, the meeting not quite over. "Why didn't you say one thing that 'ole time?" Claire asked. She was angry. "What is 'appening with you? You don't even . . ."

"Sshh, wait," Sylvia said as the final announcements were still being made. She felt suddenly foolish. She had missed the entire meeting. Not only had the discussion about interpreters taken place, she realized, but the reports on housing—her committee—had been given, as well as transportation, there had been an evaluation, and people were getting up to leave. Claire was disgusted with her for not participating in the language discussion, and god knows how long ago she had dozed off.

"Were you sleeping?" Claire was asking in a louder voice now that the meeting was breaking up.

Sylvia turned as Rikki came up and, putting her arm around Claire, said, "Good work, Claire."

Claire smiled as she returned Rikki's hug and said, "Well, you know, I think the point is worth the effort, but, the conditions define the work."

Rikki laughed. "Oh, exactly."

Rikki tapped Sylvia on the cheek. "Hey, Syl, you're certainly out of it. I missed all your salient comments tonight. Maybe these Saturday night meetings are too much for you too."

Sylvia laughed. "Maybe they are," she said, half-serious and almost rueful. She turned to Claire. "Let's go out."

"Oh. *Oui.* Sure. In a minute," Claire threw back at her, and waving a hand at Sylvia, walked back along the outer circle of chairs to the other side of the room.

It was at least another 20 minutes before they left the NEWS offices and it was after 10:30 when they arrived at Claire's apartment building on Church St. and 17th. As they walked up the stairs to the third floor, they kept to the silence of the dark hallway.

"*Voilá*," Claire said, as she had said at least a hundred times before with the click of her key from the lock. The apartment door swung open and Sylvia snapped on the light as Claire leaned to pick up her satchel of books and the stack of papers she had laid on the hall floor before opening the door. Sylvia threw her daypack and handful of notebooks and papers on the table in the front room.

"OK, Sylvie," Claire said, shutting the door. "So you don't want to talk about the meeting. But the fact is, I want to talk about these goals and objectives." She threw a stapled few Xerox copies on the table in front of Sylvia. "I 'ave a big problem with these," she finished.

Sylvia, her hands leaning on the table edge just in front of her daypack and notebooks, looked down at the Xerox copies that had just landed on top of her things.

"You want to talk about them now?" Sylvia asked.

"Sylvia, god, what?" Claire was losing her patience. "I understand you. You say you are too tired at the meeting to speak. But, of course, I know that in fact you don't want to fight with me about the interpreters. A shame you listened not at all, because finally I said OK, we cannot 'ave the interpreters as it is best, but so. We will do what we can." She stopped. "Ssss, I don't know. I looked at you then, Sylvia, just as we decided that, and your face . . . as if you didn't see a thing, so stupid, god. What can you want?"

"Claire, please," Sylvia responded, exhaustion in her voice. She stood back from the table and folded her arms, her back still to Claire who was rummaging through her satchel on the chair by the door.

"Claire," she began.

"Enh?"

"We have until one o'clock tomorrow before meeting with Ellen and Gwen at the computer room. I know you're going to be at their office all day Monday, and the first Goals discussion is that night." She paused, and turned to Claire, who was thumbing through a notebook. "Did you get the key? Are you going to be able to get in Monday?"

"*Oui*, yes. Jill told the guard lass night when she left that we would be working on a special project on this Labor Day. 'ee will let us in the front door, or leave word for 'oo ever is working there. I 'ave the key to the office, though I tell you it was not so easy to get after all. It seemed someone was always standing by that cabinet. Every other day, no one is ever by there, but of course, when I want to take something, it becomes everyone's 'ang out."

Sylvia laughed. "Well I'm glad you got it. Jill is going to go with you, isn't she? I'd hate to think of you there alone."

"Oh, yeah. It's sure. *Ne t'inquiéte pas*, Sylvie," Claire gave her a tired but sincere smile.

"Well, Claire," Sylvia began again hesitantly, rubbing the palm of her hand with her thumb. Claire had stopped going through her notebook and stood, watching Sylvia, waiting.

"I'd like to wait until tomorrow morning," Sylvia continued, "to talk about the Goals draft."

"You're still so tired?"

"No, no. God knows, I slept long enough at the meeting. I'm sorry, Claire, I . . . Actually, I had been thinking about you and me tonight . . . at the meeting. About our relationship. I feel we really need to talk about it. I want us to talk about ourselves, Claire . . ."

Claire was watching her still, one eyebrow drawn in a high arch, her thin lips pressed together. She did not look pleased.

But neither did she look unconcerned. Now Sylvia waited.

Claire was deliberating. Then, she relaxed her shoulders and said quietly, "OK," as she walked to the kitchen. "You want a Perrier, some tea?" she asked.

"No thanks," Sylvia answered. She walked to the bed and sat down, leaning her back against the wall.

Claire returned and, setting her Perrier on the floor, stretched out across the other side of the bed, her head propped on her hand, her elbow sinking into a large pillow. "So?" she said.

"Well, Claire, I feel . . . I feel that . . . something is just not quite right with us." She paused. "Tonight when you got up to speak, I just started thinking, I don't know why, about that night we met, at that CECO event. I thought it was over three years ago. It's been over three and a half, in March, in 1980. Do you remember?"

"Well, yes, of course," Claire answered, unsure of Sylvia's point. "I 'ad just arrive from France," she added.

"Yeah, you were staying in that hotel. But then, after a few weeks you moved in with me on Harrison Street, and I'd only just moved in there myself, from the CECO house . . . Somehow I always think of that place as both of ours. And I was thinking, while I was waiting for you after the meeting tonight, about that year we lived there together. Before we started work in NEWS."

Claire watched Sylvia, who was rubbing her fingers against the tip of her thumb, staring down at her hands, as if she were struggling against her own agitation. She seemed moved, upset, almost distressed. Claire laid her arm gently across Sylvia's outstretched legs.

"I remember that year, Sylvie. It was such a beautiful year for us both. *Hein?*"

"Yeah . . . it really was," Sylvia answered and looked away from Claire, a tear resting on her lashes. She brushed it away impatiently, continuing in a stronger voice, "It seems like such a luxury now, all the time we had then. All the walks we took, and even trips to the beach, the country. We even had the time to wander around thrift stores and garage sales, fixing up that place . . . It was so lovely there."

"*Oui*, yes, Sylvia. But you know we both always agree our work, our *politics*, that is what we live . . . " Claire stopped. "What are you saying, *mon choux*? You wish we still were living on 'arrison Street? That you were still working with that little CECO? And I am still juss studying, trying to learn about these States, doing some small things for CECO?"

"No, no, Claire," Sylvia stopped her. "I know that NEWS, our work in NEWS, is the most exciting . . . the most revolutionary work either of us ever could have hoped for." She looked away again and then, back to her hands, her voice less sure. "And I know that it was the most progressive decision we could make, politically and personally, to live separately. I know how you felt about your experience with Katrine. I respected that you didn't want to repeat that kind of . . . to lose yourself, or your sense of purpose in some cloying, obsessive kind of love. Though honestly, I don't think we ever would have gone that route. We were really both independent. Even then, Claire." She looked at Claire for the first time, with an almost accusing look.

Claire shifted on her side, taking her arm back from Sylvia's legs. "And so?"

Sylvia looked down at her thigh, at the place where Claire's hand had been. "I know, Claire, that our work in NEWS is all-important. It's very rightfully the center of our lives. In fact, in this past six months especially, it *is* our lives." She stopped. And then looked at Claire again. "But do you realize that for almost this whole past year every single time we see each other it's at a meeting, or we are doing NEWS work at the computer room, or at the office, or we are talking about the meetings, or about the work . . ."

"Oh, Sylvie. Come on," Claire interrupted. "We went to dinner with your cousin, Linda . . ."

"Six months ago! It was my birthday!" Sylvia's voice rose.

"OK. But what! We took a long, long walk at the beach . . ."

"Last *spring!*"

"So what, Sylvia!" Claire was losing her patience again. "What do you want me to do? We should drop out of NEWS, I guess? Forget the conference! Forget the action in February that is going to turn this goddamn world around! Let's move to Tahiti tonight, my darling, enh? You want that? Maybe we can find some native girls to do our work for us, enh?"

"Fuck you!" Sylvia shouted back and, jerking herself up from the bed, stomped into the kitchen, her eyes burning with tears.

Claire leapt up after her. "Sylvia!" She came up behind her and taking her arm, swung her around to face her. "Don't you walk away from me like szat. Fuck you! What! Fuck you!" She was furious.

But Sylvia was crying now, her face covered with her free hand. "Claire," she struggled to say, "I don't think you love me anymore."

Claire loosened her grip on Sylvia's arm and let her hand drop to her side. Sylvia stood, still crying into her hand but, trying to end it, to dam the tears back, she took a breath, and then said, very quietly, "It's not just all the work, Claire." She sighed heavily, then taking her hand away from her face, she lifted her head to look at Claire, who stood before her, watching her, her face drawn in a troubled, sad expression.

Sylvia, calmer now, went on, "I do believe, I really do believe, Claire, that we don't spend enough time together. As friends. Not just as comrades, and not just for sex late in the night after endless meetings. But as caring, loving friends sharing something of what little joy there is on this earth. One walk on the beach a year just doesn't do it, Claire!"

Claire stood still, still watching her.

"I don't think it's just about the work, Claire," Sylvia said. "Or even just about time. We could find the time, I know we could. At least three times in just this past month I've known there was the time for us to just take a walk, get together with old friends, see a movie, like we used to do, and yet . . . I didn't even ask you. You always seem so far away now. It's not just that you're thinking about the work . . . Claire, it's like you don't even *see* me anymore."

Claire's eyes rested in Sylvia's; her face softened. They looked at each other, silently, for the first time in—how long, Sylvia wondered.

"I love you, Sylvie," Claire whispered, but for a moment, as they embraced, Sylvia couldn't help but feel that it had taken her too long to say it, that the whisper was a measure of doubt, not intimacy. But as she felt Claire's warm, soft lips against her cheek, her ear, she let herself believe the words were true, and that filmy pane of antagonism slipped away from her heart as she let her love for Claire flow through her, to her.

At 8:00 in the morning Claire was up making coffee. Sylvia could smell the dark roasted beans as Claire ground them in her hand mill. Her beloved coffee, Sylvia thought, as she lay looking at the morning sky through the top half of the front window.

"*Et voilá, ma chérie*," Claire said as she brought a cup of thick, steaming coffee to Sylvia and, in her other hand, the draft of the Conference Goals, which she placed between Sylvia's fingers as they lay loosely atop the bedsheet. Sylvia smiled and, with resignation, scooted herself up to a sitting position in order to reread the draft. But just as she had placed the pages firmly in her lap to look at them, she suddenly looked up, "Oh! Claire!" and she scrambled up from the bed.

Claire, who was seated at the table with her coffee, contentedly watching Sylvia prepare to read the draft, her own copy before her, screwed her face in a look of displeasure. "*Merde*, Sylvia. Now what?"

Sylvia had pulled a robe around her and was rummaging through her daypack. "I completely forgot. Friday night at Linda's, Steven gave me this letter for you." She pulled a long, narrow, thick manila envelope from the pack and turned to hand it to Claire. "He said it had been mailed to him, inside another envelope, at his office. He wanted to know what it was about, but I really didn't know what to tell him."

Claire's expression had quickly altered as she saw the envelope emerge from Sylvia's pack, and her keen interest, an almost eager excitement, did not escape Sylvia. "Ah. *Bon*. Thank god," she was saying, her relief as intense as her interest. She stood up and took the letter over to her desk.

Sylvia waited for her response to move into an explanation, but as Claire slipped the letter into a bottom drawer and turned around, it seemed she did not intend to discuss it.

"Claire," Sylvia said, more firmly. "Steven wants to know why the hell you're using his office address for your personal mail? *I* want to know why you're using his office address, and where you even got it? I don't remember your asking me for his address."

"No. I know, Sylvia," Claire answered. She stood, her narrow forefinger rubbing across her thin, slightly parted lips, deliberating. Sylvia knew the look well, and waited.

"Sylvia," Claire began finally. "Steven cannot know what this is about. 'ee cannot be told about it."

"Claire!"

"I know, but . . . you 'ave to 'elp me about this, Sylvia. I will explain it to you. But *promise* me. You will not tell Steven," and as

Sylvia opened her mouth to object, Claire added quickly, "We will sink of somesing to tell 'im." She was nervous, Sylvia knew, and not just by the lapse in her accent. "Will you promise me?" Claire looked sternly at Sylvia.

"Do I have a choice?"

"Not really." And as Sylvia waited, "It's about the February Action, Sylvia," Claire said.

"All right. What is it?"

"You promise? About Steven?"

"I'll tell you, Claire," Sylvia answered. "There better be a pretty good fucking reason why you're putting me in this position."

"Do you promise, Sylvia?"

"Yes," she promised angrily, and stood, waiting.

"OK. Well." Claire hesitated. She seemed to be trying to decide, thinking of just what she would or wouldn't tell. Finally, with a shrug, she said, "OK."

Sylvia knew she had decided to tell her the complete story. Or most of it.

"The letter is from Chela," Claire began.

"From the Managua Headquarters? But Steven said the return address, the postmark, was from Paris."

"I know, I know," Claire replied. "Chela sent it first to Vivienne in Paris through a friend in Mexico. Then Vivienne sent it 'ere, to Steven."

"Why to Steven?"

"Sylvia, you know we are under surveillance. Our mail is no secret, enh? You think Chela is going to send her son all the way to Chiapas, to mail this letter all the way to Vivienne's post office box in Paris, to 'ave it sent 'ere into the 'ands of the CIA?"

"Why can't she use the codes, like everyone else?" Sylvia asked. "Or the couriers? I'm still not getting you, Claire. Why Steven had to be involved in this, or how Vivienne ever heard of Steven . . ."

"Sylvia, I sent to Chela by courier, seven weeks ago," she emphasized, "a request for 'er to send us this by this way, because we could not risk this information to be even in the 'ands of a courier through the customs."

Sylvia bit her lower lip, watching Claire. "What is it?" she asked.

Claire hesitated.

"Only you know?" Sylvia asked.

"And Ruth, in San Francisco. Also they 'ave receive this in Amsterdam. Through Vivienne."

"And the Allies?"

"They are the ones 'oo 'ave made this."

"What is it?"

Claire pressed her lips and nodded. "Ah, *bon*, OK. Ruth 'as been right. She told me you would demand to know, now, before the conference. She said OK, so. I tell you. Chela 'as sent the Azanian master for the February Action," Claire answered.

Sylvia's eyebrows dipped to a frown, her face confused. "The Azanian master! What do you mean? I thought the February Action was going to come out of the proposals put forth at the conferences! What the hell are the conferences for then? I thought we were purposefully having the two Christmas conferences, here and in Amsterdam, with members of every Allies Headquarters and NEWS chapter at each one," she restated the plan slowly, stunned, as if she had not gotten something right, had been deluded all these past months, "so that we could plan this Action together . . . under total security, behind closed doors, in person. There was to be *nothing*, absolutely nothing, by phone, mail, telex, codes or couriers." She was verging on anger now.

"*Oui*, yes, Sylvia."

"So what is this master plan? Why in hell are you sending couriers to Chela back in July with anything at all about the February Action?"

"Can you let me tell you, or you juss want to talk?"

Sylvia shot a glance to the ceiling and sat down on the edge of the table, her arms folded. "OK. Tell me."

"So," Claire began. "The Azanian and Namibian Allies from Southern Africa met with Chela when she was sent there in June. They told her they were afraid they would not receive exit visas, that they would not be allowed to leave Africa for the conferences."

"Not even three of them?" Sylvia asked.

"*Sylvie!* Come on," Claire said impatiently. "You know that the repression increase there each day. You are going to doubt . . ."

"No, I'm sorry. Go on."

"They wanted to be sure, in case they could not be at the conferences, to 'ave the location of their target installations there at least, and the plans for their computer linkage."

"So they gave them to Chela?"

"*Oui. C'est ça.* Also, they ask that Chela coordinate communication among all Allies Headquarters so that our network *schématiques* can be taken into South Africa as soon as they are . . ."

"Claire," Sylvia stopped her. "I understand the problem for the Azanian Allies, honestly, but even if they have had to take the precaution of finalizing their plans for the Action before the conferences and transporting them via Chela . . ." She paused. "I don't know. It seems to me that the purpose of the conferences—to have collective input and approval of each other's targets, to coordinate our linkages and software, to develop the schematics together, with maximum security, without having it written all over the place, in or out of code . . ."

"Sylvia!" Claire interrupted.

" . . . is really undermined," Sylvia went on. "Why couldn't the Azanian Allies send out their program with Chela, have her get it to the conferences some—"

"Because 'ow then would Azania get back the network *schématiques* and coordinate their program to it in time for the Action? You know 'ow many weeks it takes, Sylvia, come on! They do not 'ave the access to computers like 'ere in this country, god! 'ow many weeks it took them just to . . ."

"All right," Sylvia answered. "I just . . . I don't know why I feel so resistant to this. It's not that I don't understand the danger the Azanian Allies face, honestly, I'm not trying to minimize that."

"Well, it sounds like . . ."

"No," Sylvia went on. "It's just I feel that . . . the schematics . . . that hundreds of NEWS members who've been planning this Action think they're going to be developed at the conferences. And they're *already* worked out, practically *finished*. And about to be circulated so elaborately, secretively among a few chosen members . . ."

"Sylvia, god!" Claire was exasperated. "The conferences are not undermined. This communication is only a preparation, a design for the Action to make sure that the Azanian and Namibian Allies will participate! You don't think that is so important? Maybe the South African targets should just be forgotten? As if South Africa is not the most brutal, repressive center of colonialism and international capital. Their nuclear weapons . . ."

"I know, Claire. I know. That's not what I'm trying to say."

"Sylvia. *All* of the Allies 'eadquarters agreed in July to draft their plans, deliver them, in code, by courier, to Managua. Chela put the draft together and it will be taken to Azania, maybe they 'ave already taken it." She paused. "They know this in Amsterdam. And we know it 'ere. All Allies and NEWS 'eadquarters know of this. At the conference, it will all be presented to all the Action Committees. There will still be the input, the collective approval, and the final *schématiques* will be made *at* the conferences. Only Azania's program, if they cannot attend, must not be changed. Changes we make at the conferences can be communicated to Azania because our computer linkages with them 'ave been determined through this preliminary work. Yes, OK, it is a risk—a chance—to 'ave certain things on paper now, even in code. But the Allies believe it to be a greater risk to lose Azania's participation."

Sylvia nodded. "OK. So in July you and Ruth . . ."

"Ruth and I met with Chela in the end of June," Claire began.

"June? Chela was *here* in June?"

"Yes, juss for the day. I took Ruth to the airport to meet with 'er. Ruth was not exactly sure what it was about and, really, it was juss because I was there, I know all this. But Chela and Ruth both wanted me to 'elp them coordinate this work. And also Vivienne is ideal to pass through the information."

"Are our targets still the same? As we developed last month?"

"Yes, yes, Sylvia," Claire answered. "No one is trying to work be'ind the back of each other, I promise you."

Sylvia was quiet, her chin resting on her hand. Claire walked back to the desk, opened the drawer, took out the envelope from Chela, and set it on the desktop. She stood looking at it as they both stood in silence for several minutes.

"I'm sorry, Claire," Sylvia said at last. "I was just so surprised. I didn't mean to argue. Of course I understand."

Claire turned to her. "Sometimes you are so . . . so stubborn, Sylvia. Or I don't know. You almost sound reactionary."

Sylvia flushed. "I'm sorry," she repeated. And then, after a moment, "But why Steven, for god's sake?"

"'oo else?" Claire asked. "We needed a public, an office address. And of course none of ours. Ruth couldn't think of anyone. I took 'is address from your book. I knew 'ee would pass the letter to you without question. Also I was going to begin to check their mail each day if it did not arrive by . . ."

"But he does have questions, Claire," Sylvia said.

"Oh, *ben*, we can tell 'im something, Sylvia."

Sylvia sighed. "I haven't really had to lie to them yet. I mean . . . omission, of course. I just don't tell them." She frowned as she bit the tip of her finger. "But to deliberately lie . . ."

"Sylvia. Don't you think Steven would understand? Would say yes, sure, yes. . . if 'ee knew."

Chapter IV

Labor Day in Los Angeles brought a brilliant sun, as if ordered by god, or at least by the AFL-CIO, to the millions of workers at home in their beds across the megalopolis. A hazy languid hand of smog rested gently across the limitless borders of the L.A. pancake, slipping softly down from the Sierras in the east, stretching its generous palm to the south across Santa Ana, Redlands, Riverside; then, to the north it reached, over Burbank, Glendale, the San Fernando Valley, to the Conejo just at the tip of its grasp; and at its center, East L.A., Downtown, Hollywood, even Beverly Hills felt its density only slightly less than the oil-choked skies of Long Beach and San Pedro as it draped out to the western sea, fading to a pale yellow blue at the horizon of the central beach towns.

Redondo, that Monday morning, sat listlessly at the edge of the ocean, bathed brightly in a cloudless sky. The private beach of the Ocean Palms Condominium Complex lay smooth and clean, its pallid white sands untouched, as if no man had ever dared to tread across its breadth before the receding tide. Tall slim palms, graceful and absurd, swayed in the morning breeze high above the tiled roofs that jutted up behind the beach. White, gold, and magnificent magenta blossoms tumbled down their vines, clinging to the beige stucco walls as if to challenge the brilliant blue, then green, endless expanse of the Pacific. A mild, inviting surf broke evenly in hollowed half-tubes of aqua glass, shattering into their own white, frothing thunder.

Steven sat alone, reclining on a chaise lounge at the edge of the long brick terrace that extended back to the sliding glass doors of the Delgatto's living room. There was no one—to his left, right and beyond, of course, except the vague image of a distant ship too far out at sea to tell. His shirt off, flung to the foot of the lounge, he lay back into the vinyl webbing, finally, relaxed. Amazing weather, was as much of a thought as his mind would carry—for nine o'clock in the morning, he managed to add. Only just a bit hung-over, he had gone to bed early; he felt almost . . . what? . . . happy? He let the idea linger, not even bothering to develop a firm yes or no. Just that the word would even cross his mind was, after all, rather something in itself. The crash of the surf . . . and its noisy building, crash! building . . . crash! . . . building . . . What? That was a car horn! Droning surf, bullshit. He jerked his head around, betrayed. That freeway's about ten feet from here probably, Christ . . .

"Hi, Steven," Linda grinned at him, her head just appearing

through the narrow width by the opened glass door as he had turned, and, startled by the look on his face, she asked, "It's so bad?"

"Oh . . . well. No . . .it's . . ." He turned back to the beach, at a loss .

"Breakfast's almost ready," she said, the smile gone from her voice, and turned back into the room.

Steven lay still, probably less than a second, and then reaching for his shirt, thrust his arms through its sleeves and, pushing himself up from the lounge, he walked back into the condo.

"Hi," he greeted cheerfully, his eyes on Linda, as the smell of bacon that Rhonda, in her red silk robe, was patiently poking and turning, brought a fuller smile to his face.

"Daddy," Justin actually screeched from his high chair, the very same high chair that Linda and Jeff had splattered their meals from some 30 years before and that Rhonda had brought out of storage one week before for this very occasion.

"Don't screech, Jus, Daddy's tired," Linda quietly admonished as Justin smacked his hand into his bowl of cereal, continuing to screech, "Daddy, Daddy!" and Rhonda, laughing and drowning them both out, jumped back from a spray of hot grease that shot out from the frying bacon, hitting Steven precisely in the narrow inch of flesh exposed by his open shirt.

"Aagh!" He couldn't suppress the sudden anguish as Justin smacked his cereal again, still screeching, but no longer bothering to form a word.

"Hey!" Nick's deep baritone almost stilled the chaos as he walked into the kitchen, slim, tan—impeccably dressed, Steven noticed as he quickly buttoned his shirt and, discreetly, he hoped, rubbed the singed flesh of his chest.

"Steven," Nick nodded to Steven's hurried half-smile and, turning, he patted first Rhonda's then Linda's behind, really rather gracefully, Steven thought, as Nick then raised his arm and rested it lightly across Linda's shoulders. "Good morning, doll," he said, lifting his arm away; and Linda, just turning to him, caught the back of his head as he fixed his attention on Justin, who, cowed now, sat back in his high chair sucking on his fist. Nick gave a doubtful smile to Justin and lightly chucked his dribbly chin, then, reaching for a towel to wipe his hand, asked, "Where's Jeff?"

"Oh he just ran out to the 7-11 to get some half-and-half for the coffee, hon," Rhonda answered, laying out the bacon on a paper towel. "Has Dana gotten Evie and Tim to stop their squabbling?"

"Oh, she's up there doing something with them. She said she'd be down in a minute," Nick answered as Linda turned on the blender full of orange juice and turned to Steven. "Get some plates out of the cabinet,

Steve, will you, and put them on the table."

Steven, still leaning against the frame of the kitchen door, straightened up and glanced around.

"In there," Linda pointed with her wooden spoon dripping orange juice, and, following the spoon, he turned around into the dining room and found the walnut china cabinet.

As Steven began to set the table, Nick walked back through the dining room to the adjoining living room and, settling into a deep leather chair, opened up the morning paper.

"Looks like the Russians still aren't admitting shooting down the 747," Nick said, either to Steven or to no one.

"Pardon me?" Steven said, turning to Nick from the china cabinet with his hands full of plates.

"Oh, I, uh, say that, the Russians haven't admitted shooting down the 747," he repeated.

"Has the pilot made any statement?" Steven asked.

"Not that I'm aware of," Nick answered as he turned the page.

"Well, uh," Steven began. "As someone very familiar with the airline industry, do you have an opinion that . . ."

"Oh, pilot error," Nick answered. "The whole thing is pilot error. On both parts. The Korean jet was radically off course. His latitude and longitude readings were reversed. His course called for a latitude of 42° and longitude of 146°. He was flying at 46° latitude and 142° longitude. It's perfectly clear."

"So, you don't think there was anything at all . . . uh, fishy? About the Korean jet being off course for over two hours?"

"No. No. Pilots aren't infallible you know," he answered and, with a laugh, added, "Though they like to think so."

"And the Soviet pilot?" Steven asked.

"Well, now. Of course, that's harder to read. The Russians are such a lying pack of devils. We can only speculate on their motives," Nick began.

"But wouldn't you agree that there's no way it was in the Soviets' interests to shoot down a commercial airliner?" Steven asked. "All they've gotten from it is the worst press they've received since Afghanistan. And zero political or military gains."

"Well, yes, in fact that is true," Nick answered. "Which is part of why it's obvious that it's pilot error. Pilot error on both sides."

"Pilot error?" Steven asked. "You mean the Soviet pilot just . . . pushed the button by mistake?"

"No. No. Come on, Steve. You were in 'Nam, weren't you? I certainly remember my days in the Pacific War Theatre. WW II. How hyped up you can get. Under attack. In sight of the enemy. You can misread a command. Use bad judgment."

"You mean," Steven looked closely at Nick, "you think that the Soviet pilot wasn't ordered to shoot? He just, sort of, jumped the gun?"

"Well," Nick answered, "let me put it this way. I don't think the order to shoot came from Moscow. After all, as you say, it would have been an idiotic decision. Not at all militarily effective. Now. The order may have come from the fighter's home base in Sakhalin . . ."

"From some hawkish major with hypertension," Steven interjected.

"Or it simply may have come," Nick continued, "from the pilot's own overwrought nervous system. He may have been worked up so intensely in the chase that, physiologically, he had no choice but to complete it. To shoot."

"But, Dad," Linda said as she walked into the dining room with a tray of glasses and began placing them around the table, "do you think human beings can be just programmed to kill like that? To kill over 200 people? That it's a physiological response?"

"Linda, I'm saying that in combat, which I don't think you have experienced, the nerves are on a very sharp edge. It's the 'fight or flight' tension. Adrenalin is pumping through the body. A split-second judgment means life or death. Human beings make errors," Nick answered.

"Well, errors are one thing," Steven said as he brought cups and saucers from the china cabinet to the table, "but acting like a robot is something else." He thought a moment, as Nick rattled his newspaper in front of him, looking slightly disturbed, brooding. "I don't care where the order came from," Steven went on, "Moscow, Sakhalin, the man's own mind . . . I believe he still had some choice."

"I agree, Steve," Linda said. "I mean, Dad," she turned to Nick, who sat still, the newspaper in his lap. "Somewhere in the man, no matter what his training for combat or his involvement in the 'chase' —somewhere in him must be that emotional or moral function of the mind that is free will, that could have decided, despite *everything*, I will not kill 244 innocent people. Period."

"See, I think," Steven began, "that your dad is right."

Both Nick and Linda turned and looked at Steven questioningly.

He went on. "That it was pilot error. But the error was that he really didn't think it was a commercial airliner. He just saw that dot on that screen, the radar screen, and—maybe that is where some programming comes in—but he just saw it as an enemy plane. He didn't see it as a jumbo jet full of people. But as a dot on the screen. A symbol of the enemy."

"Oh, are you talking about *that*," Rhonda asked as she came through the dining room door with a big platter of bacon and scrambled eggs. "I'll tell you what it's all about," she announced, placing the platter in the middle of the table. "Reagan, Brezhnev—or whoever it is now, I don't know—the generals. They're all just a bunch of little boys. Little boys, pushing and slapping, grabbing toys from each other. *You did it! No. You did it!* Playing nasty tricks on each other." She sighed and shook her head as she surveyed the partially set table. "Unfortunately they're going to blow us all up."

"Hi!" They all looked to the front door in the living room as Jeff walked in.

"Oh, good," Rhonda said. "Nick, honey, come and sit down. Linda, put some napkins on, the cloth ones in that drawer, and some salt and pepper. Jeff, run upstairs and see what's keeping Dana. Here, give me the cream . . . Steve, hand me that cream pitcher on the buffet, will you dear? Oh! Justin!" she finished as she heard him starting to cry from his high chair in the kitchen and turned abruptly to go see to him.

After breakfast as Linda was sipping her third cup of coffee at the table, Nick had returned to his newspaper in the living room, Jeff and Steven were speculating on who would play in the World Series, and Dana was tending to a still cranky Evie, Rhonda suggested, "Linda, would you and Steve like to take a walk before your Aunt Maureen comes? I'd love to watch Justin for you. It seems you just got here and now you're leaving tonight." She sighed. "And you've hardly had a minute to enjoy the beach."

Linda's eyes lit with pleasure. "Oh, Mom, that would be wonderful. Thanks." She smiled warmly at her mother, and getting up from the table said, "Steve. Come on. Let's take a walk on the beach."

Steven looked up from his discussion on baseball, only slightly relieved, and said, "Sure. Great."

As they left the long brick terrace of the condo and plodded through the soft sand toward the still receding tide, Steven gently rested his arm around Linda's shoulders. "How you doin', Lin?"

"Oh fine. Fine. And you?"

"Pretty good. Actually, I'm having a good time. Your mother's great. She's so . . . energetic. And really seems to care about everyone, wants everyone to be enjoying themselves. She really puts herself out. And your dad seems a little less hostile than last time I saw him, last year."

"Oh, yeah," Linda said. "Dad's a little hard to read, but, he's trying."

They were silent a moment, both thinking of Rhonda and Nick, as they reached the hard sand at the surf's edge and headed south along the rim of dark shore meeting the blue curl of ocean.

"Do you think their relationship will hold up?" Steven asked.

"You mean that they'll stay together for the rest of their lives?"

Linda asked him.

"Well," Steven thought. "Yeah. That's what I mean."

Linda looked down the long beach before them and, with a soundless sigh, answered, "I don't know, Steve. I'd always thought, when I was a kid, when I lived with them . . . I just assumed, of course, Mom and Dad would live together forever. That's what married people do. It never occurred to me that divorce would be a possibility for them."

"Well, that's partly your Catholic upbringing," Steven said.

"Yeah. And maybe that's part of why Mom and Dad are together again now. Their separation was really a shock. To all of us. To me and Jeff—and to them. We were such a perfect, typical little nuclear family. You know?" She turned and looked at Steven.

"Well. I do and I don't," he answered. "I mean, I know what you mean, hell, I watched Donna Reed. But as far as actually living it . . ."

"I know, Steve," Linda said as she put her arm around his waist and, for a moment, leaned her head softly against his shoulder. "I wish I could have met your father."

"Oh, you're lucky you didn't," Steven said quickly, bitterly and then, with anger, "I wish he'd died sooner. Then maybe my mother could have lived longer."

"Oh, Steven," Linda said, almost with distaste, "that's pretty harsh."

"He was a harsh man, Linda. Plus, he was totally pickled by the time he kicked. His mind was just demented. I hate to think of what he put my mother through those last years."

"Why did she stay with him? I remember her as being . . . really quite intelligent."

"Oh, she was. She was. A very fine, sensitive woman." Steven looked down at his feet as they made each step an impression in the sand, and Linda, looking at him, felt the tears of sadness that lay behind the dry, thin lines at the corner of his eye.

"Whoa!" she half-shrieked as a frothy film of surf rushed up the hard sand and chased their heels as they both ran, laughing, narrowly escaping the errant wave. Leaning on each other, they took off their shoes and socks and then, looking around, threw them back from the water, in the sand, and, arms back around each other, continued on down the beach.

"I guess," Steven said, "I guess that's why she stayed with him. She couldn't just leave him . . . to the dogs. I guess she felt she had to take care of him."

"But Steven," Linda asked, "do you think if she had cared as much about herself as she did about him . . ."

"She would have left him?"

"Well. Yeah. If he was really as bad off as you say, she could have put him in a home or a hospital."

"She didn't have any money, Linda. In the last years, all they had was his veteran's pension."

"But there are veterans' hospitals."

"That's true. Yeah, I know. I wish she had done that. I really do. But I just can't believe that it was something lacking in her that kept her with him. Like her lack of self-respect or something. I think it was something else, something bigger than that. I don't know. Not her love for him, but . . ."

"Her loyalty?" Linda asked.

"Well . . . yeah." Steven nodded, again watching his feet imprint the sand.

Linda looked out over the green-blue sheen of ocean glancing white lights in the sun. "I don't know, Steven. It seems to me she should have left him. Have saved what was left of her life and lived it, fully. For herself."

"Well, now who's sounding harsh, Linda?" Steven asked, stepping away from her a little as their arms fell away from each other. He looked at her. "And, I might remind you, you didn't really know them."

"Oh, Steven, I know," Linda hurried to say. "But, really, I'm thinking of Rhonda just as much as your mother, or a million women—a million people's mothers. I just . . . It's just something I've thought about."

"What?" he asked gently, sincerely curious.

In unspoken agreement they sat down in the sand a few feet from the breaking waves and Linda, sifting the warm sand through her fingers from hand to hand, continued, "I guess, Steve—don't laugh—but you could say I've been thinking about the 'sanctity of marriage.'"

"Oh, that Catholic stuff?" Steven asked with an edge of annoyance.

"Don't dismiss it as that, Steven. And that's not really what I mean. I also mean this thing you're trying to talk about—about your mother. Love, or loyalty . . . or whatever it is that keeps two people living together, year after year, until their deaths. No matter how much their communication fails, or how much they grow to hate each other, or be bored with each other, or disrespect each other . . ."

"OK. OK," Steven answered. They were silent for a moment, both looking out to sea, both a little frightened.

Linda looked down at the little pile of sifted sand in front of her and began to pat it into a hill shape. "I really wonder, Steve, if Rhonda and Nick wouldn't be better off divorced. I really do. And, from the little I know, your mother might have been too. But Rhonda . . . Mom doesn't respect Dad anymore. I know that. And he doesn't love her. I think she drives him crazy. They just don't have the same feelings about life. They don't want the same things, not deep down. I don't mean their lifestyle, their superficial lifestyle—the condo, the car, the grocery store. I mean their view of the world, their deepest response to life. It's just not the same. They are not in harmony. I think they just stay together out of protocol or some Catholic guilt, or . . . maybe they think they don't have any other choice."

"Well, Linda, do they?" Steven asked. "What would they do on their own? What did they do during that year or so they were separated? They didn't know what to do with themselves. I don't know what my mother would have done if she had left my father. She would have been totally lost, at sea. He was the purpose of her life."

"That's what I mean, Steven. But why was *he* the purpose of her life? Why wasn't *she* the purpose of her life?"

"She loved him, Linda," Steven answered, not impatiently, but incredulously. He looked at her. "What are you getting at? That people shouldn't be loyal to each other? That they shouldn't try to take care of each other? In sickness and in health? As they say," he added, with a note of cynicism. "Is that what you mean? That you're starting to question the 'sanctity' of marriage? That you question those vows?"

"No. Steven. No. I . . ." Linda ran her hand back and forth through the warm sand, reaching down, deeper, to the cool sand beneath. She watched her wrist as it, too, began to disappear beneath the white sand. She seemed confused, uncertain, Steven thought. He watched her a moment, then reached in his front shirt pocket and pulled out a cigarette. As he lit it, Linda looked at him. "I guess I need to think about it some more, Steve. I know I'm not articulating it very well. It's just something about . . . something about thinking things are a certain way, because they have to be a certain way, they always have been a certain way, and you just go along making your life fit into that way . . . without even thinking about it."

"Well, you're right, Linda," Steven said. "That's not a very eloquent argument for divorce."

"Steve, I'm not arguing for divorce," Linda rejoined, "and please don't feel threatened by what I'm trying to say, because I love you and want to be with you. I'm talking about when, I'm talking about . . ."

"When you stop loving me," Steven finished.

"No," Linda answered.

"Hallooo," they heard and, looking up the beach they saw Jeff and Dana walking toward them.

"To be continued," Steven said as he raised himself up from his seat in the sand and, brushing himself off, waved back to his in-laws. Linda kissed Steven on the cheek and brushed off the back of his shirt and pants before they set back up the beach to meet Jeff and Dana.

"Mom's great," Jeff smiled to Linda and Steven as they approached, "she's got all three kids playing some kind of game with potatoes or something."

"Yeah, and she's having a great time," Dana added. "It's nice to get a break from the kids." She looked meaningfully at Linda.

"You haven't started either of them in childcare?" Linda asked.

"No," Dana answered. "Tim will be ready for school in another year, for kindergarten. I might put Evie in a toddler program once he starts school and go back to work, but it's been so long, god, I hate to think . . ."

"How about you, Linda?" Jeff asked. "Are you thinking of putting Justin in childcare?"

"Well, yeah, actually, Steven and I had hoped to be able to get him in a toddler program this fall. He'll be two and a half at the end of October. In two months."

"How long have you two been married?" Dana asked.

"Seven years," Linda answered. "Longer than you and Jeff, my little brother here," she said as she gave him a light pinch on the side flesh of his waist.

He smiled and backed away. "Well, Linda, you'd better hurry up and catch up with us. Give Justin a little brother or sister."

"You mean before I'm too old to reproduce?" Linda asked, pinching him again. "Listen, little brother, I have a few good years yet!"

"So how do you like living down here in the Southland?" Steven changed the subject, directing his question to Jeff.

"Oh. Well. We live down in Laguna, another 40 miles south of here," Jeff answered. "Can't beat it, I figure. Best climate in the country. I might feel a little different if I lived in L.A. though. It can get pretty hard to take. Ask Dana, she was brought up in Hollywood."

"Really?" Steven asked her, his eyes lighting.

"Don't get excited, Steve," Linda told him, "it's not what you think."

"Oh, Hollywood has really gotten seedy," Dana informed him. "Everything's run down and dirty. Actually it just looks like a slum. Not at all what people from the Midwest are expecting when they come out here. 'Where are the movie stars? Where are the limousines?' That's what my cousin said practically the minute she got off the plane. Boy, was she disappointed."

"I'll bet," Steven answered.

"Well, I hope you took her on a few movie studio tours or something," Linda said.

"Oh yeah, we did. But she never really quite got over the fact that Hollywood and Vine looks like East Cleveland. I think she expected something like Disneyland. She was happy when we went there."

"Movie studios. Disneyland. She's lucky she didn't grow up with it," Linda said. "I remember the first time I saw a real fishing village in New England I thought it was a movie set. I just couldn't believe it was real."

"I know what you mean," Jeff nodded. "Every time I see a lake or a waterfall I think it's man-made."

"Well, Jeff," Dana said, "that's because every lake and waterfall in Southern California *is* man-made."

"Well, how do you think the Olympics are going to affect this area?" Steven asked them.

"Oh god," Jeff groaned. "It's going to be a madhouse. It's at least ten months off and people are already talking about how they're going to rent out their apartments for $1,000 a day or their front lawns for parking."

"I just hope there's not some crazy incident," Dana said.

"What do you mean?" Linda asked.

"Oh like that thing with the Israelis in Germany that time?" Jeff asked.

"Oh, that was awful!" Linda remembered. "When was that? In the '60s?"

"No, it was 1972, I think," Jeff answered. "In Munich. I'd been stationed at our army base there a year before . . ."

"What was it? Some German Nazis killed the Jewish athletes?" Dana asked.

"No, no. They were Arabs," Jeff corrected.

"Actually, they were Palestinian," Steven reminded them, "Palestinians who'd been living in prison camps in Jordan and the Gaza Strip."

"Where?"

"Areas that Israel occupied after the 1967 War. The Israelis put all the Palestinians in camps," Steven answered.

"My god, how ironic," Linda began.

"Oh, it's a horrible mess over there," Dana concluded. "I just hope and pray they don't bring their terrorist murderers over here next summer."

"Why not? We send ours over there year round." Steven laughed as Linda shot him a warning glance.

"Well, it looks like the Russians won't be showing up," Jeff was saying as they plodded through the soft sand toward the condo complex.

"I thought the Olympics were supposed to *ignore* politics," Dana complained. "How else can we have any peace?"

As they crossed the terrace and went through the sliding glass door to the living room, they saw Maureen sitting in Nick's leather chair holding Justin, who seemed to be happily playing with the tie on the front of her blouse.

"Maureen!" Linda called to her as she ran over to the chair and, bending down, gave her aunt a warm hug.

"Linda, dear." Maureen returned her hug with affection as Justin squirmed to regain his position and began to cry, "Mommy." Linda picked him up as Steven came up to shake Maureen's hand. He was always curious at the difference between Maureen and Rhonda. Though Maureen was five or six years older than her sister, in her mid-'60s, that was not what struck him, but her . . . what? It wasn't that she had less vitality than Rhonda exactly, but that it was so differently channeled—inward, as if some part of her, behind the eyes, were looking inward to a depth or to the glow of an ember burning in darkness. He thought of Sylvia, Maureen's only child. Maureen must have been 32, 33—Linda's age—when Sylvia was born. And Louis, her husband, dead for over ten years. She must be a lonely woman, Steven thought. But she did not look unhappy. Nor did she look happy. She was a well-preserved woman, thin; the lines of her dry, taut skin spoke well of the years that had drawn them. Interest. A keen interest. That's what seemed to emanate from her, he realized.

"Maureen, I got the books you wanted from Sylvia," Linda said as Jeff and Dana completed their perfunctory kisses of greeting.

"Good. Good," Maureen said, her grey eyes softly shining and a mild smile on her lips as Linda, turning back from the bookshelves, brought the frayed ledgers to her aunt. She laid them in Maureen's lap and sat on the arm of the leather chair, waiting for her to open them. But Maureen folded her thin, veined, still graceful hands on top of the black leather book covers.

"Justin is a lovely child, Linda. You two must be very happy," she said looking at Steven and Linda.

Steven smiled as Linda said, "Oh, thank you, Maureen. We really are. It hasn't all been a bed of roses, of course." She laughed, looking at Justin who had wandered over to Evie and Tim playing in the dining room.

"No doubt," Maureen acknowledged, "but worth every minute, as I'm sure you know. He seems like such a gentle, thoughtful boy."

"He is, actually," Linda agreed. "Though these are the 'terrible twos' everyone has warned us about, for the most part, he hasn't been that demanding . . . yet."

"Yeah, it's kind of amazing," Steven added. "He seems quite contented a lot of the time. Almost reflective. Sometimes I worry."

Maureen laughed. "Steven, don't worry. Probably one of the worst things parents can do for a child, or for themselves, is to worry. A hard lesson to learn, I certainly know. But one I truly believe. If your child is a little different than the others, or doesn't follow all the phases just as they are in the book—whatever book is the creed at the time—please believe me, the biggest mistake is to worry about it. Rejoice in his uniqueness. Love him for who he is and the path he chooses to follow . . ." She hesitated a moment, looking at Justin plopped down next to Evie and Tim, quietly watching them squabble over their Legos. "Sylvia was a quiet child too," she said, her voice distant as it reached across the years. "A very sweet child, and reflective, as you say, Steven." She looked back at Steven and Linda and, laughing again, quietly, more to herself than to them, she said, "I'm afraid I worried too much about her, about her 'difference' from the other children. It took me many years . . . many years to accept her ways." Linda, and Steven standing beside her, watched Maureen's face, intent, waiting for her to go on. "But Sylvia would do as she would do. As she would choose." Maureen laughed again, more fully. "Don't we all know!"

Linda laughed too and put her arm around Maureen's shoulder, giving her a quick hug. "That's the truth," Steven nodded.

"Well, I'll tell you," Maureen went on. "We have both, Sylvia and I, been much happier since I . . . I chose to stop worrying about her. Her ways, and her choices. Stop the worrying, and accept her for the very unique . . ." she paused again, and wrinkling her brow as if looking for just the right word, "quite courageous young woman she is."

Linda leaned back into her side of the chair. "Maureen," she said, "it makes me really happy to hear you say that. I mean, I know things have not always been easy."

Maureen patted Linda's knee gently as if to say "enough said," and with her other hand turned back the frayed black cover of the book in her lap.

"Sylvia called me just the other night. She had quite an amusing story about her encounter with the attorney. Apparently he was not such an easy fellow to deal with. But I'm glad to have these accounts. I think I'll find quite a bit of information here."

"Just what are you looking for in those ledgers?" Rhonda asked as she and Dana walked in from the kitchen carrying trays of hors d'oeuvres and drinks. Nick and Jeff were sitting out on the terrace with the portable TV watching the Labor Day football games.

Steven took the drink tray from Dana and, setting it on the coffee table, asked the women what they would have.

"Just a small glass of vermouth, thanks, Steven," Maureen answered and, turning to Rhonda, replied, "Don't you remember, Rhonda? I'd mentioned that Louis' father had had a small business, some sort of delivery or transport business in San Francisco. Louis was raised in San Francisco," she said to Steven, and then looking back to Rhonda, " . . . just for a few years. It didn't do very well at all. It was just at the end of the Depression, I believe. Well let's see," she said, looking at the first, then last pages of each book. "It seems to have been from sometime in 1927 . . . to . . . well, just after the crash, early 1930." She looked up at them.

"Yes, yes, I remember, Maureen," Rhonda said, a little excited. "But what do you hope to find in there?"

"Well, Rhonda, you know Louis' father was Italian," Maureen laughed, "and, as I'm sure you know, the Italians frequently mix family and business, as many cultures do. I imagine I will find many of the accounts, the customers, in these books are Louis' relatives, on his father's side at least and, possibly, on his mother's."

Linda, sitting back on her armchair perch, was studying Maureen with a pensive, slightly doubtful look on her face. "But Aunt Maureen," she began. Maureen looked around to her. "What are you trying to unearth through all this?" Linda paused, clearly not wanting to offend her aunt, yet not sure she could leave Maureen's pursuit unquestioned.

"Oh, I know, Linda," Maureen answered. "Sylvia already gave me quite a lecture. Genealogy is a silly thing at best, I imagine you think. And Sylvia takes it quite a bit further, of course . . . It's dangerous. Something about 'white nationalism' and the Mormons and the 'ruling class.'"

"Well, it's true," Steven said. "The Mormons do have quite a corner on the genealogy market. They have incredible libraries with masses of records at their various temples. And in Salt Lake City, I've heard people who are really into this thing have spent months in the Mormon Temple there."

"Well, I have a friend," Dana said, "who found out her great-great-great-great-something or other was actually on the Mayflower, which is supposed to be some kind of big deal."

"To the D.A.R." Linda said.

"Who?" Dana asked.

"Daughters of the American Revolution," Steven answered.

"Definitely ruling class type folks," Linda added.

"I think it's kind of interesting," Dana went on. "I mean, what's the matter with going back and seeing where you came from, who all your relatives were and everything? I mean, it's kind of like history or something."

"Well, I think what Sylvia means," Linda said, deciding to be bold, "is that genealogy, as a sort of fad that's increasingly popular . . ." Steven gave Linda a warning look himself as Maureen sat back in her chair, though the older woman's expression was patient. Linda went on, " . . . has mainly been taken up by middle-class or well-to-do white people who seem to want to . . . to prove something that . . ." She paused, and then, despite the tense silence and the look on Steven's face, she continued, "Well, for example, to prove that their great great whatevers came over on the Mayflower, or . . . well that they are . . ." She thought again and then, remembering Sylvia's comments to her that day she had first heard that Maureen wanted the ledgers, she decided to go the whole way with it, to speak for Sylvia. Looking at Rhonda, Linda picked up her thought to continue. "Well, Linda, really," Rhonda began, but Linda was speaking again.

" . . . that it's as if genealogy represented a movement among affluent white people in this country to hold on to, even to make sacred, their colonialist roots. I mean, it *is* a kind of white nationalism, or some kind of effort to prove and glorify that they are all snowy white, that they have a direct line on the European take-over of this country, that they . . . Well. It just seems really racist."

"Well, now Linda!" Rhonda began again as Steven poured himself another whiskey and Dana walked back into the dining room to watch the children.

"Yeah, but Mom," Linda had decided to play her role to the hilt, "it's got to mean something that genealogy is the favorite activity of the Mormons—next to keeping women out of heaven. I mean, the Mormons are the most racist, capitalist . . ." She stopped, searching for an appropriately pejorative term.

"And what's more, they own the Safeway stores, the Marriot hotels, and, apparently, Las Vegas," Maureen said.

Linda and Rhonda looked at Maureen, startled, as Steven laughed.

"In fact, Linda," Maureen said to her, without antagonism, "Sylvia has already told me all this . . . and much more, as you might imagine."

"Well, I've certainly never heard that!" Rhonda said, still amazed. "The Mormons own Las Vegas? How strange! I thought Frank Sinatra owned Las Vegas."

Steven laughed again as Linda relaxed her shoulders and leaned back once more into her edge of the armchair back.

"I appreciate your information, Linda," Maureen said, looking at her with apparent sincerity, "though, as I said, I have heard a similar, possibly more detailed lecture from Sylvia." Linda flushed slightly, but Maureen went on, "And no doubt much of what you both say has truth. But the fact is . . ." She paused, reflecting.

"Well, I think it's fine, Maureen, if you want to . . ." Rhonda began.

"Thank you, Rhonda," Maureen acknowledged, but, picking up her thought again, she looked at Linda. "The fact is that, just because a certain method, or mode of investigation, of historical investigation, is adopted by a particular group—a group that may have very unsavory purposes, that is to say, racist, sexist, all the rest of it—does not mean that the method, the mode itself, is evil. The *method* is simply a tool, and a tool is a neutral thing. It is how the tool is *used*, dear, don't you think, wherein the evil lies." She looked at Linda. "Certainly, Linda. I am not a Mormon. Nor do I intend to convert."

Steven smiled as Rhonda looked approvingly at Maureen and then, with a glint of challenge in her eye, to Linda.

"I think that's true, Maureen," Linda answered sincerely and then, with a still questioning crease in her brow, "but sometimes I wonder, well, where the 'tool' stops and the 'use' begins . . . Do you know what I mean?" She looked at Steven, and Maureen and Rhonda followed her glance.

"Well," Steven was actually following Linda's train of thought, "if you mean that old question we've talked about, how 'form' and 'content' shape each other, that they are not really separate . . ."

"Yeah," Linda nodded as Maureen sat forward in her chair, more interested in this new vein of the conversation. Linda picked it up, "You know—the meaning is the message and all that. Or that you can't really separate your method from your outcome. I mean, your method of analysis determines the content of your result as much as the actual data itself . . ."

"Oh Christ, you've lost me," Rhonda said. "Steve. Pour me another little bit of scotch . . . uh, uh! That's it. Thank you, dear," she said as she took her glass back from Steven. "Personally," she said, rather emphatically, "I'd like to hear just what Maureen intends to do with these names she comes up with in these ledger books."

Maureen smiled, and Linda and Steven, in unspoken agreement, dropped their argument and sat back in their respective seats as Dana, having settled the latest squabble with the kids, came back into the living room holding Justin.

Maureen, all eyes upon her, gazed at Justin, apparently lost in thought. After a moment, she responded. "At some point," she looked at Linda, then at Steven, "I'd like very much to continue this discussion—this idea—it's very interesting. Although, I'm not sure it exactly applies here." She paused, setting her glass on the table and, as Steven freshened her drink, she went on, "However, this idea of the relationship between the method of investigation and the object being investigated . . ."

Dana frowned and Rhonda interrupted, "Oh, not now, Maureen. What about the . . ."

"Yes. OK, Rhonda. Well," Maureen began again, "the fact is, it's really no great mystery—and I'm certainly not looking to see if Louis' ancestors were on the Mayflower, god knows, I could care less, I . . ."

She paused and, her voice changing tone, somewhat saddened, she said, "I'm simply looking for . . . for family. *Living* family."

"But Maureen!" Rhonda began, as if insulted.

"Mom," Linda quieted her. "You mean Louis' family, Maureen?"

"Well, yes," Maureen said. "You know, Louis was an only child. Like Sylvia. And . . . after we were married, you know, we always lived in this area, and . . . though we did visit with his parents in San Francisco from time to time. But then they both died within, oh, I don't know, four or five years after our marriage. Louis and I were both 30 or so when we met and . . . Well . . ." She seemed uncomfortable, not quite sure if she could, or if she wanted to explain herself on this issue, especially after such an unexpected build-up.

Linda looked at her with sympathy and began to speak but Maureen went on. "Beyond those few visits with his parents, I never really had any contact with Louis' family, and I simply . . . I simply would like to meet with some of his living relatives," she paused, a sadness in her soft grey eyes that made Steven wish he could erase all that had been said, ". . . to remember him better I suppose. So many years have passed," she finished, and, with an almost girlish innocence, she looked up at them and shrugged.

For a moment the silence that followed unnerved them all, but Linda, shifting on the arm of the chair to look more fully at Maureen, said with a cheerful enthusiasm, "Maureen listen. Steven and I could really possibly be of some help to you, honestly. I mean, since we live up there, maybe we could do some leg work, or . . ."

"Yeah, for sure." Steven was nodding as he poured himself another drink.

Maureen smiled and again patting Linda's knee as if to quiet her, said affectionately, "Thank you, dear. I just may take you up on that."

"Rhonda!" Nick called from the terrace.

Rhonda, who had been leaning forward in her chair watching her sister with, what Steven thought, a rather doleful expression, sat up abruptly on edge and answered, "Yes, Nick?"

"Shouldn't we be getting ready to go?" he yelled back.

"I guess the game's over," Rhonda said to no one in particular as she looked at her watch, then, "Oh yes! My god, it's 4:00. Our reservations are for 5:00." She stood up and began putting bottles back on the tray as she called to Nick, "Yes, honey, let's get going!"

Steven turned a questioning look to Linda who responded, "Oh, Steve, we decided last night after you went to bed. I'm sorry, I forgot to mention it. So much has been going on . . ."

"Decided what?"

"To go out to dinner."

"But don't we have plane reservations for 8:30?"

"Yes, Dad's going to take us to the airport from the restaurant. We're going to The Tides, aren't we, Mom?" Linda looked back at Rhonda, and then turned again to Steven. "It's only about six blocks from here. Actually, we thought we'd walk over, or whoever wants to. Dad's going to drive the car over so whoever wants to can ride with him."

"When is the sitter coming?" Dana asked.

"Sitter?" Steven said.

"For the kids," Dana answered.

"Oh, I see," Steven nodded, and then turning to Linda, "Well, Lin, I knew you were anxious to get Jus in childcare, but it seems a little extreme to fly back home without him."

"Ho ho, Steven," she returned. "I know you think Mom and I can't make a coherent set of plans—the sitter is for Evie and Tim. We're taking Justin to the restaurant. So go up and start packing."

He sat still a moment while the women bustled around him, straightening up. "Steve. Move it!" Linda added.

He set his half-filled glass on the table with reluctance and rose slowly from his comfortable seat on the overstuffed sofa. He couldn't help but feel a sluggish wave of depression as he realized the holiday was coming to a close. As he made his way to the staircase, three thoughts hit him with almost simultaneous and deadening force: his postponed murder trial; his vandalized, possibly useless Toyota; and his unmailed billings superimposed over the three-digit balance in his checkbook. Trying not to groan aloud, he stopped halfway to the stairs and looked back at his unfinished drink just as Rhonda whisked it up onto a silver tray balanced in her hand, and Linda gave him a little push back toward the stairs.

Forty-five minutes later, when they had all reassembled in the living room, Rhonda began directing, "Justin can come with Nick and me in the car. Now, Maureen, you want to walk, I know, it was your idea . . ."

"I'll ride," Dana said emphatically, almost drowning out Linda who announced that she and Steven would walk with Maureen. "I guess I'll ride with Dana," Jeff said as the doorbell rang and Rhonda, who happened to be standing a foot from the front door, flung it open.

Dana gasped audibly as a 13 year-old girl with purplish spiked hair, peddle-pushers, high heels and a badly torn T-shirt smiled at Rhonda—sweetly enough, Steven thought through his initial surprise—as she walked into the room.

"Dana. Jeff. Steven. Linda. Maureen. Meet Gloria," Rhonda said in a no-nonsense tone. "She's the Martins' daughter."

Jeff looked visibly relieved, knowing that the Martins were his parents' best friends; though Dana had not yet recovered herself, which did not escape Gloria. Nor did it faze her in the least.

Rhonda continued, "Gloria lives just down the street and has very kindly agreed to help us out on such short notice. We're very, very grateful, Gloria."

"Oh, like, that's OK, Mrs. Delgatto. I mean like, hey, where are the kids?" And seeing Evie and Tim in the dining room with Linda, she walked in and sat down with them, a youthful, happy grin lighting her face.

Steven continued to study her as she bent over their coloring books and, with a surprising quickness and maternal skill, became involved in their child's world. He had not really been in such close proximity to a modern adolescent and was still struggling with the contradiction in his mind. For Gloria's manner and her way with children, she could have been the Virgin Mary, as sweet, polite, modest and capable as one could wish, and yet her get-up! Christ, it was grotesque. The cactus-like hair, the layers of brooding make-up, almost violent in its starkness, its defiance. He was shaking his head, though certainly not as disconcerted as Dana, when Linda nudged him. "Let's go, Steve. Maureen is waiting."

"We'll see you at The Tides," Linda called back to the rest of her family as she, Steven and Maureen, who seemed oblivious to the apparition of Gloria, strolled out into the afternoon. They crossed through the gardens of the condo complex and Steven felt his good humor return as a warm breeze wafted lightly, gently mussing his hair and, as Linda linked her arm through Maureen's, he gazed at the lush lavender bloom of wisteria falling so delicately from its mass of tangled green vine on the arbor before them. Hedges of oleander and plumbago guarded the front of the complex, opening out to a long curving drive lined with Italian cypress tipping to the breeze. To their right just beyond the drive, a plane of gold late summer grasses sloped off and up to the curve of a muted-yellow hill, a lone scrub oak sprawled at its base.

"So the conference had nothing at all to do with genealogy!" Linda was saying to Maureen.

"No, no, dear. I don't know where you got that idea," Maureen answered.

"Well, Mom said . . ."

"Oh, Rhonda never can seem to get things straight sometimes," Maureen sighed. "Well," she pressed her lips, then continued, "as I was saying, it was a two-day conference, yesterday and today. I skipped the plenary session this afternoon."

"Well, I'd love to hear more about it. I had no idea there were that many people interested in the United Nations. I guess I've just always thought of the U.N. as a big building in New York."

"Well they do turn out a few million dollars worth of paperwork every year," Steven entered the conversation.

"Tst. Now Steven." Maureen gave him a look, not without affection. "Actually that's the point," she went on. "It's true, the U.N. has little power. And yet it is the only body in existence where representatives of every world government, or at least 99 percent of them, meet on a regular basis. I mean to say, there is a foundation there, a structure already established which could be the embryo for one world government."

"Oh, Maureen. Do you really think that's possible?" Linda asked doubtfully.

"It has to be possible, Linda," Maureen answered simply. "The alternative is . . . world war." She looked off at the row of white stucco houses they were approaching, the orange tile roofs slanted against the cloudless blue sky, and then down at the sidewalk in front of her. "We survived the last one. It's true. But a lot has changed in 40 years. Technology, communications, weapons. The world is a much smaller place, and the interrelationship of everyone and everything in it is no longer something we can ignore." She looked up again, ahead of her. "I believe we can use this knowledge, and the communications systems we have developed—either to destroy ourselves—or to form a united world government."

"But it seems like that's light years away, Maureen. There are so many differences among people, cultures," Linda began.

"Well, how does this organization plan to . . . What's it called?" Steven asked.

"The Campaign?" Maureen asked, recalling her original point, "Oh, it's the Campaign for United Nations Reform. Actually, Steven, their goals are much more modest." She began to rummage in the cloth bag that hung from her shoulder. "I was just rambling on about my own thoughts on the matter, really. . . which, I should add, are not totally devoid of Sylvia's influence. Though we haven't really talked politics in quite awhile. She used to send me this and that leaflet or tract, you know. A lot of it I couldn't really make head nor tail of . . . ah, here we go." She produced a leaflet of her own and handed it to Steven and Linda. They skimmed over it.

An elliptical world, its cluster of continents bound by meridians, headed the sheet of paper. Under the title, *A More Effective U.N. System: A Program for Peace*, were a series of small sketches, each illustrating one of the points of the program: the scales of justice, a commercial jet, a refinery, a courtroom, a diamond mine. Each image depicted objectives such as:

Create U.N. Global Resources Program
Set-up International Disarmament Program
Strengthen U.N. Environment Program
Provide More Effective Human Rights Machinery
Modify Use of the Veto in Security Council

Steven fingered the knot of his tie as he looked over Linda's shoulder at the leaflet. "I don't see anything in here about one world government. Though these seem like good ideas," he said. "I just wonder if it's not more bureaucracy."

"Possibly, Steven. Possibly." Maureen nodded patiently. "But I suppose I'd rather work toward building an international bureaucracy whose goals are peace and justice in the world, than an international war zone, more and more weapons, enough to blow up every square inch of the planet a hundred times over."

Steven shrugged.

"The fact is, Steven," Maureen went on, "I don't know that I have a great deal of hope for this particular organization, the Campaign, either. They certainly don't have a very large following. Certainly the Los Angeles football team . . . what are they? . . . the Rams have a thousand times the following that the Campaign has."

Steven laughed as Maureen continued, "But there are others interested in this idea of the possibilities of the U.N. were it to have more power. I've been doing some reading on the subject on my own. One man's ideas in particular I've just come across—very interesting, very hopeful I thought. He's a Pakistani man who is a director at the World Bank, actually. He's critical of the World Bank and the International Monetary Fund, too. Of course not nearly as critical as Sylvia, I'm sure." She smiled. "But he believes that . . . well, perhaps I shouldn't speak for him. Let me say that *I* believe that we cannot possibly have world peace until there is a more just economic system in the world. Until starvation is abolished. Over 400 million people in the world are suffering from starvation—now—in 1983!" She shook her head.

"But so," Maureen recalled her point, "this man from Pakistan—Mahbub ul-Haq is his name—believes that economic equality can never be achieved as long as the World Bank and the International Monetary Fund are dominating world trade as they do. Their interests are too tied up in the affluent nations. As Sylvia would say, they are bleeding the poor countries dry. Making loans on top of loans with higher and higher interest rates; then imposing austerity measures on the countries involved."

"All the while taking out the natural resources of those countries at below market prices," Steven added.

"Stealing them, Sylvia would say," Maureen added.

"Well what is this Ul-Haq's theory?" Linda asked.

"Well, yes," Maureen went on, her eyes lighting with enthusiasm. "His theory is that the functions of the World Bank and the International Monetary Fund should be taken over by the General Assembly of the U.N., which would become a global decision-making body. This would give a majority vote to the poor nations who have so long been crushed by the few rich nations' authority in world trade. He even suggests that national reserve currencies be abolished and that there be *one international currency.*"

"Good lord," Steven said, bemused by the thought. "Well that would certainly put an end to currency gambling, black marketing."

"But he goes on." Maureen stopped on the sidewalk, a little out of breath. "The General Assembly would take over, own and control all international transport, run all international trade, allocate food proportionally to populations, and perform economic planning on a world scale."

"But how would this ever happen, Maureen?" Linda asked, afraid that her aunt was on another wild goose chase.

"Well, dear," Maureen answered, starting again, slowly, to walk toward the busy intersection ahead of them. "I know from our perspective in this country it does seem quite impossible. But there are intellectuals and economists from the poorer countries of the world, where there is so much suffering, who are developing these ideas. And where there are ideas, there are ways to make them true."

"What does Sylvia think of all this?" Linda asked. "Does she know you've been looking into these things?"

"Oh, well." Maureen gave a little shrug. "I mentioned something of it to Sylvia a few months ago. She was not very enthused, really." Maureen paused, remembering that conversation with her daughter. "In fact, she had some sort of analysis about it. To be honest, it sounded like Marxist rhetoric to me."

Steven smiled. "What was it?"

"Oh, let me see now if I can get it right." Maureen did want to do her daughter justice. "Yes. It was that . . . it was that it is futile to try to create economic justice by altering the relationships between nations."

"What? That doesn't sound like Sylvia!" Linda interrupted.

"Now wait, dear. She said that changing the relations among nations would only make changes in the 'superstructure.' And that real change had to come from the . . . what was it? . . . from the 'base.' Yes. That was it. You see what I mean? These Marxist terms." Maureen paused. "But what I think she was saying was that—I looked it up later—the 'base' is the masses, the people within the nations. And that if the changes did not originate from the people themselves, then these changes at the international level would only be superficial. People's lives would not change."

Maureen stood a moment, gazing at the stream of traffic as they stopped at the red light on the corner. "Actually, I suppose I can vaguely see some sort of sense to what she was saying." She turned to Linda. "But then, it's very difficult for me to accept that the creation of one world government, whoever set it up, would have *no* effect on the people of the countries involved."

"Well, I'm sure it would have an effect!" Linda agreed.

"Well, now, you know," Steven began, guiding the two women into the crosswalk as the light turned green. "I can sort of see Sylvia's point. It's sort of like what I was saying about bureaucracy. What's the difference? What does it really have to do with anyone's life? If there's one big international bureaucracy, or a few hundred odd smaller ones . . ."

"One-hundred and sixty, Steven," Maureen corrected. "There are 160 countries in the world today."

"Oh Steve, come on!" Linda turned to him. "Of *course*, it would make a difference. If there were only one government in the world . . . well, who would they have a war with?"

"Oh, Mars. Jupiter. God knows, they'd find someone," Steven answered.

Linda turned away from him, a frown on her face. "This way," she said as they turned left down the block. "I think it's fascinating, Maureen," she said to her aunt. "And I think it's really great that you've gotten so involved in this . . . pursuit. If more people would take an interest in these things," she glanced at a shop window's display of fall fashions, "there might be more . . . more . . . "

"Hope," Maureen finished for her.

"Is that it?" Steven asked, pointing just ahead to a large building with a facade of old weathered wood. Fishnets and green Japanese floats were draped from its roof, and scrawled over the tall doorframe in large red neon letters: *The Tides*.

Steven held the heavy wooden door open, then followed Maureen and Linda into the dark foyer. Blinking, he heard his name called, and looking to the right, he saw the rest of their party seated in the lounge. Nick was beckoning to them, and as they took their seats in the large oak chairs, Nick said, "Steven, I think you got a phone call just as we were leaving."

"You think I got a phone call?" Steven asked, looking to see what Nick was drinking.

"Well, Gloria took the call," Nick explained. "We had all just walked out the door. She said a woman called asking for a Mr. Walton. Apparently Gloria assumed it was a wrong number, but the woman was persistent and asked for Steven. Steven Walton, she . . ."

"We were getting Justin in the carseat, Steve," Rhonda overrode Nick, "when Gloria came out to tell us, she said . . ."

"She said," Nick continued, a little louder, "that she told the woman there had been a Steven there, but he had left. The woman wanted to know when you—if it is you she was looking for, I don't know—would be back."

"Did she leave her name?" Steven asked, looking very tired.

"Well, I don't think Gloria asked if . . ."

"She left the strangest message!" Rhonda interrupted again.

"It wasn't really a message," Nick corrected.

"I thought you weren't going to tell anyone we were going to be here this weekend, Steve," Linda interjected. "You didn't want to be bothered with . . ."

"I didn't tell anyone," Steven answered, irritated. "What was this message, or . . ."

"Something about using our address," Rhonda began as Steven wrinkled his brow trying to understand.

Nick broke in, "Gloria repeated it as best she could, I suppose. What she said—Gloria said—was that the woman wanted to use this address, our condo address, as your mailing address. And would you be able to pick up your mail there, or . . .?" He looked at Rhonda. "What was it?"

"Well, something like that, honey, I . . ." She looked at Steven. "Justin was getting tangled in the straps of the carseat, it was really . . . well . . . rather a chaotic moment."

"What?" Linda asked, bewildered. Steven turned his head and, looking nervously about the room, found the waitress and caught her eye.

"I'm sorry, doll. I don't know if we can be much clearer than that."

"She didn't get the woman's name?" Linda asked, not bothering to hide her frustration.

"No, she didn't," Nick answered. "She just said that it was a woman and this thing about Steven getting mail at our address, or . . ." He looked at Rhonda again, who smiled rather blankly, giving a helpless little shrug.

"Whiskey and water," Steven said to the waitress standing beside him.

Chapter V

The early morning clouds still shone a pinkish grey as Claire
strode quickly up Shrader Street. The peeling bark of a eucalyptus
colored the air with its mentholated fragrance and the silver-blue acorns
dotting the crabgrass beneath caught her eye but did not alter the
expression on her face. If she had come upon anyone in the still empty
street, she might have frightened them, her raging eyes seeming lost to
any presence of mind. She kicked at a straggling brown leaf from an
elm struggling to survive in its sidewalk cage. Orange pumpkin faces
and ghoulish cardboard bats winked down at her from the front windows
of a large Victorian flat, unnoticed, as she strode past to the porch
nextdoor and, climbing the stairs, jammed at the front door buzzer with
her thumb.

As the buzzer rang again, JoAnn quickened her pace down the hall,
throwing a robe around her and yelling at the door, "It's the middle of
the night, goddamit! Wait a minute!"

She fumbled with the lock, still half asleep, and opened the door to
meet Claire's pinched, angry stare.

"God, what's the matter with you?" JoAnn asked with alarm,
standing back to let Claire in.

"They 'ave invaded Grenada," she answered, her voice trembling and
tears coming to her eyes.

"Fuck! I knew it!" JoAnn said, though her face turned ashen.

"Is Sylvia up?" Claire asked.

"It's not even 7:00, Claire. She's still asleep," JoAnn answered,
still rooted in her position at the door, her hand on the brass knob; and
then with the full force of her strength she slammed it back into its
jam. "Fuck! Goddamit!" she cried.

"We've got to move faster," Claire said quietly.

"We can't, Claire. We can't possibly." JoAnn stared at the door.
"What's happening? How many troops?"

"Two thousand."

"Marines? 82nd Airborne?"

"Of course. *Salauds!*" Claire half-spat the word and then handed a
folded newspaper to JoAnn. "I 'aven't read it yet, I juss found it on the
way over 'ere. I 'eard first on the radio this morning at 6:00. I
expected, too, I know. I guess we all did."

"I don't know, Claire, I . . . I did and I didn't. I guess I'd thought
maybe they felt they'd done enough with the coup. And Bishop dead. I
guess I thought they would just hover around like the fleet outside

Nicaragua, or I hoped . . ."

"Yes. Yes. Me too, I know," Claire answered as she looked over JoAnn's shoulder at the front page of the paper.

"President Reagan said the reason troops from the United States invaded Grenada today is to thwart a bloody takeover by what he called 'a brutal group of leftist thugs.'"

"Funny, he doesn't mention that they've been planning this for two years," JoAnn said, her bitter tone not hiding the awful sorrow in her voice.

"Don't joke," Claire said quietly, reading on.

"Let there be no misunderstanding. This collective action has been forced on us by events that have no precedent in the eastern Caribbean and no place in any civilized society," Reagan announced after briefing congressional leaders.
'American lives are at stake,' the president told reporters . . ."

"Oh Christ," JoAnn flung the newspaper down on the hall table. "I can't read this *shit*. The motherfucking liars!"

She looked at Claire. "How in the hell are we going to find out what's really going on?"

"We 'ave to try to get through to the Allies," Claire began.

"We've been trying since the coup four days ago! We haven't heard a thing since that half a message before the curfew was clamped down. You know the Allies couldn't begin to get into the front door of the hotel now."

"Olina could be still at the office."

"But if she didn't, couldn't get to the computer up to now . . ."

"I think she did not send any message because she couldn't let us know where, or even when it could arrive. But maybe now . . . now she will take the risk," Claire said, a questioning hope in her voice.

"No. I don't think so, Claire. It would not be a wise risk," JoAnn answered firmly. Claire winced, recognizing the truth of JoAnn's words.

They stood in silence, the helplessness they felt seething within them. JoAnn ran her hand through her pale brown hair, clutching it by the roots as if to pull some brighter vision up to mind. The crease that lined her high forehead deepened as her narrowed blue eyes stared intently, unseeing, at the discarded newspaper on the hall table.

"And what about Olina?" she asked Claire, her voice little more than a whisper.

"We 'ave to 'ope she 'as already left for Trinidad," Claire answered. She was silent a moment. "Maybe yesterday, if she 'eard the fleet 'ad been redirected from its course to Lebanon. Eleven ships! They sent 11 ships! It's more square feet of fucking 'ardware than the 'ole island itself!" She slapped her hand hard against the wall of the dark hallway, then, sighing heavily, "We 'ave to 'ope Olina 'as already left. Or, if she is still there, that they will not find 'er."

"If she's still there, Claire, if she was there four days ago, after the curfew, she'll never be able to get out with the information."

"The photographs, maybe no," Claire answered. "But the rest. The rest she will know." Claire paused, her thin fingers stroking the side of her cheek. With a determined certainty in her full brown eyes, she turned to JoAnn. "I am sure of it, JoAnn. Remember. Olina is clever. And she is very brave."

"Claire!" JoAnn was impatient. "Clever or not, she has been on eight different islands in less than a month! How anyone could remember each location, each building, each room, each electronic system . . ."

"*Oui*, yes, I know," Claire answered, exhausted, though not defeated. "But at least we know she 'as already presented the information, all of it, to the Grenadian Allies. There are still 12 weeks before the Action. We will get the information, JoAnn. I am sure of it," she said, her determined eyes still looking steadily at JoAnn's. "Because now, it is more important than ever."

They both turned and looked down the long narrow hall as they heard a door open and Sylvia, dressed for work, emerged from a room in the back of the flat.

"Hi," she said, squinting as she made out JoAnn's and Claire's dark figures still standing by the door. "What are you doing here?" she said to Claire, her voice pleased.

"Oh Sylvie," Claire said. "There is 'orrible news."

Sylvia stopped where she was, looking at them both. "Grenada?" she asked.

"Yes. This morning at 5:00 a.m. Two thousand troops."

Sylvia's hand shot up to cover her eyes, pressing them closed. JoAnn and Claire moved down the hall toward her, and the three of them, talking in quiet angry voices, moved into the living room. JoAnn turned on the radio.

"There is a demonstration called for noon today," Claire began over the droning of the radio report, "at the Federal Building."

"Who's calling it?" JoAnn asked, sitting on the couch next to Sylvia who sat slumped back into the frayed cushion as her grey eyes lit with an anger that belied the dejection in her pose.

"Well, NEWS, of course. Ruth call me this morning juss after 6:00. Also CECO, the solidarity movement . . . it's not sure 'oo all yet. I think also the anti-nuke," Claire stopped at the sound of the telephone and Sylvia rose quickly from the couch and, hurrying to the kitchen, said, "Maybe this will be more news."

"Hello," she answered tersely, the receiver held closely to her ear.

"Hello . . . Sylvia?"

Sylvia waited a second, unsure, then, "Mom? Why . . . How are you?"

"Oh . . . I'm fine. I'm well, dear," Maureen's gentle voice, with that slight broken tremble that spoke of her age, left Sylvia silent, suspended between two worlds.

"How are you, dear?" Maureen asked.

"Oh . . . I . . . I . . . God, I . . ." Sylvia struggled. It had been at least two months since she had spoken to her mother, since just before Labor Day. She had been so busy, so much going on, she didn't know whether to feel guilty or angry that Maureen was calling, *now*, of all times.

"I know you've been very busy," Maureen went on. "I've spoken with Linda once or twice. I know it must be a tremendous amount of work to prepare for a conference. In fact, you know, I just heard about your organization—NEWS, isn't it?—on the radio this morning."

"What?" Sylvia asked, focusing more clearly on her mother's voice.

"Well, yes. I was listening to that university radio station, you know, what is it? . . . UCLA. They were announcing a demonstration to protest the invasion of Grenada."

"In L.A.?" Sylvia asked.

"Yes. Downtown, at the Civic Center."

"Good. Good. Were other groups mentioned?"

"Yes, well. I didn't get all the names. Something about colonial oppression. And then, a workers' party, or . . ."

"Mmmm," Sylvia answered, looking at the door to the living room and the radio beyond. "Well, Mom, uh . . . how are you?"

"Well, Sylvia, to tell you the truth . . . I know this may not be a good time to call, but . . . I've been up since early this morning listening to the news. It's so difficult to know what's going on and . . . I know this invasion is probably very upsetting to you."

Sylvia's face softened as she relaxed her tense grasp of the telephone receiver, and lent herself over to her mother's words.

"I find it quite upsetting myself," Maureen continued, less hesitantly, as if she had seen the change in Sylvia's expression. "Though I don't know much about this island—Grenada. It seems that to send in the Marines . . . it's such a crazy move. Bringing us closer and closer to war. Why on earth have they chosen this little island? I understand it has a very small population."

"A hundred and ten thousand," Sylvia said quickly. "It's only 50 square miles."

"Well, what were they doing there?" Maureen asked, urgency in her voice.

Sylvia hesitated a moment, feeling surprised at herself for how suddenly moved she felt. Her mother was genuinely concerned. Frightened. And she was asking her, Sylvia, for some explanation, for some truth.

"The newspaper really doesn't give any kind of clear account," Maureen was saying. "Well, of course, they have great detail about the military maneuver. But about the country itself, this little island they are attacking . . . Of course, there's this talk of leftist thugs or whatever, but who knows what that means?"

"Well, Grenada," Sylvia began, her voice calmer now, "well originally, it was a lot like the other Caribbean Islands. It was colonized—taken over—by the French who killed most of the original population, the Carib Indians. Then they brought African slaves over to work in plantations . . ." She paused, wondering if this were the information her mother wanted.

"Yes?" her mother answered, waiting.

"Well the French ruled Grenada until the British moved in and took over in the late 18th century. At that point the slaves and Creole farmers staged a major rebellion, but it was crushed by the British who then brought over thousands more African slaves and continued the plantation system—exporting nutmeg, bananas, cocoa—for huge profits that went straight back to London."

"But surely that wasn't still going on?" Maureen asked.

"Well, slavery was abolished, in name anyway, in 1838," Sylvia answered, leaning against the sink counter, "but it wasn't really until just after World War I that the people's protests and strikes were able to really change anything. After the war there were some reforms, but protests continued until the British had to get out of Grenada in the early '50s. They were replaced by the Grenada United Labour Party led by Eric Gairy."

"So this was a labor government? or a socialist government?" Maureen asked.

"Well, neither really. It started out as a strong popular movement for independence from the British. But Gairy turned out to be more of a friend to the British than to Grenada. Once he was in power, he secretly cooperated with the British and helped them maintain control over Grenada's economy. His administration became really corrupt. In the end he was just a puppet. He was even knighted by Queen Elizabeth."

"So these are the leftist thugs that Reagan . . ."

"No, no. The United States loved Gairy. But he was overthrown in 1979 in a revolution led by the New Jewel Movement, where only three people were killed—that's how much support they had. In the '60s and '70s, a strong black liberation movement had been developing all over the Caribbean similar to the one here, and the New Jewel Movement grew out of that. The population of Grenada is almost entirely African and so, of course, they supported the Black Power activists who wanted to break the control of the minority white capitalists and govern themselves."

She paused and, as Maureen was silent, she continued. "JEWEL stands for Joint Endeavour for Welfare, Education, and Liberation. In 1979 when they revolted against Gairy, only three people were killed because Gairy's militia handed over their guns. The Grenadians *wanted* the New Jewel Movement." Sylvia took a breath. "Mom. If you knew what an inspirational, *exemplary* new society they were creating in Grena—" her voice broke.

"Sylvia, dear," Maureen said softly, moved for her daughter, though still unsure.

Sylvia went on. "Mom, it really was, and nobody in this country knows a thing about it—except black people, of course, but everybody else never even *heard* of Grenada until yesterday. We're kept so ignorant about what's really going on in the world, and probably most people will believe this insane blabber about 'leftist thugs,' but the real *thugs* are Reagan and his *Marines* that could go destroy . . ."

Sylvia's voice had lost its gentleness and, to Maureen, its clarity.

"Sylvia, dear," Maureen said patiently, "what exactly were the policies of the JEWEL government?"

"Oh, well, my god," Sylvia said, as if not knowing where to begin; but calming herself again, she said, "Well, education was a major priority. They immediately began a literacy campaign in 1979 and developed a text book called *Let Us Learn Together*. Thousands of Grenadians learned to read and write and started to participate in developing the country. They built childcare centers where for seven dollars a *month* a child could be cared for, and that included breakfast and lunch every day. All the anti-worker laws passed by Gairy that prevented striking or having mass meetings were repealed, and workers could join any trade union they wanted.

"And the Agricultural Workers Councils," Sylvia's voice grew more enthusiastic as she forgot for a moment that U.S. Marines governed Grenada now, "Almost every estate in Grenada has organized councils of agricultural workers where they discuss their working conditions, the management and laws, and give direct input into the decisions of the government. And the Women's Organizations. Well, there were 60 women in the National Women's Organization before

1979. Now there are over 6,000. And they're responsible for getting laws passed, like the one that gives three months for maternity leave with two months fully paid."

"I see, yes. I see," Maureen said quietly after a moment. "That does seem so much better for the people there. Certainly their democratic rights . . . Sylvia, where is this information available? Is there a book or some articles?"

"Yes, sure, I can send you several articles." Sylvia glanced again at the kitchen door, frowning at the sound of the radio still droning and Claire's and JoAnn's voices involved in discussion. "Actually, I should be going, Mom, but listen, I'll send the articles, and a long letter, soon. Within the next couple days."

"I would appreciate that, Sylvia," Maureen answered. "It's been so difficult to find any information about Grenada, even though it has been in the news since the coup there last week. And I must say, the reports of that coup don't really give any sense at all of the kind of government you've been describing. Rather it sounded like ultra-leftist factions battling for power, without any concern for the people."

"I know. I know," Sylvia answered, her voice tired. "And truthfully, Mom, I don't think anyone, except those directly involved, can know exactly what took place. But—I can't go into it now—but please believe me, there is definitive evidence that the coup was *not* simply the result of internal party dissension. Grenada was such an inspiration to the people of the Caribbean, and to black people in this country and all over the world, the United States had every reason to want to see it destroyed. It was too much of a threat to U.S. domination in the Caribbean . . . But, Mom, I do have to go. I'll write you more about it as soon as I possibly can." Sylvia thought a moment. "Or maybe I can call you later this week. How are *you*?"

"Oh, I'm fine, dear. Fine," Maureen answered quietly. "I know you have to get to work, dear. I appreciate your taking the time to discuss this with me. I've had so many questions about it. Do send me a letter, dear, and more of your thoughts on it." Maureen paused. "And you, Sylvia? How are you doing?"

"Oh, fine, Mom. Just really busy."

"Are you getting enough rest? and eating well, Sylvia? I hope you're not skipping meals."

"No, no, no. I'm eating plenty, really. I'm doing fine," Sylvia answered, not curtly but clearly wanting to end the conversation.

"I'll look forward to hearing from you, Sylvia."

"You will, Mom. Later this week. For sure." Sylvia's answer was sincere. Maureen almost believed her.

"OK. Take care now, Sylvia."

"I will, Mom. Bye-bye."

Sylvia put the receiver back in its cradle and stood a moment next to the phone contemplating the strangeness of the moment, the meeting of the two worlds within her now—her mother, her childhood history, and herself, Sylvia, now, in total commitment to revolution, to international transformation. Two worlds, so separate so much of the time. Or so much she had separated them! she thought, for wasn't Maureen, too, seeking justice and peace. Though Sylvia had fought to break through, as if from a cage, the notions and attitudes Maureen had longed she would hold dear—marriage, a career, a liberal acceptance of society as she found it, flawed, and, even cruel, yes—but she heard Maureen's voice, "Sylvia, don't fight it so, you will make yourself miserable, please." But that had been . . . when? Four, five years ago? In fact, it had been a long time since Maureen and she had actually argued, or that Maureen had been so saddened—or was it frightened?—by Sylvia's choices. And still too it had been a long time since Sylvia had talked very honestly with her mother. Claire had told her three years ago, "Give it up, Sylvie!," one night after Sylvia had had an especially difficult, painful argument with Maureen about the Puerto Rican Independence Movement and about Lolita Lebron. Maureen had been horrified. It was unclear to Sylvia, thinking back, whether Maureen's fear was for herself or for her, Sylvia, or for whom exactly when Sylvia had insisted angrily—not too clearly really she remembered now—that Lolita's attack on the U.S. Senate—she and her three *compañeros* sitting in the Senate gallery, drawing out their automatic weapons, opening fire on the sick, rich old men who at that very moment were sitting complacently while, by their decree, atom bombs were being dropped on the Micronesian Islands as a "test" that would leave the islands contaminated for centuries, the indigenous peoples radiated and giving birth to mutants—Lolita's act, Sylvia had almost shouted, was the most courageous, significant act of any woman in this century! Maureen had been horrified, frightened. "Give it up with her, Sylvie," Claire had said, comforting her, or so Sylvia had thought at the time as Claire had insisted, "She is an old woman now, set in 'er ways. You cannot expect 'er to understand zese sings. Never!" But in fact it wasn't at all long after that awful argument that Maureen had begun to read about the United Nations and had even visited New York. But Claire had shown so much disgust for that when Sylvia, even then, had wanted to believe that her mother could, and would understand. "What kind of reformist bullshit!" Claire had almost sneered when Sylvia, with pride in her voice, told her about Maureen's trip to the U.N. But Sylvia knew, she had thought then, that Claire was right—that her mother, Maureen, was hopelessly lost to the ways of the imperialist culture. And she had never even tried to have a serious discussion with her again.

But now, it was almost as if some veil had lifted. Sylvia hugged herself, smiling with the moment; she felt so near, so close to Maureen. She seemed to know. She had really seemed to *know* . . .

"Sylvie!" Claire called from the living room and then, walking through the kitchen door, "You are off the phone? And so?" Tense expectation clipped her words.

"Oh." Sylvia looked at Claire and then, walking past her back to the living room, "That was my mother," she said.

"What?" Claire was truly shocked, and speechless for a moment, she studied Sylvia with an awed expression. "Your *mo*zere!" she repeated. A slow anger filled her eyes, superimposed on her morning's grief. "You are chatting wis your mother? Oh sure. Why not? It's a nice day." She looked up at the ceiling, not as if to verify her remark, but rather to quiet her outraged nerves, then back at Sylvia, in measured control, "Sylvia. We are waiting 'ere, listening to the radio . . ." Tears filled her eyes. "Of course we thought you were receiving news from Ruth, or . . ." She looked at JoAnn, too frustrated to go on.

JoAnn looked with a doubting concern at Sylvia's set jaw, and then to Claire, tired and distraught, and, leaping from the couch as the phone rang again, she shot a questioning glance to Sylvia as she brushed past her to the kitchen.

Claire, somewhat relieved by the ring of the phone, glared silently at Sylvia, whose lowered eyes still struggled to hold the moment she had felt, the sound of her mother's voice as she had said, "Oh I see, yes. I see."

"Sylvia," Claire's voice continued in its measured tone, "you 'ave been tying up that phone . . ." She broke off her sentence and stood watching Sylvia—like a cat watches a stranger, Sylvia thought—when JoAnn called from the kitchen. "Claire!" The urgency in her voice turned Claire on her heel and she slammed through the kitchen door.

Sylvia stood still, alone, in the living room. Still she sought that sensation she had felt just seconds before, but it had given way to an empty, nervous strain. She looked at the closed kitchen door, the radio racking on about the troops, casualties. She struggled to clear the jumbled motion of her mind and then, a frown twisting her dry lips, she strode quickly through the kitchen door.

"What is it?" she asked Claire, who stood close to JoAnn, nodding an emphatic Yes as JoAnn, eyes on Claire, said, "Yes, right," into the receiver.

Claire glanced at Sylvia, then with eyes back on JoAnn, she waited for her to complete the call. "Yes, OK," JoAnn finished and, hanging up the phone, turned to face them both. "We're to do whatever we can to mobilize NEWS MASS for the demo today at the Federal Building, and the one called for tonight in Berkeley. Eight o'clock, Acton and

Shattuck. Just the usual, the phone tree. We want everyone out, of course." Claire nodded impatiently. "NEWS CLAN," JoAnn went on, "will meet at 11:30 tonight at the Oakland office."

"That's all?" Sylvia asked as Claire, her head tipped in a sidelong glance, watched Sylvia closely, just barely giving her the benefit of the doubt.

"Nothing from the Grenadian Allies," JoAnn answered. "Though there may be something from Olina. We'll know tonight."

"And that's it?" Sylvia asked, looking coldly, she felt, at Claire, and then searchingly at JoAnn.

"For now, yes," JoAnn answered; and, as Sylvia's eyes did not leave her face, she added, "Nothing's changed, Sylvia. NEWS CLAN will just meet to assess. Plans for the Action are as is. We are not to move differently. Only to mobilize NEWS MASS."

"And everyone else we can," Claire said, her emotion beyond Sylvia now. "Our work today is to fill the streets, enh? With our anger."

"We're to build for the mass demonstrations now, Sylvia. And," JoAnn looked at Claire, "whatever, if any, the news from Olina, the mass work will still be our emphasis for the present. The conferences, and the Action, are still as planned."

"According to Ruth?" Sylvia asked, her eyes wide.

"According to the Allies, Sylvia," Claire answered, impatient.

"Ruth heard from Chela just before she called," JoAnn explained.

"And Chela speaks for the Allies?" Sylvia asked.

"Sylvia." Claire pronounced her name with finality. "You know Chela speaks for the Latin Allies. She 'as receive word also from the Allies 'ere and in Africa."

"All the Allies got word through?"

"Sylvia!" JoAnn too was losing patience. "For now the word is: *no change*. We can't know anymore now, for god's sake!" She shook her head at Sylvia, though with more love than Claire's eyes showed, she was still exasperated. "Can't you wait until tonight, Christ! Of course we can only piece together now . . ."

Sylvia dropped her eyes and, shaking her head too, though not with JoAnn's simple clarity, she looked up again at Claire. "I'm going to work," she said. "I'll see you at noon." She turned and, opening the refrigerator, picked up a small green apple. Taking a deep crunch into its side, she walked down the hall.

As the front door closed, Claire looked at JoAnn, her anger vivid in expectation; but JoAnn waved a hand after Sylvia's departing figure, more forgiving than dismissive.

"Give her a break, Claire," JoAnn said coolly.

"Break! Break of what!" Claire demanded. "She is so . . . god, I don't know what. Reactionary! She is driving me crazy!" Claire said, the break in her voice convincing JoAnn that Claire was sincerely distressed by Sylvia.

"Claire," JoAnn said quietly. "I've known Sylvia a long time, you know. And I know she is with us as much as anyone could possibly be with us, Claire. God, *you* should know *that*!"

Claire looked at the kitchen door, the sound of the radio still droning on beyond.

"Sometimes," JoAnn went on, "she seems like a stubborn bitch, I know."

Claire laughed or, more aptly, snorted, and with a curl of her lip, let her full brown eyes dwell on the closed front door down the hall as JoAnn said, "She has her ways, Claire, we all do."

"Not such stupid ways," Claire answered, with a disdain that silenced JoAnn.

As Sylvia pushed the button for the 14th floor and picked a dangling fuzz from her black sweater before raising her eyes to the lights of the elevator console—two, three, four, five—her mind again went back to Claire and that cold, grave look on her face so without understanding. Again a sharp, hurt anger brought tears to her eyes. She shook them off as three more passengers boarding at the seventh floor crowded the already full elevator, pushing her back against the rear wall. Give me strength, give me strength, give me strength, she repeated silently to herself as the elevator hummed up to her floor, and visions of the Grenadian People's Army battling the onslaught of the U.S. war machine played before her eyes.

As she made her way to the front of the elevator and out onto the 14th floor, she knew that her clarity, her certainty, was slipping away, getting lost in the confusion of the morning's emotions. She paused in front of the office doors—"Hansen, Rykoff & Shaw/Accountants" scripted in gold across the high walnut transom. Looking at her watch, she was ten minutes early, she walked past to the restroom down the hall. Alone in the small sparkling-white women's room, she locked the outer door and leaned back against the wall, still fighting back the tears that threatened to dissolve her exterior calm.

Grenada, the Allies, Olina, her mother, Claire, all vied within her, claiming the intensity of her anger, love, fear. She took a worn leather purse from her shoulder and rummaged in its depth for the half-empty pack of cigarettes she had borrowed from Rikki a few days ago. She extracted one from the crumpled pack, and lighting it, wrinkled her nose at the scorched, harsh sensation. Grenada. Grenada. The Allies. The JEWEL. Like a blow to the pit of her stomach, she felt their beauty, the brilliance and courage of their vision bombed, raped, crushed; and suddenly reeling, she pushed her way into the restroom stall, dropped the half-smoked cigarette, and vomited into the toilet bowl.

"God, oh god," she whispered, righting herself, and wiping her mouth with a crumpled wad of toilet paper, she flushed the toilet. Standing back against the cool tile wall, she brushed her hand across the beaded sweat on her forehead.

For the moment, she felt nothing, and then remembering the cigarette, walked out of the stall and, seeing the still-smoking ember on the floor, crushed it with her heel.

She sat against the sink counter, fighting off the weakness that seemed to overwhelm her. NEWS. Think of NEWS, she told herself. There are thousands of us. We are growing. We'll stop them. She closed her eyes. The Action, yes. She saw Ruth's face as she had spoken at the meeting last night, her eyes so clear and determined as she assessed their plans, their weaknesses and strengths, without false hopes or false fears. Her realism, and her understanding of the possible and the impossible, so acutely developed, was a model for them all. A model of faith.

Remember that, Sylvia told herself, her head beginning to clear. She sat up straighter. And JoAnn. Think of all she's been through, and she just keeps going on. She never loses hope. Her commitment is so unshakable after 14, 15 years? of meetings, tasks, demonstrations; she works so hard and gives her total attention to the smallest details, no matter what happens. She just takes it on, without a complaint. Because her vision, it's almost simple—it's so deep and certain.

JoAnn was one of the first in the late '60s to understand and then dedicate herself to that small grouping of the U.S. Left that recognized the leading revolutionary force of colonized people. "This is the period," she had told Sylvia when they had met six years ago, "of the ascendancy of the slave." Five hundred years of European domination and enslavement of non-white people was coming to its end. A new age of international economic and political equality is being born. "Our role," JoAnn had told her, "is to support the liberation movements throughout the world. And to bring down the empire from within."

Sylvia nodded her head slowly as she remembered that conversation with JoAnn, when she herself had first begun to understand the truth of those words. And at the same time, how she had marveled at JoAnn's total faith in the face of such odds, because even then, in 1976, CECO had been so small—just a handful of people in San Francisco, New York, Los Angeles. But JoAnn had never let her conviction falter and never left off the endless tasks of building a movement that never seemed to take hold. No wonder she had felt such joy when those first meetings of NEWS MASS almost three years ago drew 50, 100, then 200, 300 women. The split from CECO had been difficult and painful for her. CECO had been so disdainful, or its highest leadership, its male leadership had been so disdainful of the women's movement, the anti-nuke movement—"the mass movements of bourgeois liberalism."

Yet the fact was, as JoAnn was the first to see, it was women, hundreds of women who had rallied to the call of the NEWS declaration, even though at that time NEWS had called themselves the Worker's International for People's Sovereignty. Only two or three men had shown up at that first meeting. Yes, it was women—feminists, peace activists, women from the solidarity movements, the labor movement, and even women who had never worked in the left before—that had come to those first meetings. And they were ready for unity, and action. To stop racism, sexism, the arms race, and to build a new international social order founded in trust, cooperation, and peace. Within weeks NEWS had changed its name to the Women's International and, within a year, cadres had founded chapters in Europe, Canada, Australia—the industrialized nations of the North. And with that sudden leap, the People's Liberation Movements of the South had responded; and they believed that finally, possibly, white people were beginning to grasp the inevitable motion of history—that white people, through the voice of women, were ready to divorce themselves from their ruling classes and side with the overwhelming majority of the people of the world. And hadn't it been, really, the women revolutionaries of the South who had inspired the Northern women to mobilize? The women of Cuba, Zimbabwe, Nicaragua, Grenada, El Salvador, Puerto Rico, and the women revolutionaries fighting for their people's liberation here in the U.S.—Assata Shakur, Dylcia Pagan, Ellen Movescamp—who had provided the inspiration to the founders of NEWS in San Francisco: Ruth, JoAnn, women from CECO, together with Carol, Adrianne, Laura, Susan, women from the solidarity, feminist and peace movements.

How much they had learned from the Allies in the South, and here too, Olina, Vida, Cristina . . . Sylvia suddenly felt as if Cristina were present now; she could almost hear the sound of her voice as she had read the letter from Chela to the NEWS CLAN meeting last week. None of them had known until that moment that Cristina's husband had been found days before, on a roadside outside San Salvador, his arms and legs gone, his face slashed, the work of a Death Squad. Cristina's eyes had seemed on fire as slowly she had translated Chela's words.

> " . . . I grieve for you so, compañera, far from your
> family and your country. Thank god your son Jorje is with
> you and still I feel my own heart could break as you must
> see in him the eyes of your husband. Now our spirit must
> rise higher, to the mountains, beyond the mountains . . .

*Your work in that country, though how can you not
despise that country that is destroying yours, especially
now? But even there, we have compañeras, and your work
is very critical to all of us. Remember we are everywhere
in the world. We will take their machinery of death, and in
our hands, it will become the machinery of life ..."*

A sharp knock on the door brought Sylvia back to the moment.
She looked at her watch, then quickly in the mirror, running her hand
through her hair. She opened the door.

Patti, one of the receptionists, smiled at her, "Sylvia! Here you
are! We thought you weren't coming in today."

"Oh . . . I . . . got hung up in traffic. The streetcar got stuck."
Sylvia cleared her throat and moved past Patti out to the hall.

Walking back to the massive walnut doors, she turned the brass
handle and moved quickly past the receptionist's desk to the back of the
suite of offices. Opening the door to her cubbyhole office and hanging
her purse on the back of her chair, she looked at the stack of reports on
her desk. "Sylvia," a young man, suited in beige linen, leaned his head
in the door.

"Yeah?" She turned around.

"I've just put the Turnbull's audit report on your desk. I want you
to get it out right away. They're expecting it by the end of the week."

"Yeah, OK," she said and turned back to her word processor.
Flinging off the black vinyl cover, she plopped herself into the swivel
chair at the desk.

The man frowned, looking at her back. "Are you sure now?
You'll get it done by Friday?"

Sylvia snapped on the word processor and then, feeling the man
still standing there, staring at her, turned slowly around as she struggled
to force her lips up into a smile. "Yeah. Sure, Glen." She looked at
him. "Why not?"

"Well," he cleared his throat, "I see you have several other reports
there and . . ." glancing at the gold digital watch on his wrist, "it is
almost 9:30."

"These reports aren't due until mid-November. They're just recaps.
Don't worry. I'll do yours first." She smiled again.

He nodded and moved away from the door as Sylvia got up from
her chair and closed it after him.

Sitting back down in her chair, she opened the middle drawer of her
desk, pulled out a box of disks and, inserting one in the disk drive, put
Glen's audit report on the typing stand. As her fingers moved quickly
over the keys and her eyes studied the report on her right, her mind went
back to NEWS. NEWS CLAN. Clandestine.

It's hard to believe, Sylvia thought, smiling now, that we've been operating only a little more than a year. We're such a force. And none of our fears of splitting the organization have even remotely come true, not yet anyway. And it's not just that it was theoretically the right thing to do, either. It's what we've actually accomplished that's making it work, and that's influencing the entire mass organization of NEWS.

It did seem at first like it would split us though, she thought, remembering those first long months after NEWS had formed, when their relationships were so tenuous. It hadn't been easy to bring together the broad-based peace movement members with the revolutionary anti-imperialist cadres. Both in Europe and in the U.S., the strategies of the two tendencies had seemed so different. And then we did all our arguing by mail, she shook her head, or telephone or cross-continent meetings. No wonder it took so goddamn long. But when we discovered we could access mainframe computers and communicate internationally in seconds—thousands of us, networking around the world—our debating became really refined and the issue somehow got so much simpler. Well it was a simple issue, in a way, even though the strategy of the mass movements—peaceful protest, education, building organizationally—seemed so different than the strategy of the revolutionary cadres—militancy, confrontation, sabotage. But they're really not mutually exclusive. Why were we so sure they were? Her hands slowed on the keys. In fact it was us, the CECO cadres, who seemed so bent on defining NEWS one way or the other. But we'd been so close for so long to the national liberation movements of the South, we felt that our militancy had to equal theirs. She stopped typing and sat a moment. But by ignoring the movements in our own countries, CECO, and the revolutionaries in Europe too, were so isolated. It felt like we were having almost no effect. It was joining forces with the broad-based peace movements that actually gave the revolutionary strategies meaning, because then, finally, they were part of a mass mobilization throughout the North that gave them body and strength.

It hadn't been easy though. For the first year the mass-based leadership and the revolutionary-cadre leadership had gone back and forth over what strategy would characterize NEWS. In fact, that's the irony, Sylvia smiled again. It was learning how to use computer networks to communicate better that made us see we could actually have *both* strategies, simultaneously. The mass work continued to build and NEWS grew as an organization, and at the same time, those who believed in another level of struggle . . .

Sylvia sat back in her chair, remembering that meeting in New York a year and a half ago. Eighty-five women, the international leadership of NEWS. It had been at least 2:00 in the morning, all of them crowded in that little apartment when, who had made the proposal? Ruth? Or the Amsterdam cadres? Yes, it was Ruth. "We propose that the mass membership of NEWS continue under the leadership of the mass-strategy cadres in its current direction—to build the organization internationally and to coordinate tactics along the lines of traditional mass protest. And we also propose that, as of this meeting, another emerging level of NEWS operations be consolidated by those in NEWS leadership who support a new strategic phase, in heightened anti-imperialist unity and militant confrontation. These cadres, while still working closely within NEWS MASS, will form NEWS CLAN, the clandestine arm of NEWS."

It was amazing. Everyone had supported it. Every single woman in the room had voted yes, and we hardly even discussed it, Sylvia thought. Well, we'd been discussing it for two years, in a way. But thank god, thank god we've done it. And there are at least 300 of us now, every one of us having come through NEWS MASS.

And NEWS MASS has been influenced by NEWS CLAN, though most of the membership may not be aware of the full extent of what we do, but they do know about the sabotage campaign, and they are participating—more and more. Some 40,000 women are involved at some level. She smiled. Even if it's just occasionally taking a few reams of Xerox paper or stealing whole drawers of files from government and corporate offices, NEWS MASS is getting really daring in commandeering resources and information at our jobs, yet so subtly—it's great how we can act the docile little clerk or secretary—and not one of us, not a single one, has been caught. It's fantastic really, Sylvia thought, and then, recalling herself to her own office she stared at the half-page of typing before her.

Christ, she hadn't typed a word for . . . She looked at her watch. Here I am thinking what perfect little workers we all are and that bastard Glen is going to be here any minute to check up on me. Her fingers began their quick tapping over the keys. But her heart felt lighter than it had an hour before and, as she typed, her mind repeated, NEWS, yes, NEWS. We can do it and we will. In fact, this thought was the only thing that could quiet the sound of Claire's angry voice, the picture of her mother, sleepless, listening to the radio news, and worst of all, the image of 2,000 Marines desecrating the island of Grenada. NEWS, NEWS will stop them, NEWS CLAN . . . And Olina? Was she still in Grenada? Cornered somewhere by some maniac Marine? No. God, please no. Again she felt the tightness in her chest. Wait, she told herself. Wait until tonight. We will find Olina. But still Olina's twinkling black eyes danced before her. Sylvia shook her head, trying to shake it off. She turned the page of the audit report and typed more quickly. But still, there was Olina, at breakfast the morning she had left. She and Cristina, Tuwanda, JoAnn, Ruth, Claire, all of them sitting in the airport restaurant that late September morning before Olina had left, never dreaming at the time that the danger she would face in the Caribbean would be in Grenada. Olina. Her face happy and strong as they had kissed her good-bye at the gate . . . Olina. So many years her work in the Black Liberation Movement, first in Los Angeles, then in San Francisco, had been so admired by CECO, by all of them. And now, to work with her so closely as an Ally, but also as a member of NEWS CLAN, it was . . .

The com-line on the office phone buzzed. Sylvia swung around in her chair. "Yes?"

"A call for you on six-eight," Patti said.

"Thanks." Sylvia pushed the flashing button.

"Sylvia?"

"Ruth. Hi."

"Are you clear?"

"Let me get back to you. Clark?"

"No. Thomas."

Sylvia hung up the phone. Quickly blanking the screen on her processor and turning the audit report to page ten, she grabbed her purse and left her office. Taking the elevator to the lobby, she found a single phone booth and dialed a pay phone in a residential area of East Oakland.

"Hi," Ruth answered.

"Hi."

"You have ImCopy there, don't you?"

"Yes."

"And what's your network?"

"GTE. I can get TELNET."

"You can? Good. I thought so. Can you possibly get in to receive at 12:15?"

"Today?" Sylvia asked, alarmed.

"Olina's in Trinidad."

"Oh, thank god!" Sylvia said, the extent of her relief evident. "But is she OK? How did she get out?"

"There was a chartered flight arranged by the Grenadian officers evacuating foreigners from the island last night. She's fine. A message came through on the PC at the office this morning. But she wants to send the photographs. She needs a system with Facs. Allies at the General Food Corp. subsidiary—they're on TELNET—are going to get her in to send at 12:15 our time, if we can receive."

"But Christ! What a risk!" Sylvia felt her empty stomach knot.

"I know. I know. But the Allies want to get them out, to us, and destroy them. As soon as possible. The island is crawling with military, and Olina's not sure that when the crisis atmosphere is more under control she can avoid surveillance. The Allies want it here. With us."

As Ruth explained the urgency, the necessity of risk, Sylvia's thoughts were on the right wing of the 14th-floor suite, on Hansen, Rykoff & Shaw's IBM 370 computer housed in an office at the far end of the north hall—usually empty at the lunch hour, yes, but would it be today? And would it stay empty? Could she safely operate for up to 15 minutes, unnoticed? Would other users discover their node in use on TELNET and intrude? Or report it? And could she even articulate the linkage or manage the reception without error? She had never operated alone—and this particular computer, her office's computer, she had only even attempted once, late that evening in August with Claire. They had hid in the building until the last hard-working accountant had locked the massive walnut doors behind him, and Sylvia, using her key, had . . .

"Sylvia? What do you think?" Ruth was waiting for her answer.

"Ellen can't get TELNET at the Alcoa Building?"

"No. And they can't gateway in Trinidad."

Sylvia was silent. She had two hours to somehow make sure, absolutely certain, that she could get to the computer for up to 20 minutes—from 12:10 to 12:30—absolutely unnoticed and alone.

"OK," Sylvia said. "Tell them to send. At 12:15. What encryption, for salutation? Is there more than the photographs?"

"Some text. Swahana."

"I just hope to god if they don't get my response *immediately*, they'll get the hell off."

Ruth heard the strain, the fear in Sylvia's voice.

"Of course they will, Sylvia. They know what they're doing. You know that. If it's not absolutely safe, don't receive. Leave the building."

"All right."

"Call me at 12:45. Here."

"All right."

"Good. Take care."

"Yes. OK. Bye."

Sylvia hung up the phone and slowly walked back toward the elevator, her mind racing, searching for a way to clear the office. She stopped abruptly a few yards from the phone, turned and, with her hand flying through her purse, she found some change and hurriedly redialed the Oakland number.

It rang once, twice, three times. Come on, Ruth. It's me! she shouted silently. In the middle of the fifth ring, she heard the receiver lifted . . . and silence.

"Hello? Hello, is Tom there?" she said, her voice high and thin.

"Sylvia, what on earth . . ."

"Ruth. I'm sorry. I had to get back to you."

"All right. It's all right. No one's around."

"Listen. I'm going to go back up to the office now. I'll find out what's happening at lunch. But I feel I just can't be sure that everyone will leave. Or that no one will be in the right wing . . ."

"Have you changed your mind?"

"No. No. Listen. I want you to get someone to phone in a bomb threat. At noon. Or just a minute or two before."

Ruth was quiet.

"It will clear the floor, Ruth. It will clear the building, if they do it right."

"And you?"

"I know where to hide. I've done it before." She waited. "It's the only way to be sure, Ruth, that I can receive undiscovered. And even so, there's still the possibility that other users will question our node presence, though that's so unlikely I think it's a risk worth taking, and by the time it shows up on the phone bill . . . I'll deal with that later."

"All right. Who should receive the threat?"

Sylvia thought a moment. She looked at the Directory across the lobby, struggling to make out the half-familiar names. The 13th floor. A law office. Perfect.

"Vincente, Ryan, Barsotti & Wall. And the security of the building itself. Say it's on the 13th floor. The north wing." She paused. "Make it real, Ruth."

"All right. At 11:57. So you'll definitely receive?"

"Yes. Unless something else . . ."

"I'll send someone to meet you to pick it up."

"When?"

"What do you think? 12:40?"

"You'd better make it 12:45. I might have trouble getting out. And tell them to wait. The deli on California and Market."

"All right, Sylvia. You take care now."

"I will. Bye."

Sylvia hung up the phone again, this time walking quickly back to the elevator, her mind calm, sure. This will work. She smiled to herself.

As she walked back to her office, she ran into Glen, his thin shoulders hugging his neck, rigid with irritation. He glared at her. "I've been looking for you. I want to add a paragraph to page seven. I couldn't find your copy. Where have you . . ."

"I just got my period. I had to find a Tampax," she said walking past him.

Glen's eyes went cold, his face flushed; he turned and rushed off down the hall to his own office.

Sylvia found Glen's scribbled addition clipped to page seven of his draft on her desk. I better get this fucking thing finished, she mumbled as she snapped the processor back on and her fingers flew across the keys.

At 11:45 she was halfway through Glen's report. She left the processor on, but turned to her small metal desk and, unlocking the bottom right drawer, pulled a file from the back, took three Xeroxed copies from the middle of an old audit report, folded them carefully and put them in her wallet. As she put her wallet back in her purse, her com-line buzzed.

"Shit," she said, picking up the phone.

"A call for you on six-six," Patti told her, waiting. "Will you take it?"

"Yeah. Thanks." Sylvia snapped the flashing button.

"Hi, Syl. How are you?" a friendly voice inquired.

"Rikki! Hi. Listen, I'm just on my way . . . What's up?" Sylvia wondered suddenly if by some chance Rikki knew. There had been talk in NEWS CLAN of Rikki possibly coming over, but not for . . . She looked at her watch; she had less than five minutes.

"Oh, we're working on the leaflets for tonight's demo. I'm going to skip the one at noon to get this out. But I want to ask you a couple things. Do you think we can meet for lunch?"

"Oh, god, well. I can't, Rikki, really. Can we meet for dinner instead?"

"Well that would be too late for the leaflet."

Sylvia looked at her watch again. "Rikki. I've got to go. I'll meet you for dinner, OK? Then we can go over to the demo after. 5:30, OK? Same place we were the other day."

"Well, OK. If we can go by the printers. I'm going to the same one, it's pretty near there, so . . ."

"OK. OK. Fine. See you then. Bye." Sylvia hung up the phone. Rikki'll think I'm totally neurotic, she thought, but who can think about it now? She took her purse from the desk and put it over her shoulder, looking at her watch again. 11:48. She sat in her chair, going over in her mind the computer terminal, the modem, the baud rate set, 1200 . . . She looked at her watch again. 11:50. She took a note pad from her desk and printed "Back at 1:15" and, getting a piece of scotch tape, she switched off her processor, taped the note to the front of her office door and walked down the hall.

She stopped at the reception desk. "Patti, I've got a lunch date and won't be back till about 1:15. If Glen gets in a snit, tell him to relax, his report will be done by 5:00 today. Do you mind?"

"You mean I have to talk to Glen?" Patti made an exaggerated face of disgust. They both laughed.

"See you later," Sylvia said as she closed the walnut door behind her. Seeing two men in suits waiting for the elevator, she stood a few feet from them, then boarded the elevator when it arrived. She got off on the tenth floor and quickly walked to the stairwell. Opening the heavy door, she took the steps two at a time as she returned to the 14th floor through the empty well. On the landing off her floor, she quietly turned the knob of the stairwell door and held it less than an inch out of its jam. Through the tiny crack she saw another secretary from the office leaving the small women's room she had been in earlier that morning. It must be empty, but god, who knows, sometimes two or three women go in there to use the mirror before lunch. She looked at her watch. 11:56. She looked behind her, up, then down the staircase. Should she go in now? If someone were there, she could pretend to leave again. But would she have time to get back before they began to evacuate the floor? She waited. Then she heard a door open above her in the stairwell. Oh shit. Some fucker's getting his exercise. How far up was it? She heard the quick clack of shoes trotting down the steps—three, possibly four flights up. Then she heard a voice—loud and authoritative: "Leave the building. Everyone please leave the building." Another secretary emerged from the women's room, looking around. "What's going on?" she asked the people walking out of the walnut doors down the hall. The footsteps above quickened, only one flight away. Sylvia slid through the door and into the empty women's room, unseen in the growing commotion. She locked the door behind her and, sitting back against the sink counter, looked at her watch. 11:58. Bless you, Ruth, she said with a quick exhaled breath of relief. She listened to the activity on the floor. The low din of voices, some laughter, the same loud, authoritative male voice repeating, "Leave the building. Everyone please leave the building." They must be evacuating the whole place, she thought. Great job, Ruth! She looked at her watch again. 12:00. A din of voices grew slightly louder, coming toward the restroom. Sylvia looked up at the door, alarmed, then realized they were going beyond to the stairwell. The elevators must be packed, she thought. The voices had only the slightest edge of fear; for the most part, it sounded like a school fire drill. She waited for the voices to die down. 12:04. It was quiet. Totally quiet. But it didn't feel empty, not quite. She wrinkled her brow and strained her ears for any sound as she quietly turned the lock in the doorknob and then, very quietly, the doorknob itself. She began to pull open the door, then she hesitated. It didn't feel empty. Why not? She pulled the door open just a crack and just then heard the elevator doors down the hall open, then close. She stood still, listening. Yes. Now. Now it was empty.

She slid out the door and walked softly through the plush carpeted hall to the large walnut doors. The brass handle turned in her hand. They had left it open; she didn't even need her key. She shut the door behind her and then walked briskly through the suite, as if she had come to retrieve something, just in case. But the suite was empty. She turned into the right wing and walked down to the end of the hall. The computer room door was closed and, yes, she tried the knob, locked. She reached in her pocket for the key. Thank god she and Claire had gone through all this before. It had taken her weeks to get a copy of this key. She opened the door and closed and locked it behind her. 12:09. Plenty of time.

She sat down at the terminal, opened her purse, took out her wallet and, taking out the Xerox copies, placed them before her. She leaned closely over the small print, located the baud rate for General Food Corporation's Trinidad dial-up, and checked her own computer's modem. They agreed, thank god; she wouldn't have to adjust it. She turned the computer on and logged into the central terminal, then adjusted the modem to the telephone receiver. 12:10. She turned to the second Xerox copy, again leaning closely over the small print to review the encryptions. She took a pencil from behind her ear and quickly worked out her response salutation. She checked it. And checked it again. 12:14. She coded in the TELNET exchange and then, with a silent prayer, the connection with Trinidad. She waited. 12:15. Within 30 seconds the computer began to move. She watched, her body totally still, only her eyes moving, taking in each symbol. Yes. There it was, in clear Swahana encryption. Their salutation. Her heart fluttering with excitement and anxiety, she very carefully coded in her response, encrypted: "Receiving you Allies. All clear. Send."

With lightning speed the computer clacked through its printout. Sylvia sat perfectly still, her eyes wide, tense, engrossed as 40 to 50 encrypted lines appeared before her; and then, a phenomenon she had never before witnessed, a photograph began to take shape before her eyes, there on the printout, and then another, and another, of buildings, inside offices, close-ups of terminals, floorplans. Though Sylvia could not decode the encrypted lines following each graphic so rapidly, she knew well what they were and where they were from: Puerto Rico, Haiti, Jamaica, Dominican Republic, Dominica, Martinique, Barbados and Trinidad—CIA offices. Photographs taken by cleaning women, by Allies, and by Olina. Sylvia studied them as they appeared, her grey eyes cold, steeled. Her burning anger of the morning returning, she thought of the Grenadian Allies even now, this minute, in combat with the U.S. Marines. As the photographs continued to appear before her, she pressed her lips, nodding. We will stop you. We will stop your insidious, deathly ways. The 32nd and last photograph was followed by

28 more lines of encrypted text. Then, after a split-second pause—Sylvia glanced at her watch, 12:22—the closing. She waited three or four seconds, and then carefully coded in her encrypted closing: "Received, Allies. Excellent. Love." She waited another full minute. Nothing more came through.

Breathing a slow, deep sigh, Sylvia checked her watch again. 12:28. Who knows when they'll let people back in the building. I've got to get the hell out of here, she warned herself, as she quickly and carefully lifted the end of the sheaf of paper out of the printer and, creasing its last, neat accordion folds, laid it to the side as she slowly cleared the computer, then, snapping it off, unzipped her pants and lowered them to her knees. Taking the printout and rolling it into the thinnest possible cylinder, she taped it securely to her bare thigh. As she wound the tape around her leg she smiled, for the first time grateful for the dress code at Hansen, Rykoff & Shaw's and the baggy slacks Linda had loaned her, which she had worn most every day since she'd been hired. Testing that the printout was absolutely secure because she might have to run, she pulled her slacks back up and zipped them. Then she neatly folded her Xerox copies and placed them quickly back in her wallet and her wallet in her purse. Putting her purse over her shoulder and looking around the room, checking again that the printouts were secure, that she had left nothing and that everything was as she had found it, she opened the door of the office. She stood half a second. Still quiet. She turned and locked the door behind her then walked quickly through the suite. Behind the massive walnut doors she stood still another moment, listening. Then slowly turning the brass handle, she opened the door a crack. There seemed to be no one around. She walked out to the right down the hall toward the stairwell.

The trick would be to get past the 13th floor. It might be crawling with cops. Or maybe not. They don't want to get blown up; maybe there's just a couple of them. Maybe she should just go back into the women's room and wait there until people came back into the building. But that might take hours. Or maybe everyone went home for the day. That would be nice, she thought, remembering Glen's report. She stood frozen against the wall as she heard the elevator doors slowly opening down the hall and around the corner.

"I hate this," a man's voice said. "You know it's just some crank call and now we've got to check every goddamn floor."

"Oh, I don't know, Dave. Sometimes we find 'em. And they're not always where they say. But, yeah, I think you're right this time. I sure as hell hope so, or we might get blown right out of here."

Sylvia stood just two feet from the stairwell door, still paralyzed, her back against the south wall of the hallway directly across from the women's restroom, her body washed in sweat and dread, her mind racing, cursing herself for relaxing even for a second. She watched the corner of the wall 30 feet to her right, around which and just behind, were the elevators. Directly across from the elevator foyer, at the end of the narrow hall where she now stood, were the walnut doors opening to the only offices on the 14th floor.

"Well, what the hell's this. More lawyers?" The men appeared in view. Sylvia stopped breathing.

"Fancy doors, huh?" Dave turned the brass knob, and by a miracle beyond Sylvia's wildest expectation, they walked through the doors without even a glance down the hall.

Sylvia let her bursting lungs take in a long quiet draught of air, and moved quickly, silently, to the stairwell door at her end of the hall. Thank you god in heaven, or wherever you are, she prayed from the depth of her soul. And now, in command of herself again, she quietly turned the knob of the door and pulled it open, listening. Silence. She slipped through and carefully shut the door behind her. How many of them were there? How many floors were they on? She looked up the stairwell and down. They must be in the elevators and on the floors. Anyway, she had no choice. She slipped off her shoes and, clutching them and her purse to her side, she ran down the steps, silently, flight after flight, at a speed that astonished her.

The stairs stopped on the landing of the second floor. She stood still, her chest heaving, stifling the sound of her gasps; she checked the printout, still securely taped to her thigh. Now what? she asked herself again, her mind racing. She had to go through the second floor to the elevator, to get to the first floor lobby. Maybe the building is cordoned off. Even if she could get through the second floor, down to the lobby, the minute she walked out the door they'd all pounce on her. They'd take her to jail, search her . . . The printout. She looked around the stark stairwell. There was nowhere to leave it. She looked at her watch. 12:35. She looked back up the stairwell. Should she go back up? Try to get into the women's room on her floor unnoticed? She'd barely escaped there just minutes ago. Something held her from returning. There must be a women's room on this floor too, probably just outside this door. Would it be locked? If she could get inside and lock it, maybe they've already searched it or are just neglecting it altogether. They're obviously not that thorough; they haven't found me yet, even when I was right under their noses. At least possibly I could hide the printout somewhere before they find me. Decided, she slowly turned the knob of the stairwell door and pulled the door quietly to her, leaning into the narrow crack she looked out into the hall of the second floor. Her eyes widened with amazement. Two men in suits and a woman in a sharp tailored dress and heels stood talking not 15 feet away.

"So they're still up there looking around?" one asked.

"Yeah, they've closed off the tenth through the 15th, I guess. You know Mutual's too cheap to shut the whole place down. They'd rather see us all get blown away."

"Well, this is my fourth bomb scare, fellas, how about you?" the woman interjected, a wry, flirtatious smile on her lips.

"Oh, yeah, when I was over on Montgomery, we had one. Supposed to be right in our offices. Somebody bitching about their PG&E bill or some . . ."

Sylvia let the door move softly back into its jam and slowly turned the knob back. Not letting the relief she felt fully flood her wracked nerves, not yet, she slipped her shoes back on and walked back up to the third floor and out into the empty hallway toward the elevators. Pressing the down button, she brushed her tousled hair back from her face and rummaged in her purse for a Kleenex. Slowly, with the descent of the elevator, she let the relief ebb through her, and as she walked through the lobby out the front door, it was all she could do not to leap into the air shrieking with delight. Still, composed, she casually checked the printout on her thigh and headed for the deli.

Despite the last hour she had been through, possibly the longest of her life, Sylvia couldn't help a quick intake of breath as she saw Claire sitting at the counter of the deli, nervously looking out the plate glass window to her side. Sylvia looked at her watch. 12:45. Why hadn't Ruth sent someone else? She walked in the rear door of the deli, and just as she approached, Claire turned and saw her. Claire's eyes widened, anxious, asking. Sylvia nodded. Claire's tense, compressed lips broke into a smile and the warmth and admiration in her eyes filled Sylvia with a joy that washed away her morning's anger. They smiled fully with each other for the embrace they could not have; and then, carefully hiding their emotion, Sylvia turned and looked out the window as Claire took a dollar bill from her small woven bag and laid it on the counter.

"Shall we take a walk?" she asked Sylvia, smiling again.

Chapter VI

Steven's new shoes, Linda's birthday gift to him, tapped smartly across the scuffed linoleum of the sixth floor of the Hall of Justice. Standing in front of the elevator, he stubbed his cigarette out in the ashtray. Impatiently, he hit the down button again with his thumb.

"You look like a man in a hurry," a voice behind him said.

Steven turned around. "Oh, hi, Mark. How's it going?" he answered, without enthusiasm.

"Oh, not too bad. Not too bad." Mark smiled cheerfully as the elevator doors opened and, walking in to the back, they headed for the first floor.

"You look like you just had a rough one," Mark added.

"Well. I didn't win it," Steven answered grimly. "Not much you can do about a lying cop."

"Now, now, Steve. That's part of the game, you know that. Just makes it more of a challenge." Mark clapped him on the shoulder as the elevator opened to no one at the fourth floor.

"I didn't want a challenge, Mark. I just wanted to get the guy off. Believe it or not, this one didn't do it. He'd been up before for a fight in a bar. A Mexican man. Easy mark for the cops. So they decided to pin him with a two-month-old robbery of a liquor store in South City. Apparently the owner's a cousin or something of somebody in the D.A.'s office, so the pressure was on for a conviction. Didn't matter who."

"Oh, come on Steve, it's easy to blame the other guys." Mark gave him a reproving look.

"Look, Mark. I got enough crap from the judge. I don't need it from you." Steven's tired eyes were cold.

"Hey, OK. Listen. Let's go have a drink at the Jury Room. On me," Mark said with a friendly smile as the elevator opened at the first floor. "Come on, Steve," Mark added as Steven hesitated. "I know what you're talking about. Believe me, I do. I just happened to win one myself. So of course I'm high on the justice of it all."

Steven replied with a short, hard laugh, and then, "OK. What the hell."

"Who'd you have? Cranston?" Mark asked as they walked down the front steps of the Hall and headed across the street.

"No, worse. Whitmore again. Third time in two months. The asshole hates me. Wouldn't find with me if I was defending his own mother."

"What'd you do to get on the old fart's bad side?" Mark asked.

"Oh, that appeal last winter. Got him kicked off the case for bias."

"Oh, yeah. Yeah, I remember that one," Mark nodded as they walked into the dark, smokey bar. "Still drinking whiskey, Steve?"

"And water," Steven answered as he sat down at the bar.

"Well. Here's to justice, pal," Mark said, raising his scotch rocks to Steven's whiskey and water.

"Yeah. Yeah right," Steven said without a smile and took a long draught of his drink. Reaching in his front pocket, he found a cigarette and, putting it between his frowning lips, snapped his butane lighter to its tip.

"Hey, you've got it bad, Steve. This stuff really getting you down?" Mark asked, watching his old law school friend.

Steven turned on his stool and faced Mark, whose expression held as much concern as curiosity. It had been months since he'd seen Mark, beyond a nod or a quick remark when they ran into each other at the Hall. Mark, also a criminal lawyer, had managed to do quite well for himself, opening his own practice with another law school friend a few years before. They had expanded to the defense of white-collar criminals, a plush downtown office and, as Steven had noticed some months before when he saw Mark driving down Eighth Street, a brand new Mercedes Benz.

"Yeah," Steven answered. "Yeah, it is." He turned back to his drink.

"Well, what's it about, Steve? What's got you down?" Mark asked sympathetically.

Steven had thought he'd already explained, but maybe Mark had forgotten what it was like to defend a common criminal, not to mention trying to collect fees. He finished off his drink.

"Two more," Mark said to the bartender, then turning back to Steven, "Steve, my man. Maybe you're in the wrong business," he said, joking, but still sympathetic.

Steven, staring at the endless shelves of bottles before him, raised his eyebrows and exhaled a thick stream of smoke.

"How much did this Mexican guy give you, Steve? How many hours did you put in to watch him get hauled off to the joint?" Mark asked as Steven, still staring ahead, twisted his lips to a tighter frown.

"Whew, boy!" Mark went on. "I don't think I want to know!"

They were silent a moment as Mark stirred his swizzle stick around the ice in his drink.

"He was court appointed," Steven finally answered.

"Oh, uhhuh. You're still doing those, huh?" Mark said, not exactly paternalistic, but with a tone that made Steven wince. "I thought you gave that stuff up when you left the Public Defender,

Steve. God. I'll tell you. That is *one* dead-end street. No wonder you're down, Steve. God. I got out of that as *fast* as I could. Working your butt off for peanuts. And the truth of it is, Steve, come on, we both know it. You could work up a defense worthy of the Supreme Court itself trying to get any of these low-lifes off. What's the point? It all comes down to what the judge had for breakfast. Or say you do get lucky and get one of 'em off. Three weeks later there they are again. This time it's drugs, or assault, or murder. It's a waste of time, Steve, let me tell you. That's not the level where the law really *operates*. Where you can sink your teeth into a case because you know—if you're smart—you can make it work for you." Giving Steven a sincere, advising look, Mark said, "Where the law works, Steve, really *works*, is where the money is."

Steven looked at Mark, wondering if he understood the meaning of his own words, but Mark was beaming now, remembering his own triumphs. "God, I remember when I finally crawled out of that hole. When I took my first case with Drew. A PG&E exec retained us on a misuse of public funds," he paused, catching the look of distrust in Steven's eyes. "Look, Steve, I know what you're thinking. But tell me this. What's the difference between clearing some two-bit mugger who's grabbed some old lady's purse, and clearing some bigwig who's bilked the taxpayers for a few thousand? I'll tell you the difference. At least the PG&E exec didn't knock down any old ladies. Nobody's gotten hurt. Yeah, the taxpayers have to pay another nickel a year, so what? Hell, I pay taxes. The difference, Steve, the real difference is two things. One, you get to practice *law*. Real law. The judge *listens* to you, Steve. You get to use your brains. To really outwit the other guys. And *win*." He paused again, signaling the bartender and laying a $20 bill on the bar. "And two, you make a living, Steve. A decent, goddamn living." He looked at Steven closely. "How much do you still owe the government for your three years at Boalt, Steve?"

Steven frowned again.

"No, tell me, Steve. I know how you had to scrimp and starve all the way through school. I remember, I was there. And still I bet you're paying for it. How much, Steve? Fifteen thousand? Twenty thousand?"

"Eleven. Eleven thousand," Steven answered.

"And you've got a family, don't you, Steve? A little boy? How is Linda anyway?" Mark asked as the bartender set another round in front of them.

"She's OK. She's fine," Steven answered.

"God, Steve. I remember what a bright boy you were in law school, too. One of the best, Steve, really." Mark looked at him with admiration. "You were so sharp, shit. I half-expected you'd be a judge by now. But then you always did have that bleeding heart." He nudged Steven with affection.

Steven sighed and sipped his drink, remembering himself those first years after law school, his hope, his enthusiasm.

"Well, how is it going for you, Steve. Tell me," Mark asked again, still curious, and concerned.

"Oh. Well." Steven thought a moment. "It's not that good, Mark. Not too good, really."

"How do you mean, Steve?"

"Well . . ." Steven sipped his drink again. "You know how it is, doing PD work. And now . . . now that I'm on my own, well. The truth is . . . it's worse. I think I'm making less. I just can't get any damn money out of it. There's no money in it." Steven paused. "And it *is* bullshit. It really *is*. There's no 'justice' in that courtroom. It's just a game of wits and egos. Between us. The lawyers. And the clients are the pawns."

"Well, now, Steve." Mark was uneasy.

"And I'm sick to death of it, Mark. You're right. I've got *nothing* to show for it. Nothin'. The fact is I can hardly pay the rent, and Linda wants to put Justin in childcare so she can look for a job. That would help. But I just can't afford it, Mark. I can't afford the fucking cost of the centers. They're over $400 a month! At least the ones she's looking at. She wants the best for him, and so do I. I just don't know how to tell her. I keep putting it off. And then, god. I've had this crazy run of bad luck." Steven watched the bartender set another drink in front of him and, reaching in his pocket for another cigarette as Mark listened attentively, he went on. "First some assholes dumped sugar in my gas tank a couple months ago. I never did figure out who or why, but the goddamn fuckers practically destroyed my engine. This is one dangerous town, I'll tell you," he said, lifting his full drink carefully to his lips.

"Sugar in your gas tank? Geez, that's weird," Mark said. "Have you got the Mafia after you, Steve? Or some side dish is pissed at you, maybe?" He winked at him.

"No. Christ. No. Just some random nut, I guess. Linda says I should be grateful, that it wasn't worse. I could have been shot by the Zodiac killers or something."

"Well, that's a hell of a way to look at it," Mark answered, puzzled. "Anyway, it must have set you back some."

"A thousand dollars. And riding buses for two weeks."

"You've just got one car between you?" Mark asked, surprised.

Steven sighed. "Yeah."

"Well, that is a rotten break, Steve. You've really gotta watch your ass in a town full of crackpots like this."

"Hey, listen, that's not all. It didn't stop there. Then about a month ago—this one's really nuts—Linda told me, she just happened to mention one day, that some neighbor had been by. Supposedly this woman lived down the street from us, and she came by giving Linda this line that she was a sociology student at some community college, or out at State or somewhere, and that—get this—she's doing a survey on young married couples for some research project, and was Linda married? Supposedly she's going around asking all the neighbors, right? So Linda says yeah, and the next thing the woman's in the house giving Linda the third degree about her family, their relationships, blah da blah . . ."

"You mean Linda talked to her?"

"Yeah, well, she didn't know. She'd been in the middle of giving Justin his lunch and the woman more or less connived her way in, I guess. But listen, this family stuff, all these questions about her relatives and shit were just to get her off guard." Steven lit another cigarette. "Then she starts asking about *me*, my family, my background. My *financial* situation, right?"

"And Linda *told* her?" Mark was incredulous.

"Well, not that much, but enough for her to know we rent our place, we've only got one car, we don't have any money in the bank."

"So this woman wrote it all up for the school newspaper?" Mark grinned.

"Huh! I wish that was all!" Steven answered. "Three days later I get a letter from MasterCharge. They canceled our credit. Zap. The bitch was checking our credit."

Mark wrinkled his brow. "That is a weird one, Steve. I've never heard of any company running credit checks like . . ."

"How else can you explain it?" Steven asked, setting his empty drink back down on the bar. "Why in hell would MasterCharge just cut us off? Like that! Without any warning? You can bet Linda and I had a few scenes about that one. Her talking to some stranger. No wonder I don't want to talk to her about money!"

"Well, Steve," Mark looked embarrassed. "Maybe your payments, uh . . ."

"No, goddamit. Our account was *fine*. We don't have much, Mark, but we get by. I pay the bills, for Christ's sake." Steven's face was flushed with anger.

"OK, OK," Mark said hurriedly. "It just seems kind of wild, I mean. I mean maybe it was just a coincidence, or . . . I mean, maybe the bitch really was just writing a term paper."

"Nah!" Steven shook his head. "See I put the whole $1,000 for the Toyota on MasterCharge and I think they decided to check us out. But we don't have any credit accounts anywhere else."

"You don't?" Mark asked, incredulous again.

"Well. No." Steven answered, ending his story, deciding he had said enough.

Mark thought a second, then seeing Steven's empty glass, "One for the road, Steve?"

"What time is it?"

"Oh, it's still early. 5:30," Mark said, looking at his watch. "Still happy hour."

Steven hesitated. "Yeah. Sure. Let me make a phone call." Getting up from his stool, he walked to the back of the bar. A minute later he returned. "It's out of order," he said as he settled himself back in his seat.

"Listen, Steve," Mark said, leaning forward on his stool, his folded arms resting on the bar. He turned his face close to Steven's. "I just had an idea."

"Yeah?" Steven said, reaching for his new drink.

"Drew and I've been picking up more and more clients. Drew's been in this for several years now, you know. He's a sharp man, Steve. Brilliant man."

"So?" Steven said, not enjoying the turn of the conversation.

"But, listen, Steve. There could be a place in this for you." Steven moved his stool closer to the bar as Mark went on. "I know Drew's been thinking, though he hasn't said anything yet, I know he's thinking that we could grow—that we could use another attorney with us. This is just the beginning, Steve. Drew's reputation is just getting around in the really important places," Mark paused to sip his drink, "and I'll admit, I'm bringing in quite a few clients myself. I'm pretty damn good myself, Steve."

Steven nodded, waiting.

"On my recommendation, Steve, I think Drew would consider taking you in with us." He looked happily at Steven, moved by his own generosity.

Steven looked at the clean, neat cut of Mark's blue Yves St. Laurent suit, the thin silk tie clipped to his shirt with a small gold stud matching the slightly larger gold cuff links on his crisp, white shirt cuffs.

"Of course, it's demanding work, Steve. It's no gravy train, I'll tell you. We're playing hardball, here. You've gotta be sharp, tough, put yourself on the line." Mark was beginning to sound like a drill sergeant.

Steven turned away to exhale a long stream of smoke, then back to Mark. "I'll think about it, Mark. Thanks."

Mark sat back a little, nonplused by the lack of gratitude in Steven's response. "It's the chance of your life, Steve," he said with a petulant severity, "and you know it."

Steven raised his eyebrows, staring again at the rows of bottles and then, with a start, looked more closely at the mirror above them. "Well, I'll be damned. There's Sorrenson!"

Mark followed Steven's gaze to the mirror, then turned around to see the figure in its reflection, a tall, well-built man in a loose sports jacket and jeans, his tousled, curly dark hair graying at the temples above a strong dimpled jaw. "Christ! You're right! I haven't seen him in years."

"No. Me either. He's been in New York since, oh, '74, '75. At least, that's the last I heard."

"Yeah. Working with the pinkos. That's what I heard."

"Well, I don't know 'pinkos,' Mark," Steven said.

"Oh, yeah, Steve, it's true. He always was a radical, even at Boalt. If it wasn't Viet Nam, it was the Black Panthers. I mean, I guess we all were a lot of bleeding hearts in those days, but he got worse, I swear. I heard he got in with Charles Garry and that bunch."

"The National Lawyers Guild," Steven said.

"Well, yeah, but a lot of them are pretty tame compared to the company Sorrenson keeps. Black radicals, some of these cult Marxist groups. He defends 'em all."

"Oh, get off it, Mark. He's a great guy. You talk about putting yourself on the line. There's a man you can respect, can rely on. He always does exactly what he says he's going to do, sticks to his principles."

"How the hell do you know? You haven't seen the guy in ten years."

"Hey! Sorrenson!" Steven ignored Mark and, turning on his stool, raised his arm to wave Sorrenson over to join them.

"Oh, Christ," Mark muttered, signaling to the bartender to bring another round.

Jack Sorrenson looked across the crowded room. His eyes focusing on Steven, he grinned and, leaning over to exchange a few last words with the people sitting at the table where he stood, he handed them a sheet of paper and made his way over to Steven and Mark at the bar.

"Steve! How are you?" He shook Steven's hand warmly, the amber light in his hazel eyes smiling affectionately at him, and then, seeing Mark next to him, his back half to him, "Hey! Mark. How's it going?"

"Long time no see, eh, Jack?" Mark returned with a nod of greeting.

"Are you just here for a visit, Jack? or here to stay?" Steven asked, moving his stool back to make room for Jack to stand between them at the bar. "Hey, let me get you a drink," he added. "What'll you have?"

"Oh, I don't think I've got time for a drink, Steve," Jack answered. "Actually, I just stopped into this place to try and get some people out to a demonstration in Berkeley tonight."

"Still at it, eh, Jack?" Mark laughed, shaking his head.

"Oh." Steven looked somber. "About Grenada, I guess."

"So you came all the way from New York to organize a demonstration for us?" Mark asked, not too kindly.

Jack laughed. "No, I'm in town for some Guild work. Just for a few weeks. Though several of us left the meetings this morning when we heard about the invasion. Want to get some people out in the streets." The gold twinkle in his eye turned dark, angry. "Can you believe it, Steve? Not even Congress knew about this until the troops were on the island."

"I wouldn't be surprised if they still didn't know," Steven answered.

"Steve." Jack looked puzzled.

"Oh, our boy Steve here doesn't believe in the law anymore, didn't you know that, Jack? Thinks it's just a big game," Mark informed him.

"Well. I don't entirely disagree with that," Jack said, his eyes thoughtful as he looked at Steven. "So you're not practicing anymore, Steve?"

"Oh, yeah, yeah, I am," Steven said uncomfortably. "So what's this paper you're passing around?"

"A call to a demonstration tonight and some facts about the invasion," Jack answered. "We didn't have much time to work on it, but we want to at least counter this crap about the U.S. invading to 'save the lives' of the American medical students." He laid his leaflets on the bar.

"Reagan's getting pretty wild, don't you think?" Jack asked. "Calling for a news blackout. Christ. Talk about totalitarian."

"Yeah." Steven reached for his drink. "Maybe he thinks he's in a Nazi movie."

Jack half smiled. "No, he's got a lot to hide. Like how Grenada sent *three* requests, to him and to Canada, to airlift their citizens out *days* ago. Canada did—yesterday." Jack shook his head. "Reagan didn't even acknowledge the offers. Even the medical school administrator said the students weren't in any danger, until the Marines got there!"

"Nobody's gonna believe we're in there for the medical students anyway, Jack," Mark told him. "Everyone knows we invaded to get rid of the Communists. Who needs another Soviet base in the Caribbean? Besides, most of the countries down there asked us to come in. They don't want the Commies down there either. They're just using that line about the medical school for all the people in this country who just don't understand politics. Face it, Jack. There's a lot of people out there who just aren't too bright."

Jack was silent, then turned and looked around the bar.

"Wait a minute, wait a minute," Steven said. "Who asked us to invade?"

"Six members of the Organization of Caribbean States," Mark answered with an impatient shrug.

"The fact is," Jack decided to try again, "under international law it is illegal for a nation to invade another nation and change their government. The U.N. Charter, the OAS Charter, the Organization of Caribbean States all make that very clear. And the Caribbean pact on military assistance states that the islands shall call for intervention only in the case of external threat, and only by unanimous vote. Grenada was not under external threat—until the Marines got there." He looked at Mark. "Only four of the islands had voted to call on the United States—in violation of the pact."

Mark sat stiffly, staring at nothing in particular, while Steven watched Jack, listening. "You know these stories about Grenada building an airport for a Soviet base are pure bullshit too," Jack said. "Grenada had been planning to build that airport for years, to increase tourism and trade. The specifications for it are so obviously for commercial use . . . The World Bank was doing a feasibility study back in 1976, planning to give them a loan for it. But as soon as the New Jewel government took up the *identical* plans, the U.S. blocked the loan. In fact we have attempted to prevent Grenada from getting any loans of any kind through international agencies since 1979."

"Well, Jack." Mark looked disgusted. "What do you *expect*? Why should we help build a Communist country in our own backyard?"

"You tell me, Mark." Jack looked at him sincerely. "What do you mean by 'communist'? What is a 'communist country'?"

"Come on, Jack." Mark almost laughed. "You've been around the block. A Soviet puppet. That's what a Communist country is. A country where the Soviets shove everybody up against the wall, tell them what to do and line the goddamn place with missiles aimed right at the U.S.A."

"Sounds more like the U.S. in El Salvador. Or Lebanon," Steven said, laughing, as he added, "With the missiles pointed the other way of course."

Jack looked at Steven, somewhat relieved, then to Mark. "Mark. Are you aware that the Grenadian government had almost total popular support? That they are all people born and raised there—black people who threw off centuries of slavery to reclaim their own country. Since they've been in power Grenada has had the greatest economic growth of almost any country in the Western Hemisphere."

"Well, if they're so independent, Jack, why was the place crawling with Cubans?" Mark asked. "Same thing. Same as Soviets."

"No, Mark. Not the same as Soviets. Cubans are Cubans."

Looking frustrated, Jack glanced at Steven, who sat quietly watching, enjoying the debate. He looked back at Jack, a hint of challenge in his smile, as if to say, 'Oh yeah?'

Jack took a breath, and in a calmer voice said to Steven, "Look, you know, Steve. If the Cubans are closer to the Soviet Union than to the United States, it's because we've pushed them there. At the very beginning of the revolution Castro publicly stated that Cuba was 'neither capitalist nor communist,' and that he was *not* opposed to capitalist enterprises, as such. So long as they didn't conflict with Cuban law. But when Cuba began to take more economic control of their country, the United States completely cut off trade. It wasn't until 1960 that Cuba began relations with the Soviet Union and then only because the Soviets had agreed to trade sugar for oil."

"Are you trying to tell us that Cuba isn't a Soviet puppet, Jack," Mark said with a sneer.

"What I'm saying, Mark, is that the United States and Europe have dominated world trade for centuries. If a sovereign state like Cuba, or Grenada, attempts to develop its economy in its *own* interests it has to contend with the United States blocking it *every* step of the way. Look at Chile! Allende's popular government was being suffocated by U.S. economic maneuvering—cutting off trade relations, denying them access to essential technology. The coup was just the last straw—the CIA's favor to Western financiers who wanted Chile's copper and sulphur back in their control. And the Chileans weren't looking to make mega-profits from their own resources, you know, but just to turn them into food, education and health care for their people. Hell, when a small nation working for the development of its own people is put in an economic *stranglehold* by U.S. corporate powers, and the Soviet Union offers them reasonable trade agreements that will allow them to survive and still maintain their own political program . . ."

"Jack, Jack. Don't try to tell me that we're the big evil ogres and the Soviets are just your everyday innocent Good Samaritans," Mark interrupted.

"No. The Soviets put their own interests first. And, yeah, Mark, their interest in defense is probably behind a lot of the aid they give. But still, by the *nature of their economy*, the interests of the Soviet Union are *not in direct opposition* to the autonomous economic development of smaller nations. That's the crux of it, Mark. Regardless of the Soviets' role in the arms race—their *economic structure* does not *demand* the total subjugation of the rest of the people in the world! And capitalist profit-making *does*!"

"I'm sorry, Jack," Mark answered. "I'm just *not* going to buy it. You *damn* well know if the U.S. lets up for a minute, *one* minute, its vigilance in this hemisphere, it would create a vacuum here that the Soviets will move in and fill before you have time to think up another quote from Marx."

"Oh, Mark," Jack groaned. "Have you really gotten as racist as that? You really think a white guy always has to be in charge? If not the U.S., the Russians? You really think that the people of Latin America, left to their own, are a *vacuum*? The Cuban revolution was a movement of Latin and African people determined to control their own lives. Likewise for Grenada, Nicaragua . . ."

"Look, Jack." Mark set his empty glass on the bar and looked at his watch. "I've got to go." He stood up from his stool and nodded gruffly at Steven, then turned back to Jack. "And listen you son of a bitch, don't you ever call me a racist again. I give more money to the NAACP than you've probably seen in a year." With that he pushed his way through the crowded bar and out the door.

Steven watched him go, his face drawn in a surprised, though slightly amused expression. "Have a seat," he said to Jack, pushing Mark's empty stool toward him.

Jack, annoyed and flustered, sat down at the bar. "God, I wasn't trying to offend him . . . I . . ."

"S'all right, Jack," Steven said. "Mark was always a little over-sensitive." He looked at his empty glass for a moment. "In fact, he's an asshole."

"Well, I don't know." Jack still looked concerned. "I haven't seen the guy in over ten years probably. I guess I was pushing my point but, it just really gets to me when I hear that kind of 'red-scare' talk from another lawyer, a man who has the responsibility to be better informed than that, for god's sake!"

Steven felt his face flush and reached in his pocket for a cigarette. "Well, Jack, everyone's entitled to their own opinions. Speaking of the rights of man."

"Everyone's entitled to access to the facts and unbiased information to form his or her opinions, and I'd think that after 20 years of education, a man like Mark would know how to get beyond the distorted, self-serving propaganda from the Pentagon."

"Not if it serves his own interests, Jack," Steven said.

"I don't remember Mark as being a candidate for the Republican Party, Steve."

"You've been gone a long time. What can I say?"

"Well. I know this isn't the '60s . . ."

"Jack, the fact is a lot of people, most people in this country I would say, feel very threatened by 'Communism' and by the Soviet

Union."

"Yeah, I know that. But there's a place where anti-communism stops and racism begins. This idea that the only two *real* countries in the world are the United States and the Soviet Union, and all the other people of the world are their puppets and pawns, it's just too simplistic, Steve. It's like the guy had never heard of the Nonaligned Movement."

"The what?" Steven asked.

"You guys really did forget about politics after school, didn't you?" Jack looked at Steven, beginning to accept the gap that the last decade had formed between them.

Steven felt his face flush again, and thought a moment before he answered, "I think that might be a little simplistic, too, Jack, in my case anyway. I wouldn't say that I've 'forgotten' about politics. Though have I been involved in politics to the extent, or in the way, that you have? No."

"I'm sorry, Steve. I didn't mean it to sound like that. I guess I just thought, when I saw you two guys sitting over here, the last ten years just sort of slipped away, and I expected us to get into one of our old discussions . . ."

"So, what's the Nonaligned Movement?" Steven asked.

Jack smiled. "Well, it's got quite a history, Steve. Maybe we can get into it some other time." He looked at his watch. "Why don't you come on over to this demonstration with me? We can catch up on each other's lives a little."

"Sorry, Jack, I can't. I told Linda I'd be home early tonight. What time is it?"

"After 6:00."

"Oh Christ, yeah, I have to get going." Steven picked up one of Jack's leaflets from the bar and, folding it, put it in his pocket. "Listen, Jack. How long are you going to be in town? Why don't you come over for dinner some night before you leave?"

"That would be great, Steve. Though I don't exactly know my schedule right now. Actually, it's possible I may be staying on longer than a few weeks."

"Good. Good," Steven said warmly. "Let me give you my number." He pulled a pen from his pocket and jotting down his number on a napkin, handed it to Jack as they left the bar.

Fifteen blocks away Rikki hurried up Market Street to the corner of California. She grabbed at her hat as a fierce gust of wind threatened to rip it from her head. And they think it's cold in New York, she thought, pulling the wool cap tight over her mass of black curls. As she shifted the two heavy boxes of leaflets she carried to her other arm, she caught her own image reflected in the dark plate glass of the

Crocker Bank. For a moment, she hadn't even recognized her own small frame, had thought it was a teller, a worker inside the bank, but no, that face, so intent, even purposeful, was her own. And when she smiled at the realization, that ironic half-smile, she had to laugh—so here I am, Ms. Revolutionary. If my mother could see me now. She hiked the heavy boxes up a notch in the crook of her arm, walking quickly up the street. Or Mrs. Caldwater. She always thought I was destined for doom. Rikki laughed again, remembering her high school counselor, Mrs. Caldwater, her chiseled face, perplexed and annoyed as she told her, "We're going to have to suspend you again, Rikki. I've spoken with your mother. I just don't understand how you can . . ." Of course she didn't understand! She didn't have to sit through all that *boring* crap, like a prisoner, chained to those highchair desks for seven hours a day, listening to those . . . Well, the teachers were probably just as fucking bored. If it hadn't been for Miss Bernstein I never would have shown up at all. Rikki smiled, her black almond eyes alight. At least that woman could think for herself. Of course everyone thought she was a crazy communist, just because she knew something about what was going on in the fucking world. She stopped abruptly. Shit, she had walked right past the restaurant. Oh what the hell, I'm only carrying 600 pounds of paper, she said to herself as she turned back. Leaning her shoulder into the aluminum-framed door, she pushed it open and stood in the entranceway, her eyes quickly scanning the long narrow cafe as she shifted the boxes of leaflets once again.

A glass-encased counter half the length of the room held plates of parsley-garnished quiches, small bins of light, buttery croissants, trays of thick chocolate and cream desserts, and bottles of imported beer and wine. Grouped across from the counter and beyond were small wooden cafe tables and chairs, most filled with downtown workers having a glass of wine, a light snack, and, oh, there she is, back in the corner, Sylvia. No wonder I didn't see her, Rikki thought, she didn't say she would be with Claire. They seemed engrossed in conversation. As Rikki started to make her way toward them, Claire stood up from her chair, and leaning over Sylvia, her arm around her shoulders, whispered something to her, and then, oh uhhuh! Rikki thought, as Claire, smiling into Sylvia's upturned face, kissed her slowly, then stood back, her hand resting on Sylvia's cheek. As Rikki neared the table, Sylvia said something, grinning to Claire, who burst into laughter, a rich, fluted sound that Rikki, honestly, had never heard from her before.

Claire turned and, seeing Rikki standing just behind her, said, "Oh Rikki! *Allo*, 'ow are you?" She smiled warmly as Sylvia looked up. "Rikki. Hi! How'd it go?"

"OK. You two seem happy," Rikki said, raising her eyebrows at Sylvia as she dumped her load of leaflets onto Claire's empty chair.

Claire smiled again. "Things are not so bad." She stepped back to look at the clock above the cafe counter. "But in fact, I 'ave to go, I am going to be late. I'll see you in Berkeley, enh?"

"Yeah, we'll see you there," Sylvia answered as Claire picked up her satchel and with a last smile to them both, "Bye-bye," she said and left the cafe.

Rikki, pulling up an empty chair, sat across from Sylvia. "God. I've never seen Claire so . . ." She glanced at Claire's departing figure as if to find the word.

"What?" Sylvia asked, straightening the clutter on the table.

"Well . . . Nice."

Sylvia looked at her. "Rikki!"

"Well, I mean, Syl. I mean, usually she's so," Rikki made a serious, grim face. "You know. Business-like."

"Oh come on, Rikki. She's not like that!"

"Well, no, I mean. Well when I walked in here, she was laughing, and . . . Well I don't know if I've ever heard her really laugh before. You know?" Rikki looked at Sylvia sincerely, and then seeing the hurt in her friend's eyes, she said, "But I think Claire's great, Sylvia, really! I mean she totally knows what she's doing. Like *all* the time. And I get the feeling she doesn't take *any* crap. From anybody. Ever."

Sylvia was quiet a moment, studying an empty glass as she held it in her hand, her other hand running the tip of a finger around and around the rim.

"Oh, Syl," Rikki began.

"No. I know what you mean, Rikki." Sylvia looked up at her. "You haven't known her that long though. She's not . . . well, she's not how she used to be really. But Rikki, I've known her a long time. She wasn't always so *serious*, or, so intense about . . . Well, she was, but . . . She has another side, you know. She does. A very sort of, playful, loving side. She can be really warm, Rikki. And fun. Funny. She used to . . ." Sylvia looked away, as if not sure she could explain herself. Or her lover.

"Oh, I'm sure, Syl. I didn't mean to . . ."

"Honestly, though, Rikki, I do wonder sometimes." Sylvia kept her gaze on the cafe door. "We used to have such good times together," she looked back at Rikki, "really happy times, you know? Even though we were always working so hard. Our political work always came first, of course. Comes first. But we could laugh, and . . . I remember when, especially when we lived together, but after too, we'd spend hours just—making things up really. Cooking all kinds of concoctions, some of them were ridiculous, or sometimes we'd get out my art supplies from school and draw all kinds of crazy pictures, or friends came over—" Sylvia stopped herself short, glancing at Rikki who watched her quietly, listening. "Well anyway," Sylvia flushed slightly, "she does have that side. It wasn't *all* work. *All* the time. Like now." She thought a moment. "Yeah. Today she's happy. This afternoon." She remembered Claire's jubilance as they had walked to the Market Street NEWS office, the Allies' information safe in her satchel.

"I don't know why the fuck she's happy today of all days," Rikki said. "What about the fucking Marines in Grenada?"

"Oh no, no, she's very upset about it. Something else happened, I don't know," Sylvia said hurriedly. "But I know what you mean, Rikki. In general. Claire is just too serious now."

"Well now, Syl, I am getting confused. How come you're always telling me: 'Rikki, get serious. Be serious. This work is serious. Take yourself seriously.' And now you're saying . . ."

"Well, now . . ." Sylvia smiled despite herself. "That's kind of different, Rikki. There are extremes in everything you know. I guess, in terms of you," she looked at her friend with affection, "I worry about you sometimes. That you don't really think that anything's going to work, or, like you don't really have faith that we can *do* it. I mean do what we believe we can because we're just not up to it or something." Sylvia looked at Rikki questioningly. "Do you know what I mean? That's what I mean by taking ourselves seriously. We're creative, intelligent adults. We can make a difference. A *big* difference, and we *will*. We're not a bunch of insignificant 'girls,' like we've been told all our lives. Not if we take ourselves . . ."

"OK, OK, Syl," Rikki answered, "I've heard it before." Her dark eyes flashed, piqued now as Sylvia seemed to be changing her position when it came to her, Rikki, her own attitudes, her humor, and doubts. "But sometimes I think Claire, and most the other women I've met in NEWS, are just *too* fucking serious, or 'dedicated,' or so 'holy, holy,' 'goody-goody,' like the whole world would fucking collapse without them."

Sylvia sat back. Maybe she had pushed her point too far this time. After all, Rikki worked hard, as hard as any of them. Just because she wasn't always sure, because she often made the wry comment or ironic remark, sometimes disparaging, yes, sometimes seeming to mask her own uncertainty . . .

"Well do you know what I mean?" Rikki said, irritation in her voice.

"Well . . ." Sylvia began hesitantly.

"I mean sometimes I just don't think people are being real in this organization. Everyone's so fucking 'dedicated' all the time. Yeah, people get bitchy or pissed off, but they don't *do* anything about it. I mean they don't sit around badmouthing each other, or have screaming fights, or . . . just act like normal people! Hardly ever!" Rikki was silent, then laughed at her own words, less angry now. "Well, it's not like I think we *should* exactly."

"And it's not like we never do, either, Rikki," Sylvia said, remembering some of her own confrontations in the past. "Stick around. You'll see," she added with a tired, grim expression.

"Well it's not like I'm looking forward to it."

Sylvia laughed. "But you know, too, Rikki," she began. "There isn't as much of that kind of thing in NEWS as there might be. Well there *can't* be. We couldn't exist if we were all bitching around at each other all the time. That's the point. We've got more important things to do. Really. I think it's that simple. Sure, there are problems and antagonisms and conflicts. But it's just because we really *do* believe in what we're doing, and that it is 'good'—even 'holy' if you want—that we keep it together and stay above a lot of that petty bullshit. We just don't have the time for it. We can't afford it. That's why you don't see that much of it. No one's interested in it. And we do have the choice—to be different."

Rikki shrugged, but not without interest, as she gazed quietly at the poster against the wall, a still print of blue and violet flowers. "I guess," she answered finally. And then turning to face Sylvia, "Yeah, I guess that's good." She smiled. "So for that I won't tell my friends what a shit I think you are."

"Oh don't be too sweet, Rikki." Sylvia grinned. "Should we get something to eat?" She looked at her watch. "Oh yeah, we better hurry."

"Oh why, we've only been sitting here for an hour."

"I've got to make a couple calls about the demonstration, too," Sylvia said, worried now as they got up from the table to order their dinner.

Linda was just helping Justin down from his highchair when she heard Steven come down the hall and walk into the bedroom.

"Steve?" she called.

"Yeah. Hi, Lin," he answered through the half-open kitchen door.

"I thought you were going to be home by 5:00," she remarked, casually.

"What time is it?" he said, still from the dark bedroom.

"It's almost 7:00, not that late, but I thought we were going . . ."

"Oh, Mark and I went for a drink after court. I ran into him at the elevator," Steven answered as he came into the kitchen, his tie loosened at the neck and his tired eyes a pinkish blue. He had a tall, narrow paper bag in his hand and, taking a fifth of whiskey out of it, he set it on the counter. "I don't really feel like a movie tonight, Lin. I'm beat.

Really a lousy day in court. Want a drink?" he asked, getting a glass from the cupboard.

"Well," Linda said. "I guess I'll cancel the sitter."

"Yeah, I tried to call. The phone was out of order." He opened the freezer door and took out an ice tray.

"Steven!" Linda turned from Justin, her angry eyes fixed on him. "Look. You can be late. You can mess up our plans. But don't start lying to me!" her voice rose.

Steven dropped his hands to his side. Still facing the counter, he said quietly, "I'm not lying, Linda."

Linda felt the anxiety of the last two hours fighting its way to her throat and eyes, disappointment filling them with tears. She bent to help Justin get his car from under the table.

"Where Daddy go?" Justin asked, looking at Steven.

"Goddamn you, Steve," Linda said, turning to him. "You couldn't find a phone that worked?"

"Linda. We were at the Jury Room. It was crowded. Jack Sorrenson was there." He sipped his drink, turning around and leaning back against the counter.

"I'm going to call Ann," she said. As she walked toward the telephone it rang and, quickening her step down the hall, she picked it up. "Hello?"

"Hi, Linda."

"Sylvia, hi."

"Are you OK?" Sylvia asked, unsure of the note in her cousin's voice.

"I've been better," Linda acknowledged, her voice clearer.

"How're Justin? and Steven?"

"Justin's great. Steven just came in late . . . I was worried. How are you, Sylvia? It feels like months since I've seen you."

"Oh, I know, Linda. So much has been going on. Actually, I'm calling to ask if you'd be interested in going to a demonstration in Berkeley."

"About Grenada?"

"Yeah. It's tonight. At 8:00."

"OK. Sure. I'll go. How are you getting there?"

"You will? Great! Well . . . are you going to leave Justin with Steven?"

"I'll be coming alone," Linda answered.

"Well, I'm downtown with a friend, Rikki. We're going to take BART. Do you want to meet us?"

"Oh, I'll drive. I can pick you up. Where are you?"

"On Drumm. Between Sacramento and California. We're at that little cafe . . ."

"Boudin's? Where we had lunch?"

"Yeah, that's it."

"What time is it now?"

"7:00. We should go about 7:30."

"Well, I'll be leaving here in about ten or 15 minutes."

"Great. See you, Lin."

Steven was sitting on the floor with Justin building block houses when Linda came back to the kitchen. "Steven, I didn't cancel the sitter. I'm going to go over to Berkeley with Sylvia."

"You're going out?" he asked, looking up from the blocks.

"Yeah, I'm leaving in about ten minutes. As soon as Ann gets here."

Steven got up from the floor as Justin, watching him rise, began to chant a whining, "Daddy. Daddy. Daddy."

"I hope you're not trying to punish me, Linda."

"Ppphh. Don't flatter yourself, bud."

"So fine. Go out. I can take care of Justin. We don't need to pay for a sitter."

"I want the sitter, Steve."

"Linda! Why should we pay ten bucks for a sitter when . . ."

"Because you're drunk, Steve! That's why!" Linda was alarmed herself at the sound of the words, ringing loud in her ears. She looked over at Steven's empty glass on the table as if to vindicate herself.

Steven lowered his eyes, giving Linda a surly look, shaded with the distance of betrayal. The doorbell rang, and Linda turned and left the room.

When Linda brought Ann into the kitchen she found Justin playing alone with his blocks on the floor. Steven was gone, behind the closed bedroom door, and so was his fifth of whiskey Linda realized, the angry anxiety she felt masked behind a reassuring smile to Ann as she showed her Justin's things.

Leaving Ann with Justin, Linda stood a moment outside her bedroom, her and Steven's bedroom. She could hear the low drone of the television beyond the closed door. Finally, with a quick turn of the knob she walked into the dark room, straight to the closet and, rummaging through it, pulled out a sweater and her jacket. Steven, lying on the bed, the television screen casting its greyish light over him, said nothing. Linda slipped the sweater over her head and, putting on the jacket, she turned to Steven, watching him a moment. He held a half-filled glass in his hand as he stared ahead, a deep frown on his lips and forehead as he watched the reports on the Marines in Grenada and Lebanon. Linda saw herself walking over to him, laying her arms gently around his shoulders and lightly kissing his taut, drawn brow, brushing the hair back from his temples; but still she stood, silent, in front of the closet, longing to comfort him while still something stronger held her there, unmoving. She turned and, taking her keys from the top of the bureau, left the room and closed the door behind her with a sharp click of the knob.

Linda drove quickly down Market Street smiling, despite herself, at the bright lights in the night darkness. She felt as if it had been months since she'd been out, on her own, going to Berkeley. She pulled into a red zone near Boudin's and ran from the car to the front door of the restaurant.

Sylvia saw her as she walked in and, taking Rikki's arm, hurried to meet her. "Hi Linda." She smiled and hugged her cousin, who rested a second in Sylvia's arms, feeling a comfort in their close, warm embrace. Then smiling, Linda said hello as Sylvia introduced her to Rikki, who grinned at them both, her dark eyes looking with interest and pleasure at the two cousins.

"It's great that you could come, Linda," Sylvia began as the three of them got in the Toyota. "I just called you on the off chance . . ."

"Well, I'm glad you did," Linda answered, turning the car around and heading toward the Bay Bridge. "I've been watching television reports on and off all day. It's really hard to tell what the hell is going on." For an instant she saw Steven, laying alone, morose, in the grey light of the television.

"I'll bet," Rikki said. "They don't mention how they've been planning to invade Grenada for years now. Or their practice run in Vieques." Her voice, though mocking, belied a deeper anger.

"Their what?" Linda asked.

"In March of 1981. 'Operation Red,'" Rikki answered. "The Marines acted out the whole thing they did in the invasion this morning. They even called their pretend target 'Amber and the Amberdines!'"

"Grenada has two other little islands, Carrikou and Petite Martinique," Sylvia explained. "Together they're called Grenada and the Grenadines. So: 'Amber and the Amberdines.'"

"What? Two years ago?" Linda repeated, trying to grasp exactly what had gone on, "The U.S. military pretended to invade Grenada?"

"Yes, they did a mock invasion on the island of Vieques," Sylvia answered. "There's a NATO base there. It's the largest military base in the Western Hemisphere. The people of Vieques have been trying to get NATO off their island for years. Some of them have even blown up a few Air Force jets."

"They're incredible," Rikki added. "They go out in their little fishing boats—Vieques used to be fishing villages before NATO moved in and started acting out all their war shit—so they go out in these little wooden boats and try to fuck up the maneuvers of all the destroyers and battleships. They've really got guts."

"So the Marines in Vieques were practicing how to invade Grenada—in 1981?" Linda asked, incredulous.

"Yes, really," Sylvia answered. "The exact maneuvers they used today. The 82nd Airborne—the same troops who did it for real this morning. The CIA's been trying to destabilize Grenada since 1979. Remember when that bomb went off under the stage at a political rally in Jamaica? Maurice Bishop was on that stage. That was just one of their . . ."

"Oh, Sylvia, you know, I've been reading that book you gave me last year, finally. You know?" Linda interjected. "The one on the CIA in Latin America? I'm just half way through it, but I can hardly believe it! I mean the things that go on!"

"I know," Sylvia said. "Anytime a country gets a little freedom or control for itself, there's the CIA, right there, fucking with them."

"They're demented," Rikki said.

Linda was quiet a moment. She wished, actually, that Steven were with her—that he could experience this too. What would he say about this 'Operation Red?' She glanced in the rear view mirror as she changed lanes and saw Rikki's face, troubled, but . . . what? Not irreverent, exactly. But, close. "Rikki," Linda began. "How did you get involved in all this? I mean NEWS. Or, I mean politics, I guess." She laughed.

"Oh, well," Rikki said, turning to look out at the night sky. She thought, recalling again, Elsa Bernstein, the woman who had been her only real teacher in the entire New York Public School System. "Actually, I was just thinking about it before, kind of."

Sylvia turned in her seat to look back at Rikki.

"I guess it started with this teacher I had in high school in New York."

"But Rikki. I thought you cut the whole four years," Sylvia said, laughing.

"Well, I tried. But there was one teacher. I really liked her. I told you about her, Syl. Her class was great. I never missed it. It was supposed to be history, but everyday we talked about what was going on right then, in the newspapers or on TV. And she brought in all these articles from magazines and news clippings from all over the world—a lot of leftist papers too. It was just completely different than anything else. It seemed more like 'reality' than anything else."

"So, well was she in NEWS in New York?" Linda asked.

"NEWS didn't exist then," Sylvia said.

"Yeah, this was five or six years ago," Rikki continued. "And then, just my general attitude at the time . . ." She smiled at Sylvia, then looked up at Linda's eyes in the rear view mirror as they glanced at her. "Mostly I wasn't too involved in school. I hated it. And I got in a lot of trouble. In fact," she hesitated, looking at Sylvia, who nodded. She went on, "I spent some time in Juvenile Hall. I mean 'Youth Guidance.' A real piss-pot of a place." She turned again to the window.

"Maybe that's what did it more than anything," Rikki said, looking back at Sylvia and Linda in the front seat. "I always swore that when I finally got to be 18 I'd go back and burn that fucking place to the ground." She laughed. "But that's not really what I meant. I didn't want to go to any more prisons, for sure. Unless it was for something really great. What I meant was, I wanted to do something to get rid of places like that. To change things. Though I didn't know what."

"Well what did you have to go there for? Linda asked, slightly shocked, curious.

Rikki shrugged, and, remembering that time, her voice more angry now, said, "Oh, really evil crimes you know? Like smoking a goddamn joint in the hall at school. I got suspended and my parents just totally freaked. They decided they needed to 'save me from myself.' So they had me locked up. I mean, like that's going to make me a good citizen or something. They were so fucking scared of everything, just paranoid—about cops, money, the president—you name it. And they tried their fucking hardest to put that fear in me."

Linda, glancing up to the mirror again to see Rikki's face, saw the anger in her eyes, as pained as it was fierce. "The next time it was even worse," Rikki said. "I mean the scenes, my father flipping out, telling them to lock me up forever, but fuck, at that point I'd take the Hall any day to get away from him and his paranoid fits, smacking me around." She was quiet a second, and then, to Linda's surprise, started to laugh. "You know what it was for that time? Some shit had come down at school where this guy, a black guy from the East Side, had gotten framed up by some white jock boys for stealing a bunch of stuff from the gym. I mean everybody knew about it, but the 'authorities' are programmed to only believe white boys, you know, and they completely got off. So a bunch of us," she laughed again, "we really got elaborate. We trapped these guys in the boys' john after we'd stopped up all the toilets and sinks and started a flood. I mean, it was a total mess, and they were swimming in it." She grinned, remembering the sight. "That didn't go over too big."

"Rikki, I can't believe you," Sylvia said, laughing, as Linda, not sure whether she felt shocked or amused, asked, "But . . . that's what got you into politics?"

"Well it was all this stuff," Rikki said. "And then a friend I'd met around then turned me on to this anarchist group. In fact I left home and lived with them—on my 18th birthday to be exact. It was a pretty small group, but we started doing some street actions, mild stuff. Pouring blood on the steps of the jail, you know. But, after awhile, well, I couldn't really see the point. Nothing ever changed anything. I dropped out and was doing nothing for a long time, more or less. But then I decided to come out here. A woman I met here, Carol, told me about NEWS. So I joined." She grinned at Sylvia. "And am I *glad!*"

"Rikki," Sylvia said.

"No, I really am," Rikki said, sincere now as she turned to Linda's eyes in the rear view mirror again. "I've learned a lot. I mean, I'd read a lot of stuff before, studied a lot even. But I never knew just what to *do* about it. And now I do."

"Hmh," Linda answered, thoughtful a moment. "It's great that you've found something that means something to you. I mean sometimes, it's so easy to feel like there's nothing we can do. You know?"

"Oh yeah." Rikki nodded.

"I mean I know how angry, or helpless . . ." Linda turned to Sylvia, "You know that book, too, it really makes me feel like this has just *got* to stop. About the CIA I mean. I really didn't know how they're all over the world! And the things they do, it's like the sickest spy movie. But so much sicker."

"I know," Sylvia said. She watched the huge steel girders of the Bay Bridge span as it loomed over them. "It's really . . . it's awful to know that human beings can be so depraved."

"Their training schools," Rikki said, "and they're all over the place, are where all the police and military torturers in Latin America learn their sick shit, like that one in Texas . . ."

"Oh please," Sylvia stopped her, feeling that tightness in her chest again.

"Yeah," Linda said. "I was just . . . Sylvia, what exit?"

"Oh, University. It's on Shattuck and Acton."

Linda changed lanes. "Actually, I used to think you exaggerated, Sylvia, about the CIA's role in the world. Or their powers or whatever. But reading this book and seeing the history of it, how they've murdered leaders and destroyed democratic movements, and their connections with the Mafia, and controlling the media with outrageous, *insane* lies. It's terrifying!" She paused. "And the torture."

"I know." Sylvia studied her hands, remembering the coded text and the photographs as they appeared one by one on the printout that afternoon. "But it's important to remember," she looked at Linda, "that there is resistance. People can and *will* change it." She couldn't say more. She turned to the window. *Would* they? The Allies, NEWS, NEWS CLAN. She almost shuddered with the enormity of it, of what they were going to do . . . But we will, yes, yes, she repeated to herself, we will, as her eye caught sight of a narrow, ivy-covered brick courtyard on Shattuck. The entrance to Vivoli's, that evening—when was it?—years ago came back so vividly to her, she and Claire, they'd gone for ice cream, and standing outside on that warm, sultry summer night, they'd barely been able to stop themselves, eyes on each other, licking the soft, sweet chocolate, barely able to . . . Oh Claire. No. No it was NEWS. The Action, that's what mattered. All that mattered. They were going to . . .

"I guess I should park," Linda said as they approached Acton and, turning down a side street, she drove a few blocks west.

"There's a place," Rikki said, "behind that truck."

Linda was thoughtful as they got out of the car and she locked the doors. "But Sylvia, I don't want to be pessimistic, but I don't know if anyone can fight the CIA. Because, for one thing, most people just don't care."

"Well what do people care about then? They're just so in love with their own lives? Their house or car or . . ."

"No, Sylvia, listen. There are whole countries full of people who are so in love with some god, or religion that they're too busy fighting each other . . ."

"But if it were real love, Linda, real love has to embrace *all* people, don't you think? You can't just pick one person, or god, or whatever, and say you love it, and then laugh when everybody else is getting killed. We *have* to care. About the entire Earth. That's what real love is."

"International love," Rikki summarized.

"Well, if that's love, Sylvia. If that's the only kind of feeling you call love, then there is damn little love in this world," Linda responded.

"But don't you think the potential for it's in everyone?" Sylvia asked, her voice suddenly full of an emotion that Linda could not quite interpret. "I mean we are all . . . all of us want the Earth to survive. All of us can love peace and community—if we feel we're a part of it. And for the first time in history the entire world is linked by mass communication and we *are* part of a world community. To *deny* that, to *hate* that, to hate the Russians, or the Chinese—or the Grenadians—is to hate ourselves. And to destroy them is to destroy ourselves."

"Literally," Rikki added as they heard the raised voices of a milling crowd on the corner ahead and she handed Sylvia a stack of leaflets.

"The Reagan Administration thinks they can win this one," a loud, angry voice rose over the crowd through a rasping microphone. "Six thousand Marines have more weapons than the entire island of Grenada! They suffered a defeat in Lebanon, so they want to prove they're still the tough guy by shafting a tiny country with a population of 100,000! Reagan and the Pentagon are flexing their muscles to show the world we're still king of the mountain. Let's show Reagan what we think of his wars! Let's show the Pentagon whose side we're on! Grenada's! Victory to the people of Grenada!" he shouted as the crowd cheered, their anger and emotion filling the cold night air.

"God," Sylvia said to Rikki as they passed out their leaflets, "Who's he with? He sounds like . . ."

"U.S. OUT OF GRENADA! U.S. OUT OF GRENADA!" A column of people marching up Shattuck Avenue drowned out Sylvia and the speaker on the platform. The crowd turned, alarmed, then enlivened by the clapping, chanting marchers, picked up the beat and chanted, banging pans and sticks. "U.S. OUT OF GRENADA!" The 500 people turned as one and followed the hundreds of marchers that had joined them out into the street.

"U.S. OUT OF GRENADA!" They flooded into the four lanes of Shattuck Avenue, stopping traffic, their angry cry, "U.S. OUT OF GRENADA!" resounding through the downtown corridor. They moved, striding, ten, 20 abreast, fists raised and placards held high. "U.S. OUT OF GRENADA!"

Cars backed up in intersections with drivers honking, some angry, but more cheering, raising their fists with the crowd. Within four blocks the marchers had doubled their ranks, over 1,000 strong, their angry storming mass moving to the east toward the student community.

Rikki grinned at Sylvia, her eyes shining, and Sylvia returned her glance, excited by the bold, determined motion of the demonstrators.

"I haven't seen anything like this since the '60s!" Linda said, her own eyes glittering in the night as they marched past the student housing—the march swelling as groups of students came out of their rooms picking up the chant, "U.S. OUT OF GRENADA! CIA OUT OF NICARAGUA! U.S. MARINES OUT OF LEBANON! NOW!"

As they turned up College Avenue, the demonstration had grown to over 2,000 people, filling the streets, backing up traffic, their chanting voices raised as one angry call for an end to imperialist war.

"Where are the cops?" Linda asked, catching her breath between chants, her voice hoarse as she watched Rikki hand out the last of her leaflets to a group of students on the street.

"They won't be here," Sylvia answered. "The mayor of Berkeley, he's a black man, supports the New Jewel Movement. In fact he's a member of the Grenadian Friendship Commit . . ."

She was interrupted as a Chevy Vega driven by a middle-aged crew-cut man appeared from a side street and began to plow its way into the crowd. Rikki was just in front of his bumper and as she turned angrily toward him he gunned his motor, knocking her off balance as Sylvia grabbed her and pulled her to her, just escaping the forward lunge of the car as it parted the crowd, barely missing the scattering people. Rikki, furious, grabbed at the side mirror of the passing car, wrenching it from its casing, as Linda kicked at the door and a tall man in a loose sports jacket just behind her flung himself on the trunk of the car banging the rear window with his fist. The car spun to the right, throwing him off the trunk and sped off down the opposite side street, its side mirror dangling. Linda, Sylvia and Rikki ran to the man in the sports jacket who, picking himself up from the asphalt, brushed off his jeans, cursing, "Fucking ex-Marine." The marchers just surrounding the incident stopped a moment, then, seeing that no one was hurt, surged on, their angry shouts echoing through the streets.

"Are you OK?" Linda asked the man as Rikki, still fuming, glaring at the now empty side street, yelled, "What an asshole!" Sylvia put her arm around her, still trembling with rage herself.

"Yeah, I'm OK. How about you?" He looked at the three women, concerned.

"We're fine," Sylvia answered as Linda added, "I wish you'd broken his goddamn window. Nice try, though." She smiled at him.

"He's a real nice guy, huh?" The man laughed. "A real advocate of the people's right to peaceful protest."

"Yeah, and he'll probably be back here in a minute with an M-16 he got in 'Nam to finish us off," Rikki answered as she turned to rejoin the marchers still sweeping by.

The man laughed. "Well, you women certainly put up a good fight." He held out his hand. "I'm Jack Sorrenson."

"Jack Sorrenson!" Linda said, shaking his hand. "I'm Linda Walden."

"Rikki," Rikki said, smiling, "and . . ."

"Sylvia," Sylvia finished, smiling at him with a friendly nod.

"I think you know my husband," Linda went on.

"Walden? . . . Steve Walden?" Jack asked, a happy, surprised expression lighting his face. "I just saw Steve a couple hours ago! In fact I asked him to come on over here with me, but he had to get home," he stopped, confused now.

Linda nodded and smiled as, back in the stream of marchers, the still angry chanting made further conversation impossible. Jack marched with them, past the university campus on Bancroft where crowds of students and people in the streets watched them, some cheering them on or joining them, others watching, unsure, while a few fraternity jocks sneered and flipped them off.

As they marched back beyond the campus toward Shattuck, many who had joined them drifted off back to their homes, but even so, as they approached the major intersection of Shattuck and University, they were over a 1,000 strong, their voices still ringing through the night. In the middle of the intersection the thronging demonstrators in the front lines stopped to burn a flag, forming a widening circle around the fire.

Approaching the flaming pile, fed by trash and newspaper, Sylvia saw Claire, JoAnn and other NEWS members standing to the side, engrossed in discussion. Two blocks ahead down University, a few police stood in the middle of the avenue directing traffic to the north and south.

"Linda," Sylvia turned to her cousin, who was talking to Jack, "I'm going to see what's happening. We'll be right over there." Linda nodded as Rikki and Sylvia walked across the street to the NEWS grouping.

"Look. The mayor's *in* the march. I saw him. There's not going to be any confrontation," Evelyn was saying.

"That's right, I agree," JoAnn said. "Look," she glanced back over the demonstrators still crowding up to the intersection, "Half the people have already left."

"But the ones who are still here are still moving, are still ready to act. Listen to them!" Carol said, surveying the mass of people stretching back down the avenue.

"Where's it going from here?" Sylvia asked.

"Some of them want to take it back to the City Hall," JoAnn answered, nodding at four or five young men and women holding a banner in front of the circle of flag-burning demonstrators.

"The federal offices," Claire said. "We should move to the federal offices."

"We'd lose too many people, Claire. A lot of these people support the mayor. It will split the march," JoAnn answered.

"So we are going to the City 'all and listen to the mayor and some more speeches? And then we all go 'ome to write our congressmen, enh?" Claire asked.

"We don't have to go to City Hall, Claire, but *I'm* not going to try and lead this demonstration to the federal offices," JoAnn answered. "We've been marching for over an hour, half the people have left, and the *fact is*, I think most everyone who's still here will follow the mayor's supporters. Let's take this for what it is."

"I agree," Evelyn said. "But also, from what we've seen tonight, we can build on this spirit."

"I agree," JoAnn said. "We need to make this happen again—in San Francisco—where the mayor will definitely not be marching with us."

Claire laughed. "OK. So we begin, tomorrow, to plan for another demonstration in San Francisco?"

"Yes," JoAnn and Evelyn agreed as the others nodded.

"And we will take the streets again, without the mayor, no matter 'ow many cops, enh?" Claire asked.

"Yes. With more time, we can mobilize all of NEWS at the very least," Carol said.

"*Bon*, OK, we can meet tomorrow, in the morning? At Market at 7:30?" Claire asked. They agreed as the demonstrators began to move away from the smoldering ashes of the flag and garbage fire, shouting, "To the City Hall! To the City Hall!"

"Sylvia, you are 'ere with Linda?" Claire asked, seeing Linda and Jack walking toward them. She smiled at Linda, then turning back to Sylvia, "I don't want to go to the City 'all." She looked at her watch. "It's almost 10:00. We could 'ave some tea or something before going to Oakland."

"Hi," Linda greeted Claire, a little surprised by the tired lines under Claire's deep brown eyes. She hadn't seen her in months it seemed, and she looked thinner, her hollow cheeks almost gaunt.

"Linda, I have a meeting tonight over here, but Rikki will ride back with you," Sylvia began.

Rikki shook her head, "I can't, Syl. I'm going over to Carol's tonight, I'm staying in the East Bay. I thought you'd be riding back with Claire and JoAnn."

Linda looked annoyed with her cousin, then Jack, standing behind her, said, "Linda, if you don't have a ride home, I'll be glad to take BART back to the city with you."

"Oh, no, I have a car. But I can give you a ride." The annoyance left Linda's face.

"Well do you want to go get some tea or have a drink, Linda? I still have an hour," Sylvia said.

"No, I really have to get back, Syl, there's a sit—Well, I've got to go, but thanks," Linda answered.

Sylvia linked her arm through her cousin's as they walked a few feet from the group. "Linda, this day has been so . . . demanding. I haven't even been able to find out how you are or what you've been doing."

"Well, Sylvia, we'll just have to get together some time. I feel like I've seen less and less of you in this past year, though I know, these last months you've been working on the conference."

"I'll call you soon, Linda, I promise." Sylvia kissed her cousin's cheek. "I love you," she said as Linda, with a glance to Jack who had joined her, walked down the street in the direction of her car.

Chapter VII

A cold wind howled around the corner of the back of the house, rattling doors and windows, flinging sheets of rain into the glass as Sylvia lay in her bed contemplating staying home from work. She glanced at the clock. Six more minutes before getting up to dress. She closed her eyes, the stack of audit reports on her office desk appearing on the inner face of her eyelids. She was not behind now, but if she didn't go in today . . . her barely conscious mind went through the motions, wrapping her robe around her, walking to the bathroom through the heatless flat, shivering by the sink as the water took its endless time to warm. She was walking through a large old building, in another city, London or New York, on the fourth floor, there were rooms, classrooms, no, offices. She began to walk quickly, realizing, yes, she began to run, that she had to get out, she had been held prisoner, there, in the building, some armed unit had held her. She looked around her shoulder, running, escaping. Voices sounded behind her, three men running behind her, catching up with her, she turned into one of the rooms and found her mother and father, sitting at a table, they smiled at her, and then, as suddenly, her father looked angry, it seemed she had not been doing her part in keeping up the building, he began to yell and she flew at him, to silence him so that the three men wouldn't find them, but then they were there, pulling her back down the corridor, one holding a cord, an electric cord around her neck, across her breasts as she saw her mother's face watching in terror. She tried to scream, her mouth open, her whole body pushing to force the scream through her lips, but no sound came as they dragged her to a room at the end of the hall, a storage room filled with machinery, innards of clocks and televisions, massive circuit boards unrecognizable, she saw them as still her whole body raged in a soundless scream, bound in powerless terror, paralyzed. Then, as suddenly, she broke from them, their dreadful being just inches away, she kept them at bay, wielding slowly, heavy in her hands, she found in her hands, the television-innard-thing, and lifted it, slowly, heavily, and then, just as slowly, though their rapist presence hovered, surrounded her, she brought it slowly back down onto their skulls—once, twice, three times—with each strike the weapon growing lighter, she saw the blood gush from their skulls, and then she knew that it was fine, that it was right, and that she was dreaming, and then, lucidly dreaming, she left the small room, her feet just above the ground, floating, she glided through the broadened corridor, out, through the building, high now in the air above a glistening, glittering blue lake, her arms outstretched, she glided 40, 50 feet above the clear blue lake toward shooting geysers of colored, luminous water breaking through the air in splendid shafts of light and power, she glided, faster now, flying, Sylvia, Sylvia, a voice called her name . . .

"Sylvia!" JoAnn stopped knocking and, opening the bedroom door, came in the room.

Sylvia, as if drugged, her lips parted, fluttered her eyes open, thick with the sleepless dream.

"Sylvia? Are you sick?" JoAnn asked, leaning over her, concerned.

"I . . . I'm not going to work," Sylvia answered. Her eyes closed again, as the rattling windows and pounding rain brought her back, more fully, to consciousness.

"Are you sick? Do you need something? Linda's on the phone, should I tell her . . ."

"All right. All right," Sylvia said, her mind now fixed in its wakened state. "Tell her I'll call her in a minute. I'm not sick." She rolled over to her side. "Thanks, JoAnn."

Sylvia lay still a moment, trying to reclaim the vision of the clear blue lake, the magnificent fountains, the wondrous sensation of flying toward them as her mind ticked off the list of things she would have to accomplish if she stayed home from work and, slowly, with a groan, she rose from her bed and walked to the closet.

Fifteen minutes later, dressed in jeans, socks and sweaters, a notebook in one hand and a glass of juice in the other, Sylvia sat down on the living room couch to make her phone calls. She picked up the receiver, listened to the dial tone and then adjusted a small black box attached to the telephone. She watched the tiny unlit bulb on the black metal box, waiting a moment. It did not light. The phone was clear. She glanced at her notebook. Then, remembering Linda, she quickly dialed her cousin's number.

"Hi, Linda?"

"Sylvia, hi, how are you? I wanted to catch you before you went to work, but JoAnn said you're not going in?"

"No, I'm taking a day off. I've got so much to do. I thought I'd get a lot of it done last week over Thanksgiving, but, god, Linda do you realize the conference starts exactly *four* weeks from today?"

"Sylvia. That's what I wanted . . . Well, what day exactly does the conference start?"

"December 26th. The 26th through the 30th. It starts that Monday, the day after Christmas!"

"Well . . . How's it going?"

"Oh, it's OK. It just seems there's so much work to do, but a lot's been done. At least all the logistics. I mean housing, food, transportation. We finally got the high school for the full five days, you know, St. Joan of Arc's, the Catholic girls' school out by the beach. They *finally* agreed to let us use it with access to all the facilities for the entire time, thank god! Well, Cristina, the Ally from AMES, talked them into it. Actually the nuns have turned out to be really cooperative."

"Oh that's good. Last time I talked to you—when was it? Not long after that demonstration in Berkeley. You were afraid you were going to have to go out of the city."

"Yeah, I know. It was just after that, a few weeks ago, that it all got settled, and what's really great is the nuns are going to let us use the dormitory space, which really helps with housing."

"What order are they? I don't remember the nuns who taught where we went to school being that . . . that . . ."

"Oh, they're connected to the Maryknoll order somehow. Some of them—and, luckily, the one in charge—are really into Liberation Theology, you know?"

"I think I've read something about it. It's mainly in Latin America, isn't it? Don't they say Christ was actually a revolutionary, because he wanted to get rid of sin, and since sin is really social injustice, fighting against it is really what Christianity is all about. Isn't there a priest in Nicaragua who's written a lot about it? Ernest Cardinal or something? And the Vatican's having a fit over it."

"Yeah, they are. That's why they keep sending the Pope over there. But it's a huge movement. Thousands of nuns and priests and even bishops are totally involved in it. It's so different than what we grew up with."

"Are you going to have workshops on it at the conference?"

"Well, yeah, actually we are. Basically we're having workshops on about every mass movement there is. I mean, progressive mass movement—in each of the countries represented—liberation, peace, labor, women's rights, gay rights. We want to determine what our level of cooperation with them should be. And out of that, our own strategy for mass action, education and coalition work."

"Sylvia. That sounds like it'll take forever!"

"Tell me!" Sylvia agreed, watching the wind and rain flailing the boughs of the tall pine outside the living room window. "But, Linda, there are 1,200 women expected to attend, and each of those women has been doing research and preparation. And each national grouping has discussed and prepared position papers and had them translated, so our real job, besides preparing our own goals and positions, is just to schedule it all. Which, true, isn't easy."

"How many nations are represented?"

"Over 50 at this point."

"Good lord!"

"Well that's North and South America, the East Indies and Asia and Australia," she said studying the tiny bulb, still unlit, on the black box attached to the phone.

"What about Europe and Africa? And the Soviet Union, are they invited?"

"I told you, Linda, we have members in Moscow and Kiev—though their ties are more with our European chapters. Didn't I tell you that there's a simultaneous conference of NEWS chapters from Europe and Russia and the African Allies being held in Amsterdam the same week? Christmas week?"

"I don't think so."

"Well, they're going to be going through the identical process there. The European Chapters are sending representatives to our conference to take information back just as we're sending members from here there."

"I really didn't realize it was so complex, Sylvia."

"Well, it's not all *that* complex, Linda. There are international summits and conferences all the time. I mean, people do it. Why shouldn't we? Of course, it's harder for us—we have less resources. That's why we've been planning for this for, well, since we first became organized, really."

"Oh, I know, I know, Sylvia. It seems like I've been hearing about this conference for years, though I never really did understand its purpose exactly, or what was involved."

"Well besides what I've said, it's also to develop more cohesion as an organization. Some of our connections with other chapters, especially in areas difficult to reach, have been pretty loose, or vague sometimes. We want to be sure we are all basically going in the same direction."

"How *are* you paying for all this?" Linda asked.

"Well. It's not easy, it's tens of thousands in plane fares alone. But we have a very major fundraising program. And also most all of us in NEWS work, so we've been able to put in a lot over the past year or so and finance the Allies, who can hardly even live on the wages in the South, much less fly around the world."

"I wondered what the hell you were doing with all your money, Sylvia." Linda laughed.

"I'm not paying for it alone, Linda. Maybe next year, when I get a raise."

"How's it going at your job?"

"Oh, OK. Boring. How about you? How are you doing? And Justin and Steven?"

"OK. It's OK." Linda's voice sounded distant.

"Well, did you get Justin in a childcare program?"

"Oh, no. Not yet."

"Well, how are you feeling about staying at home, and not working? Are you getting any time to yourself?"

"Oh yeah. His nap time every day, a couple hours. And Steven helps. Sometimes." Again her voice seemed to trail.

"How is Steven, Linda? I haven't seen him in months!"

"Well . . ."

Sylvia waited. "Linda. What's happening with Steven?"

"Oh, I don't know, Sylvia. It's been . . . it hasn't been easy . . . lately."

Sylvia heard the tears in her cousin's voice and asked gently, "What, Linda? Tell me."

"Well, I . . ." She took a breath. "It all seemed to start around the end of the summer. I mean. Steven's always, since I've *known* him, liked to, you know, have a drink now and then. I mean, when he'd come home from work he'd have a glass of wine or two. So would I. We'd just relax at the end of the day with a couple drinks and then have dinner. And then sometimes on the weekends he might buy a bottle of whiskey and, maybe even drink the whole thing by the end of the weekend. I hate whiskey, I . . ." Her voice closed again.

"But now, he's drinking more?" Sylvia asked, tentative.

Linda cleared her throat. "Well . . . Yeah."

"And it started around the end of the summer?"

"Well, I don't know, maybe before then. But now, now every night he has four, five, six drinks. Of whiskey. Stiff drinks, Sylvia!"

"Yeah, that's a lot."

"And it's not just that! I mean, it was around the end of the summer, or just after Labor Day, around then. Well it was after something happened to the engine of the car—it cost a lot, about $1,000, and it really depressed him. He works so hard, Sylvia. But, gradually, he just started getting real cynical or . . . Well then about a month later some woman from the community college, a neighbor of ours, came by to ask me some questions for a survey. She was writing a paper . . . And Steven! Well a few days later our credit . . . our credit with MasterCharge was canceled, and Steven was just *furious*. He was just *sullen* for days, and he kept insisting it was because I had talked to that woman! I mean, Sylvia, he was just . . . so *paranoid*!"

Sylvia closed her eyes, her hand tensing its hold on the receiver. "Well, what kind of questions did she ask you, Linda?"

"Oh, nothing, for god's sake! Just about family, my family, his family. Nothing to do with MasterCharge! And it's not just that, Sylvia, that's just one example. I think, I mean I know, his drinking is making him paranoid! And then, you know, remember at that demonstration about Grenada in Berkeley, and we ran into that man who jumped on the car? Well, he's an old law school friend of Steven's, and Steven himself, that very day, had invited him to dinner. His name's Jack, Jack Sorrenson. So, remember I gave him a ride home afterwards? Well we made arrangements for him to come to dinner the next week. And when I told Steven about it the next day, he got really angry. He was furious. I mean, maybe he was mad because I went off to the demonstration. I didn't tell you then, but I had to have a sitter stay with Justin that night because I was actually afraid to leave him alone with Steven! He had come home two hours late, without calling me, drunk . . . And his excuse was that he had run into an old friend! But then when I happened to run into that same old friend, he was furious! It's just not like him, Sylvia, I mean Steven has his ways, but this . . ."

"Well, Linda, do you think it's just his drinking that's making him paranoid? I mean losing $1,000 on your car, and then losing MasterCharge. Those are financial problems that could . . ."

"Sylvia, if it were just about money. I mean people can be *reasonable* about money. Steven is not being reasonable." She paused. "Believe me, Sylvia. He's getting *way* out there. I mean just a couple weeks ago Jack finally did come to dinner, and before he'd even shown up at the door, Steven was on his fourth whiskey! The dinner was . . . a nightmare! I had been cooking all afternoon and tried to make something really sort of elegant—you know, for a change—and Steven was just, well, he was just really hostile! To his old friend! I mean Jack had hardly sat down when Steven said, in this really surly way, 'Well, I know about your Nonaligned Movement, Jack,' or something crazy like that, not even hello, or how are you. And it just degenerated from there. It was almost humiliating, except that Jack seemed so understanding. He really tried to make light of it and to humor Steven. He even got him to laugh a couple times."

Sylvia's face was drawn as she listened to her cousin and watched the rain, calmer now, still falling outside.

"But even when he's not drinking, Sylvia, he seems so unhappy. I mean. Sometimes it just breaks my heart—" her voice caught, struggling again against the tears.

"Well, Linda . . ."

"But Sylvia," she went on. "Do you know what he said to me the other day? This was just the other day, in fact, we had been talking about—about war, and Reagan—politics. You know. He said, 'You know, if you don't care—if you don't care about life, like a junkie, a wino, a lifer in prison. You die.' And then he said," Linda continued, incredulous now, "then he said, 'And if you do, if you do care very much about life, like Sylvia, I guess, or our friend Jack, you still die.'"

"Mmmm," Sylvia murmured through her cousin's outraged silence. "That's . . . pretty cynical."

They were both silent.

"Well, what did you say?" Sylvia asked.

"Well, I said . . . I guess I wasn't that sympathetic at the time, I said, 'That's really brilliant, Steven,' I said, 'If a flower smells just heavenly, all the petals fall off. Or if it smells like dogshit, all the petals still fall off,' or something like that, I don't know."

Sylvia smiled. "That's not bad, Linda."

"But I don't know, Sylvia. I want to do something to *help* him. I just . . ."

"Well, have you talked to him about his drinking?"

"I've tried, but . . . it's hard. He won't really talk about it. And well, to be really honest, I was sort of ignoring it myself for a long time. I just wasn't acknowledging or accepting that he was getting so into it. The first time I even said anything was about a month ago, and, I really haven't talked to *anyone* about it, Sylvia. Except you now."

Sylvia thought a moment. "Linda. I think the first thing to do, and as soon as possible, is to get clear with him that he has a drinking problem. I mean, it sounds really serious. I know it's hard, but, if you want to help him . . ."

"I do, Sylvia! But I *have* tried. It's like our communication just freezes in mid-air whenever I even vaguely try to bring it up."

"Well maybe you have to get someone else. A friend of his, or, does he have any family out here now?"

"No. Not really. He had a sister somewhere in Florida, but, I don't think he even knows where. And his friends, his old law school friends he hardly keeps in touch with now. Or if he does, it's to go out and drink with them!"

"Mmm." Sylvia's eyes searched the rainy sky beyond the misted window pane. "What about a counselor, or . . ."

"First he's got to believe he's got a problem before he'll ever agree to go to a counselor, Sylvia. If I suggested that, he'd just think I'm trying to say he's crazy or something. Honestly, you don't understand. He really is becoming paranoid. He's different than when you saw him at the end of the summer."

"Well, what about someone in our family? Rhonda or Nick?"

"Or you, Sylvia," Linda said, as if the idea had just occurred to her and yet, at the same time, as if she had been meaning to suggest it all along.

Sylvia said nothing, but Linda went on caught up in the notion, as if, in fact, it actually had just occurred to her and sounded right, yes, the very thing that had to happen. "You've known him a long time, as long as I have, and, I know you haven't seen much of him in the past couple years, but still, you're family! And he really does respect you. I know sometimes he likes to give you a hard time about your ideas, but I know he respects you, a lot. It just . . . it could really help."

"All right," Sylvia answered with a quickness that both surprised and relieved Linda.

"Oh, thanks, Sylvia, it would just be such a help to me. Whatever I'm doing is just not working. When . . . when do you think we could get together?"

"I'll have to check. I'll have to call you about it later, Linda. As soon as I can."

"Well, Sylvia," Linda hesitated, "There's something else I need to talk to you about. Actually, the reason I called . . . Have you talked to Maureen recently?"

"Well, yeah, I have actually, about ten days ago. Is everything all right?" Sylvia was finding the conversation increasingly disconcerting.

"Oh, she's fine, she's fine. But, I guess she hasn't mentioned to you the Christmas plans?"

"What plans?"

"Well, Mom and Dad decided that since Steven and I couldn't get back down to L.A. for Christmas, they would come up here, and Maureen is coming with them. We're going to have Christmas dinner and everything at our place. You won't have to do anything, Sylvia. Except show up."

Sylvia's face looked as if she had swallowed a pepper, tears stinging her eyes. Suddenly the strain of the past months was becoming overwhelming.

"Oh, Sylvia, I hear Justin. I've got to go. We can talk about it when you call me back."

"Wait! How long are they going to be here?" She tried not to voice the panic that she felt.

"Just a few days."

"Well I can't possibly . . ."

"Sylvia, I've got to go, I'll talk to you soon, OK? We'll work it out. Bye-bye."

As the phone clicked, Sylvia sat still, the receiver still in her hand, her mind screaming at Linda. How in god's name could you arrange a family reunion at the same time as the conference and expect me to come? What's the matter with you? Don't you understand anything? Don't you know me at all? She jammed the receiver buttons down and furiously began to dial her cousin's number as the thought of Steven—his drinking, his 'paranoia'—stilled her hand and she sat motionless, her face set with a cold fear. Again she pushed down the receiver buttons, slowly this time, holding them down as she glanced again at the black box, still clear, and her mind went over the conversation with her cousin. Then, resolutely, she began to dial the telephone again.

"*Allo?*"

"Claire?"

"Sylvie. I've been trying to call you, maybe for one 'our. At your office too. They said you didn't call there."

"Well, Claire, I . . . Are you going to Fowler's today? Or did you finish their books yesterday?"

"I finished them. But I 'ave to drop them off by there today sometime, and also to pick up the books for Daley. But I 'ave something important . . . I wanted to meet you at your work for lunch."

"I'm not going in. Can you come over here? Soon?"

"Ah, *bon*, maybe. If I go by Fowler's first."

"He's on Divisadero, right?"

"Yes, OK, 'ee's on the way, more or less. I can see you pretty soon."

"Good, thanks, Claire. I'll see you soon."

Sylvia dropped the receiver back into its cradle as she sat forward on the couch. Oh, god, god, Steven, she said half-aloud and bit deeply into her lip as Linda's words, fragments, images from her cousin's conversation forced her mind to form the inevitable conclusion. No, no, no. Wait for Claire, she told herself. Don't even . . . Just wait for Claire.

Sylvia picked up the phone once again and dialed her office.

"Hansen, Rykoff & Shaw. Can I help you?"

"Hi, Patti, this is Sylvia."

"We've been wondering where you are, Sylvia. You just got a phone call . . ."

"I just woke up. I was up all night. Must be the stomach flu. Can you tell them I'm home sick?"

"Are you sure it's not just too many Thanksgiving leftovers?" Patti asked with a laugh.

Sylvia laughed. "Could be. But this feels a little more serious than that. I think I'm going to be spending the day in the bathroom, you know?"

"Oh. What a drag," Patti answered sympathetically. "Well, I hope you feel better soon, Sylvia."

"Thanks. Thanks, Patti, me too. I'll probably see you tomorrow, though. Bye-bye." She put the telephone down and leaned back into the couch, gazing out through the tall bay windows that overlooked the neighbors' yards. The rain was letting up, though the sky was still a dull, cloudy grey. She tried to think of what she could get done, the whole day free before her. Finalize her report for the conference, make those phone calls about translations, oh, and the calls about transportation from the airport. It wasn't too early for that. Especially since the Security Committee plan was complete.

Security. God. Was it even really possible to have enough? Especially if . . . No. They had 200 women doing security around the clock, from the minute everyone would begin to arrive until the last woman had left. But what *did* this conference mean to the *State*? How much of a threat would they find it and how would they try to retaliate, and undermine it? How many hundreds of times have we asked that question, she thought, remembering their meeting in late October, just after the invasion of Grenada, when they had all been shocked, and especially frightened for the Allies, all of the Allies. They had seriously considered canceling the conferences, but no, the Allies had said to go on with it, it was more important than ever. The risk must be taken. And, so far, she grimaced at the irony, the fact that they were all women had worked for them. Worked very well for them. For the male-dominated 'intelligence' establishment had yet to really take them seriously. She almost laughed. From what NEWS CLAN had been able to discover through their, so far, very limited computer intrusions, the FBI and CIA files on NEWS defined them as "essentially made up of women pacifists, with a sprinkling of more militant members, frustrated lesbians, who could breed hysteria and fanaticism and bear watching."

That had been one of the first reports, just after they had formed. But even according to the file that Ellen had tapped just last week, NEWS was a "loosely connected network of women's groups and organizations with little power or relationship to mainstream society." Though there were "certain radical lesbians who have previously been involved in small, self-styled revolutionary cults." They were so fixated on lesbians it was absurd. She stood up. Walking to the window, she opened it, letting in the sweet rain-washed air. She stood, watching the grey sky.

But what had really given them pause and made them consider canceling the conference again, just last week, was the statement, in that same file: ". . . planning a conference for 12/26-31, 1983, involving female national minorities and foreign nationals from Communist movements and regimes in this hemisphere . . . furthering Communist subversion internally . . . potential for perverting the minds of women pacifists in this country who are currently of little consequence . . ."

And how many hundreds of other files were there that NEWS CLAN hadn't been able to tap? She turned back to the couch, putting her hands, suddenly cold, in her pockets and stood staring at her open notebook on the table. Even what NEWS CLAN did get showed that the State thought NEWS had gone from a bunch of irrelevant pacifists to potential Communist subversives in about 28 months—the State *was* beginning to take them seriously as a mass movement, even assuming they were completely unaware of NEWS CLAN—which wasn't exactly a safe assumption, though nothing at all had shown up on the . . . But if they had any idea we existed, any at all, Sylvia's lips tightened, we'd know. We'd know because they'd be all over us.

No, it's because our relationship with the Allies is building that the State's changing its perception of us, she thought, and even given that, the amazing sexism of the male mentality still just doesn't really get it. She sat back down on the couch, remembering the last statements of the file: ". . . conference involves women only, none of whom have any significant role in their respective nationalist movements or Communist regimes. Primary goals to protest nuclear arms race, eliminate national boundaries . . . Characterized by feminism, idealism and pacifism . . . May become significant adjunct to mass international anti-nuclear movement, provoking unrest and civil disobedience."

So they had decided to go ahead with the conference. Amsterdam had decided the same. Proposals to move the San Francisco conference to Havana had been definitively voted down, especially by the Allies, because the invasion of Grenada had only proved that holding the conference in an Allied nation would even more seriously endanger the conference participants to individual CIA attack, and, more importantly, it could endanger the Allied nation as a whole. Here at least, in the United States, a CIA attack on the conference itself, or its participants, could not be so easily ignored or lied about by the Northern press.

But the Security Committee has got to make its plans absolutely airtight, Sylvia thought, thinking now of the debates she'd heard were troubling that committee. Who exactly would be responsible for detecting infiltration? Everyone at the conference? Only the security cadres? A small committee with only that task? But they've got an entire month to work it out and the biggest acting committee in all of NEWS right now, and 30 Allies advisors—they'll do it. It'll be good, she decided. It'll be just fine.

Feeling finally more assured, she rose from the couch and, walking to the kitchen, turned the gas on under the kettle. As she leaned back against the counter by the stove, her eye caught the poster above it, a tall African woman, her expression so intense, and yet serene as she clenched her upraised fist. Sylvia thought of Olina—in Managua now—and the day, over a month ago, that she'd received the communication from her and the Allies in Trinidad. She half-smiled, remembering the fear she'd felt, racing down those 13 flights, the printouts taped to her thigh; and at the same time she felt strengthened as she remembered that they'd all managed that communication completely undiscovered.

She looked again at the poster above the stove. The woman did resemble Olina, the hair so short and the long neck, and that expression, so . . . what? Beyond things, somehow. That was what had impressed her, well, almost intimidated her, when she first met Olina years ago, when CECO had just begun work on the Campaign Against Apartheid. Olina, a member of the Black Action Front, had worked closely with CECO to coordinate their role. And, yes, at first Sylvia had felt almost startled by Olina's presence, but her humor and her warmth proved even stronger than that other quality—that detached sense—and as Sylvia had gotten to know her, and know her well through their work and what eventually had become a friendship, her admiration for Olina had only grown deeper.

It's just been the past few years though, Sylvia thought, that she felt so close to Olina and a really loving friendship had formed. She remembered the long evenings over the years that Olina and her lover then, Maimouna, had spent with her and Claire. Yes, talking politics most of the time, but there had been other talk, laughter. And even when Maimouna left last spring to live in Zimbabwe, Olina still seemed to glide through her work, to feel and do so much with a kind of grace Sylvia could only wonder at.

Olina. She would be in Central America one more month, until just before the conference. Working as she had in the Caribbean, traveling as a 'liberal American journalist,' gathering the invaluable information from the Allies in Guatemala, Honduras, Belize, El Salvador, bringing it back to Managua . . .

And would the same events be repeated? Would the U.S. invade Nicaragua as they had Grenada? Sylvia's eyes closed, shutting out the thought, unsuccessfully, as the rumors from Washington ran through her mind: "Nine thousand U.S. troops are massing on the Honduran border." "The State Department feels, after Grenada, public opinion is on their side." "The holidays will divert international attention . . ."

A new front of the winter storm sent a torrent of rain against the small kitchen window as it rattled in its frame and the wind took up its howling cry behind the house. Sylvia took a cup from the shelf and a small bag of black tea. Pouring the boiling water into her cup, she struggled once again against the paralyzing sensation of defeat. The destruction of the Sandinista society—the greatest inspiration to Latin America since the Cuban revolution—it would be devastating, a near deathblow to the liberation of Central America, isolating and threatening Cuba . . . She started as the front door buzzer cut through her thoughts. Putting the kettle back on the stove, she hurried down the hall to the front door.

"*Bonjour*," Claire said as she set her dripping umbrella in the hall corner and gave Sylvia a quick kiss and embrace. "So you decide to take a day off?" she asked, smiling.

"Yeah." Sylvia linked her arm through Claire's as they walked back to the kitchen. "I just couldn't wake up this morning. I had another one of those strange dreams."

"Ah *oui*? What 'appened?"

"Oh it was that same thing. Evil rapists are chasing me, dragging me away. I'm trying to scream and can't."

"*Aie*, Sylvie. That one." Claire put a comforting arm around Sylvia's shoulders.

"Yeah, but then, like the last time I guess . . . I killed them. With some machine. And then I rose up out of the building, floating . . ."

"Ah, you 'ave been flying again?"

"Yeah. And this time there were magnificent, beautiful . . . Powerful fountains of water and light."

"That's so good, Sylvie," Claire said, her hand reaching up to touch Sylvia's cheek, resting a moment. "Stay in contact with these forces, *hien*? They can be 'elpful to us all. To give us 'ope."

"Well, actually," Sylvia said as she turned to take a cup from the kitchen shelf. "Do you want coffee?"

"No, no. I've 'ad some already." Claire draped her damp jacket over the back of a kitchen chair and sat down at the table.

"Well, actually," Sylvia continued as she picked up her cup of tea and joined Claire. "I was just feeling sort of the opposite of hope. I was thinking about, if they invade Nicaragua . . ."

"Ah, OK. That's what I want to talk about with you."

"Well, I was thinking about, if they destroy the Sandinistas . . ."

"Sylvie. They *cannot* destroy the Sandinistas." Claire looked at her questioningly. "Remember, you know? Sandino is dead, but Sandinismo *lives*. OK, sure, the Pentagon, the CIA, the Contras, the Marines," she waved her hand impatiently, "they can try, they can bomb and invade and use all their money and weapons and covert action. But they can never destroy liberation. There will always be resistance. In Grenada now there is resistance. Look at Chile, enh?" Sylvia listened intently, studying Claire as she spoke.

"They thought they 'ad destroy Chile when they kill Allende, when they murdered three, four thousand of the Popular Unity in Chile, tortured them, killed them. Pinochet, for *ten* years strangling that country, with the 'elp of the States, South Africa, Israel. And still, you know? 'ow many? One *million* of Chileans protest last week in Santiago! You know that. They cannot destroy the spirit of the people. They cannot destroy Sandinismo, even if they put the 'ole of the military there."

Sylvia watched the steam rise from her cup, letting it warm her face as the cup warmed her hands, and Claire's words now warmed the cold stark fear that had gripped her. "You're right, Claire. I know that. But sometimes I just feel . . ." She looked at Claire a moment, hoping she would understand.

"Well, in fact, Sylvie, of course, nobody wants to see Nicaragua invaded. The thought, it drives me crazy too. That's why I want to tell you the idea we are thinking. In fact, it was Rikki's idea. She told it to me and Ruth last night after the Security Committee meeting. We are thinking to propose it to NEWS MASS this week, through the Steering Committee, of course."

"Well what? What's the idea?"

"To establish a women's peace camp on the Nicaraguan/Honduran border. And to send as many North American women as we can possibly afford to this camp to prevent an invasion." Claire watched Sylvia's eyes as they widened, intrigued, and yet unsure.

"But what will that do to the conferences? Will that replace the priority of the conferences?"

"Sylvie." Claire looked disappointed. "Are you going to be stubborn again? First you tell me you feel so 'orrible about a possible invasion, you are losing all your 'ope. Then we talk about making the NEWS priority to prevent the invasion and you are afraid for your sacred conferences! Why can't you be flexible? You cannot 'ave a strategy that is rigid, that does not look to the conditions of the moment . . ."

"Claire, wait. Just wait a minute. I just asked! We've been planning the conferences for almost three years! And you know there are more than the Central American Allies involved in the conferences. And the February Action! You expect me to forget all that in five seconds! Or them to forget it!"

"'oo said anything about forgetting all that, Sylvia? We are not talking about forgetting, we are talking about prioritizing! The conferences will still take place, enh? OK? The Action, of course, is still the very first priority for NEWS CLAN. That does not change. But maybe some of the Canadian and U.S. NEWS members 'oo were going to attend the conference 'ere will instead be at the peace camp in Nicaragua. And still many of the rest of us will be 'ere, at the conference, as planned. OK?"

Sylvia was quiet, letting the idea take shape in her mind. In fact there was a brilliance to it, and if it didn't coincide with the conferences, she would be 100 percent for it. What could be more effective in deterring the State Department from deciding to invade than the prospect of slaughtering several thousand white women in the process? The very racism of the public's 'opinion' in the U.S. would make scandalous the deaths of their own white women, though they wouldn't bat an eye at the massacre of millions of Central American people. The problem was that, to be really effective, it would have to be a mass effort involving thousands of women. Fewer than that would be dismissed as lunatic fringe, Soviet agents, or whoever made up the 'they' that mainstream U.S. culture thought was the 'left.' No more worth saving than foreign peasants and savages. In fact, all the better if the Marines could wipe them all out in one neat maneuver. Clean up the place for democracy.

"So what do you think?" Claire watched Sylvia's grey eyes, their dark clean brows cocked as she gazed again at the storming sky through the kitchen window.

"Well." She looked back at Claire. "In some ways, I think it's a great idea. But it would have to be done very carefully, with mass participation, and not just NEWS. The liberal sector would have to be really behind it before it's even mobilized, or the whole effort would be lost. I mean it could go either way."

"What do you mean?"

"I mean that if there wasn't broad enough support, it could make things worse. It could potentially have no effect on public opinion and only encumber the Sandinistas in their defense of the border."

"But, Sylvie, I think even several 'undred women is enough! When 'as it ever 'appened before? So there are women's peace camps in Japan and Europe and 'ere too, NEWS is in them. But never 'as a peace camp of white women gone into the South, saying NO! You want to destroy these people, but first what are you going to do about us, your own citizens!"

"I know, Claire. I think that's true. It would be a whole new level of solidarity—for a mass expression. But that's just it. It has to be *mass*."

"And it will be, Sylvia. Just in the very beginning it will be a few 'undred, until we can send more."

"I don't know, Claire. You know that all of NEWS CLAN is going to be involved in the February Action, and we have to train at least 500 NEWS MASS members for it too. And mainly it's just going to take so much of our resources that if we can only have a few hundred women in the peace camp through the Conferences, then we can only have that many right on through February. And after the Action. Well. You know."

"We will not need a peace camp."

"Hopefully not."

"*Bon*, I don't know. I think we 'ave got to stall off an invasion until then. We just 'ave to make the camp without such a big participation, that's all. Because to 'ave thousands of women there, and more thousands working 'ere to support it, we cannot do it. The conferences must be just as planned for NEWS MASS."

"That's the thing, Claire, NEWS MASS has *got* to be optimally unified and our relationships to all sectors of the left, liberals and mainstream perfectly clear. *Everyone* has to be ready to carry through toward transformation after the Action. I mean, you know it, Claire."

"I know." Claire's eyes rested in Sylvia's. "We cannot risk even a moment of confusion . . . or chaos."

Sylvia was silent, eyes in Claire's, as the sound of rain, falling hard again now, seemed to make the room suddenly cold. She got up from the table and walked to the stove, turning on the oven. "Let's get some heat in here." She turned to Claire. "Do you want something to eat? I'm going to have some toast and eggs I guess."

"Yes, OK." Claire rested her chin in her palm, leaning back in her chair, her deep brown eyes contemplating Sylvia's teacup.

Sylvia moved toward her, standing just behind her, and, resting her hands on Claire's shoulders with the light touch of comfort, she bent slightly and kissed her hair, her temple.

Walking back to the stove, she said, "We can discuss it at the Steering Committee. Maybe you're right. Maybe it can be done with a smaller force. In any case, it's for the Allies to decide. Has anyone talked to Chela yet?"

"I 'ave sent 'er word. We expect a response by tomorrow on the Oakland system. Ruth will bring it to the Steering Committee." She paused. "Yeah. We will see."

As Sylvia beat the yellowed viscous eggs in their bowl she held herself back from the question that clamored in her mind. And if we agree to do it, will you go, Claire? And if you go. Will you come back? Without a green card, with a visa that expired three years ago? A member of NEWS, a cadre in a peace camp in Nicaragua, do you think they will ever let you back in this country? No. Never. Not until we eliminate national boundaries, and February Action or no, that is a long, long time from now. Sylvia tried to stop the question pounding in her mind. Will you go, Claire? Will you go? She snapped the bowl of egg over the hot skillet, its contents spitting and sizzling as it hit the seering iron.

"But, Sylvia," Claire turned to her from her reverie. "What was it you wanted to talk with me about? I 'ave been so much in this idea since lass night." She stood up, and walking to the stove, put her arm around Sylvia's waist. "Can I 'elp you?"

"Get the toast if you can," Sylvia answered. Claire moved back to the cupboard, the gentle touch of her hand, gone now, bringing Sylvia dangerously close to tears. Wait! she commanded herself. Wait and see. She turned her thoughts to Claire's question, as Claire asked again, "So? Tell me, *hien*?"

Sylvia turned the half-congealed egg in the pan, pushing through the tumult that the thought of Claire's leaving stirred in her, struggling to recall what had seemed so urgent only an hour ago, and then, she remembered. Steven.

"Oh, god," she said aloud, her conversation with Linda flooding back to her now.

"*Quoi*? What is it?" Claire asked again.

"Actually, Claire," she said as she spooned the scrambled eggs onto two plates and Claire laid the buttered pieces of toast beside them. "It's really serious."

Claire ate her breakfast slowly as Sylvia recounted her conversation with Linda: Steven's drinking, the vandalized car, the 'neighbor's' questionnaire, the canceled MasterCharge.

"CIA," Claire said, her voice low, foreboding.

"I know," Sylvia answered.

"When it began?"

"Around Labor Day. Just after the letter."

"*Aie*," Claire winced. "You think they 'ave seen the letter?"

"I don't know."

"*Bon*, even if they 'ave, they will never fathom the encryption. Even if some day they do, we 'ave never use it since . . ."

"But the content!"

"But Sylvie, I really don't think they 'ave seen it, or the Azanian Allies would 'ave been arrested immediately, tortured. But nothing 'as changed with them. In fact, they 'ave not yet been denied exit visas, and they 'ave applied lass month."

"I know. I know. I thought that immediately when she told me what . . . when I realized what was going on. It has to be one of two things. Either it's a coincidence that they began surveillance of Steven around the time of the letter . . . But no."

"No. It's the letter. They would not go to such an extent otherwise. But this is the first time you realize this is going on?"

"Well, *yes*. I mean, Linda told me months ago that something had happened to their car, that they thought someone had actually put sugar in the gas tank. But to be honest, I didn't really think about it. And I haven't seen much of either of them since then. I haven't seen Steven at all! And Linda didn't tell me any of this until today. I had no idea Steven was drinking so much—or any of this. I feel bad, I mean I just haven't been able to stay in close touch with Linda lately. And I think too, well, she was really embarrassed. It's hard for her to talk about Steven, her problems with him. Especially the fact that he's becoming an alcoholic."

"OK, OK, first. If it's the worse thing. If they 'ave understood the letter, decoded the content. What does that mean?"

"It means they know that women in the African National Congress and Pan African Congress have access to computers and use them. And that those women know where the offices of the CIA and South African secret police are located in Johannesburg, Cape Town, Port Elizabeth, Durban . . ."

"No, wait, Sylvie. That envelope contain only the locations of the offices and the computer linkages. Nothing more. And that envelope came from Vivienne in Paris. From a post-office box that she no longer 'as. There is nothing about African women. They can 'ave no idea from where the information was sent. Only that it was from someone, somewhere in Paris."

"And that it was sent to you. To NEWS."

"Yes."

They were both silent, the rain still falling in a steady downpour as the wind, calm now, then gusting up in a squall brought a tree branch crashing against the side of the house within inches of the small kitchen window. They both jumped in their chairs, turning to stare at the window. Neither spoke for a moment.

Finally Claire turned back around. "But wait, Sylvie, you know? Nothing in the files Ellen tapped last week indicate that they suspect anything beyond the usual. Anything more than the mass conferences. OK, she 'asn't tapped all the files, but enough to know, if they suspected, there would be some mention . . . some allusion . . ."

"I know, I know. I really feel that they still don't know, Claire, that they don't get it."

"In fact, yes, it has been three mons since that letter arrive. We would know if they knew. We would see it. Their tactics with us would be very different. It's sure, they took the encryption for exactly what it appeared, you know?"

"That they just accepted it as a plan for marketing Atari products in South Africa?"

"Yes, why not? They don't think we women could get much beyond something like that. They think NEWS is maybe monitoring corporate investment in Third World countries, you know? That is why the encryption was chosen."

"I know. I know, Claire. And the truth is I've been counting on just that all morning. That the encryption worked. And they took it at face value and assumed that the Paris Chapter was just sending us some more data on capitalist expansion. But, then, I don't know, when I was telling you everything Linda said . . . It seems they really are on Steven's ass. In a big way. Why? Why would they be trying to break him for simply receiving and passing on Atari's marketing strategy?

What in hell could we do with that besides make some dull point in some unread pamphlet about U.S. corporate expansion and exploitation in Africa?"

"Well, Sylvie, I think," Claire's eyes shone with relief, sure now that the letter had not been understood, "they are 'arassing Steven in their way because 'ee is a lawyer and 'ee is a man."

"What?"

"I mean, OK. Yes, Atari's marketing strategy is no big deal, but to 'ave it does mean that someone in a position to attend their strategy meetings is sympathetic with us, no? Even if she is juss the secretary 'oo take the minutes, or 'ooever. It can make them angry. Like, you know, what are they? They use a whistle, or, what is it?"

Sylvia looked at her, doubtful, then, "Oh! A whistleblower."

"*Oui*, yes, that. They don't like leaks, you know? And then. What they don't like even more is a lawyer 'oo *does* like that kind of thing. What they know—this is what I think—they know that Steven receive the letter. Vivienne should not 'ave use that P.O. box. It was too old, even then, but so, we can talk about that later. So they know that Steven receive the letter, that it was directed to me, and that it contain the Atari information. This means to them that Steven is—one, sympathetic with corporate leaks, *hien*? Two, sympathetic with NEWS because 'ee is going to pass it to me. And three, so . . . 'ee is a symptom, a sign of a new turn in the NEWS organizations that they do not want to see. Men. And men in positions of power, working with us, 'elping us. This they must discourage. They must . . . what? Nip it in the bud, you know?"

"Mmm," Sylvia nodded. "It makes sense." She pressed her lips tight, thinking a moment. "And it's true, I have really felt, because their files haven't changed, and because there haven't been any arrests or crackdowns, that the encryption held, that they didn't break it. Or even get that they should try to. Chela was really brilliant for using that."

"That's sure. She is," Claire agreed. She sat back in her chair, the rigid tension in her shoulders subsiding.

"But what really has been worrying me more," Sylvia still sat forward, her eyes still intent on Claire, "is Steven. What about Steven?"

Claire looked down at her empty plate, remembering that hurried day in July when she had taken Sylvia's address book from her desk while she was out and jotted down Steven's office phone, just in case. And then two days later, when with no other possible options, she had called the number and carefully written down the address as the secretary recited it over the phone. "I didn't expect this, you know," she said, her full brown eyes apologetic as she looked up at Sylvia.

"I didn't either, Claire. I really didn't. I'd really totally forgotten that the letter had come through him at all until Linda told me this morning about that 'neighbor' interviewing her. I mean, the car thing—I never even gave it a thought. It's such a fucking hokey thing to do!"

"Ah, *bon*, that's what they are best at, you know?"

"I know. I mean, if I didn't know what idiots they are, I wouldn't recognize this whole pattern as theirs."

"But they are very powerful idiots, Sylvia. These are their amateur 'dirty tricks,' that's true. They keep their dirtiest tricks, their torture, for people of the South . . ." Claire paused. "But, you know. You are right." She almost laughed, a broken breath low in her throat. "I read this some weeks ago, in the newspaper, that the CIA 'ad sent an interpreter to Grenada during the invasion to translate the language for the Marines, you know?"

Sylvia laughed aloud, "What? Oh no!" She shook her head. "You'd think with all their surveillance they'd have noticed that the Grenadians speak English."

"Anh, maybe the Marines don't."

"Claire."

"OK, OK, let's not fight again about the French Academy and all that stuff."

"But that is the point. I mean it is hard to believe some of the adolescent things, like fraternity stuff or something, that the CIA thinks up for their secret spy games. I swear some of them have this comic book mentality . . . "

"Not that funny."

"And they act it out in *real life*. Like with Steven, right now. Shit, it's so . . ." Sylvia grimaced, a look of both anger and remorse. She looked at Claire. "We're responsible, you know."

"Sylvia. Pardon me. But I am not responsible for the actions of the CIA. As a matter of fact, that's exactly 'oo I am trying to fight against."

"But Claire! If you hadn't taken Steven's address . . ."

"Oh, Sylvie, listen. 'ee is related to you, enh? 'ow long before you think your 'ole family is under surveillance, if not now, enh? What are you going to do about that? You are going to stop your work? You are going to leave NEWS? We should all give up the transformation because Steven lose 'is MasterCharge? Ppphh! All the great social change of Chile, Grenada—so many destroyed by agencies like the CIA. And we are suppose to feel so awful because Steven lose 'is credit card!"

"It's more than that, Claire. They're really trying to break him. It's like you said. They don't want any man, with any kind of power, or men in general getting involved in NEWS, and especially assisting us in any kind of clandestine capacity. They want to discredit him, make him look like a chump, a loser."

"Yeah, I know, Sylvia. But we can't feel guilty for that! It is exactly the work of NEWS to stop such kind of things, to stop all the force of destruction that keep the imperialists in power. That is our work. If one or some of us get 'urt by them, even killed, or our family—we cannot feel guilty for that! It would paralyze us! It is not you and me 'oo are 'urting Steven, it is the CIA! If we want to feel guilty, let's feel guilty for the thousands and thousands of people 'oo 'ave been killed, imprisoned, tortured by the CIA for trying to free their own countries, or 'ave a decent life for their people."

"OK, OK. Let's not feel guilty. But what the fuck am I going to do about Steven, Claire? I mean the fact is he apparently has no idea that he is under surveillance and is being harassed. I *do* know that, primarily because I have information about it, such as the letter you had sent . . ."

"What did you tell 'im about it? Did you explain something?"

"Yeah, I called him the next week and told him it was something about your passport, that you needed a legal office address for the officials in Paris, that you'd been in a hurry, you'd never do it again without asking, blah, blah. Like we'd decided."

"And 'ee accept that?"

"Yeah, he was in a hurry. He was on his way to a murder trial or something."

"OK, so 'ee 'as no idea . . ."

"No. He doesn't. And in the meantime he's drinking more and more, really becoming cynical and . . . wrecked out, according to Linda."

"Yeah, that's not good."

"And, Claire, he *is* family to me. I know you haven't seen your family in years, and they have nothing to do with your life anymore, but I still do care about the people in my family! I can't just sit by and watch Steven go to hell—be driven crazy by CIA harassment—knowing full well what is going on and say *nothing* to him or Linda!"

Claire was silent a moment, looking at her hands as she turned the silver ring on her forefinger round and round. "*Bon*, Sylvia. I know you care about your family. I 'ope you don't really think that I don't care about my own." Sylvia felt suddenly moved, the solemn dignity of Claire's tone made her wish she could take back her words, but Claire went on. "I don't think it means a person does not love their family, love them very much, *hien*? because they choose to put first their love for all people, for the Earth. Isn't that what you say is international love?" She looked at Sylvia, her eyes searching. "Where we get beyond the egoism of loving juss ourself and the ones close to us, juss the things around us that we know are ours? If we love a justice, an 'armony for all people, and we make this the work of our life, whether our family agree or no . . . Does that mean we don't love our family? I don't think so."

"No. I know, Claire," Sylvia said quietly and, listening to the rain, falling evenly now in a lapse of the wind, she thought of Linda, and of the urgent sadness in her voice as she talked about Steven's 'paranoia,' his drinking.

"Sylvia. I think we need to find a way to do something about Steven, to 'elp 'im. But nothing that would endanger the work of NEWS CLAN, not in any way." She paused, looking at Sylvia. "You know?"

Sylvia nodded. "I know."

"And if 'ee is drinking all the time, we cannot trust 'im with any kind of information. We cannot tell 'im anything."

"But . . ."

"First. 'ee muss stop drinking."

"Oh god, I don't know."

"But 'ee drank a lot before this, *hien*?"

"Well, more than some people, maybe. But it was under control. Now it's not." Sylvia thought a moment. "You know, I told Linda—well, actually she asked me to—I'm going to meet with Steven and talk to him about his drinking."

"You are?" Claire looked surprised and somewhat horrified.

"I know. Listen. It's the kind of role I just hate. But she asked me to. She said that nothing she says gets through to him at all—just starts fights. And he won't go to a counselor. He doesn't have any family here. She said I'm the closest one to family. I would've put up a fight, really, I mean, I don't know what to say! But I agreed to because . . . because I do feel responsible."

"Sylvie, please. Forget this thing about being responsible and guilty! You will make big mistakes if you keep feeling that kind of thing. Mistakes that can 'urt so many more people than Steven!"

"Anyway. I agreed to talk to him."

"When?"

"I'm going to call her later and find a time."

"Well, it's good. Maybe you can convince 'im to try to stop drinking. And if 'ee stop, maybe then we can tell 'im more and 'elp 'im to get the CIA off 'is back. Try to, Sylvie. Try to 'elp 'im decide to *stop* drinking. That's the real way you can 'elp 'im."

Sylvia hesitated. "Well, I mean, what you're saying makes sense, Claire. But how in *hell*, in a two hour conversation, am I going to convince someone who's been drinking for years to *stop* it all?"

"You can try, Sylvia. Try to give 'im some inspiration. To care more about 'isself, and 'is family, enh? If he cannot care about things beyond that, 'elp 'im see 'ow 'ee makes 'imself so *powerless* to be drunk all the time. If you can juss get 'im to stop for awhile, for some weeks, 'ee will feel so different."

"OK, Claire, I'll try, but god. I mean it's a full time job and I have so much to do."

"No, no. You cannot make it your big priority. Meet with 'im and see what 'appens. If 'ee doesn't stop, then, there is nothing we can do. Until after the conferences and the February Action. *C'est ca!* You agree?"

Chapter VIII

The sound of shattering glass brought Steven back to consciousness. "What! What's that?" he called out, his voice thick with sleep.

"Nothing. Nothing!" Linda answered from the kitchen above the sudden burst of Justin's tears. "I dropped a glass."

Steven turned heavily in the bed, his face deep in his pillow. He opened his eyes and looked at the clock—8:15. Had the alarm rung at 7:00? What the hell? He remembered, or had he dreamt the clock radio blaring out its news, his hand shooting out to silence it—was that this morning? What day is it? December 5th, 6th? Tuesday, yeah. He should be leaving for the office. With a barely audible groan he turned again. His head, uhh, would hardly move. He shut his eyes, shutting out the feeling, too familiar, that began to seep slowly through him as his mind wakened to the fog that thickened it and that feeling, his eyes so swollen, and his mouth intolerably dry, like cotton, dull, stupid. Hatred. He hated it. Everything. The noise in the kitchen would drive him mad. Can't she keep him quiet, for god's sake? Didn't she know he needed to sleep? Why the hell else had he overslept? She didn't give a shit.

The office loomed before him like a prison, a tiny stark cell, to enclose him, trap him in its empty vacuum, a heartless, cold cement tomb. He hated them all. Mark. He winced, his face tight, to slap back the flash of Mark leaning close to him in the Jury Room last night, his styled, sprayed hair like a model's wig even after his tenth drink. Tenth? How long . . . No. Forget it. Paint it out. A big thick paint brush full of white paint covered over the scene. It disappeared. He turned to his other side. Linda had quieted Justin and only the sound of his gentle prattle drifted through the cracked bedroom door. I told him I'd take the job, sounded loud in Steven's mind, against his will. He winced again, repulsed. Why did I even go have a drink with him in the first place? he asked, disgusted. Why do I even talk to that sold-out asshole? Did I really say I would work with him? Under him? He pulled the blanket up, covering his mouth, his eyes closed against the dull throbbing just behind them. He's going to have Drew call me today. That arrogant sucker, I'll just hang up the phone. I'll just call Mark and tell him to fuck off. I don't need their motherfucking condescending dirty con-game ass-kissing—Ugh. He brought his hand slowly to his forehead, running it down his face as if to pull away the bloated, foggy smell of stale smoke and whiskey.

They can go to hell. He repeated, over again, his litany of hatred against them, while just beneath he asked himself why he had been spending time with Mark lately anyway when he had about as much respect for him as a slug. Because he bought him free drinks and listened to his problems and badmouthed Jack Sorrenson—Shut Up! his voice of litany shouted him down. I hate them all, he repeated as the memory of Linda talking about Jack appeared again, her face flushed and glowing that night after she had come back from Berkeley, and the night that Jack had come to dinner, her face angry, accusing as he had argued with Jack, and her face, defiant, when she told him she had had lunch with Jack the week before, the day he had told the secretary at the office to tell Jack he wasn't in when he called. He threw back the blankets and, lunging up from the bed, walked over to the chair where his suit jacket lay, thrusting his hand in its front pockets. He found his cigarettes and, lighting one, leaned back against the bureau, letting the smoke stream evenly through his lips. Why shouldn't he take the job. What the hell? They'd have ten times the money they had now. He could keep clear of Drew and Mark, just see them when . . . No. The image failed. He just couldn't see himself standing in court, pleading the case of a Bechtel executive. It was hopeless. Things were just fucking hopeless.

"Steven?" Linda called from the kitchen as the smell of smoke, its acrid odor, wafted through the room.

"Yeah?" his voice answered, almost gruff in its groggy hoarseness.

"Are you going to work?"

"Yeah."

She came to the bedroom doorway, pushing it open, a dish towel in her hand. She smiled at him. "Do you want some breakfast?"

"Some coffee. I'll get it," he answered, not looking at her.

"Let me fix you some eggs, Steve. I don't think you had any dinner last night, did you?"

"Well, I . . ." He looked at her, guarded, wondering why she was being so nice—he'd come in late, drunk—he shut his eyes, painting it out. What had he said to her?

"It'll just take a minute. Have some breakfast, Steve," she said, her eyes entreating now.

"OK," he answered. He watched her turn back to the kitchen, his look still guarded. He'd called her and told her he'd be late. She'd been sleeping when he came in, or trying to. They hadn't talked. Maybe she was getting used to it. But usually he could feel her anger, her coldness the next morning. Maybe she'd just as soon he wasn't around, god knows he'd just been so bad, so miserable these past weeks. He stubbed out his cigarette, shaking his head, as if to shake off the tired, empty sadness he felt.

After a shower, dressed and shaved, he came into the kitchen. Justin was playing in his room and Linda had set the table prettily with cloth napkins and flowers from the yard. Feeling both pleased and uneasy, he sat at his place as she brought an omelet, toast and coffee to the table.

"Can I help?" he asked.

"No, no. It's all fixed." Linda sat across from him at the table and served them both. She put her napkin in her lap and then, fingering the handle of her coffee cup, she said, "Steve."

"Yeah?" he answered, thinking, here it comes.

"Do you remember that you agreed to be home for dinner at 6:00 tonight?"

Steven felt his cheeks flush hot. Was that bastard Sorrenson coming to dinner again? Linda paused as she saw his shoulders tense and his mouth harden. She took a sip of coffee and, setting the cup back in its saucer, began again. "Steve, I told you last week that Sylvia was going to come to dinner tonight. We haven't seen her in months. I just . . ."

"Oh, yeah. Yeah." Steven's shoulders relaxed and he took a bite of omelet, vaguely recalling that Linda had said something about Sylvia coming over days ago. He nodded. "Yeah, I remember. I'll be here."

"Well, Steve," Linda hesitated. "Are you sure? Because Sylvia is really busy these days, you know that conference she's been working on is in a few weeks."

"Well, sure, I'll be here, Linda. I mean I'm here most nights, aren't I? Look. I'm sorry about last night. I ran into Mark again, I, you know . . . I called you."

"At 8:00."

"Well, look! Nobody was coming to dinner at 6:00 last night. At least as far as I knew." He looked at her.

"Oh, god, Steven, will you stop that!" Linda put her fork on her plate, her eyes tearing with exasperation. "We have been over this thing about Jack a hundred times, and there's *nothing*, nothing to even go over! He came to dinner a month ago—you had invited him yourself! I went out to lunch with him *one* day, after he had tried to reach you at the office too! And I talked to him on the phone twice. *So what!* You're going to drive me crazy with that, Steven!"

"OK, OK. Let's drop it. So I'll be here at 6:00. What's the big deal? You've had plenty of evenings with Sylvia in your life without me."

"Sylvia wants to see you, too. She said so. She'd like to talk to you about some things." Linda looked at her plate, her breakfast hardly touched, and, calming herself, she looked at Steven gently. "I really want you to be here, Steve. I want us all to have dinner together."

"OK. Fine. I'll be here." He looked at her with raised eyebrows and a shrug of the shoulders. "Why not?"

"Well, good," Linda answered, smiling, not happily, but relieved.

"It'll be a great dinner, Steven. I'm going to make a kind of couscous, it's a Moroccan dish, and we'll have a special kind of mint tea with it."

"Sounds fine." Laying his napkin on the table and taking a last sip of coffee, he stood up. "I better get going. It's after 9:00." He took his plate and cup to the sink, and, stopping to give Linda a quick kiss, he went into Justin's room, picked him up and, giving him a hug, said, "See you later, little man."

"Daddy going to court?" Justin asked as Steven set him back down in front of his cars and blocks.

"To the office. The office. Bye, Jus," he answered and, leaving the room, walked down the hall and out the front door. He hurried down the porch steps and up the street to his car, glancing at the headlines on the newspaper stand outside the corner store.

MORE MISSILES IN EUROPE
WHITE HOUSE CHALLENGES NICARAGUA.

He looked away, cursing himself for having looked at all as the white paint brush blotted out the words in three quick strokes. He got into his Toyota and pulled out into the street.

A cool winter sun shone in a bright blue sky as Steven turned onto Dolores Street, frowning at the knock of his engine as it pushed itself up the hill. The city lay bathed in the crystal light of air freshly cleaned by the storms, a sparkling luminescence one could almost reach and touch. In the distance the downtown buildings glistened a nearly summer white. A travel poster. A post card, Steven thought, depressed by its two-dimensional familiarity to him. He was sick of it. He hated it.

There in the skyscape on the 14th floor of the Mutual Life Building, Sylvia sat at her word processor, her fingers flying over the keys. She was finishing the last Spanish translation of the position papers for the conference. If things went well, she could spend a good part of the afternoon Xeroxing this and the others assigned to her.

Another secretary in the office, Janet, with whom Sylvia had begun to develop a friendship in recent months, had become interested in NEWS and had been helping with some of the conference preparation work. Fortunately her desk was close to the Xerox room and she had agreed to keep guard while Sylvia Xeroxed several thousand pages of documents for the conference. Janet had been following the Nuclear

Freeze campaign before Sylvia had ever mentioned politics on their occasional lunch dates, and it was Janet who had brought it up—her fear of the building arms mania—tears in her eyes as she had talked about her two-year old daughter. In fact, it was Janet who had brought her a list of the planned military spending for 1984. Over $2 billion for MX missiles, over $6 billion for B-1B aircraft, a half a billion for 95 more Pershing missiles, the list went on and on, and Janet had been livid. When Sylvia had told her of the work of NEWS, its goals, the plans for the conference, Janet had been intrigued, hopeful. And her husband, an unemployed teacher who had lost his job with the most recent funding cutbacks in education had, when Janet told him about NEWS, himself urged her to join. She had gone to her first general meeting two weeks ago.

Sylvia was elated to have found a comrade among her co-workers. It had taken her months to develop the relationship because she was usually working alone in her office during lunch and every other available moment, but on Ruth's advice she had recently made more of an effort to get to know other women in her office. So many of the mass members of NEWS had come from contacts at cadres' workplaces, offices, schools, hospitals. And the fact was, as Sylvia had learned, resource appropriation was so much more effective when they could work together. Janet had been of tremendous help as they juggled their office workloads between them, covering for each other as they did their 'real' work, the work of NEWS.

These past weeks they had accomplished much more for the conference than they had for Hansen, Rykoff & Shaw, thank god. And between all the office workers on the Conference Coordinating Committee, they would come up with over one million pages of reports on progressive organizations in their region in 15 languages, collated and bound. It was a huge amount of work, and yet most of it had been done on the paid time and equipment of some of the largest corporations in the world. The Bank of America alone, whose corporate headquarters on Jones Street employed eight NEWS members, had unknowingly contributed over $40,000 in salaries and supplies in the last three months, according to Carol's calculations.

Sylvia smiled as she typed, thinking of Teresa on the third floor of her own building and how she had managed, slowly, week after week, to transfer an entire supply room to the NEWS Oakland office and also use her firm's printing account for some very unusual publications, thanks to her friend at the quick-print across the street. And Los Angeles NEWS, hadn't they managed to get over $10,000 of medical supplies through their hospital workers in less than two weeks and deliver it all, intact, to Chela and the Allies in Managua? In fact, if NEWS decided to go through with the peace camp, the L.A. chapter had guaranteed enough medical supplies for the duration of the camp. Though it was unlikely that would be necessary now. And yes, Sylvia had to admit, she was glad, even though Claire had seemed disappointed. But what? she thought, it's NEWS, the Allies and their best interests we've got to think of, always. And working to build for the conferences, just in itself, is building NEWS, everywhere, all of us are getting more involved and daring in transferring resources. Because to see how international cooperation can work and acting on it gives us all such hope, such a sense of power. Her fingers danced across the keys as she nodded her head. Yes, we can create the future.

The buzz of her com-line stopped her hands in midair as she turned in her chair and picked up the phone.

"Call for you on six-six."

"Thanks, Patti. " She clicked the flashing button.

"Sylvie?"

"Hi, Claire," Sylvia answered, smiling. "Are you at work?"

"No. No, I'm not."

"I thought you had to do the books at Fowler's again."

"Yeah, me too, I thought so. And I went by there to do it, and when I arrive 'ee told me I need to fill out a paper, some stupid form. So I look at it, and I ask 'im, what is this for? 'ee told me it's a new law, passed by Reagan of course, that everyone, even an independent contractor like me, must fill out this form—a 1099—so they are sure to pay taxes. So 'ee needs my social security number. Of course, I don't 'ave one. I told 'im, 'Look. You pay me only $3,500 a year. Not even enough to live. You want me to pay taxes on that! For what! So we can 'ave some more MX missiles so you can die?'"

"Claire, Claire. Didn't you try to talk to him about it? I mean, you just started talking to him like that?"

"No, no, not really. First I say, OK. But why do you need this and you never needed it before? 'ee said, because it's a new law so . . . Oh, I don't want to say the 'ole thing to you now, Sylvie. In fact, I called to ask if you can meet me for lunch."

Sylvia looked at her watch. 9:30. She could finish her typing by noon, then Xerox after lunch. "Sure, OK. At noon? At Goldy's?"

"*Bon*, OK. I see you then."

"But, Claire, wait. What happened in the end with Fowler? Are you going to work for him anymore?"

"No. It's finished."

"Oh. OK. I'll talk to you at noon. Don't worry about it, Claire, we'll work something out. So relax, love, OK?"

"Oh yeah. I'm not worried about it. I'll see you at lunch, Sylvie. Bye-bye."

"Bye." Sylvia hung up the phone and turned back to her typing, her mind still on Claire. Something in her voice when she had said good-bye . . . She didn't seem worried at all. As if it didn't matter that she'd just lost over a third of her income. How in hell was she going to pay the rent on her apartment? It had gone up to $400 last summer and was still a good deal. Rents were so disgusting. Let's see though . . . she still has the Daly and Worcester accounts. They bring her about $6,000 a year, maybe a little less—what is that. $500 a month. Impossible. She can't pay $400 rent, then have $100 left for everything else. Sylvia stopped to turn the page of her copy as she typed. She'll have to find another client. Maybe she could do it in my name and use my social security number. That could work. Though it could take her awhile to find another client. Especially now. Christmas is a horrible time to look for a job. And what if Daly and Worcester hit her with this thing too? She'll have nothing. It'll definitely take some time to find new clients. She may just have to give up her apartment. God, she'd hate that. But . . . Sylvia's hands slowed on the keys. She could come and stay in our flat. She could live with me again. She let her hands drop to her lap and sat back in her vinyl chair a moment, remembering that first year they had lived together.

So much had changed since then. NEWS hadn't even existed then; it was hard to believe. And now NEWS CLAN, the Action. Yes, things were different now. Of course they were. And, yes their relationship wasn't exactly the one of blissful unity it had been then. But still. Still they were so deeply connected. More than ever really, after all they'd been through. If they just had more time, just get through this . . . Sylvia folded her arms as she sat. Though Claire does seem more . . . what? Hard, now, or . . . what did Rikki say? But Rikki doesn't know her. Not really. Sometimes people just don't understand Claire. Not like I do. How could they? They don't see her in those moments that . . . only lovers know. There's such a tenderness, and joy in Claire, and humor. That was it. Rikki said she never laughed! That's absurd. Sylvia looked incredulous, dismissing the thought. Hadn't Claire given her such pleasure, such happiness in her life? And a whole new sense of—an emotional quality that she hadn't experienced in years. Certainly not in her affair with JoAnn. And even with her first lover—woman lover—Rena, it was never as deep, or not deep, but . . . exciting as with Claire. Always, even when it seemed so hard, it was still there, that fire, the intense soul-knowledge between them.

The love she felt for Claire filled her as she slowly brought her hands back to her keyboard and began to tap out the words on the pages before her. All the love she felt for her, despite the harsh words they'd had, their differences, their impatience with each other. It was hard! It wasn't easy to work so hard all the time and never lose your temper.

And if they had more time to spend on their own relationship . . . if they lived together again, just even to share more of those simple, happy moments, resting in each other's caring and knowing of each other. Claire. Sylvia almost laughed. What a wild one she can be, so strong. Sometimes her mind was like a flash of brilliance, lightning, and yet her eyes, those warm, liquid eyes could melt the earth. Though she was getting too thin, she'd lost even more weight and she wasn't sleeping well. And there was grey now in her hair, that blonde curly hair with always the rebellious strands wisping by her temples, the hollows of her cheeks. She is so thin though, Sylvia thought, seeing Claire suddenly with a concern that almost alarmed her, that she hadn't taken the time to feel . . . If we just had more time, to care for each other, Sylvia thought. Couldn't it work? To live together again? To have more than just those few nights a week after meetings. Though still, their schedules were so full, they might not even see that much more of each other. But even just to share a meal more often. I wouldn't mind at all, she thought. We'd probably argue less, not more. We could give each other more comfort. And if not? Well, it would only be temporary, anyway. Sylvia smiled as her fingers moved more quickly over the keys. It could be great. To have more time together, just to relax, to laugh . . .

At ten minutes to 12:00 Sylvia took her work from the machine and locked the manuscripts in the bottom drawer of her desk. She grabbed her coat and bag and, leaving her office, went to Janet's desk to check with her about the afternoon Xeroxing. After a few quick words she turned, and humming to herself, left the suite.

As she rushed up the street to Goldy's, she saw Claire standing at the front door of the crowded deli. "Hi," she greeted, a warm smile lighting her face.

"*Allo*, Sylvie," Claire answered with less than a smile, agitated.

"Look. It's so busy, 'ere. Let's take a walk, *hein*? I need to talk with you. I don't think we can 'ear anything in there."

Sylvia glanced around at the street packed with Christmas shoppers and the flood of lunch-time workers. "Well . . ."

"Let's go to the end of Market. To the bay. We can cross 'ere and go by Mission."

"OK."

As they moved south of Market and the crowds began to thin, Sylvia said, "Claire, you know I've been thinking . . . about your job and this problem with Fowler."

"*Bon*, Sylvie, I don't care about that."

"You don't?" Sylvia looked at her, confused.

"No, no. I want to talk with you about something else."

The gravity of Claire's voice and the look in her eyes stopped the flood of ideas Sylvia had been waiting all morning to express. "What?" she asked.

"Well, you know that the Steering Committee decide, after we 'eard from Chela, to wait about the peace camp."

"Yeah?"

"Well, as Chela said, it could take away too much from the conferences and the Action. And it seem that the probability of an invasion is growing less . . ."

"Yeah, I know. We decided not to do it unless we heard differently from her. From the Allies."

"Well, yes, we decide not to mobilize for it now. But, you know, we also decide to 'ave an ad 'oc committee to prepare for it as a possibility, in case the threat of invasion will become more serious again."

Sylvia felt an uneasiness as they stood at the red light, waiting to cross Embarcadero. "Yeah. Didn't you meet Sunday night? I guess I haven't talked to you about it since then."

"Yes, we met." They moved quickly across the wide street, silenced by the torrent of cars speeding along the overpass above. Turning, they headed west along the bay, the great wharf docks stretching out to their right.

"And?" Sylvia asked finally.

"So. We are recruiting members of NEWS, internationally, 'oo are willing to go on a very short notice if we 'ear from the Allies that they decide, yes, it is necessary."

"Mmhmm."

"And also we are reserving some flights on a sequence of days, and looking to see even about a special charter flights, if that is possible to arrange . . ."

"But these are just preparations, right? I mean they probably won't be necessary, didn't Chela say . . ."

"*Oui*, yes. It is just a preparation. In case. But also we decide that . . ." Claire stopped at an opening between the wharves to look out at the broad expanse of blue bay glistening in the winter sun. She rested her hands on the wooden railing in front of her, the sound of the water slapping at the rampart below seeming to gauge her words as she spoke. "We decide that part of the preparation should be to send some cadres to Nicaragua, to the border area, to determine an appropriate site, to find where there can be access to water and food, to prepare for . . ."

"I see." Sylvia leaned against the wooden barricade, looking down into the rippling depths of sea water below. She knew the rest. Claire was silent.

"When are you going?" Her voice was low, cold.

"Next week."

Sylvia felt her teeth biting hard into her lip as she stared down into the steel blue water, biting back the rage, the tears. Claire stood close beside her, standing straight, looking out across the bay. Sylvia felt her nervousness, and her determination. Finally she turned to Claire though her eyes seemed as if they still studied the grey-blue water beneath, mirroring its color, as tears began to find their way, each in its lone path along her face, she looked hard at Claire. "Why you? You don't have to go. No one asked you to. You know they'll never let you back in this country!"

"Sure they will, Sylvie."

"Fuck, Claire! The minute you go through customs and they see your passport stamped for *June 1980!* Are you crazy? And a three-month visa that expired over three years ago! They're going to say good riddance to you, you saved us the trouble of deporting you, and plug you into their computers as *persona non grata*, which will correspond just fine with the FBI and CIA files. You *know* it Claire! You'll never get back in here!"

"Juss see. Wait and see, Sylvia. We 'ave other ways, you know. I expect to be back. Maybe not by the conferences, because in fact the threat of invasion is most 'igh at Christmas. We must 'ave some solidarity forces in Nicaragua at that time. And possibly we will 'ave to mobilize the entire peace camp on short notice and bring women down from the conference 'ere."

"Claire." Sylvia had stopped her tears. She stood straight, looking at Claire, evenly, "There are others who would go. No one is assigning this to you." She looked closely, intently, searching her lover's eyes. "Why *you?*"

Claire looked out across the water. "I want to go there." She glanced at Sylvia. "I want to *feel* it."

Then turning away, back to the horizon, her voice not so much hurried as intense, she went on, "I want to experience the revolutionary society, the feeling of the people I 'ave 'eard so much about. It seems so big there, the motion, the commitment of the people. There the revolution is so *alive*. The 'ole nation, not just the cadres, or a small organization . . ." She turned to Sylvia. "I love NEWS, Sylvie, you know that. I will always give my life to NEWS, but I just want to feel this for awhile, to go there . . ." She paused. "And also, you know. In fact, I was asked to go. Chela ask that I come there."

Sylvia, her eyes still on Claire, stepped back as if struck. "Chela! Chela asked you knowing your problems about visas here! Knowing it means you can't return to NEWS here in this country! Goddamn Chela! Who cares what Chela wants!"

Claire's eyes hardened, an anger building in her. "I do. I was 'appy that Chela ask that I work with 'er. I want to work with 'er. It . . . it can be a great opportunity. I can learn so much! You don't care about that, Sylvia? You juss want me to be 'ere by you? Be honest, enh? You don't care what is good for NEWS, or for me! You are juss caring for yourself! For what you want!"

Sylvia stood silent, her lips parted and eyes still on Claire. Struck motionless by hurt and disbelief, she stood and then, her voice low and cold again, "I'll talk to you later, Claire." She turned and walked back down the Embarcadero toward her office.

She walked quickly, unseeing, stunned by a pain too sharp for tears, she made her way through the crowds along Market Street, jostled by shoppers, their arms full of packages, her mind empty—then flushed hot as her fantasies of the morning came back to her, humiliating her. She felt sick, as if beaten, slapped and kicked. She rode the empty elevator up to the 14th floor and walked alone through the suite to her office.

Closing the door behind her and hanging up her coat and bag, she sat at her desk still numb, disbelieving. Claire was leaving. And she would not be back.

Always Sylvia had carried the small fear with her that Claire would be discovered by immigration, through CIA and FBI surveillance; and they had taken great care, all of them, NEWS, to keep her underground, unidentified. Though the letter that came through Steven had brought her to the State's attention, obviously they preferred to leave her here, to wait and see what else might be revealed through her. But the fear of her deportation had always been there, a small, usually unconscious fear because Sylvia had always believed—she had never really doubted at all—that if it were to happen, if Claire were threatened with deportation, the problem would be both of theirs. They would resolve it, find solutions, together. Claire would return to France, work with Paris NEWS, and Sylvia would go with her. She had never doubted this. Of course she would go with Claire, and so that small fear had never really been of great consequence to her; though at times, when they had had their worst arguments, Sylvia had wondered if she would really want to leave her family, her friends here in NEWS, comrades she had worked with for years, her home, California, where she had lived all her 33 years. But still she had known that, yes, she would go with Claire, so strong was the bond she felt with her, so deep was her belief in the strength of their relationship, and her commitment, her loyalty to that belief. It wouldn't have been forever. They could have returned here one day, or maybe Sylvia, alone would return; but first, she would at least try. She would have gone with her.

Sylvia sat still, staring at the empty wall above her desk. She shook her head slowly, her face still blank, stunned. Of course she'd always known Claire and she were different. Yes, they had their differences, and one of them was about—what—how could she say it—family, or loyalty, or some kind of feeling for personal love. But never, never had she thought that Claire had so little—what—what was it! Sylvia clenched her fists in her lap feeling the outrage, the betrayal rise like hot liquid steel in her veins, burning her eyes. Hadn't Claire left Jean Marc overnight? For Katrine? And then Katrine! She left her too. Both of them. She'd left, when she felt—what? Restless. Or that her own personal development was stagnating. And did she try to work it out with them? Her lovers? No! Had she even tried to grow, to break the patterns that held them back. Did she feel any responsibility for those patterns? No. No she just walks out. Walks out and moves on to the next stage of her life and doesn't even look back at the person who's seen her through the last one. Fuck her! And then she moves on to the next lover to see her through the next stage. Just like now, she's leaving. Leaving me to run off and "experience the revolutionary society." With Chela. Bitch! Sylvia slammed her fists on the top of the desk, the tears released now—the hot steel behind her eyes searing through with a pain she could hardly stand. She lay her head in her arms on the desk, her thoughts gone, dissolved into the stinging tears, the words shaken meaningless as her body gave itself over to the sobs of an ancient sorrow.

Held in her grief it seemed for hours, she lay finally still, drained; her body calm now, washed in its sadness. She sighed a deep trembling sigh and raised her head, looking at her watch. One o'clock. With a small moan she rested her forehead in her hands, and then, wiping her eyes, opened her top drawer and found a Kleenex. Her word processor sat on its stand, a hulking slab of metal and keys, and again her face flushed hot, humiliated, as she remembered her foolish daydreams of the morning. Blissful days with Claire. Fuck! She wrenched her bag off the hanger on the back of the door and found more Kleenex and a mirror. Janet would be by any second to see about the Xeroxing and, just as she'd finished dabbing at her swollen eyes, she heard her knock at the door. Bracing herself, knowing she looked a mess, she opened the door.

"Hi, Janet, I'm almost ready." She turned quickly away to unlock the bottom drawer of her desk.

Turning back again, her arms piled high with manila envelopes holding the conference documents, she saw the look of concern in Janet's eyes. "Sylvia? Has something happened? Are . . ."

"Oh. I've had some bad news, actually, I . . ." She half-laughed. "I know. I look awful."

"Oh. I'm sorry." The gentle sympathy in Janet's voice could have sent Sylvia reeling again but she set her mind fast on the conference, NEWS, the significance of the documents in her hands to their future.

"Is there anything I can do?" Janet asked, still taken aback at seeing Sylvia so shaken.

"No. Thanks, Janet." She offered half a smile. "We should get going on this. I'll go to the supply room and get some empty boxes for the copies."

As she walked down the hall, she wished that she could just say it, tell Janet, "My lover just told me she's leaving and she's not coming back." It would be a relief. To say it. The awful truth of it. But Janet, as yet, wasn't aware that Sylvia was a lesbian. In fact, Sylvia had no idea what Janet's thoughts about lesbians were. Of course, she must accept it on some level, in the abstract, as it was obvious that a good 20 percent of the members of San Francisco NEWS were gay. But as far as personal friends . . . Was Janet homophobic, afraid of lesbians, as so many straight women are? Who knows. In any case, it wasn't worth the risk.

At 4:45 Sylvia and Janet had finished the last of the Xeroxing and were in Sylvia's office taping shut the cardboard boxes. They would have to be stored there until Rikki could come by with her car the next day at lunch and pick them up. As they piled the last box in the corner behind the desk and taped the front page of an audit report to its top, the com-line on Sylvia's phone buzzed. She picked it up. "A call for you on six-seven."

"I'll get it in just a second, thanks Patti." She turned to Janet who stood at the door. They smiled at each other, pleased with their work.

"See you tomorrow, Sylvia. You take care now," Janet said warmly and left the office.

Sylvia pressed the phone line. "Hello."

"Sylvie! I 'ave been trying to call you all the afternoon, at your 'ouse too."

"Mmm," Sylvia answered, not knowing what else to say.

"I need to talk with you. Can we meet now?" There was an urgency in Claire's voice that Sylvia couldn't help but appreciate.

"I can't, I have to be at Linda's at 6:00. I'm meeting with Steven tonight. Remember?"

"Oh, yes, OK. *Bon*, do you think we can meet afterwards? At 9:00, or 10:00?"

"Well, I guess . . ."

"OK, I will be at 'ome. Maybe Steven can give you a liff to my place . . . or can you take the streetcar?"

"Well. OK."

"Good, OK, I'll see you then. I love you, Sylvie," Claire said and hung up the phone.

The tears came again as Sylvia put her hand to her eyes, trying to stall them back. She couldn't keep breaking apart like this. But still, she felt a warmth from Claire's words that soothed the sense of awful void that had loomed before her all afternoon. Taking her coat and purse from the back of the door, she closed her office securely and left the suite.

Leaving the lobby of the building she wrapped her coat around her. The early winter dusk brought a sharp chill to the evening air. She walked down Market Street, still crowded with Christmas shoppers, the city's strange tinselly ornaments dangling down from the street lamps overhead. She made her way through the crowds at the Embarcadero MUNI terminal, riding down the escalator patiently to the tracks below, and stood waiting for the 'J Church' car. Her thoughts, usually running in step with her busy schedule, idled now and she let them, watching the mass of workers about her waiting to go home. Bits, fragments of their conversation filtered through to her.

" . . . I had $50 on that game, $50! Beginning of the fourth quarter I thought I was set, then Davis intercepts . . ."

" . . . oh, I saw that, yeah, he was so cute in that, I just love him, I wish his show was still on . . ."

" . . . well, we don't have that kind of thing in real estate, once your deal's gone through they can't try and throw that back at you . . ."

Sylvia followed the line of passengers as they surged forward to the front of the coupled streetcars. Boarding with them, pressed tight among the standing bodies, she swayed back as the cars lurched forward into the dark tunnel ahead. She looked at the faces around her, tired, cold, some bitter, others almost dead, as a gloomy silence filled the car—taut nerves, almost visible, waiting to be released.

"To experience the revolutionary society," she heard Claire's voice and remembered now, Olina's letter, "The people are so alive here, so warm. Everyone in Managua is talking about the revolution, and the new society they are creating. Everywhere, there is so much hope and inspiration. These people know that they are creating their own destiny. And a model for the future of the world."

But NEWS was that for her. It was. In fact it was so much her life that she rarely even noticed the society she actually lived in; this—what she heard, saw around her—that she never really let in.

Except tonight, it all seemed so *there*. Because it is, she thought—this is reality, in this country. Television shows, football games, business deals, deadened, alienated workers watching the world rot before them on their TV screens . . . No, don't! She closed her eyes, swaying with the motion of the car as it made its way through the underground passage. That was exactly the kind of thinking she'd found so disgusting in the more cynical cadres of CECO. That faithless disrespect for people in our own society. Assuming they were incapable of change. How could she think that? Everyone is capable. Every human soul can feel hope, and inspiration, and love for life, *all* of life. Everyone can feel that love. And act on it. It's just to break through this 'reality' of drugs, apathy, consumerism . . . But it can happen. It can be done. It just takes faith, and example. And it *is* being done. All over the world. Even here, yes here too. For one thing, there's NEWS. And NEWS CLAN.

The streetcar nosed its way out of the tunnel up onto the street into the dark night sky, turning left onto Church Street. Sylvia looked out the top of the tram window as they neared the corner of Church and Market. There, the building on the left, on the third floor Claire's light shone through her small apartment window. She was home.

And me, Sylvia thought, why? I love her, yes, but *why* do I feel such a *terror*, an emptiness at the thought of her not being in my life anymore? What kind of narrow love is that? Why doesn't the whole of love, transformational love, fill me still so that the loss of her, that one *single person*, doesn't feel like the end of the *world* to me. Maybe she's right. I'm just thinking of myself. Caught in a kind of egoism that only holds me back, holds her back. It makes me powerless. And to feel powerless is to feel hatred, and I hated her today. I really did. But I don't hate her. That's not what I want to feel. I want the greater love, the entire creation of love to flow through me, move me, always. I don't need Claire for that. I don't need her. I don't.

Yes, I need closeness, caring. And I have it. Without Claire. In NEWS. Comrades, and good friends, JoAnn and Rikki, Olina, Ruth. And my family, Linda, and, yes, my mother. I'd have more time for them, all of them, and I've missed them, I really have. It's more than enough, more than many have in this country of 'individuals.' And more than anything, at the center of everything, the feeling of the greater love, the whole creation of love will carry me through. Yes it will. As I give it in my commitment to NEWS, the conference, the Action. She closed her eyes again, feeling herself calm now, at peace, she smiled; yes, this is the love that is truth. And comforted, for the first time that day since her meeting with Claire, she felt strong. Herself. She had reclaimed, she knew, that central part of her that the thought of Claire's leaving had seemed to destroy, no, she would be all right. She would be fine.

She looked at her watch as she stepped down from the streetcar door on 26th Street. 5:40. She was early. Well, good, maybe she'd have a few minutes alone with Linda before Steven came home. She almost laughed. What a time to have to try to talk somebody out of drinking; she'd never wanted a drink more in her life.

As Sylvia walked up the street, Linda was just putting a few last touches on the table setting in the dining room. She had gotten out her wedding china and silver for the occasion and put fresh flowers all over the flat—daisies and chrysanthemums in the kitchen, iris and gladiolas in the living room, and tea roses and baby's breath for a centerpiece on the dining room table. The rooms sparkled from her thorough morning's cleaning, the couscous was fully prepared and only needed to be warmed for serving, and she had two large pots of mint tea brewing. She had even taken Justin to a neighbor's for the evening. And she had also removed every bottle of alcohol from the house. She found herself humming a little tune as she rearranged once again the roses in the centerpiece. She felt . . . almost happy, for the first time in months. Steven would have to see. He would have to see how much she cared, how good their life could be together still. She was doing everything within her power to make things nice for him. This was his home. She knew he loved her, and Justin, more than anyone, anything. He would have to see that it could still be good, his family. His marriage. If he could just stop drinking, pull himself together. If only . . . if only he can hear from Sylvia what he can't hear from me. She turned as the doorbell rang. Good. There she is.

Linda's smile was warm and grateful as she opened the door to her cousin. "Hi, Syl."

Sylvia rested a moment in Linda's warm embrace, reassured, comforted. "Is Steven home yet?" she asked as they walked into the living room.

"No. What time is it?" Linda asked, a note of trepidation threatening her mood.

"Oh, I'm early. It's about a quarter to six," Sylvia answered. "How are you, Linda?"

"Fine, at the moment. I'm glad you're here, Sylvia. Believe me, I really appreciate this."

"Oh, don't think about it, Linda. I just hope that . . . You know, I don't know if we're really going to be able to accomplish anything with this. I mean, if he's not hearing it from you. Or, I mean, if Steven's really far, far gone into this, it may take a lot more than an evening with you or me to change it."

"Oh, Sylvia, come on! You're the optimist, remember? We've got to make every effort to convince him that . . . Fuck! He's killing himself! He's killing me!" Linda's voice rose, as the tension she had held so long within her was sparked by Sylvia's doubts.

"OK, Linda. Dear, we'll do our best." Sylvia looked at her, realizing that she had never seen her quite so strained, on edge. She looked around the living room and the dining room beyond. "Everything looks beautiful, Linda! What gorgeous flowers!" She put her arm around Linda's shoulders and felt a taut, almost brittle tension in her cousin's narrow back.

"Where's Justin?" Sylvia asked as for the first time she began to grasp not just the severity of the crisis Linda was undergoing, but also the kind of 'last hope' expectation she seemed to have for this evening's encounter; and as she listened to Linda explain that she had taken Justin to a neighbor, Sylvia felt a sinking dread. Her own exhaustion from Claire's news, the knowledge of the 'covert' aspect of Steven's problems that, in all good conscience, she could not yet disclose, together with the general improbability of an event such as this having any real effect gave her a feeling that, though she fought hard against it, she recognized as futility.

Linda saw the distress on her cousin's face and, torn between concern for her and a desperate insistence that some kind of miracle be worked on the stage she had set, she said, "Sylvia. Sylvia, I know you're probably tired, but please, try and really be *here* for this. How do you think we should proceed? I mean, should we just start right in? Or wait until after dinner?"

Sylvia looked again at Linda, the streaks of grey in her black wavy hair, the thin lines deepening at the corners of her usually shining blue-grey eyes, her forehead creased and drawn and a tremble, an agitation in her finely tapered cheek and jaw. She had always been something of a beauty, in a kind of classic, Anglo-Italian way; and it had brought her a privilege, not, of course, as tangible as that of her upper-middle class background, but a privilege nonetheless. The privilege of deference from men, their service and protection in instances where other women would be ignored or belittled. Yet Linda never played on this privilege, nor used it to her advantage at the expense of others, as many women do. Never consciously, and rarely even unconsciously, did she rely on it; but rather she rejected it, disgusted by the injustice of it. Despite the privilege and protection in her life, she did seek justice and she did have an interest, a caring for life beyond her own needs. But now, she looked almost haggard, or even, crazed, as if she were waiting for her world to collapse, trying frantically to shore up the walls against an indomitable sea. Sylvia felt a quick and firm resolve: futile or no, she would do her best to help her cousin now, to help her get through to Steven, somehow.

"Well, so?" Linda asked, impatient with Sylvia's silence. "So? How should we do it?"

"Oh. Well, Linda. Does he have any idea what this dinner is about or . . ."

"No. Not yet. He just thinks it's to get together with you, because we haven't seen you in so long. Though, actually, this morning I might have said that you had something to talk to him about, or something like that."

"Oh no. Well, I don't think it should be like *that*. Like I came over here to tell him how to live his life. That stinks. He'd just tell me to get the hell out. I mean, so would I." She thought a moment. "Look, Linda. Let's just try and have a normal conversation and both of us be looking for a way to get into it, and once we do, once it's out in the open, both just be honest, as honest as we can." Sylvia stopped as she heard the front door open. Linda started, her eyes widening, and, giving Sylvia a meaningful look, she walked into the hall.

"Hi, Steve." Linda gave him a warm kiss as the smell of his first drinks of the evening filled her nostrils and left her standing, deflated, as he smiled and walked past her to the living room, setting a paper bag on the coffee table.

Looking at Sylvia he said, "Hi, stranger, how's it going?"

"Oh . . . up and down I'd say. How about you?" Sylvia asked as they embraced. Smiling, she stepped back, trying not to show the genuine shock she felt at Steven's appearance. Not that he was any less good looking, his dimpled chin still charming beneath the sensitive curve of his mouth and his fine straight nose; but yes, he was less good looking, for the skin of his cheeks sagged heavily and his eyes, which had struck her as so keen that first day she had met him years ago were alarmingly dull by comparison, sadly dull, and his skin was not sallow so much as a pastey, mottled grey, as if he hadn't seen the sun in god knows how long. But even with all of this there was still nothing, no single thing she could identify that caused her quite the level of shock she felt when she stood back and looked at him, full in the face. He was not well.

She moved back toward the couch, feeling a sad anxiety as she glanced back at Steven busying himself with his paper bag. She had always had a special fondness for him, he was an unusual man. He had a certain grace, lovely really, that so became what otherwise might have been a too-proud sensitivity; yet he seemed unaware of his own gifts or his own powers. And now, now he seemed to be losing touch with them altogether as if even his kind, fine spirit were breaking. "They're trying to break him," she heard herself tell Claire, and her mind fairly swam in the difficulty, the impossibility of the moment. It was awful to see what was happening to him, to Linda. For now, face to face with them both, she could only see the reality of their experience and feel the love, the years of love, and loyalty she felt toward them both. Of course Claire could say not to tell them. It wasn't just because she wasn't family to them either. Claire was cold. Very cold.

"A glass of wine?" Steven asked as he popped the cork from a half-gallon bottle. Pushing the corkscrew back into his penknife and slipping it back into his pocket, he sat down. "Linda, are you going back to the kitchen? Could you get some glasses?" he asked, looking over his shoulder at his wife who stood, still, in the doorway to the hall, watching.

As Steven turned back around, Sylvia caught the look of defeat in Linda's eyes, her shoulders slumped. Sylvia, looking at her, shrugged with a glance that said, "Go ahead. Just for now," and sat down facing Steven.

"Well, what do you mean 'up and down,' Sylvia? I thought things were always *up* for the dedicated revolutionary," Steven said as he lit a cigarette and shifted restlessly in his chair, waiting for Linda to bring him a glass.

Sylvia raised her eyebrows. This was not going to be easy. She had gotten her first taste of what Linda had meant by his 'cynicism.'

"Oh, well, Steven, even Che got depressed sometimes," she returned.

He laughed, looking her in the eye for the first time. "Well, what's been getting you down, Sylvia?"

She hesitated. The evening was not supposed to be about her, her problems. And could she even trust herself to bring it up without breaking down again. And yet . . . maybe it was the best approach. What the hell. There had to be *some* honesty this evening.

"Claire," she answered. "Or I should say, Claire's decision."

"What decision? You two haggling about how to run the conference again?"

His determination to belittle her froze the rest of her words in her throat, but as she heard Linda's slow step coming back down the hall and looked beyond at the dining-room table, set with such care, she went on.

"No, no. Claire won't be at the conference. She's leaving the country next week." She paused, steeling herself for the words. "I probably won't be seeing her again." It hadn't worked. The tears came and, as Linda stood by the coffee table, the glasses in her hand, looking stunned and dismayed, Sylvia threw her head back, shaking off the tears and summoning everything within her to focus on the purpose of her presence here at this moment. She gathered the pieces that those words seemed to shatter and taking a breath, said to them both, "So . . . that's been on my mind."

"Sylvia! You didn't tell me!" Linda began.

"Where's she going?" Steven asked. "Why won't you see her again?"

"Oh, I . . . I could see her again, I don't mean to be dramatic. She's going to Nicaragua. I could go there to see her, or to France, if she goes back there. I just don't think she'll get back in this country. Not in the near future." She was surprised herself by the lightness she felt just for saying the words, as if some dense, murky weight had begun to lift.

"Oh, Syl." Linda set the glasses down and came over to her cousin, leaning to her and holding her in her arms. Sylvia felt near tears again, not just by the comfort Linda offered her, but knowing the troubled, anxious state Linda had moved herself beyond to do so.

Steven poured the glasses full from his half-gallon bottle as Sylvia returned Linda's warm embrace and, giving her a kiss, said, "It's OK. I'll know more tomorrow. We can talk about it later." She gave a nod of assurance to Linda who sat down on the couch beside her.

"Why does she have to go to Nicaragua?" Steven asked, handing Sylvia a glass of white wine, his own gesture of comfort.

Sylvia took it and set it on the table. Suppressing the anger the question called up to her, she answered briefly, "Some women from NEWS are going down to investigate the situation at the border."

"But why now? With the conference just a few weeks off?" Linda asked.

"To see what can be done to prevent an invasion."

"Sylvia. Nothing can be done to prevent an invasion. If the generals decide to invade—Bye-bye Sandinistas," Steven said as he took a sip of wine. "Tell Claire she's wasting her time. She's better off up here organizing a conference than down in some Central American jungle trying to fight off the Pentagon. Christ."

If she hadn't known Steven was trying in some strange way to make her feel better, she would have been livid. "Actually, Steven, even the Pentagon generals can be outsmarted. Or should I say, especially the Pentagon generals."

Linda laughed. "Say 'especially.'"

"Outsmarted, yes," Steven agreed. "Outnuked, no. What's our friend Sorrenson say, Linda? That quote from the Department of Defense Guidance. From last year . . ."

"Oh." Linda looked somber. "Yeah. Actually they said, quote unquote, 'If conventional means are insufficient to ensure a satisfactory termination of war, the U.S. will prepare options for the use of nuclear weapons.' Honestly. That's their policy, as of 1982."

"Yeah, I know it, believe me," Sylvia answered. "But that doesn't mean there aren't ways to stop them."

"Well, you tell Steven that, dear, I'm going to go get the couscous. Do you want to sit at the table, Steve?" she asked, giving him a nudge as she left the room. Sylvia couldn't tell if Linda had just totally given up on the evening or thought it was going well; but somehow she seemed almost carefree now, with an air of abandon, as if Sylvia's own distress over Claire, and then the talk of nuclear war had put some kind of perspective on her own problems. Or else made life itself seem meaningless. It did seem more that, actually. It seemed that possibly Linda was getting into her own brand of cynicism, of not giving a fuck, rather than entering into some enlightened state of detachment; and Sylvia felt herself beginning to sink again—without moorings, what was there to hope? What could she say?

"Shall we?" Steven glanced at her as he rose from his chair and picked up his bottle and glass. Sylvia followed him into the dining room, carrying her and Linda's still-full glasses and setting them at their places.

"So, Sylvia, what are these 'ways' to stop them? You know what the ways to stop them are? There are none." He poured his glass full. "There are 4,200 nuclear warheads lining the earth and how many hundreds of satellite weapons mining the skies? We're sitting on a fucking time bomb, and you know it! Why pretend it's any different? What does your group of Pollyannas think they can do? Who the hell does Claire think she is, going to Nicaragua as if she could make a damn bit of difference?"

He was getting drunk. Sylvia bit the inside of her cheek. If you had any idea, you asshole, just what we're going to do . . . She looked at Steven, waiting for the anger to pass through her. "Steven," she began.

He waved her off. "I hate to see you wasting your time. I really do. You all work your butts off, it seems like, and, really, you should be out there having a good time! While you still can! You and Claire should go to Hawaii, not Nicaragua. Go and see it! It's beautiful! That's where Linda and I went when we got married. It's really beautiful! Go see it before it gets blown off the fucking map."

"Oh. Giving your apocalypse speech again, Steven?" Linda asked as she set a copper pot full of the steaming couscous in the middle of the table. The edge in her voice made Sylvia uneasy. It was not abandon, as she had thought after all; it was no holds barred. She could see it. Any minute, Linda was ready to pull out all the stoppers.

"What's the matter, Lin? I'm not enough of a visionary for you? Like your friend, Jack? 'Cuz I'm not pumping out a lot of bogus lefty slogans? Well, listen," he leaned over the table, "at least I speak the truth!"

Sylvia saw Linda turn rigid where she stood, her fists clenched, the knuckles white, and, turning back toward Steven, Sylvia decided to beat Linda to it—to pull out the stoppers herself. "Truth! *Truth!* And where do you get your *truth*, Steven?" Her voice was hard, direct. "In the courtroom? From those bought-off old judges who think their family dog is more important than the human being standing in front of them, or you either, for that matter! From that idiot box television that would go bankrupt if murder and violence went out of style? From the newspapers? Journalists who rather kiss ass and sell their mothers before they'd ever tell the facts that might expose the corporate pigs that own them? Death and doom, yeah, they blab it out every day just like they try to pump us all full of drugs and booze to keep us all down, stupid, numbed, paralyzed—and powerless. That's your truth, Steven, and that's no truth at all. The real truth is what we *make* it. We *make* the truth, brother! And you're making yours with that bottle." She stood up and grabbed the serving spoon from the copper pot, slapping down a pile of couscous on each of their plates. "Eat something, Steven. You look like the bomb's already dropped on you."

Steven sat back in his chair, not sure if he had really heard correctly, if this was really Sylvia, yelling at him about truth, yelling at him to eat. He looked at Linda. Linda too, sat still, her face expressionless, not sure if she liked what was going on. This was not what she had expected from Sylvia.

Sylvia felt the thick, embarrassed tension in the room and, without looking at either of them, picked up her fork and began to eat. At a loss for what else to do, Linda followed suit. Steven—looking again at Sylvia, then at Linda, not really able to tell which side his wife was on—sat another moment then leaned forward and picked up his fork. The three of them sat in silence, eating their dinner.

As Sylvia reached for the serving spoon to take a second helping, she said, "I'm sorry, Steven. I really am. I . . ."

"Oh . . . that's OK, Sylvia," Steven answered, forgiving, sobered now by his plate of couscous. "I didn't know you had such a temper!" He laughed.

"Me either," Linda said, giving a warning look to her cousin.

"Well, I just felt, I just felt so . . . More?" she asked them as she held the serving spoon in her hand.

"I'll have a little," Steven answered as Linda shook her head.

"I just felt so frustrated by some of the things you were saying, actually," she went on as she served him again.

He looked at his glass of wine, then Sylvia. "About nuclear war?"

"Well, and the hopelessness of it all. Or this idea that absolutely nothing we do matters at all, because it's all locked up."

"Well, in some ways, Sylvia, I honestly don't know how you can think any differently? I mean, it frustrates me that you try and tell me that it's all going to change."

"But, Steven, everything changes. Life is change. Motion."

"Well, yeah, I'm not saying there's no motion. I just happen to believe that the current motion is moving right toward one vast, all-encompassing set of explosions."

"Oh, Steven," Linda sighed.

"What? How not! You saw that movie the other week. What was it? *The Day After*."

"But, Steven, that was a melodramatic enactment . . ."

"It wasn't the movie, Linda. It was the panel discussion afterward that convinced me it's all over. You heard it! That was no movie! Those guys were for real! They run the fucking country! Or assholes just like them—worse! You heard Kissinger *say*, liar though he is, he let it slip that this government will consider first-strike use of nuclear weapons. Come on! What about that quote from the Defense Department you recited half an hour ago? And when I saw those guys sitting around the table, those parochial, simple-minded con men, and realized they have their finger on the trigger. Hey! Kiss it good-bye."

"But, Steven," Sylvia began as she watched him look at his glass again, then at hers and Linda's, still untouched, and reach to his pocket for his cigarettes with a glance at the bottle of wine. Sylvia looked at Linda, "Should we have some coffee?"

"Oh!" Linda answered, "I forgot about the tea!" She started to get up from the table.

"I'll get it, Linda," Sylvia said, reaching a hand to stop her and getting up from her chair. "Where is it?"

"Well . . . it's on the stove. I hope it hasn't all simmered away to nothing."

Sylvia left the room, walking down the hall to the kitchen, wondering what could be said to Steven's argument. The answer to her, of course, was NEWS, but . . . Well though, if the conference did pass New York's proposal to involve men . . . But, no. God! What was she thinking? Anybody who thinks we're a 'bunch of Pollyana's.' Her mind flared at the thought of it. If he had any *inkling* of the kind of risk, the absolute *precision* that no drunk could ever—no, wait. No, OK. Maybe he could . . . maybe he could see if he's interested in some kind of anti-nuke group. Isn't there a Lawyers for Social Responsibility or something? She searched her mind as she found the glass tray with three china cups sitting on the kitchen table and the Pyrex teapot, still fairly full, bubbling on the stove. But would he even be open to the idea, in the state he's in now? At one time, he might have been. But now . . . She heard Linda and Steven talking quietly as she approached the dining room with the tray of tea. Entering the room, she noticed with relief that Steven's wine glass was still empty and, setting the tray on the table, she began to pour them tea.

"I was just telling Steven, Sylvia. What do you think?" Linda turned to her. "That the more people who believe that nuclear war is inevitable, the more inevitable it will become."

"Well, you know it's really hard for me to believe," Steven countered, "that it makes any fucking difference at all if I happen to believe the bombs are going to blow or not. What's Steven Walden—one person in four billion's personal opinions—have to do with any goddamn thing, really." He frowned at the steaming cup of tea Sylvia set before him.

"Maybe, Steven," Sylvia agreed as she sat down. "As long as you're just one person, in four billion. But what if you and the other billions really didn't want to see the Earth blown up and believed that you could stop it."

"But that's not the case, Sylvia. Half the other billions are just trying to keep from starving. There's not a fucking thing they can do."

"But there is, Steven! Actually, it's exactly the starving people who *are* fighting off the lying con men like Kissinger. That's what people's movements in the Third World are about. And it's not just because they don't want to be nuked. They don't want to be killed *now* just for refusing to be slaves. It's *us*, Steven, the well-fed who refuse to take power. Who sit around drugging ourselves with TV, cocaine and . . ." She stopped, looking tentatively at Linda.

"Sylvia, I don't know if that's totally true," Linda said. "There is a very *large* mass movement opposed to nuclear war in this country, and in Europe too. There are people here who believe that they can do something about . . ."

"Look," Steven interrupted. "There's some tiny percentage of politicos in every country. And then there are normal people. I personally don't think the various politicos of any country, even if you put them all together, have a chance in hell to get rid of all the nuclear weapons in the world."

"Come on, Steven," Sylvia said. "You know that's not true. That's totally ahistorical. You're just talking about your own culture. In a lot of countries most of the population is politicized and involved in developing their societies. Look at Cuba, Nicaragua. Even in Europe a lot more people than in this country care about their governments' role in foreign policy. The population of the United States is the most politically uninformed . . ."

"I don't know, Sylvia," Steven said. "I think most people are the same, whatever country they live in. They just want to get by. That's all anybody really cares about."

"OK. But there are a whole lot of people in the world who know you *can't* get by alone, in a vacuum. Or by murdering everybody who gets in your way. People are beginning to understand that, in fact the opposite is true. *Nobody* can get by—unless *everybody* gets by. That's just the way it is now. Thank god."

Steven frowned as Linda nodded her head. "I think that's true, Sylvia. I mean," she turned to Steven, "I also think it's true that . . . I mean I disagree with you, Steven, that there are just a few weirdos in the world who get involved in organizations, and then there's all the normal people. I think politics is part of all of our lives—whether we acknowledge it or not. And really we'd be better off if we *did* acknowledge it and decide what to do about it. Instead of just letting the state of the world eat us alive. Steven, don't you think you would feel better if you were doing something to try to prevent nuclear war instead of sitting around brooding about it . . . and drinking all the time."

Steven looked at her. "Linda, I don't think going to a couple meetings a week would do much for me at all. Just make me more tired than I already am from working 50 hours a week."

"Well, Steven," Sylvia began cautiously, "if you don't have the energy. I mean, if you're too exhausted to even check it out. Maybe it's your diet, or if you got more exercise, or . . ."

"Quit drinking. Right?" Steven looked at her, not pleased with the turn in the conversation. "Is that what all this is about? Is this the thing that Sylvia wanted to talk to me about?" He turned to Linda, an edge of anger growing in his voice. "And special pots of tea? And you two sitting like a couple of teetotalers. Give me a break. Really. Give me a break." He stood up from the table and, reaching for a cigarette, walked into the living room.

Sylvia looked at Linda whose eyes, filled with tears, followed Steven to the dark living room, watching him stand gloomily in front of the window staring into the street below, smoking his cigarette. She got up from her chair and went to him as Sylvia sat still at the dining room table.

Linda stood a second behind Steven, then encircled his chest in her arms, leaning her cheek against his back. "Steven. I just want you to be happy. I really do." She was crying now, and Sylvia got up quietly from the table and walked to the hall to get her coat and bag. She heard Steven murmur something, his voice gentler, as she quietly opened the front door and left the flat.

Chapter IX

Twenty-fourth Street smelled of pine and rain as Linda, Justin and Steven came out of Gladrags onto the crowded sidewalk. "Look. Singing," Justin said, standing still, wide-eyed as a group of carolers on the corner strained to the high notes of "Oh Holy Night."

"Now, let's see," Linda was counting her fingers, two large shopping bags draped from her arm, "that's Jeff, Dana, Tim, Evie, Mom, we still have Maureen, Nick, Sylvia, oh, and I really want to get those books for Justin, Steven. And what about the secretary at your office?"

"Linda, look, it's still a week until Christmas. Do we have to do everything today?"

"Steve, we can't do it next weekend, that's Christmas Eve! Mom and Dad and Aunt Maureen will all be here, I . . ." She stepped back as an anxious shopper pushed past her to get in the door of the boutique.

"Well, Lin, maybe you could take care of the rest of this during the week." Steven looked tired, strained.

"Oh, Steve, I want to do it with you. I love having you with me. Let's just go up to Children's World and look at those books for Jus. And your secretary, don't you want to pick something out for her?"

"Well, I hadn't really," Steven looked at Linda's shining eyes, she really was excited, "OK, OK, let's do those. Come on, Jus." He tugged at Justin's hand as they made their way up the street.

On the corner of Noe Street, Steven heard his name called, "Hey! Steve! Walden!" He looked down the block. Of course. Jack Sorrenson.

"How are you, Steve?" Jack smiled warmly at him, shaking his hand. Steven couldn't help but return his smile.

"Pretty good, actually, Jack. How about you?"

"Not bad. Hi, Linda," he greeted her with the same warm smile, shaking her free hand.

"So you decided to stay in town," Steven said.

"Yeah. Made up my mind about the same day I talked to you last week. I've been wanting to thank you, Steve, for the information you gave me. It certainly helps having someone set the scene for you when you're trying to find a niche."

"I thought you were staying in practice for yourself."

"Oh, I am. I mean, just in terms of getting my bearings here, a feel for who's on what side. You know."

"Have you found a place to live?" Steven asked.

"No, no. Not yet. It's a terrible time of year to look, and I can still stay with my friends from the Guild in Potrero. They've been very generous. And, it won't put them out too much, they're leaving in a couple days for a week or so. Going to spend Christmas in Florida, if you can believe it!" Jack laughed.

"Well, they sound like dedicated leftists." Steven couldn't resist.

"Oh, well, Steve. We're all still products of our privilege, I guess. Though, I have to say, it wouldn't be my choice."

"So what are you doing for Christmas, Jack?" Linda asked.

"Oh, probably just lying low, getting some work done. In fact, I'm looking forward to a little solitude and time on my hands."

Linda looked at Steven, who, sensing her thought, decided, after a moment, to go with it. "Well, Jack," he said, "why don't you at least come over to our place for Christmas dinner. We're having some family and friends over, we'd love to have you."

"Oh, Steve, I don't know, I'd hate to . . ."

"No, Jack, really, it would be fine!" Linda smiled happily. "It'll be fun. Sylvia, my cousin, will be there. You've met her, remember? At that demonstration in Berkeley."

"Oh, yeah, I do. Well . . . if . . . I wouldn't want to be intruding."

"Not at all, Jack, not at all!" Steven almost laughed at his own heartiness. He was going to play this to the hilt. If he was going to be a good boy, why not be a good boy all the way? "Come on over. What . . . around 2:00, Linda?"

"Oh, or earlier if you're free, we'll all be there. Dinner will be around 3:00 or 4:00. I'm not sure, we haven't got the turkey yet. But come over early, Jack, it would be great to see you." The warmth and sincerity in her voice managed to change Jack's expression from doubt to agreement.

"Well. Fine. Good, then. I'll come by around 2:00," he said with an appreciative nod to Linda, and clapping Steven on the shoulder, he smiled. "See you then."

Steven smiled back, still laughing inside at his own cheery manner as Jack strode on by down 24th Street. Linda gave Steven's arm a warm squeeze. "Oh, that's nice, don't you think, Steve? I hate to think of anyone being alone on Christmas." She kissed his cheek and left her hand resting on his arm as they walked on up the street.

Steven continued to smile and nod pleasantly as Linda, feeling gay and happy, pointed out things in the store windows, chattering to him and to Justin, stopping to give the carolers some change. She had always loved holidays, with a devotion to their celebration surpassed only by Rhonda's, for whom their successful enjoyment had some mysterious meaning that Steven had yet to grasp. But somehow, it seemed, it was as if the very survival of the family itself, whether its joys or its woes would dominate, hold it together, or break it apart, would be foretold by the holiday experience, manifested by the family's ability, or more specifically hers, the mother's ability to make every possible tradition, symbol, meal, the quintessential expression of the feast, to enforce the 'magic' of the season come hell or high water. And yet sometimes, too, he did feel the magic. Linda's elation was real, and it was also contagious. He couldn't help but feel touched and warmed by her excitement as she pulled him gently over to yet another shop window, wouldn't this be the perfect thing for Sylvia, wouldn't she love it, oh, and Steven, we'd better get something for Jack, if he was going to be there, let's just look for a few more things. The fact was, Steven wanted a drink. As he smiled at her again, returning her quick kiss, the desire for a whiskey and water rose more strongly in him than it had in the entire ten days since he had quit drinking. And, of course, that's part of why Linda was so happy. He had not had a drink or been in a bar since that dinner with Sylvia. He had been home every night after work, helping with the cooking, playing with Justin, helping make out Christmas cards. And he had even dragged out his old resume and begun work on rewriting it. He had decided, after one of his recent long discussions with Linda, to look for a new job. He had cut off his talks with Mark, given Drew a flat no when he had finally called last week, and had begun to seriously consider seeking a new position in an area of law that was both palatable to him, as well as less defeating, possibly teaching, or even returning to the Public Defender's office where he had at least had a consistent income. And it had been, he had to admit, an almost wonderful feeling. Just in these past ten days, he felt like he was seeing his son for the first time in months, and he hadn't seen Linda smile and laugh so much in, he couldn't remember when. Although he had agreed with her, that night they had really talked, to just quit for a week, to stop drinking for one week, when the week was up there had really been no question for him but to continue. He did feel better. Much better. He had begun to feel hope again. Hope even that he could get a different, not just different, but more fulfilling and sustaining job. In fact, after the first day or two, he'd hardly even thought of taking a drink. It had been such a change, the change itself had been an adequate distraction.

But that was not the feeling he was having now, as he held the door open for Linda at Children's World. He really wanted nothing more than to walk back down the street to Finnigan's and order a double. Why? It wasn't because they'd run into Sorrenson, he'd well gotten over his paranoia about Jack. Linda had been right, it was paranoia, and the happiness and love they had been experiencing, more than they had felt in—how long?—since Justin's birth probably, had convinced him of that. Anyhow, they'd had it all out about that the night of the mint tea. Linda just liked Jack as a friend, the same as he himself did, really. Jack was a good man, an interesting man. And hadn't he bent over backwards to be friendly to Jack, help him out, both last week when he'd called, which he'd told Linda all about, and today, he'd invited him over for Christmas dinner, for Christ's sake. But still, why did Linda's eyes, that light in them when she looked at Jack . . . No.

"This is the one, Steve." Linda was holding a children's book, showing him the pictures of women fighting fires, men changing diapers. "Don't you think it's great?"

"Oh, let me see," he answered, taking it from her and flipping through the pages, pushing it down, down, that impulse, stronger than any he had yet had to fight, that said, have one, pal, on me, what the hell, what is the truth anyhow? There is none, it doesn't matter. Shut up, shut up. Later, he told it, as the big paint brush, thick with white paint, covered over·the look on Linda's face as she had invited Jack to dinner, and it disappeared.

He smiled at the picture of a little girl flying a jumbo jet and, closing the book, looked for the price. He would have gagged when he saw the figure had he not begun to get used to it, this being their third shopping excursion. He had not argued long with Linda when she had insisted on selling the bond her father had given her for her birthday last spring to finance this Christmas occasion. He had decided to do things her way for awhile. Hadn't she been right about the drinking? The fact that he could think of a thousand more important uses for the money really did seem irrelevant. To her, for some reason, this Christmas, with her family coming up, seemed all important. And it was her money. What could he say?

"Oh, god, Steve, it's almost 1:00!" Linda said, alarmed, as she saw the clock over the counter. "We've got to get back to give the car keys to Sylvia. She's coming at 1:15!"

"Oh, that's right." He brought the book over to the counter and pulled out his wallet. "Let's go home and have some lunch. We can come back this afternoon." He took his change from the saleswoman, returning her thanks and Christmas greetings, and looked at Linda, smiling at him, elated again, almost childlike in her pleasure.

As they opened the front door of their flat and Linda set her packages on the hall table, Steven put Justin down and picked up the pile of mail on the hall floor.

"I'll start lunch, Steve. Listen for the bell, will you? Sylvia should be here in about 10 minutes." She turned to him with a smile, giving him a warm kiss, her rosy cheeks glowing from their brisk walk in the winter afternoon, cool as they brushed his face. He watched her as she stepped lightly down the hall, Justin toddling after her to the kitchen.

Walking to his desk in the corner of the dining room, he glanced through the pack of mail. Some junk, only one bill, and Christmas cards. He began to open them. A slick Santa with an embossed sleigh from his secretary, he turned it over, no note. A homey Yule scene and Xeroxed letter from Linda's old friend Cheryl, still in Michigan, three kids now, Lord. What's this one. No return address. The card looked hand made, with just a candle burning at both ends pieced together from magazine pictures. Really more ominous than cheery, how bizarre. He opened it. Letters cut up from a magazine, glued in, no signature. He turned it over, blank. He opened it again and read the odd letters' message: "Jack be nimble, Jack be quick, Jack jumped over the candlestick. And you. Merry Christmas." He turned it over again. Nothing anywhere on it but the ghoulish magazine cut-outs. He picked up the envelope, turning it over and back again. Nothing but the stamp and cancellation, and his name, typed, by a processor apparently. Who the fuck? What kind of fucking crap? He threw the card and envelope back on the desk, away from the others, he didn't even want to be touching it. What kind of sinister shit? A candle? Jack? Well, he only knew one Jack. Oh god. If there was only some goddamn whiskey in the house. Fuck. He walked away from the desk over to the window, looking down into the street. Who the fuck? It wasn't Jack himself, that's for sure. Mark. That asshole! Pissed at him for giving Drew the brush-off. For not hanging out in the Jury Room with him three nights a week like he had been. That's just the kind of adolescent, sick thing he . . . But Mark wasn't crazy. This thing, it . . . His lips twitched in repugnance, it was psychotic! But who the hell else? Hadn't he been talking to Mark about Jack? Hadn't he even told him that Jack was trying to put the make on Linda? He covered his eyes with his hand, uhh, what other bullshit had he blabbed on and on about all those drunken evenings. And what in hell was Mark going around saying about him to other people? He'd never even thought of it. Of the consequences of cutting off his association with Mark. He probably saw his turning down Drew's offer as some kind of rejection or judgment, and this was his way of getting back. The old cuckold routine. But god, it was so childish. And *weird*. Had he been so crocked all the time he couldn't even see that Mark was a lunatic? Jesus.

He walked back to the desk and, picking up the card and envelope, he smashed them into a small wad and flung it into the wastebasket by his desk. Jesus. He turned back to the window, looking again into the street, then turned back again and, walking to the wastebasket, took the crumpled wad out again, and opening the bottom drawer of his desk, stuffed it back into a back corner. Linda doesn't need to see this fucking

kind of thing. Unless . . . Mark knows something I don't know. No.
He's such an asshole. Linda always knew he was an asshole. She
couldn't stand me hanging out with him these past months, even back
in law school she could see right through him. She always thought he
was kind of a slime. A parasite. But this was so goddamn *weird*.
What's he trying to imply with that anyway? Well, it's obvious. Mark
never was too subtle. Linda's burning the candle at both ends. It's my
own fault. God, what a sick thing. Where are my cigarettes? No one
has to know about this. He searched his pockets for his lighter. I'll
just ignore that asshole completely. I'm not giving into this kind of
kid's play. I just hope he got his jollies off of this and that's the end of
it. God, what a sick bastard. What the hell else would he do? What
the hell else have I told him? What an asshole drunk I've been, he said
to himself, repeating it, standing at the window again, as just beneath
his own voice he saw himself somehow getting away from Linda for a
couple hours so he could go have a drink.

Transfixed, he didn't see Sylvia at first as she was walking, slowly,
up the sidewalk toward the house. Something about her posture, the
look on her face, brought him out of his state. She looked as if she had
lost her last friend. It didn't even look like her. But yes, that was her,
the faded jeans, the short grey wool jacket, her black full hair pushed
back from her face and her dark, clean brows drawn deep, furrowed over
her large grey eyes, so troubled now, and her mouth in a horrible frown.
He'd never really seen her so unhappy. Though 'happy' wasn't really a
word he associated with Sylvia, but alive, energetic, full of hope. But
now she looked like she'd just witnessed the crucifixion or something.
He moved away from the window as she neared the corner and, glancing
again at his desk and in the wastebasket, sure that the weird card was
gone, out of sight, he walked slowly into the living room toward the
hall. When he stopped to think about it, he never really had understood
Sylvia. She was a lesbian, and a Marxist, of sorts, and he accepted her
as that, and that's about as far as he'd ever taken it. But her private
griefs, or joys . . . He'd never even considered much whether she had
them or not. Certainly she was engaging on an intellectual level, and
he had always enjoyed that, felt that they had a pretty good
communication, or spirited one, anyway, on that level. But something
about seeing her there, just then, in that private moment of grief, gave
him pause. He realized he'd never even given a second thought to what
she must be going through now, with Claire leaving. As a matter of
fact, Claire herself never seemed exactly real to him. He'd spent so
little time with her, but even so, just who she was . . . She looked like
a woman, but she always seemed like more of, of what? A foreigner?
No. A lesbian. Or no, not exactly that. But definitely a breed apart in
some. . . A fanatic? Well, not exactly that, either, not even that real,

or common. Another Marxist, I guess, he thought, as he wondered why Sylvia hadn't rung the bell yet. Or what? A revolutionary? Maybe. He'd never really met one, actually. And though Sylvia was obviously committed to her politics, she'd always seemed more human to him, at least. She was his wife's cousin, after all. But pain, or joy, or love between her and Claire, he'd never really thought of it at all, beyond the abstract fact that they were in a 'relationship.' It had never seemed real to him. But seeing Sylvia just now, he could almost feel himself . . . The sharp ring of the front bell brought him out into the hall and to the door.

"Hi, Steven," Sylvia greeted him, with an amazingly convincing smile on her face. "Hey, you look great," she added.

"Hi, Sylvia," he answered, tense now that he'd had a glimpse beyond that smile. "Uh, can you stay for lunch?"

"Oh, no. Thanks. Claire's flight is at 3:30, and she wants to get to the airport early, in case there are any problems." She hesitated, looking at Steven and, sensing his concern for her, smiled again, though more sadly, allowing herself to share with him that much. "In fact, I think I'll just say hi to Linda and get the keys. I should have the car back by 5:30 at the latest. Is that all right?"

Linda appeared in the hall, drying her hands on a towel, and walked toward them. "Sylvia, when you come back here you're staying for dinner. I'm going to make a wonderful dinner for you," she said, coming up to her and putting her arms around her.

Sylvia returned her hug. "Oh, thanks, Lin, really, but I have a meeting at 6:00. I can't miss it. The conference starts in eight days! Can you believe it?" Her face lighted with what, Steven had to admit, was joy. "In fact at least 800 women are arriving Christmas Eve, and we're going to be running around all over the place up to the last minute. Though things are going so *well*—it amazes me! I mean I wouldn't have believed it four months ago. It's going to be great! I mean it's phenomenal . . ." To Steven, it was as if that Sylvia he had seen walking up the street minutes ago were a phantom, for she looked radiant now as she spoke. "But, Linda," she went on, "you're coming to some of the sessions, aren't you?"

Steven looked at his wife. This was the first he'd heard of this. As close as Linda was to Sylvia, she'd never gone to any of her meetings or involved herself in NEWS in any way.

"Oh, definitely," Linda answered. "I've already gone through the program you gave me and picked four or five. I haven't had a chance to talk to Steven about it." She looked at him. "Two full days of the conference are open to men, Steve, as well as a few other sessions. I'll have to show you."

Steven frowned. "Yeah. I'll look at it later." He reached in his pants pocket and pulled out the car keys. "Well, Sylvia," he asked, "are you going to be too busy to see your mother at all while she's here?"

"Oh, no. It's great, actually, she's going to come to the first day of the conference, and some of the second if she can before her flight."

Steven raised his eyebrows. "Well, you've got everyone going to this thing."

"Well, I wouldn't call Linda and Mom everyone." She laughed. "But there will be a few thousand people at some of the sessions, and a lot of them men. You might want to check it out, Steven."

"Oh, yeah, I'll look at the forms, or . . . But what about dinner on Sunday, Christmas Day? Linda said you would be coming over."

"You are, aren't you, Sylvia?" Linda gave her cousin a stern, expectant look.

"Oh yes. But I can only stay a couple hours, Linda. I've talked to Mom about it. It's all fine, really. She might come up again in the spring, or I might go down there. It's all worked out, honest. And I will be here for dinner, thank you." She looked at Steven. "I'd better go. I told Claire I'd be by at 1:30."

Steven handed her the keys. "Drive carefully."

"I will." She laughed. "See you two later." She opened the front door and, waving a last good-bye to them, ran down the porch stairs and to the car.

Pulling out onto Noe Street, she drove slowly toward Church and Market, glancing at her watch. She would be a few minutes late. A funny time to test Claire's patience about punctuality, but what did she owe Claire anymore, anyhow? Something's wrong with that attitude, I know, Sylvia told herself, but at the moment, she hadn't the heart to decide what. She let her mind run over the work she had still to complete for the conference, preparation for the sessions she would lead, and for NEWS CLAN, finalizing her part of San Francisco's role in the February Action. With the thought she felt a flutter, as if a bird had flown from her stomach to her throat. Suddenly it was all becoming so real, it *was* real, the Action, "that would turn this goddamn world around," she heard Claire's voice. And Claire? Where would she be? Still in Nicaragua? Until the end of the dry season, when threat of invasion was less severe? Or back in France? In Paris, with Vivienne, Yanick, her old friends? Or would she try to come back to the United States, to San Francisco? "If thousands of undocumented workers can cross the border at Mexico each week, can't you see it is also possible for me, Sylvie?" Claire's voice sounded again. Yes, yes, anything is possible. It wasn't so much that it was impossible for Claire to return to San Francisco, or that it was 'impossible' for she and Claire to be reunited. It was a feeling that she had, and it was a feeling that all Claire's reassurances simply did not change. It was a feeling that Claire was finished with her. Not that she didn't still love her, although when this 'feeling' had first begun to creep into Sylvia's consciousness, she had thought it was that; but no, she knew now that Claire would always love her. It's just that she was finished. Finished with their life together. Tears, again, the tears that came to her so many times in these last ten days and seemed always present, beneath the surface, even as she worked, even as . . . No, not when she worked on the conference, the Action, they did, they really did transcend this pain, but now here they were, again, the tears. I'm not finished. I still want her in my life . . . *so* much. How can she just *go*? How *can* she? Sylvia reached in her pocket for the handkerchief she knew to carry now as she waited at the red light on 16th and Church, and, as the light changed, she pulled over into the bus stop across the street and stopped the car. Leaning her head against the steering wheel she cried once again, as if to call up from deep within the ocean of tears, to get them out, once and for all. She could not see Claire like this. Not with this anguish that was half rage. *How can she just decide that she's finished when I am not!* She slammed her fists against the plastic steering wheel. Sitting back, sinking into the vinyl seat, she held her handkerchief over her eyes and, sobbing now, her mind screamed and strained against the powerlessness she felt, the injustice of it, all the values of commitment and collectivity they had shared politically, inverted, turned inside out, to this desertion. This betrayal! Her clenched fist slammed again its rage against the plastic wheel, but her tears were for the deeper pain. The knowledge that Claire had the right to go, and that she wanted to go. She wasn't betraying the Allies or NEWS. No, she truly believed she could be more effective, and inspired, working in Nicaragua. With Chela. Sylvia's face hardened, biting back the tears. Goddamn her. Goddamn them both.

She watched, unseeing, as the traffic moved through the street outside. And when she was done with that? Who knew where she'd go next. Wherever she felt the most 'effective and inspired.' Wherever her politics took her. So it's me. Sylvia shrugged. I'm the one who's inverting values, by asking her to stay. Because I happen to still be in love with her. Whose interests is that in? World justice? Or my own ego. But where the fuck is commitment in this? Why do I feel such a loyalty to her that I could *never* leave her like this. She closed her eyes. 'Loyalty.' What is it? Some kind of reactionary feeling? She threw her head back, Shit! These questions, over and over would drive her *insane*. Accept it. Just accept it. Claire's leaving. She looked at her watch. In less than two hours.

She looked back up to the street, her tears dry now. She sat a moment. Yes, Claire loved her. But it was not the same as she loved Claire. Her love for Claire still had faith, that they could change and grow, together. That that was part of being effective, and inspired. And somehow, she couldn't help feeling that, because she gave it to Claire, Claire owed her the chance. But Claire chose to move on, to other things and, though she wouldn't admit it, Sylvia knew, another lover. And as Claire saw it, Sylvia owed her that chance.

"So let her," Sylvia said aloud, her voice as hard as it was pained and starting the car again she pulled back out onto Church Street and drove up the block to find a parking place.

As she turned the key in the front door of Claire's apartment building, she refused to dwell on the hundreds of times she had made that same quick motion never guessing that today would be the last. She stood at the bottom of the stairs, searching within herself for some source of strength that would let her get through this, with love, love. The greater love. Slowly she climbed the two flights of familiar wooden stairs. Why couldn't she move beyond this awful, stagnant sadness? Life is change. Change. Change with love. The creation of love. She knocked on the door and opened it with her key.

"Sylvie?" Claire called from the little kitchen.

"Hi," Sylvia answered, looking around the always neat apartment, now perfectly clean. Claire's three bags, the same three bags she had brought from Paris almost four years ago, were stacked on the bed.

"'ey, you took your time, *hein*?" Claire said, smiling as she came out of the kitchen, her humor high, excitement in her rich brown eyes.

"I'm a little late. You still have plenty of time though," Sylvia answered. She smiled. Claire looked remarkably beautiful.

"But I 'oped we could 'ave some time 'ere," she stood close to Sylvia, "before we go." Her eyes seemed so near, deeper now, searching Sylvia's.

Quietly Sylvia put her arms around Claire as Claire held her so close it seemed that all their years of loving flowed in this moment, and the tears, again. No. Sylvia backed away. "We should go."

"Sylvie," Claire said. Her hand touched Sylvia's cheek, her eyes still so near. "It's 'ard for me, too. You 'ave to know that."

Sylvia nodded. No. She didn't know. Why go then?

"You don't believe me," Claire said with a sadness that made Sylvia believe her, yes. But understand her? Not really.

"Let's go, Claire. Please."

"*Bon.* OK." Claire's mood was somber now, the excitement gone from her eyes. She turned and walked to the bed. Together they picked up Claire's three bags, her briefcase and purse and, locking the apartment door behind them, walked down the stairs to the street.

"So, I should give the keys to Dianne at the meeting tonight?" Sylvia asked. "She's moving in tomorrow?"

"*Oui*, yes, that's what she said."

They piled the bags into the back seat of the Toyota and Sylvia, glancing at Claire's face as she walked around to the driver's seat, couldn't help but feel the sadness that now dimmed Claire's eyes, her movements slow and lifeless, when a minute ago she had been so radiant.

"Claire," Sylvia began as she pulled the car out into the grey afternoon traffic.

"Mmm."

"I know how important it is for you, and the other cadres, to be in Nicaragua now. You know, I . . . I admire all of you for taking this on now, and missing the conference, after working so hard for it." She looked at Claire a moment. "It will be an incredible experience for you to be there though." Turning back to the road ahead, she added, "Working with the Allies, and Chela. You'll learn so much, and it's really important, I know that."

Claire was silent, her head back against the car seat, motionless.

"I know," Sylvia went on, her voice gentle. "I guess I know why you have to go."

Claire turned her head, just slightly, watching Sylvia from the corner of her eye. "Do you? Really?"

Sylvia said nothing as she guided the car up the ramp to the freeway, merging into the stream of cars. They sat in silence. Sylvia shifted lanes, passing the slower traffic to the right. Finally she answered, "I don't know. I'm trying."

"You could 'ave come, too," Claire said, her voice low and her lips almost petulant—or was it simply Gallic?—Sylvia should know, but how could she tell now when Claire refused to see the obvious.

Why pretend. Say it. "Claire. Chela requested that you come there, not me."

"Oh, Sylvia! Maria, Elaine, the others decide to go there without Chela asking . . ."

"What's more important," Sylvia interrupted her, "much more important, is that you didn't ask, Claire. You didn't ask me. Or even think of it."

"Sylvia! You need someone to ask you? You can't make your own political decisions? You were not even on the ad 'oc committee that made this decision! That was not your interest. You made no effort at all to be involved in this, or delegate your work from the conference so that you *could* go. You are in the conference up to 'ere," she brought her palm sharply up to her forehead, "and that's what you want! I could see that. You think I 'ave made all the choices 'ere, Sylvia, but you are not such a powerless girl, enh? You 'ave made your choices, too!"

Oh, god. Maybe she wouldn't really miss her at all, Sylvia

thought as she changed lanes again. She was such a bitch.

"Claire," Sylvia said, fighting off her anger, "it seems to me, that when people love each other, and are trying to share their lives together, they make major decisions like this a little more *collectively*, for *god's* sake! You made this decision before I even heard about the ad hoc committee's plan in the first place! How do you expect . . ."

"Look, Sylvia. Why the 'ell didn't you ever say you wanted to go with us before now? It's because you . . ."

"Because you just announced to me what you were doing and when I even *implied* that I wished you wouldn't go, you said I was 'holding you back,' being an 'egoist!'"

"Sylvie. Sylvie." Claire put her head in her hands, her long, slender fingers grasping her forehead, her temples. "Please. Don't you see? You never wanted to go there. Why should I ask you?" She raised her head. "You wanted *me* to stay *'ere!* But I wanted to go there. So much! Like I wanted to come 'ere four years ago. I wanted to go. You wanted to stay. 'owever we make the decision, collectively or independently, the decision is the *same!* If we both are going to do what we want, what we feel is best for ourself, and our work in NEWS, it is the same. You stay, and I go. *C'est ça.*"

"Claire, no, come on, you know that's not right!" Sylvia was crying now. "I don't know about going, or staying, or what I would have done! I know I didn't want to stop seeing you! I know I didn't want you to walk out of my life! I know I would have tried to find a way to work it all out, *together!* You never gave me a chance!" She reached again for her handkerchief, almost useless now and, guiding the car steadily in the middle lane of traffic, managed to blow her nose, as the tears still fell.

"Sylvie," Claire said quietly. "I thought that when we talk lass week . . ." She hesitated, studying her hands, clasped tightly on the worn leather briefcase in her lap. "'ow many 'ours we talk about this? I thought we 'ad an understanding. I am not walking out of your life. I want to be in your life always." She turned and looked at Sylvia, her eyes insistent, incredulous. "You know I love you. You told me you knew that!"

Sylvia dried her cheeks with her hand. "Do you have any Kleenex?" She kept her eyes on the road.

"*Aie, merde*, Sylvia!" Claire turned sharply back in her seat, yanking open her purse and rummaging beneath her wallet, her passport, she found a packet of Kleenex and held one out in front of her.

"Thank you." Sylvia took it and blew her nose again, dabbing at her eyes and then, looking in the rearview mirror and over her shoulder, pulled over to the right lane and the exit for the airport. They sat in silence, Claire again studying her hands as they lay on her briefcase.

Sylvia looked at her watch as they drove into the terminal. 2:35. She followed the sign for departing flights.

"I'll drop you in front of the terminal so you can check your bags. I'll meet you there after I park the car," Sylvia said. "Pan Am?"

"Yes," Claire answered.

"Who else is on this flight with you? Karen and . . ."

"No, they left this morning, the others too, from New York and Chicago. I meet them tonight in Miami. The flight to Managua is tomorrow, but first tonight we meet with Miami NEWS, well . . . I will be late. I did not take this morning's flight, you know, with the others," she looked at Sylvia, "so I could spend that time in bed with you. You loved me then, Sylvie, enh? Why now this! Again this thing! You think I am so cold. So *brutale*. Like I am never going to see you again. In fact, I will probably see you in two mons. How are you so sure I won't, enh?"

Sylvia said nothing as she pulled the Toyota over to the curb in front of the Pan Am terminal and, getting out of the car, she helped Claire pull her bags to the curb.

"I'll be back in a few minutes," she said as she turned back toward the car.

Claire stood by her bags on the curb, watching the little Toyota as it pulled away and Sylvia, shaking her head back, the black sheen of her hair tossed back as she maneuvered confidently through the stream of traffic. Drawing her lips between her teeth, an eyebrow raised, Claire stood a moment, then turned and dragged her bags to the porter.

"No, I keep this," she told him as he reached for her briefcase. "Thanks very much." She handed him two dollars and walked through the sliding doors to the line at the ticket counter. She looked in her purse—wallet, passport, ticket. Taking out the ticket she assessed the line in front of her, an older couple, a single man, a young woman, another couple. Maybe twenty minutes. She looked at the clock. 2:45. Plenty of time.

Bon. OK. *Je m'en vais.* She looked back at the sliding doors of the terminal, a security guard catching her glance and turned back again. *Pour combien de temps? Deux mois? Comme j'ai dit? Probablement, oui. Bon, je ne sais pas. Peut-être plus. Aprés l'Action? Bon, ça dépend. Si Chela, les Alliés croient que je peux faire plus là-bas, il faut rester. Mais je vais rentrer ici, un jour, c'est sur. Ma vie est ici, aussi. Oui, peut-être il pourrait être difficile de rentrer, bien sûr, mais je peux trouver le chemin, c'est sûr. Pourquoi? Pourquoi Sylvia ne comprend pas? Je veux la voir encore, travailler encore avec elle . . . mais, il faut que cela soit différent. Ou, peut-être en France.* God. I am not going there. Why am I in French now? *Il faut parler Espagnol. Necessito hablar Español.* She checked her briefcase for her Spanish textbooks.

Her hands were trembling. *Oui*, OK, I can be afraid, a little, to leave these States. These comfortable States. She moved forward with the line of passengers, looking back again at the sliding-glass doors, and then, around the terminal. She remembered, almost four years ago, arriving here, this same terminal, her first moments in this city, the excitement and the loneliness of those first days, those first weeks, walking, walking for miles, discovering San Francisco. Yes, she had felt its magic too. They had been right, those Parisians who brought tales of the beautiful and strange city in the far West, a Mecca for gays and leftists. It was, it is, a beautiful, beautiful city. But, at some point, I don't feel it to be real. She pushed a curling wisp of hair back from her cheek. I must see more of the world than this, to know what is really life, people's lives, beyond this city. She moved forward again. The younger couple just ahead of her stood at the counter now. She looked at the flight board. Flight #309. San Francisco/Miami. On time.

San Francisco. A second home. But not her home. Again she felt those first weeks, the discovery, the color, the amazing unfolding. And Sylvia. Sylvie. Those incredible first months when they felt they must have discovered the mirrors of their own minds, souls. And all that they had shared, Sylvia opening her life, her home to her, her city. The endless walks and talks, and the work, NEWS, NEWS CLAN. Of course, I will see 'er again, I cannot leave 'er. She always is a part of me.

"Ma'am? Your ticket?" The clerk waited.

"Yes, OK." Claire quickly laid her ticket on the counter, looking at the clock. 3:05.

"Smoking or nonsmoking?"

"No. No smoking."

"Window seat?"

"Yes, OK."

He processed the papers in front of him. "You can go directly to the gate. I've given you your boarding pass. Boarding is at 3:15."

Claire took the folder from his hand and, walking away from the counter, looked at the sliding-glass doors again. So. She doesn't want to say good-bye. She stood, still, not quite believing it. Biting the inside of her cheek, she stood, waiting a moment. So. OK. Turning, she walked quickly toward the entrance to the gates. Laying her briefcase and purse on the conveyor belt, she walked through the metal detector, picked up her things on the other side and headed down the corridor to her flight.

I can't believe you, Sylvia. You want to make all our life together nothing. So. If that's 'ow you want, OK. She walked into the crowded waiting area at her gate, standing at its periphery. She looked

at the clock. 3:14. She saw that defiant shake of the head, the black
sheen of hair tossed back as Sylvia had driven off a half an hour ago.
"Oh, Sylvia," she whispered aloud, quietly, tears filling her eyes now.
Yes, she wept. Her hand shading her eyes, she felt the passengers
around her stirring, moving to form a line at the boarding gate. She
felt a warm arm around her. "Claire, thank god, I thought it was too
late, the traffic . . ." Sylvia held her fast, together they stood, locked
in time, their tears one, inseparable.

"I love you," Claire whispered, "I love you, Sylvie." They moved
apart, feeling the line of passengers receding into the boarding passage,
and, with hands still clasped, they walked to the mouth of the tunnel.
"Sylvie," Claire's eyes, deep brown, now light, looked at her,
searching.

"I'll see you, Claire," Sylvia said, smiling through her tears and
nodding, yes, "I'll see you later." She let go of her hand and, leaning
forward just a moment, kissed her, and turned to leave.

Sylvia walked quickly down the corridor, her mind surprisingly
open, light. It was over. She was really gone. Time to concentrate,
finally, on the present. For her obsession, yes, it had become that,
really, since she first feared Claire might leave, an obsession with all
its questions and doubts, as if she could create some logic that would
keep Claire with her, yet knowing that only Claire and she together
could have created that logic, and Claire preferred not to. And there was
nothing Sylvia could tell herself that would say it was not Claire's
right. But why had it felt so unfair? Why did she feel so betrayed?
The question thudded, dull now, after all its flaming blaze. What
difference did it make? Claire was gone. Really gone. Out of her life.
And she had work to do. Work to do. Sylvia looked out across the
parking complex. She'd run so fast through the bumper to bumper
garage, she'd barely had time to notice where she'd left the car. Now
she headed to the left, remembering her path through the maze. The
sound of jet engines roared close overhead and, shaking her head back,
she let the tears slip from her eyes, without anger, but for the loss.

Finding Steven's car, she drove it to the exit, patiently, the crowded
garage dark in the grey afternoon. She rummaged through her purse for
a dollar bill, calmly, and drove out of the airport toward home.

Without really noticing, her mind surprisingly quiet, she found
herself near Ocean Beach, as if the car had driven itself. Parking at the
end of Judah Street, she walked to the high sea wall, to the arched
tunnel that burrowed through it, and walking slowly through its
passage, she gazed ahead, held by the framed vision at the tunnel's end,
the dark beach sand meeting the ocean beyond, its crashing waves high
in the wind, as if soon the sea wall itself would be washed into its
tides. Their wild beauty embraced her heart, her eyes. Walking to

them, she moved up the beach alone.

The sky, its grey almost night in the late winter afternoon, loomed, barely visible, above the churning depth of ocean. Gulls cawed, snatching at each other as they fed in the whipping wind. Sylvia buttoned her jacket close to the neck, turning up its collar. She bent against the weather. The damp sea spray wet against her cheeks, she walked. Let the wind fly, blow through her. Let it clean the tangled snarl from her mind. Claire was gone. There were no more questions to ask. Only the grey sky and sea were with her now.

At 6:15 Sylvia stepped from the J Church, running against the yellow light to Laguna and pressing the front door buzzer of the building at its corner. She checked her bag for the copies of her report.

"Sylvia," she said to the voice from the speaker, pushing quickly against the door as it clicked. Running up the three flights, she found Rikki at the top of the stairs smoking a cigarette.

"Hasn't it started?" she asked her.

"Carol's giving her session's report, the one you typed last week. I've read it." She looked at Sylvia, a sweet comfort in her eyes. "How are you doing?"

Sylvia set her bag on the floor. Sitting on the step next to Rikki, she took a breath and, starting to speak, she shrugged and shook her head. Rikki put out her cigarette and, lifting her arm, encircled Sylvia, bringing her head to rest on her shoulder. Again the tears, that she had hoped the ocean had swallowed, that she had brightly held back as she had returned the car to Linda moments ago, fell as Rikki held her. They said nothing.

"Oh . . . Rikki." Ruth's head appeared at the opened hall door.

Sylvia leaned back against the wooden stairs as Rikki lowered her arm, holding Sylvia's waist.

"Sylvia," Ruth said stepping into the hall and closing the door behind her. She tipped her head and looked at Sylvia, who wiped her cheeks with her hand as her reddened eyes stared back up at Ruth. Ruth's kind eyes, filled with concern, rested in Sylvia's, sensing the hurt that looked back up at her, almost defiant.

"I'll ask that the security report be postponed," Ruth said, looking back at Rikki. "Carol's almost finished. We can hear the peace camp ad hoc report now, but in . . ." She looked at her watch.

Rikki nodded. "I'll be there." Ruth returned to the meeting, shutting the door behind her.

"Do you want me to take you home, Syl?" Rikki asked, taking Sylvia's hand and holding it in her lap. Sylvia sat up. "No. No, it's OK." She held Rikki's warm hand. "It's just so hard . . ." Rikki waited. "I don't know Rikki. You know, I . . . I keep thinking I'm getting past it, that I'll be OK, and then," she looked at her, still upset, "I just can't stop thinking about her and . . . and Chela. Do you think I'm crazy?"

"Oh hey, Syl, no. Listen. You're talking to the president of the jealousy committee. Give yourself a break."

"But it's not even just feeling jealous. I feel so guilty about feeling jealous . . . I don't know. She kept insisting she's coming back, but then the way she talks about Chela . . . she doesn't even hear herself. And I know her history."

"But Syl, maybe she will. Maybe she just kind of admires Chela, you know. Like a teacher or something. She really cares about you, Syl. I mean, you know I'm not Claire's greatest fan exactly, but I could see that much. Even when she's really being a bitch. You could see she really cares what you think. I mean you have a lot of power with her."

"Not anymore." Sylvia sat up straighter, running her hand through her hair. "Oh, I don't know, Rikki. Maybe she did go for purely political reasons. That's why I feel so guilty about being jealous. But we'd had so many fights lately . . ." She shrugged impatiently. "I don't know about love anymore. I just want to stop *thinking* about it." She turned to Rikki. "I mean, she's gone."

Rikki could see in Sylvia's face that it wasn't really as simple as that. "Listen, Syl, give me your reports. JoAnn or Ruth can give them. You can go across the street and have a drink or something and I'll take you home after Security . . ."

"No. No, I want to be here." She glanced at the closed door to their right. "It's better, really, Rikki."

"Well. You know, it is kind of exciting, Syl. Everything's happening. It's like a movie or something. I can hardly believe it. Oh, and you know what? The Azanian Allies are going to Amsterdam. We heard today."

"Really? They got exit visas?"

"Yeah. Somehow they came by them. And it looks like every single representative to San Francisco is really going to come. We have all their flight times now. Transportation's got it coordinated."

"Even the Filipino Allies?"

"Yeah. We just got it on the computer about an hour ago. Really, we heard from everybody today. Just like we were supposed to. Can you believe it?" Rikki looked at her, her black eyes lighting. "Syl, it's really going to be intense! I mean to meet all the Allies. And NEWS chapters from all over the world. I'm totally excited. I mean it's going to be incredible. It's going to change the world!"

Sylvia had never seen Rikki so animated. And the frequent half-smile, always ready for a dry remark, given over now to a happy certainty that lifted her heart as she listened to her.

"Even the school is working out perfectly. The sisters at St. Joan's let us start setting up this morning. All the kids left yesterday, so with the dorms there and our offices and houses, there's a place for everybody. And we've got the kitchens all stocked, even with food from the different cultures. And at least 80 percent of it was donated or else appropriated. Did you see Housing's report?"

"No, not yet."

"I'm just totally impressed. It's like everyone has become superhuman or something. It even makes me think that Security is really going to be OK, which . . ." She grinned. "Well, you know how I felt when I first got assigned as a squad leader."

Sylvia laughed, nodding.

"Freaked out!" Rikki laughed too, then, appreciation in her smile, she added, "But you really helped me with that, Syl. I'd just thought the whole thing was impossible. But the training—rigorous as it's been," she rolled her eyes, "but that and the contingency plan Ruth and JoAnn worked out really do make me feel OK. You know," she looked ahead of her, intent, with a maturity Sylvia had not seen in her before, "I really believe we can do this." She turned to Sylvia. "I really do."

They smiled at each other, and Sylvia nodded, "I do too, Rikki."

"And it's going to change the entire way we work. We really are, Sylvia—like you've always been trying to tell me, I guess—we're really going to be a *force*. Just the way everybody has come through on everything. All that work! And it's not just the work, I mean, the program—it's so thorough and organized, and the logistics. It just amazes me."

"I know," Sylvia agreed, quiet a moment, feeling so much lighter now, lifted beyond her small, dark sorrow. "It is transforming us. Because we've all been working so hard, at the peak of our ability. And in such harmony. It's giving our goals real meaning."

"Yeah," Rikki agreed, "we're so much more together internationally from working on the conferences that *already* we're doing what we wanted to happen at it. I mean not everything, but . . ."

"Well, we haven't heard all the reports, and voted, but, I know what you mean," Sylvia agreed. "It is like all our work so far is a kind of faith in our goals and the Declaration of Peoples' Sovereignty. And now we know we can trust each other. That's what's so important. Because it's out of trust that we'll create justice. And peace."

"I never thought I would really believe that, Sylvia," Rikki said. "I mean that we could. That—just so many women—could change the world." She gazed at the door beside them. "But I do, now. I really do. And that I'll *see* it. Worldwide transformation. In *our* lifetime." Rikki's eyes shone as she looked back at Sylvia, who reached to her, hugging her.

"I'm so glad you were here, Rikki." She held her close a moment, then leaned back. "Thanks." She smiled and, then, standing up, she asked, "Shall we go?"

Chapter X

Sylvia woke to the clock radio. Handel's Messiah. She lay still. Christ. Christ is born. The crescendo of voices was exquisite. A magnificence of harmony and joy. The men's deep baritone carrying, carrying as the soprano reached higher, still higher, breaking through to the height of heaven itself. For a moment she almost believed it. The magic of Christmas. The spirit of love. As if the Christmas spirit were really the expression of humanity's highest aspirations, redemption, salvation, all of the Earth alight with giving and sharing, blessed by the Most High, bringing each human soul to its most transcendent state of unity, oneness, love. For a single, unique moment she believed Christmas was real. The music stopped and a man's voice wished her a Merry Christmas, reminding her that if Santa did not bring her her favorite perfume today, tomorrow's after-Christmas sales would be a perfect time to exchange that present from . . .

She snapped off the radio and looked at the clock, 7:10, laughing at herself for her moment of sentiment. Christmas, and Christ himself, like most of the Christian world, belongs to capital. A celebration of consumerism. She rose quickly to dress. Rikki would be by in 20 minutes. And Olina was coming home! She smiled, happy, and relieved that she had been awake for ten minutes without a single thought of Claire.

At 7:30 sharp Rikki rang the bell and Sylvia ran down the hall still chewing her piece of toast. She opened the front door. "Hi, Rikki. Just one second." Turning back down the hall, Sylvia knocked on JoAnn's door and, opening the door she said to a sleepy JoAnn, "It's 7:30, Jo. Time to get up. You're shift goes at 8:15." She started to go, then stopped, turning back, "Merry Christmas!" she said, laughing, and then shutting the door softly behind her, she moved down the hall to Rikki and left the flat.

"Merry Christmas? Sylvia, are you finally having your nervous breakdown?" Rikki asked as they ran down the steps.

Sylvia laughed. "God, I hope not." She looked at the rainy sky and buttoned her jacket. "Rikki, it *is* Christmas Day, you know."

"Spare me, Sylvia. Maybe I didn't finish Hebrew School, but I didn't convert. I *am* Jewish, you know."

"No. I know, Rikki, I was just kidding," she answered as she got in the car. As Rikki choked her old Dodge into a slow start, Sylvia remembered all those Sundays, year after year, that she had attended Mass, enamored, really, by the incense, the candles, the long Latin chants, her father beside her with his worn black prayerbook reading the Latin as if it were his own native Italian.

"Or maybe the Catholic in me isn't dead yet," she said, to herself as much as to Rikki.

"Well, the Jew in me will never die, and I'm not into celebrating dead trees and shopping malls, no matter what religion they've been co-opted from."

"Well, then you're lucky I'm not inviting you to Christmas dinner at my cousin's today!" Sylvia smiled at her.

"Ugh! God! You're actually going to go? And there's so much happening today. How in hell do you think you can take the time?" Rikki asked, her eyes wide, almost an angry dark against her clear, fresh complexion.

"Oh, Rikki. You sound like Claire. As if it's so reactionary to spend two hours with my family. My mother, god, I haven't seen her in at least a year! She'll only be here three days and she's been here since yesterday, and I haven't even seen her yet! And I'm performing *all* of my tasks . . ."

"OK, OK, Syl. I don't mean to get on your case, really. I just think that Christmas is such a hype! But I can understand you're wanting to see your mother, I really can."

"Well, too, Rikki, you know. I think it really is hard for a lot of the Allies to be leaving their families at Christmas. It's not all tinsel and credit cards. It is about family, and deep spiritual beliefs . . ."

"Oh, I know, I know. I heard Ruth's speech about the dedication of the Allies, and everyone in NEWS, for coming to the conferences. But what's good is that right now, in most of the world, everything is sort of 'on hold.' So people can get away from their jobs, or leave their kids with other family, and sort of get lost in all the Christmas hubbub. For *security*, it's great!"

"Well, and it's probably a sacrifice for a lot of . . . Rikki, don't get off here!"

"Oh! Shit!" Rikki said as she swerved to the left lane of the freeway, barely missing the Daly City exit on her right and the blue Chevy pick-up on her left that honked its horn violently as it screeched around the swerving Dodge and roared on ahead.

"Good god, Rikki. Don't kill us yet! I want to see Olina," Sylvia said, clutching the front of her jacket and looking around at the traffic behind them.

"I'm sorry." Rikki laughed. "Come on, Syl. I've never had an accident yet and I've been driving a car for five years. Four of those years in New York City!"

"OK, fine, dear. But there's always a first time."

"What time is it?" Rikki asked as she slowed the car slightly.

"Ten to eight. We have plenty of time, her flight arrives at 8:20."
Sylvia looked out at the rows of little boxed houses lining the hills of
South San Francisco, trying not to think of her last trip to the airport,
with Claire.

"How long are you staying at the airport with Security?" she asked
Rikki.

"Until 6:00 tonight. There'll be two squads out here on this shift,
then three from 6:00 to 2:00 a.m. The last arrivals tonight are at 1:30.
Then three squads tomorrow from 5:00 a.m. to noon, and at that point
everyone should be in. Are you going to leave the car at St. Joan's, or
. . . where are you going to be?"

"Oh, I'll be at St. Joan's all day, and night, doing set-up and
security. Except for a few hours at Linda's for dinner. Though I'm
back-up for another transport shift at 8:00 tonight if there are any flight
changes, but we'll use Eva's car for that if it happens."

"Well, why don't you take my car to Linda's with you? I
obviously won't need it, and it's not being used, even for back-up,
besides this morning's run. Just be sure and put some water in the
radiator." She looked at Sylvia with mock innocence. "Do you think
everyone thinks my car is unreliable, Syl?"

"Well, it is older than you are, Rikki."

"It is *not*," Rikki answered as she pulled over to the airport exit,
and the old Dodge backfired, making them both laugh.

Sylvia and Rikki walked quickly up the escalator steps of the
Mexicana terminal, still laughing as Rikki was telling the story of her
aunt teaching her how to drive in Manhattan. They headed toward
customs, imperceptibly acknowledging Jean and Diana at their security
posts with a bag of packages in Christmas wrapping on the seat
between them, Diana dressed as a paramedic, a two-way radio on her
belt.

Sylvia checked the flight board. The plane had arrived. She felt a
surge of pleasure. It had been over three months since she had seen
Olina. She held herself back from peering through the small glass
window in the closed doors to see if she could find Olina in the crowd
of passengers that had begun to fill the customs area. She would get
through. She'll get through. She's gone too far to be stopped now.
All of her information was on mag tapes and disks, in plain view, in
her briefcase. She had an *L.A. Times* press card and a portable Apple
computer. They would believe she was a journalist. She *is* a
journalist. She'd worked on the *L.A. Times* staff for four years before
she'd moved to San Francisco with the Black Action Front, and met the
CECO cadres, and then become an Ally of NEWS. And NEWS
CLAN.

Sylvia looked up at the clock, 8:40, as Rikki lit a cigarette and

kept up her quiet banter, sensing Sylvia's edginess, keeping them cool.
Olina would have several packages, again in Christmas wrapping, to
keep the customs officials busy and her professional paraphernalia
beyond suspicion. Of course, if they had her name . . . If they had her
name, that was that. Her precautions would be useless. But she hadn't
been stopped in Mexico City; they'd heard from her on the PC just last
night. She would get through. Olina was too quick for them, too
smooth. They don't have her name. Not yet. She'll get through.

Sylvia laughed as Rikki kidded her, reminding her of the day she'd
spilled coffee on her new slacks at Goldy's and the scene they'd made,
the reaction of the two women sitting next to them. Rikki mimicked
first Sylvia, then the women. Sylvia had to laugh. 8:45. The doors to
customs opened as the first passengers came through, two older men in
suits, then a family, Sylvia glanced beyond them through the open
door before it closed. Was that Olina in the back? No. A Mexican
family came through the doors, then a single woman, blonde, tan,
sporting a large straw hat. Her boyfriend rushed to her, hugging her.
Olina would have seen Claire in Managua. She'd left Nicaragua just
three days after Claire had arrived, spending the rest of the week in
Mexico City before her flight this morning. Olina had almost stayed
herself for the peace camp preparation. She had wanted to but knew
that her past three months of work demanded that she be at the
conference. Of course she had agreed to return.

"Sylvia! There you are!" Sylvia turned, startled, as the blonde-
haired woman in the straw hat hugged her warmly, whispering in her
ear, "I have the disks. Come with us." Sylvia stood, frozen at first,
half-hugging the woman. Agents? What was this? Rikki looked on,
expressionless, alert. The woman put her arm around Sylvia's waist,
gently leading her through the crowd at the customs gate, Rikki close
behind, the boyfriend beside her. Diana stood up from her seat across
the room, watching. The woman in the straw hat took Sylvia's other
hand. "I'm so glad you could make it. I didn't expect you, really," she
said, kissing her cheek as Sylvia felt a piece of paper being pressed into
her palm and, glancing down, read, "Sylvia. This is Shelly. Go with
her. I love you. Olina." It was Olina's writing.

Shelly was talking about the fabulous beaches in Puerto Vallarta.
Sylvia looked at Diana and with a quick wink of her right eye, she
turned to Shelly. "Well, you look great! You must have had a
fantastic time." She turned behind her to Rikki. "Don't you think
Shelly looks great, Rikki?" Next to Rikki's left hand, just inches
away, there in the large-boned hand of the boyfriend, was Olina's black
leather briefcase.

"Oh, yeah, yeah!" Rikki answered with a look on her face, both
perplexed and accommodating, that made Sylvia laugh hard. They

quickened their step, as if in time to the airport's Musak blaring, "Deck the halls with boughs of holly, fa la la la la . . ."

"Jingle bell. Jingle bell," Justin sang as he bounced up and down on the living-room couch, sitting next to Rhonda. The tree standing in the corner window was sparkling with tinsel and ornaments, the lights shining dimly in the midday light, open packages and crumpled colored paper strewn beneath. Nick sat in the easy chair across the room reading the Sunday paper. "Gramma wanna play?" Justin asked Rhonda as he placed a plastic dinosaur in her lap.

"Isn't that the way, though," Rhonda mused, looking at the elaborate set of toys beneath the tree, a three-foot-long airplane—Nick's choice—a battery-operated dump truck, a rocking horse. "You give them all kinds of fancy, expensive things and they pick the strangest little nothing as their favorite. He's been just fascinated with this ugly little thing all morning." Nick made a sound of acknowledgment as Rhonda picked up the dinosaur and tickled Justin, playing with him. "Come on, Dimples. Let's go see how Mama's doing with the turkey." Rhonda folded him into her arms and, standing up from the couch, carried him out to the hall.

Linda was frowning as she took her wedding china out from the pantry cupboard. She couldn't really blame him, everyone had been drinking since the early afternoon. It *was* Christmas Eve. And it must have been at least the third time Nick had offered him a drink. But still, she had so hoped he wouldn't . . . Was it going to start all over again? Oh god. Oh no. Let it just be the holidays. But he must have drunk the rest of that fifth of scotch himself.

"Linda! What's the matter, dear? You look like you've lost your last friend!"

"Oh. Hi, Mom." Linda looked up from her china, smiling at her mother. "I'm just wondering if there are enough plates."

"Well, you have at least ten there, don't you? We're less than that. Let's see." Rhonda set Justin down and he walked over to hold Linda's leg. "There's Nick and I and you and Steve, and Maureen and Sylvia, and then this Eddie fellow that Steve and Maureen went to pick up. I have to say, I can't get over Maureen bringing some long lost fifth cousin of Louis's to the family dinner. She's never even met the boy, just talked to him on the phone last week. He's a *complete* stranger to all of us. But then, I suppose it might be interesting." Rhonda laughed. "In a way, I can't wait to see just who all this genealogy business has turned up for her. He is a Bernetti, isn't he? Didn't she say?"

"Well, Mom, I think he's a little closer than *fifth* cousin. I think she said he was Louis's uncle's grandson. Though what that makes him to her or Sylvia, besides having the same last name, I really don't know. I'm sort of looking forward to meeting him, too, though." Linda smiled with a lighter heart. "And also a friend of Steven's and mine should be arriving around 2:00."

"Oh, that's right, you mentioned that. An old law school friend of Steve's, isn't he?"

"Yes."

"So, he would be about Sylvia's age, wouldn't he? Or two, three years older? Is he married, dear?"

"Oh, Mother!"

"Linda. It's never too late," Rhonda was stern, then laughing again, "No. I suppose you're right. Sylvia's definitely into her own trip, as Gloria would say."

"Gloria?" Linda asked, confused, as she lifted Justin to his booster seat and got him a glass of juice.

"Oh, you know. The Martins' girl. Didn't you meet her when . . . Oh yes! And there was that strange phone call for Steve! About his mail or something. I forgot all about it until just the other day. Something *did* actually arrive in the mail addressed to Steve just before we left. I'd completely forgotten with all the excitement."

"What?" Linda asked, turning off the water at the sink.

"Oh, I think it's just junk mail, dear. It looked like it. You know those sales firms will hunt you down anywhere. You make the mistake of ordering a magazine or something, and get on some mailing list, and pretty soon everybody and their uncle is getting heaps of paper in the mail." Rhonda brushed the sleeve of her red morning jacket, the glint of her bracelets shining in the overhead light. "Now, what can I do to help you, Linda. I've just been lazing about all morning."

"Mother, you made the entire breakfast this morning, and you were up at 6:00 with Justin! Don't be silly. I'm just going to do these dishes and then I'll be out to have another cup of coffee with you and Dad."

"More juice, please," Justin asked.

"Well, I can get Justin his juice at least. Can't I, Dimples?" Rhonda said as she tousled Justin's blonde curls on her way to the refrigerator.

"But I still can't imagine why anything, junk mail or whatever, would be sent to Steven at your and Dad's address," Linda went on, still perplexed as she dipped a greasy bowl into the soapy water.

"Oh, well, Nick has it somewhere in his luggage. We'll give it to Steven when he gets back, just remind me." Rhonda stood back from the table, watching Justin drink his juice, then glanced at the stack of china plates. "So there will be eight of us then, dear, you have 12 plates. That's more than enough. Have you basted the turkey?"

Linda glanced at the clock on the counter. "Well, I was going to do it again at 1:00, in a few minutes. I suppose we could go ahead . . ."

"Oh, I'll take care of that, then." Rhonda opened the oven. "Oh, it's browned beautifully, Linda," she said, taking a fork from the table and poking at a thigh. "Yes, it should be ready by 3:00." She took the baster and poured the hot juices over the cooking bird. "Now, what else is there to do?"

"Nothing, really, Mom, at least not for the next hour or so." Linda placed a dripping pan in the dish drainer and emptied the sink. "I'm just going to put Justin down." She dried her hands on a towel and, lifting a yawning Justin from his chair, she carried him into his room and laid him in his crib. Rhonda stood watching them from the open bedroom door—Linda bent over her son, whispering her love to him as she gently lay his blanket over him, checking his still-dry diaper, and brushing his curls back from his sleepy eyes.

Rhonda stepped back as Linda left the crib and came back into the kitchen, quietly closing the bedroom door behind her. She turned to her mother and paused a moment, surprised and moved by the tenderness she felt from her, so rarely now, it seemed. She smiled. Rhonda patted her daughter's cheek, and then, with a quick turn toward the cupboards, said, "Now let's see, should we set the table now and have that done before . . ."

"Oh, no, Mom. " Linda leaned against the refrigerator. "Let's take a break. Let me just check the turkey again."

"I just basted it a minute ago, dear."

"Oh, well." Linda looked around the kitchen. "I think we can just let it go for awhile." She bent to pick up Justin's dinosaur from the floor as the sound of the front door opening and voices in the front hall stopped her hand—Steven. Her mind raced as she stood up, how could she possibly keep the inevitable drink tray from being served? Coffee. More coffee. "Mom, let's make another pot of coffee!"

As Linda walked quickly over to heat the kettle on the stove, Rhonda said, "Oh, here they are!" with a mock dread in her excitement, then, "What, dear? Oh, no, I'm sure Nick will want his scotch. He's so *uptight* around people he doesn't know." She watched Linda almost frantically measuring coffee grounds into the Melitta. "Are you sure you haven't had enough coffee, dear? Why don't you have a little glass of wine and relax? I'm going to. And I'm sure Steven will have a drink. Come on, now," Rhonda said, taking Linda by the arm and leading her back to the hall door.

Linda frowned as her mother led her away from her coffee pot, suddenly angry, sabotaged. But she couldn't blame Rhonda, she had no idea. And she couldn't blame Steven, it *is* Christmas. Anxious, dreading the afternoon, she felt nauseous as her mother led her gayly down the hall.

"What'll you have, Ed?" Steven was asking their guest as Rhonda and Linda appeared in the doorway. Maureen was seated on the couch, happily looking on at the men standing in the middle of the living room—Steven at his most gracious and dapper, Nick standing rigid, one hand in his slacks pocket; and Ed Bernetti, not an especially large young man yet seeming to take up quite a bit of space, his answer to Steven an unnecessary and boisterous laugh.

"Oh, Ed." Steven stepped aside, nodding toward the women in the doorway as Nick and Ed turned around. "Meet more of the family. Maureen's sister, Rhonda, and her daughter, Linda."

"Who happens to be your wife, Steve. And I'm the mother-in-law," Rhonda smiled with her own charm, extending a hand to Ed as she walked forward. "Now is it Ed or Eddie?"

"Ed to you," Ed answered with another loud laugh and a shake of Rhonda's hand as Linda seconded her mother, "How do you do, Ed," and Rhonda stepped back, a little startled, glancing at Maureen who still sat watching her family dreamily, pleased with herself. Steven caught Linda's eye as he stood behind Ed and, expressionless, they exchanged an inaudible 'egad!'

"So, uh, what . . ." Steven began as Linda said quickly, "Can I get you some tea, or coffee, Ed? Anyone else?" She looked at Maureen.

"Oh, I think Ed might like something a little stronger than that," Nick said, coming alive for a moment. "How about it, Ed? Steve?"

"Sure, I'll have a drink. What'll it be, folks?" Steven asked, smiling brightly at Nick as he moved toward the dining room.

"Scotch for me, Steve," Nick answered. "Ed?"

"Do you have any Chivas Regal?" Ed turned to Steven. "On the rocks. Can't stand that rotgut stuff," he explained to Rhonda and Linda, who quietly nodded and smiled as the hefty laugh sounded again in their ears.

"I'll have a glass of wine, Steve," Rhonda called after him as she sat down on the couch next to Maureen. Nick offered Ed a chair and sat back down in his own as Linda stood nervously a moment, then, responding to Rhonda's hand patting the cushion of the couch next to her with a look of command as much as invitation, she sat down next to her mother. The five of them sat a moment in a silence so sudden and complete it took them off guard, as if they had each lost their tongue, Rhonda and Linda straining the reaches of their minds for any possible thing to say, confounded by its utter absence, as Nick cleared his throat, a sound as helpful as the tick of the brass-encased clock on the mantle, when finally Maureen roused herself from her reverie and to everyone's tremendous relief, said, "Ed lives just three blocks from Louis' old family home, on Green Street, don't you, Ed?"

"Yep."

Silence. The more persistent for its brief reprieve. Steven, though busy with the drinks 30 feet away at the corner cabinet of the dining room, felt the edgy torpor taking hold and called to Linda, "Lin, where's the ice?" though he had put the little cooler in the cabinet himself an hour ago for just this moment.

"Oh, I'll get some, Steve." She jumped up from the couch.

"Oh, no, here's some," he answered, and Linda sat back down, barely hiding her disappointment. Nick cleared his throat again.

Recovering herself finally, Rhonda asked, "So do you work here in the city, Ed?"

"Nope." Again the laugh.

Linda felt she might have to vomit and wondered if she could escape the inexplicable paralysis that seemed to grip the room to even get herself to the bathroom, as Steven rushed in with the tray of drinks and bottles, letting them rattle and clink just to fill the stifling void. "Here we go. Rhonda . . ." He handed her a glass of red wine. "And, Linda." Another glass of wine for her. She took it. Maybe Mother's right. "Maureen . . ." A glass of vermouth. And handing Nick and Ed their scotch, he and Linda exchanged another expressionless laugh—it was certainly not Chivas Regal. Picking up his glass of whiskey, Steven sat in a chair next to Ed.

"Now that's smooth," Ed offered, after a sip of his drink. "I figure, if you're going to do something. Do it right!"

Steven shifted in his chair. "So, uh, Ed. You were telling Maureen and me on the way over about your investments in, what was it? Dry goods?"

"Oh, now, if you're looking for a tip on the stock market, I'm not your man."

Steven sat back. Nick clinked the ice in his glass in time with the clock, and Maureen began to look troubled. "Oh, I don't think Steven's thinking of investing, Ed. Are you, Steven?"

"Well, no, I . . . you . . . you were just in the middle of a story when we came in the house. About your success, uh . . ." Steven gave up, taking a long sip of his drink.

"Yes, Ed, what were you telling us about? Real estate, wasn't it? When we were talking about Louis' home on Green Street," Maureen reminded him.

"Real estate. Dry goods. I deal in both." Ed uncrossed his legs and pushed his glasses back on his nose. "All on my own, too, you know. And I'm probably the first Bernetti to make a go of it in this country."

Rhonda's mouth dropped open as the now familiar silence began to take on a new quality of tension.

Two quick short rings of the front door bell brought smiles to everyone's face, as Steven stood up, finishing off his drink, and said, "That must be Sorrenson."

"Or Sylvia?" Maureen said hopefully, longing now for her daughter and wishing, in fact, that Ed Bernetti would go home.

Rhonda forced herself to meet the still threatening silence, embarrassed to have anyone come upon them at such a socially inept moment. "Oh, I'm looking forward to seeing Sylvia. I'm not sure when I last saw her. Nick, when did we see Sylvia last?"

"Oh, uh, a few years, or, hmmm, uh. Oh, at Linda's wedding."

"No, Dad, that was eight years ago! You saw Sylvia that last spring you and Mom came up, after Justin was born, two years ago." Linda rolled her eyes, sometimes her father was just . . .

Jack Sorrenson walked in the room ahead of Steven, tall and almost athletic, just the vitality of his presence seemed to revive the fatigued family. His greying dark hair was striking against his black sweater and grey tweed jacket that must have been new acquisitions, they fit him so well. Linda fairly beamed at the sight of him, for something in his just being there brought her up, as if for air, from the stifling, sinking sensation that had been taking a deeper and tighter hold of her all day.

Steven, introducing Jack to the family, did not miss that look in Linda's eyes, a look he had hoped, these past three weeks of sobriety, that he had been imagining in the past, but it shot through him now as sharply as if she had shot him with a gun. And even Rhonda, and Maureen, had seemed to notice it, and Jack—wooing everyone with those golden-boy eyes—a darkness, thick and heavy, settled into Steven's mind . . . Jack be nimble, Jack be quick . . .

"Steve," Nick said, still standing, "I said, can you get Jack a chair?"

"Yeah. Yeah, of course," Steven recovered his poise, "here, Jack, take mine." And only Maureen, actually, heard the note of defeat in his voice, as now the family, stirred to life, all began talking at once and Steven walked alone to the back of the house to find another chair.

"Jack, would you like some tea, coffee, a drink?" Linda asked as Rhonda said, "You went to law school with Steve, didn't you?" and Nick said, "Didn't we meet at Linda and Steve's wedding?"

Jack laughed good-naturedly and, nodding politely to Linda, said, "Sure," glancing at the drink tray, "wine would be fine," and to Nick and Rhonda, "Oh, yeah, Steve and I go way back, we were at Boalt together, though, I'm afraid I missed Steve's wedding. I'd moved to New York. I believe, the year before?" He looked again at Linda.

"Oh, New York! You've been living in New York!" Rhonda said, her eyes alight as Linda handed Jack a glass of wine, smiling, and even

Ed showed a glimmer of interest.

"Well, yes, though I've just moved back here to California. And I'm glad to be back. It feels like home." He smiled warmly at them.

"So you were in New York for quite some time," Nick offered.

"Ten years, wasn't it, Jack?" Linda replied.

"Well, how did you feel about it?" Rhonda asked. "Did you find it exciting, or . . ."

"Oh, that town can eat you alive," Ed announced.

Jack laughed again, his laugh as pleasant as Ed's was not. "Well, I think people there are actually a little more friendly, or human, than their reputation might lead you to believe. And," he looked at Rhonda, his own eyes alight as well, "it is exciting! There are people, thousands and thousands, from all over the world, every nationality, religion, culture, all there in the buildings and streets of 24 square miles! Surviving. Together. It's amazing! You know you hear New York is so violent, rampant crime, berserk murders or whatever. But there's something really heartening, inspiring even, that for the most part, all those diverse people are living together there."

"You know, I had that same sense when I was there, a few years ago," Maureen said, intrigued by Jack now. "The density of the population was almost overwhelming at first, but the diversity so exciting. I remember my first ride on the subway." She laughed.

Jack returned her smile. "Were you visiting friends there?"

"Oh no, I have no family or friends there. I had gone to visit the United Nations."

"Maureen's been involved with an organization on U.N. Reform, or, what is it, Maureen?" Linda asked, looking at the hall door. Where was Steven?

"Yes, the Campaign," Maureen answered. "It's based on the idea that if the U.N. had more power in international politics that, well, that that would be a step toward world peace."

Jack sat forward in his chair. "Really? That's an organization in San Francisco?"

"No, well, yes, they have a chapter here, but I live in Los Angeles, I work with them there."

"Why, that's marvelous! I . . . well, I'm very interested in international law myself." Jack smiled, almost shyly Linda thought as she felt a growing irritation that she was going to have to leave the conversation and go look for Steven. Was he avoiding Jack? Starting that insane jealousy again, he'd only had one drink. "Excuse me," she said as she slipped around the coffee table and between Jack's and Ed's chairs to the door.

"Is that what you were practicing, uh, is that the area you were working in in New York?" Nick asked.

"Oh, no. I'm a criminal lawyer. Like Steve." Jack looked over his shoulder. Where was Steven? Then back to Nick. "But I've done a lot of reading and research on my own in the area, and especially recently in regard to U.S. policy in Central America and the Caribbean which, most people don't realize, is totally illegal."

Nick cleared his throat as Maureen sat forward slightly and Rhonda looked on, unsure, yet interested. Ed yawned loudly.

"Yes, there's a woman in our organization in Los Angeles who has traveled in Nicaragua," Maureen said, "and, Guatemala, I believe it was. But she actually lived in Nicaragua for several years. In fact, her husband was in the foreign service, the American Embassy in Nicaragua, while Somoza was still in power."

"Who, now?" Rhonda asked.

"Somoza. The president of Nicaragua before the Communists took over," Nick answered. "They kicked him out, finally shot him down in Panama."

"Well, Nick," Maureen clarified, "he was more of a dictator than a president. He and his family owned nearly the entire resources of the country and faithfully handed them over to U.S. business leaders, while literally half the children in the country died of disease or starvation before the age of two."

"Yes, that's true," Jack nodded.

"But as I was saying, Nick, this woman, Velma, was so . . . horrified, just shaken to the core, really, by the atrocities she witnessed under the Somoza regime. And our government actually promoting the tragic injustice to the people there. Well in the end, she divorced her husband. It changed her entire life. It had a terrible impact on her."

"Well, Maureen," Nick stood up and walked to the drink tray, pouring himself a glass of Steven's whiskey, "you know, many wives don't really understand their husbands' work. These things are very complicated. Sometimes our leaders don't have a choice in who they may have to support in these underdeveloped countries. The governments change down there every couple months. The *point* is, in the interests of democracy, our role as leader of the free world means that we keep the Communists *out*. Wherever they're trying to take control."

"I agree with you there, Nick." Ed nodded his approval as Jack sat back in his chair—where were Steven and Linda? Rhonda looked confused.

"Nick," Maureen spoke patiently. "If you are concerned about women having simplistic attitudes, wouldn't it be your responsibility to look more closely at the complexities of the situation yourself." Nick leaned back into his chair, looking at Maureen, guarded, as Jack raised his eyebrows. Maureen went on, "What do you mean by 'free world,' Nick? Free for whom?"

"Free, well, free. You know." Nick waved his hand impatiently. "Freedom of the press. Free for democracy!"

"No, not for what. For *whom*? For the thousands, millions actually, of poor and starving people who are ruled over by military regimes? Regimes that we keep in power?"

Rhonda shifted uneasily on the couch, and Maureen sat back, calming the deepening sense of antagonism she was feeling for her brother-in-law. Where was Sylvia? She looked at her watch. It was after 2:00. Nick looked darkly into his drink.

"Well, why don't you tell us your opinion, Jack?" Rhonda asked brightly, trying to save the moment, as she poured herself another glass of wine. "Let's hear from a lawyer."

"Well." He glanced at Nick, who nodded at him—anything but more lectures from Maureen.

"It is true that, just simply in terms of the law, not to mention the moral issue," Jack smiled at Ed who was still glowering at Maureen, "that, well, in El Salvador, for example, the presence of U.S. military personnel is in violation of our *own* Constitution." Jack paused, waiting for Ed to slowly turn his attention to him.

"To be precise, it's in violation of Article I, Section 8, as well as Article IV. And our involvement in Guatemala, as well as in El Salvador, violates Section 502B of our own Foreign Assistance Act of 1961."

Jack stopped as Linda came back into the room. Both Rhonda and Maureen could see that she had been crying, though she smiled cheerfully and said, "Well, the turkey's doing fine. Dinner's at 3:00 as planned." She looked around the room. "Sylvia's not here yet?"

"Not yet," Nick answered with relief. "Where's Steve off to?"

"Oh he's . . . with Justin. Justin had a bad dream. He'll be in in a minute." She stood a moment as they looked at her. "Can I get anyone another drink?" She smiled again.

"I'll have some more of that Chivas," Ed answered. "Where are you hiding it?" He laughed.

"Oh, uh, in here." She took his glass and headed toward the dining room.

"When *is* Sylvia coming?" Rhonda asked.

"I told her to be here at 2:00," Linda called back. "It's almost 2:30. She should be here any minute," she said as she came back in the room with Ed's drink.

"Now, Sylvia is . . . your sister, Linda?" Jack asked.

"My cousin," Linda said, smiling at him. "Maureen is my mother's sister, and Sylvia's mother."

"Ahh," Jack said, nodding, things were beginning to fall into place.

"It's not like Sylvia to be late," Linda added.

"Maybe we could call her," Rhonda suggested.

"No, she told me last night she'd be over at, what was it? St. Joan's. She's working on the conference all day today," Maureen answered.

"Oh, that's right, she's a member of NEWS, isn't she?" Jack asked Linda, as Steven came back in the room with a chair and sat down quietly on the other side of Ed, leaning forward to the coffee table to pour himself a drink.

"Yes, she's been in it for a few years, since it started. Actually, I think she helped start it here," Linda answered.

"That's quite an amazing organization," Jack said.

"What do you mean?" Maureen asked.

"Oh, it's had incredible growth! I don't think there's been such a large grassroots movement since the Third International before World War II, or Marcus Garvey's international organization for African people in the '20s and '30s."

"The Rajneeshi's seem to have a pretty big international organization," Steven offered.

"Well," Jack gave Steven a knowing look, laughing, "I guess I mean of a political nature."

"The Third International what?" Rhonda asked.

"Oh," Jack answered, "the Third International—an organization of socialists, Marxists . . ."

"You mean the Soviet Bloc," Ed announced.

"No, no," Jack answered. "The Third International had its roots back in the 1850s, long before the Russian Revolution. It grew out of the First and Second Internationals—they were just renamed after each major reorganization. They were made up of labor unions, socialists and anarchists, as well as Marxists, in the United States and Europe."

"You mean there were Communists, or Socialists or whatever in this country before Russia . . ." Rhonda began.

"Oh, sure. Socialism and communism didn't originate in Russia!" Jack answered. "Marx was a German who lived in England most of his life. Communism, as Marx developed the concept, is a blend of 19th-century European economic and philosophical thought." He hesitated, glancing at Maureen, who smiled at him.

"In fact," Jack continued, "a lot of today's communists in the West believe that the Soviet Union is no longer communist at all. Although the Russian Revolution did carry out Marxist ideals originally, it's turned into almost its opposite now, a kind of state capitalism with a privileged class."

"But what happened to the Third International?" Linda asked.

"Oh, it's a long story, but, basically World War II created national antagonisms, and the antifascist front diffused a lot of the revolutionary energy. And then the Stalin revelations after the war were so disillusioning, the international socialist movement just faded away, for the most part."

"Yes," Maureen nodded at Jack. "I remember Louis talking about his uncle who had been in a very strong labor union in the '30s. He was an anarchist, I believe. And after World War II he said so many people had fallen away . . ."

"What uncle was that?" Ed demanded. "I think you're mistaken."

"But, yes." Jack leaned forward, setting his glass on the floor and he seemed suddenly so animated that Linda smiled as he spoke. "That's why I think NEWS is such an exciting organization. Like a revival of the socialist internationals, only dealing with colonialism and the oppression of women in a much more progressive . . ."

"Well, it's a shame Sylvia isn't here to hear all this praise," Steven said, reaching for another drink and, sensing Nick's discomfort, he asked, "Would anyone like anything else? Maureen? A little vermouth?"

"Oh. All right, Steven." She handed him her glass as Linda looked at her a moment. She really looks worried, Linda thought, touched for her aunt. Where the hell is Sylvia?

"But, Jack," Steven went on as he freshened everyone's drinks, "How can you feel so excited about an organization you're forbidden to participate in? It's women only, you know."

"That's not totally true, Steven, I told you last week that men are attending their conference," Linda answered. "And Sylvia told me the other night that there's going to be a proposal at the conference to start having men in the membership."

"Though not the leadership," Jack added. "And I think that's fine. Obviously they're open to having men join, and eventually move into leadership positions, but first they have to trust that men are capable of following women's leadership. Don't you think that makes sense, Steve? I mean there's no precedent for that."

"Well, that's the truth," Rhonda agreed. "I can't think of a single place in the *world* where women are calling the shots and men are doing the work."

Nick got up and walked down the hall to the bathroom, as Maureen nodded quietly at Rhonda's statement, still looking preoccupied. Where was Sylvia?

At the moment, Sylvia was sitting in a hotel room one mile from the San Francisco airport fighting against the fear that shrouded her mind, battling the sensations of failure and defeat that washed over her like waves of the sea. She looked at Shelly again, and then at her watch, 2:45. It didn't make sense. But it did . . .

Rikki and Diana seemed to believe Shelly too, when they'd left the terminal this morning. Diana had been following them, but when they arrived at Shelly's car, she joined them as Sylvia beckoned to her. And then and there Shelly gave Sylvia Olina's briefcase, taking it from her friend David's hand, and offering it to Sylvia with a pleasant, cheerful smile. And she had been talking of Olina all the way to the car in a way that Sylvia could not help but be convinced that this woman knew Olina, in fact, knew her fairly well. Though it seemed the two had just met in Mexico City four days before; apparently they had spent much of that time together.

No, Sylvia did not really doubt Shelly then. She checked the briefcase, tapes and disks, labeled again in Olina's writing, and agreed to send Rikki back with David to check on Olina's situation at customs. It would be better to have a man asking after her, a man who's only connection was that he was Shelly's boyfriend. Diana left them to return to her security post and Shelly and Sylvia sat in the car to wait.

Shelly told Sylvia, there in the car, of how she had met Olina just last Tuesday night in the lobby of her hotel. Olina had simply been walking down the street and had stopped for a moment in the hotel's gift shop to buy a newspaper, when Shelly had come into the lobby, upset, disheveled, disoriented. Shelly had been traveling in Mexico for ten days, alone, on vacation from her job as a buyer for Magnin's. She'd stayed primarily at the resort towns of Acapulco and Puerto Vallarta, and had just come to Mexico City that Tuesday morning. She had checked into the hotel and left her room for the afternoon to walk about the city. Just an hour before returning to her hotel, she had encountered a well-dressed European man in the Zocolo and had agreed to go with him for a drink. Their date had ended in attempted rape. She had escaped from his rented car, where he had managed to force her down against the seat, pawing and groping at her, ripping at her clothes, his rigid body pinning her down, thrusting at her. She had escaped only by her furious screaming, so loud that children at the other end of the back alley rushed to the car, peering in the windows, distracting him as she batted him back, jerking herself free and out the car door. She had run down the alley, running through the streets, she had finally hailed a cab and returned to her hotel, where, standing in the lobby, she had looked beside herself, as if, in another moment, she would collapse. Olina had immediately walked up to her, knowing somehow, exactly what had happened to this well-dressed, attractive young woman. She had approached her gently, suggesting she sit down a moment and, as they sat on an overstuffed couch in the hotel lobby, Olina waited, just sitting, there with the woman. It may have been 20 minutes before they spoke, but somehow, in that 20 minutes, a bond stronger than any words had been forged between the two women. "I felt like I'd known her all my life," Shelly told Sylvia, "and I hadn't spoken one word to her." Later, after Shelly had told Olina what had happened, once, twice, several times, and then Olina had left her in her room to take a long hot bath and change her clothes, they met again for a late dinner. And then the next four days they had met frequently for long walks, lunch, dinner, "and talked about everything under the sun," Shelly said. "Olina is just wonderful. I've never met anyone like her! She's helped me just . . . tremendously. The things she knows, and understands. About everything. And about sexism—a word I'd never given that much thought to really. I mean, I knew men were 'male chauvinist pigs,' but I never really knew what that meant, and besides, David is so sweet, I never thought about it, about sexism . . . as a social problem." And the more they had talked the more Shelly—obviously an open-minded, inquisitive woman beyond her primary focus on fashion and art—had become more deeply interested in the ideas, the philosophy, as she called it, of NEWS. Friday afternoon, Shelly had decided to change her evening flight for San Francisco in order to come back with Olina this morning. And the next day, yesterday, Olina had mentioned to Shelly that she was afraid she might have some trouble in customs. Shelly had seen Olina's concern grow as the day proceeded and last night she had asked Olina what she was afraid would happen. Olina had told her that she had some very important information for the conference and she was concerned that if customs detained her or held her bags, she would be too late to get it there. Shelly, knowing that hundreds of women from all over the world were going to be coming to the conference—in fact she also had decided to attend as many sessions as possible—offered to take the information through customs herself. They had debated Olina's concern for Shelly's safety, but they both realized that the chance of Shelly's being subjected to anything beyond the most perfunctory of searches was highly unlikely. Olina had agreed. And early this morning they had made their plan, that Shelly was to try and be one of the first off the plane and through customs. She would meet David and immediately hand him the briefcase and her other hand luggage, explaining to him that she had to meet another woman there and, if she were slightly delayed, to take her things to the car immediately—she had 'contraband.' David adored Shelly, and she had convinced Olina he would comply. Shelly was then to find Sylvia, having studied a photograph of her that Olina had given her on the plane, and give her the note, getting her out of the terminal as quickly as possible and turning the briefcase over to her. If Olina were not released from customs within an hour, they were to take Sylvia to an agreed-upon hotel and wait there with the briefcase until further word. Sylvia was not to contact anyone in NEWS or elsewhere until Olina was released or able to contact her herself, and they could determine what level of surveillance had been activated. Sylvia was to keep the briefcase in her possession until it was absolutely secure to transfer it to NEWS. If Olina were detained for any length of time she would, if permitted, call Sylvia at the hotel, stating phrases she had agreed upon with Shelly that would indicate the level of danger. If Olina indicated that it was likely that Sylvia and other NEWS cadres were under heavy surveillance, Sylvia should return the briefcase to Shelly who would keep it until further notice, and Sylvia should return to the conference site. In the meantime, NEWS Security would have alerted NEWS leadership that Olina was detained and security measures should be enacted as determined. Or so went Shelly's story.

It was 10:30, two hours after the plane had landed by the time David returned to the car and told them that Olina had not yet cleared customs. He had inquired about her with the airline personnel and had only been told that some passengers were being detained for questioning. Sylvia, with nothing else to go on, the briefcase in her lap, rode with them to the Marriott Hotel where Shelly paid for the room that, Sylvia noticed, had already been reserved.

Once in the room, Shelly, asking Sylvia to excuse her, stepped outside with David. After 20 or 30 minutes she returned to say that David was going back to the airport to check further on Olina and that she had needed to let him know a little more of what was going on—though she had talked to him on the phone several times from Mexico, about the rape and meeting Olina and wanting to stay on with her and fly back together—still, he had had no idea that he would be spending the day at the airport.

"Well, I imagine he's a little upset. He hasn't seen you in two weeks, you delayed your flight a day and a half, and it *is* Christmas." The distrust in Sylvia's voice was evident, though, at the same time, Shelly's story had actually moved her. It was hard not to believe. Something about it . . . it was the sense she had that Shelly *knew* Olina, and even loved her. It had been in her voice, her eyes. Olina. God. Sylvia felt sick with worry for her. For all of them. For NEWS.

"Oh, David could care less about Christmas. He's an atheist. And it was always a hideous day for him when he was growing up, full of family fights. You know. Actually I think he's beginning to enjoy this." And Shelly seemed to be enjoying it herself—the intrigue. Not exactly in a self-important way, but as if nothing nearly this exciting had happened to her in quite awhile, and that was what made Sylvia wonder. Maybe she was telling the truth. And not knowing, Sylvia could do nothing but what Shelly told her Olina wanted her to do. But why hadn't Olina written more in her note? Written the instructions herself?

"You don't believe me, do you?" Shelly asked, looking at Sylvia then, sensing her deepening distrust.

"I . . . I don't know," Sylvia answered, suddenly not sure of anything, anything at all. NEWS CLAN had been so certain that Olina would not be detained. Ellen had tapped the San Francisco Immigration's computer three days before and only four Allies, none of them U.S. citizens, had been listed as questionable. Olina Dade had not been listed. And that had been communicated to Olina that same night. Why had she suddenly decided that her pose as a journalist wouldn't work? What had happened yesterday, even if all of Shelly's story were true, to make Olina suddenly so concerned about passing through customs? Olina. Always so sure. So perfectly sure and unafraid. She had a grace and power that moved her through situations so deftly that she was gone before anyone had time to do more than admire her. It was for that that Sylvia questioned why Olina would have decided to involve Shelly in this most important of tasks. And yet, it was also for that that she could believe Shelly's story, believe in Shelly's interest and dedication to the events at hand. And hadn't Sylvia herself feared this morning, at the airport, feared that they did have Olina's name?

"I guess this is pretty strange," Shelly said finally. "The past week has just been so wild for me, I mean, I feel I've been experiencing so many changes, that this whole thing is just a matter of course. But it is weird, isn't it?" She looked at Sylvia, sincerely. "I'm sorry you don't believe me. I feel like," and she put a hand to her elegant neck, "like you think I'm going to kidnap you or something."

Sylvia sat down on the twin bed across from Shelly, still holding the leather briefcase close to her. "I do feel confused. I wasn't expecting this," she answered, looking around at the thickly draped and carpeted room, the glasses on the nightstand still wrapped in their sterile paper covers. "Why don't . . . why don't you tell me about your job? It seems like we have some time to kill."

Shelly laughed, a little nervously, smoothing the sleeve of her amber gauze jacket. "I'm sorry you don't trust me. With Olina . . . it was so quick. We were fast friends, overnight really. And, knowing that you're such a good friend of hers—she had wonderful things to say about you—I didn't stop to think how you might feel, I . . . I was just looking forward to meeting you." She gave a quick little shrug and smiled. A sincere, charming smile.

Sylvia sat motionless. Who *was* this woman? She could have been a model for her grooming and dress, with her blonde, nordic features so fetishized in this country. Yet there was something more genuinely lovely about her—an honesty—an emotional honesty and yet naiveté that left Sylvia simply unable to judge. For the first time that day she thought of Claire—not a thought—but that longing again. Possibly more than she had since Claire left, Sylvia longed for Claire. What would Claire do? What would she think?

"Well, since Olina has told me about you, a little, I mean I would love to hear more, but . . ." Shelly looked down at her hands, folded in her lap, and then back to Sylvia. "Why don't I tell you a little more about myself."

"Sure," Sylvia answered. If only Olina would call.

As Shelly unwound her tale—growing up in Baltimore, Maryland, attending a well-known art school on the East Coast, her efforts to break into the fashion industry in New York, her disillusionment and move to the West Coast—Sylvia could not help but be interested, again, by that charming honesty with which the woman spoke, and too, her life had been so radically different than Sylvia's own, and then, of course, from the events of her life came her thoughts, ideas, on art, men, work. Sylvia let the talk distract her, let herself give over to the conversation. After all, it was pure generalities, and it eased the sick tension in her heart.

At 1:00 David called to say there was still no change. The officials only continued to repeat that a few passengers were being held for questioning. Shelly ordered lunch from room service. She seemed to be enjoying herself, as if this were one more of life's grand adventures. At 2:00 Sylvia excused herself and went into the bathroom. She thought of Olina. What in god's name was happening to her? And Claire. Why wasn't she here? And NEWS. What was happening? And her mother, dear god. What was going on? Why was she stuck in this stifling, sterile room with this incomprehensible woman? Olina, what are you *doing*? But Olina, the thought of Olina, calmed her. Her grace, and power. Taking a deep breath, Sylvia splashed some cool water on her face, drying it gently and standing a few more minutes to compose herself. She picked up the briefcase from the floor and rejoined Shelly, who suddenly seemed more worried herself. She looked up at Sylvia as she walked back into the room. "You know, I'm becoming very frightened for Olina. What could they possibly be holding her so long for? She hasn't done anything illegal."

"I don't know," Sylvia answered dully. "I just hope they'll let her call eventually." She looked at the phone sitting silent, lifeless, on its stand. "Actually, if we haven't heard from her by 3:00, I think we should begin to think of some alternative plan."

"Well, she said that I should take her briefcase, because she's afraid you might be harassed by the FBI. Though I can't imagine that they would really search your home. Though some of the things she told me the FBI *has* done to political people in this country really just shocked me. I mean to all kinds of people, whether they had done anything illegal or not. But somehow. Olina . . . Even if they did question her, I just had such confidence that she'd get out of it by now. It's been hours. I'm beginning to feel this is a lot more serious than I'd thought." She looked at Sylvia, a moment of fear in her eyes. "I just pray to god she's all right." Shelly kept her silky blue eyes in Sylvia's, as if for reassurance, consolation. It seemed the morning's excitement, the spy-drama enthusiasm she'd been operating on had given way to a less naive assessment of the situation. And again Sylvia couldn't help but feel that Shelly's concern was genuine, and that it was not for herself. It was for Olina.

"When is David supposed to check back next?"

"Just as soon as he's found something out," Shelly answered helplessly. "But I'm beginning to wonder if he's ever going to find out anything. I wish he would be a little more aggressive. Maybe I should go back to the airport and try myself."

"No, you were on the flight with her, it could just complicate things. I think . . . next time David calls, if nothing's changed, tell him to say that if he's not allowed to talk to Olina he's going to get a lawyer. Then maybe they'll be more cooperative."

"That's a good idea." Shelly lay back on the bed, suddenly exhausted. She closed her eyes. Sylvia watched her, wondering if she would sleep, and if she did, would it be possible to go quickly through her bag, and would there be anything there that would indicate that Shelly was not who she said she was? But if she wasn't, then surely she wouldn't fall asleep and give Sylvia the opportunity to find out. Sylvia sat still, silent. It was impossible to tell if she was asleep or not. The minutes passed. 2:45. 2:50.

No. No in fact the whole thing didn't make any sense. Sylvia shook her head. Why was she just sitting here? Now was her chance to do something. She looked at her watch again. 2:50. But do what?

Again she looked at Shelly. Her regular breathing seemed as sleeplike as anyone's could be. Either this woman was an incredible actress, or she was just who she said she was. But then, she looked like an actress. It's impossible, Sylvia thought. Either she was waiting here in this hotel room, like a sitting duck, the briefcase in her lap, in one of the most obvious set-ups . . . or Olina's supposed warnings were true. If she left the hotel, tried to contact anyone in NEWS, she would be walking the disks, and herself, right into a dragnet. She couldn't even think of calling Linda's house, Steven had been under surveillance for months. It was beginning to seem that NEWS CLAN was hopelessly naive. Their work had not gone undetected. She shuddered. All along we've been watched. Every communication tapped and interpreted. She sat motionless, paralyzed by the thought. And they've kept their own files clean of information on us, knowing that we were intruding looking for just that. They waited for us. Waited until today, to round us all up. They were waiting for the Allies. No, no. She put her head in her hands. She couldn't believe it. They didn't know. They couldn't! Oh god. The Allies. She could see them in her mind—500 women from half the world's nations arriving here, 500 of the most revolutionary women in the world. And 700 members of NEWS from all over the North meeting together for the very first time in the history of the planet to *reclaim* the Earth and put an end to the rule of war and obsession with the power of destruction. Twelve hundred women and all their years of planning for this week, this moment . . . If they knew, if the CIA knew about NEWS CLAN, if they had taken Olina because . . . If they knew about the Action! Her heart began to race. But how could they? No! Everyone had been so perfectly careful! She brought her head up sharply, looking at the briefcase on the bed beside her. They didn't get anything from Olina, no. But then . . . there was Claire's letter. The letter that went to Steven. Maybe they had broken the code. Or somewhere, some slip . . . They *had* only waited. Waited until today. So they could link NEWS CLAN to the conference and deny that it was a legal meeting of women, so they could charge all 1,200 of them with international conspiracy while this 'Shelly' woman kept her *imprisoned* here to keep her from warning NEWS CLAN that they *knew*, that they'd taken Olina, that the whole conference would be branded as a conspiracy of terrorists and all of them, *all* of them would be taken! Oh, god, god, god. Sylvia buried her head in her arms. For the first time in many years, she wished she were dead. She sat, motionless, silent, with only the sound of Shelly's regular breathing, so much like sleep it enraged Sylvia not to know as its perfect cadence rang in her ears, filling the gaudy, absurd room.

She must have jumped a foot from her seat on the bed, flinging herself around to face the door as it noisily opened. There were voices, "Sylvia!" "Olina!" There she stood, her dark eyes bright, just as Sylvia had seen her last, her smile light and sure. Sylvia ran to her and they held each other fully a minute as David walked over to Shelly who sat up now on the bed, brushing the sleep from her face as she looked on at the two women with a curious admiration.

"Mission accomplished," David told Shelly, proud of himself as he sat down beside her. Shelly laughed, delighted, and gave him a kiss.

Olina and Sylvia, still without exchanging a word, laughing happily with joy and relief, walked over arm in arm to join David and Shelly. Olina leaned forward to give Shelly a warm hug. "Thank you, Shelly." Shelly smiled back at her with, now Sylvia was sure, love.

"So what happened?" Shelly asked.

"Well, nothing really," Olina answered, sitting down next to

Sylvia.

"*What?*" Sylvia asked.

"I'm really sorry you've all had to wait all this time. I had a feeling I'd be stopped and questioned though." She turned to Sylvia. "Yesterday morning I ran into an old friend from the *L.A. Times* at a restaurant in Mexico City. He told me that every journalist who had been in Grenada before the invasion was being held for questioning at customs in the United States. I'd suspected that, but then another journalist I'd met in Nicaragua had told me before that all that had stopped. But, my *L.A. Times* friend turned out to be right."

"But what took so *long?*"

"Well what took so long were two other passengers who the officials decided were in a drug ring. That kept them busy for *five* hours. At least that's the story I got every time I asked what the problem was. But there were a few different things going on, I think. For one, they did want to harass me and another passenger who had to wait just about as long. He'd been in El Salvador, as a journalist. And you know, they were all in totally foul moods because they have to work on Christmas. So, liberal journalists who've been in 'controversial countries,' especially if they're black, are perfect for taking that out on when they have instructions to harass anyway. It was after 2:00 before they even called me in for questioning. And you know, when they did it took exactly ten minutes. Even if I'd had the disks, it would've been illegal for them to confiscate them, but then, I really didn't think I should count on the letter of the law." Olina finished with a glance to Sylvia, "I didn't want to risk it." Then turning to Shelly, she smiled and said, "You're wonderful, Shelly, for taking this on."

"So they don't . . ." Sylvia stopped, looking intently at Olina.

Olina shook her head, knowing precisely what Sylvia wanted to know, and she smiled with the relief in Sylvia's eyes.

"And I asked them if I could use a telephone at least every 30 minutes," Olina went on. "And everytime, the same response, 'We'll be with you shortly, ma'am. Please have a seat.' I could have made a scene, but I really thought it would make things worse. You know how it is when a cop is in a bad mood."

"So, we're clear." Sylvia still studied Olina's eyes, hardly able to grasp it, so disorienting her day had been.

"Yes, Sylvia, yes!" Olina laughed, patting Sylvia's knee.

Sylvia smiled. "So we can go!" She walked to the phone. "Let me just call my cousin."

It was after 4:00 when Sylvia rang the bell at Linda and Steven's flat, her heart full of joy and excitement. Olina was still in her mind and the sight of St. Joan's as they'd come in, filled with a spirit and activity so high, and the Allies, many of them already arrived—the whole world seemed gathered together in purpose and hope.

Maureen answered the door.

"Mom." Sylvia seemed to glow as she took her mother in her arms.

"Sylvia. Dear." Maureen held her daughter, caught in her joy. She stood back. "You look so well, dear." She hugged her again. "I was so worried after you called. Linda said you'd had an accident . . ."

"Oh, it was nothing, really, nothing at all, just a bump. I just couldn't get to a phone, you know," she said quickly as they walked to the dining room, her arm around her mother's waist.

"Well, here she is!" Steven almost bellowed as they came in the door, his glass raised in greeting.

"So, you were almost one of the holiday casualties, eh?" Nick said, leaning back in his chair.

"Merry Christmas, Sylvia," Rhonda said warmly, getting up to give her niece a hug with Linda close behind to give Sylvia a stern but loving look. She hadn't believed the accident story for a minute, but she winked at her cousin as she kissed her cheek. Sylvia laughed, greeting them all happily, leaning over Nick's chair to give him a quick kiss as he barely moved, and then turning to Steven she smelled the whiskey on his breath as she kissed him. Oh, no, she thought

"And this is Ed," Steven sat back with a gesture to Ed on his right. "Your namesake, Sylvia. Ed Bernetti." Oh right, she remembered as she shook Ed's hand. Maureen had mentioned something about a relative of Dad's being here.

"And, Jack," Steven gestured lavishly again as Jack, standing by his chair, clasped Sylvia's hand with a friendly smile and said, "I believe we've met, in Berkeley."

"That's right," Sylvia said, smiling. "Nice to see you again." She sat next to her mother at the table as Linda set an empty plate in front of her. The others had all eaten and were sipping coffee and after-dinner drinks. It was clear that, except for Jack and Maureen, and possibly Linda, everyone had had a fair amount to drink. And especially—again she felt a twinge of guilt, fear—Steven. She turned to Rhonda, who was studying her, and smiled. Rhonda, so glamorous still, she hadn't aged a day it seemed.

"Well, Sylvia, you look *wonderful*, dear. Better than the last time we saw you, even. Don't you think so, Nick?" Rhonda said.

Nick wasn't listening. He had finally managed to get Ed involved in a conversation on the stock market.

Rhonda turned back to Sylvia. "So maybe there's something to this Marxism after all," she said, loud enough for Nick to hear. "It's certainly done well by you."

"Marxism?" Sylvia asked as she took the glass of wine Linda handed her.

"Well, yes, dear, Jack was telling us about your organization earlier."

"Well, then I hope you explained it isn't simply Marxist." Sylvia smiled at him.

He laughed. "Well, I tried."

"Are you still coming to the conference tomorrow, Mom?" Sylvia turned to her mother.

"Oh, yes, dear. I'm looking forward to it," Maureen answered, smiling at her daughter, watching her with quiet contentment.

"I'm going to bring her over in the morning, Sylvia," Linda told her, "though I'll be coming back here to spend the day with Mom and Dad. But, I'll be there Tuesday, and a couple of other days."

"And what about you, Steve?" Rhonda asked. "If men are allowed to attend . . ."

"I have to work," Steven cut her off. "Though I'm sure Jack here will probably be going," he said, smiling coldly at Jack, realizing that, in fact, he probably would be. He reached for the bottle of wine and filled the glasses around him.

"Well, yes. I am actually," Jack answered.

"Well, Linda, maybe I should go with you and Maureen tomorrow and stay for just awhile," Rhonda said, turning to her daughter. "Nick and Steve can watch football or whatever."

"And take care of Justin," Linda added.

"Yes. Well, they can certainly do that. Yes. I think I would really like to go. Would that be all right, Sylvia?" Rhonda straightened her back, a look of determined enthusiasm brightening her face.

"Of course, Rhonda, it would be great if you came," Sylvia assured her, amazed at the turn of events. Although the majority of the conference sessions were closed, there were a series of educational forums each day with open attendance. "Actually, tomorrow morning's forum is on Internationalism and the Nonaligned Movement of Nations. There'll be speakers from several countries . . ."

"Oh, the Nonaligned Movement. Just your cup of tea, eh, Rhonda?" Steven fairly sneered at his mother-in-law.

"Steven," Linda warned him under her breath.

"Well." Rhonda laughed nervously. "I can't say I exactly know what that is, I . . ."

Sylvia cringed to see the look of pride and enthusiasm fade from Rhonda's face as she looked down at the table, embarrassed.

"Well, of course you don't," Sylvia said quickly. "Hardly anyone in this country has ever even heard of it. I was just going to explain, I mean, even though two-thirds of the world's countries belong to it, it hardly gets any press coverage at all in this country. Nobody expects that you or anybody else should have heard of it. How could you have? Things like that don't get in the newspapers here. They don't want us to know about it."

"'They!' *They!*" Steven shot back at Sylvia as even Nick looked up, "Who is this 'they' you leftists are always blaming everything on!" Steven demanded.

Sylvia took a breath. "You're right, Steven. I should be clearer. I mean the owners of the establishment media who are in the service of a small number of families who own most of the corporate . . ."

"Oh, get off your high horse, will you, Sylvia! Between you and Jack I've had just about enough sermons for today!" Steven shouted at her, standing up from the table, and, steadying himself, he sauntered out of the room.

Linda's face was white, her eyes following Steven with a rage even Rhonda had never seen before. Jack looked at Linda with concern, a question in his eyes as she glanced at him, how could he help? Nick and Ed looked on blankly, confused by the scene, as Rhonda looked back at Sylvia who sat, her lips pressed together, cursing herself for letting him irritate her, for her role in it. Maureen took her daughter's hand, holding it in her own, as the family sat in the most difficult silence of the day.

Suddenly Sylvia stood up from the table and, as she turned toward the hall, Linda said, "Don't, Sylvia. Leave him." Sylvia turned back. Linda's eyes were serious, cold. "He's probably passed out." Linda stood and silently began clearing the remaining dishes from the table.

"Well, I guess it's about time for me to get going," Ed announced.

"Oh, I'll give you a ride home, Ed," Nick offered.

"Don't feel bad, Sylvia," Rhonda said, coming to her side. She added quietly, "He really had been drinking much too much. You know, the holidays."

Sylvia smiled at her aunt. "Thanks, Rhonda." She turned away as Rhonda moved back to the table and, looking down the hall again, she knew she had to talk to Steven, soon. He had to know, if that was what was causing him . . . The sound of Claire's voice, strong and distinct, overrode her thoughts, "It is not you and me, Sylvie, or NEWS, 'oo are 'urting Steven. It is the CIA! If we want to feel guilty, let's feel guilty for all the thousands of people 'oo 'ave been killed, tortured . . ."

As she stood, her face drawn in a deep frown, she felt her mother's arm slip around her waist. "Let's take a walk, dear. It's been so long since we've had a chance to talk together," Maureen said to her.

She smiled gratefully at her mother. "I'd love to."

"Now, Jack," Rhonda said as she saw Maureen and Sylvia leave the room, "You're not going to abandon us too, are you? Stay and have some dessert with Linda and me. We have two whole pies to ourselves." She laughed, trying to save the occasion.

"Well, if you like," Jack began.

"Yes, do, Jack," Sylvia heard Linda answer as she and her mother buttoned their jackets and left the flat with Nick and Ed behind them.

Maureen and Sylvia bid Ed a gracious good evening, Maureen promising to phone him the next time she was in the area.

"I really didn't have a chance to talk to him at all. What was he like?" Sylvia asked as she and Maureen turned the corner, walking off into the twilit evening. The cool, damp air felt like a balm to her, smelling fresh and clean.

"Don't ask," Maureen answered with a laugh. Sylvia looked at her. "Oh," Maureen went on, "I don't know what I was expecting. Or looking for. Certainly not that fellow."

"Why? Who was he?"

"Just a young man, rather self-important, pompous, nothing much to say. No one could have bored me more."

Sylvia laughed. "But what were you looking for, Mom? I mean, what did you expect?"

"Oh." Maureen smiled, both sad and amused. She looked off into the darkening sky as Sylvia walked beside her, watching her. "I suppose I was looking for something of your father. Though not . . . not as that sounds." She paused. "I was looking for family, Sylvia," Maureen said, turning to her.

Sylvia's eyes softened, deepened, as she linked her arm through her mother's and looked ahead. "I'm not enough, Mom?" she asked, the irony in her voice not hiding the doubt.

"Oh, Sylvia," Maureen answered, "of course you are, dear. I don't mean that. But you know, you have your own life. You're very busy. We don't see each other often, at all. Though I've very much enjoyed our telephone conversations these past months. I know you're making more of an effort to keep in touch, and I appreciate that, dear."

"It's not an *effort*, Mom. I like to talk with you!"

"No, yes, I can tell that. You wouldn't do it if you didn't!" Maureen laughed, certain of her daughter's ways.

Sylvia was quiet, looking at the brightly colored Christmas lights in this window, now that, shining out to the empty street as the evening moved to night. In each house she knew a family, parents, children, relatives sat at their Christmas hearth, acting out the ritual in their own particular way. Something in it, together with Maureen's—were they accusations?—irritated her. She felt resistant.

"But why does everyone have to be so attached to their *family*, as if they were the only people in the world they can relate to?" She took her arm from her mother's, as if to make her point, folding her arms as she walked. "Why do you have to dig up some obscure person with the name 'Bernetti' to find 'family'?"

"Sylvia, Louis has been dead for ten years. You left Los Angeles over 12 years ago . . ."

"But, Mom, what is it about the name 'Bernetti' that's so special?"

"Sylvia, it's not the name." Maureen was still patient, though her voice grew firm. "It has not been easy, you know, living alone these past ten years. I miss the closeness. I miss the knowing, and sharing, that people uniquely experience with family. The bonds, the common history . . ."

"But you had about as much in common with that Ed man as with a . . . a porcupine." She shrugged, "You said so."

Maureen had to laugh. "I didn't say exactly that, Sylvia." She paused. "But yes, yes," she sounded sadly tired, "my little experiment did not work. In fact, it failed miserably."

Sylvia linked her arm back through Maureen's. "But, Mom. Can't you feel closeness, and sharing, with your friends? And people you work with?"

"Yes, Sylvia, I do, but," she turned to face her, "surely you know what it is to feel a special, a unique bond with someone, a . . . completion, that, if you insist on rejecting in blood relations, you must feel with your lovers. With Claire."

Sylvia caught her breath. Not only had it been years since Maureen had even mentioned Claire's name, but what she said was true. They walked a moment in silence. It was too true. The very thing Sylvia was so impatient with in her mother she had been struggling with mightily in herself these past weeks. And Maureen felt now that she had made her point.

"Yes. I do know what you mean," Sylvia said finally. "And the fact is," she took her arm back again and ran her fingers through her thick, dark hair, pushing it back from her face, "I'm fighting against it." Her voice was determined. "Against this thing, this feeling that so much of me has to be all caught up in *one* other person. That love has to be such a narrow, *confining* thing."

"But, Sylvia, why? If you love her, if you're happy together?"

"I have to." Sylvia sounded almost desperate. Then she laughed. "Claire's gone."

"What?" Maureen asked, confused. Sylvia hadn't mentioned . . .

"She left. About a week ago. She's in Nicaragua."

"But aren't you . . ."

"No, no. It's finished." It was getting easier to say.

"Oh, I'm . . . so sorry." Maureen looked down at the sidewalk, walking slowly now as they moved in silence.

"And you know what I can't stand!" Sylvia said, tears in her voice, though whether angry or hurt, Maureen wasn't sure. "I can't stand this sense, this *reality*, that my whole life, in all this great *world*," she flung her arm from her in an arc, "my life is all hammered down," her fist clenched at the word, "wound around this one single person. As if I am incapable of feeling anything else! I mean . . . it's not like that all the time. I mean I love my friends, and Linda and you. And I'm totally involved in NEWS. But still . . . something about not being able to share it all, or *any* of it, with Claire, is so *awful*, so hard. *Why?* Sometimes it feels like it's killing me, and *why?* It's all still there, just as real, just as full without her. NEWS is still NEWS. Olina, Rikki, JoAnn are all still themselves. Why do I feel so empty sometimes?"

"But, Sylvia, it's a terrible loss . . ." Maureen's voice broke in sympathy.

"Or is it an obsession? I mean," Sylvia was calmer now, "the other day—and it's not the first time—I was leaving work, and in the street, from the back, I saw a woman and I was suddenly just sure it was Claire, and my whole heart stopped. I could hardly breathe. And then I knew, of course, it wasn't her, and I felt so hopeless, and I thought—but really, Mom—*So what?* So what if it wasn't her? Why couldn't I love that woman, whoever she really was, anyway? I mean, how can one single person of all the four billion on the planet be so all-important that I could die for her and care less about all the rest?" She paused. "There's something really sick about that. How we do that."

"Sylvia, dear. Don't be so hard on yourself. You have lost your lover. Someone very close to you, with whom you shared a very special love. My dear, that's devastating. To *every*one."

"But it shouldn't have to be!" Sylvia was insistent. "There has got to be another way to love."

"Sylvia, why do you have to be so exceptional? I don't mean to be critical, dear, but I think you'll destroy yourself with this kind of thinking." Maureen paused. "Don't you feel there is some kind of arrogance in your refusal to accept that you have been hurt? Your lover has left you and you are hurt. You are human, Sylvia, and for as long as we have been on the Earth, all the billions of us, we have mated, paired, made *one* other person more important to us than all the rest."

"But, Mom, that doesn't mean it has to always be that way! Why keep doing it if it's so horribly painful? It always ends. Always! People break up, divorce, die. Why invest all your soul and feeling, or even most of it in just one other person, or little family unit, to the exclusion of everyone else? Why can't we spread that love around?

Surely the world would be better for it." They stopped on the curb as a car rounded the corner.

"I mean, I don't think it's arrogant," Sylvia said, more quietly now, "to doubt the value of romantic love, and familial loyalty, when it seems to be a human behavior that causes so much pain. And I don't just mean when the relationships end. I really do believe that so much of the world's grief comes from this kind of self-centered expression of love, that's really a *delusion*. One other person or little group is simply *not* so infinitely important, as if all the rest are just meaningless blobs who could die tomorrow and, as long as you and your 'loved ones' are together, you don't feel a thing. And people don't. Not really. Maybe in the abstract, but—I mean, I'm speaking of myself—I feel now, how *little* I've developed my real caring, or passion, or personal love for people. People all around. Because it was all so caught up in Claire somehow, my human identity all bound up in her. And I want, I really do want to find *another way to love*."

"Sylvia, dear." Maureen took her daughter's arm and led her to a low brick wall bordering the front yard beside them. Sitting down, she said, "I can't help but feel that you simply don't want to accept the pain that you feel. You have been hurt, dear. You are human and the loss of a loved one is extremely painful. That is human. You can't escape it."

"But, Mom." Sylvia sat down next to her. "I'm sorry, but I don't think being 'human' is a state of being that's etched in stone. It changes. We create what it means to be human." Sylvia looked at her hands. "I mean, I remember not so long ago when you told me that it was not 'human' for me to be in love with a woman.

"Now, you did," Sylvia went on as Maureen began to protest. "I know it was years ago, but you told me it wasn't 'natural,' that it wasn't really love, that that's not the way humans love. And yet I knew just how very real and natural it was to *me*. And that made it *human*. Because I am human." She looked at her mother. "And if I feel now that I can love another way, and I can experience a soulful, passionate love—this 'special connection'—for not just one other person, but for *people*, all people, and not to live to protect just me and mine, but all life, the Earth . . ." She paused, gazing up at the now pitch dark sky. "I know I'm still caught up in missing Claire, as if she were the only person in the world sometimes, but . . ." She looked again at Maureen, the profile of her mother's gentle face bent close to hear her, illumined in the street lamp light. "I do believe, I really do, that this way of loving is coming to an end. It's too small. Too narrow. It isn't big enough to stop war. To keep us all alive. It's this egoistic kind of love that *causes* war. Protecting me and mine, clinging to one lover, or one family, one nation. Isn't it just as human to love many, to love all, as it is to love just one?"

Maureen was quiet a moment. Somehow, she felt, she must get through to Sylvia for, she really believed, her daughter would drive herself mad with these ideas. She was denying something that simply cannot be denied.

"Sylvia, I understand your desire to free yourself . . . to be free of dependence on another person. But I fear you are mixing abstract ideas—political ideas—with personal needs you have as one mortal body. You cannot escape, dear, no matter how much human consciousness may evolve, that you are confined to a human body. And as such you will develop dependencies in your environment . . ."

"But, Mom, is love a state of the body? Or a state of mind? I believe it's a state of consciousness and it *is* a political, social phenomenon, and it can be expanded. We can expand our consciousness—*and* our way of loving."

Maureen thought a moment. There was a beauty in what she said. Yet still, no, it was so unrealistic. Still, Maureen believed, Sylvia was rejecting personal, romantic love as an effort to reject the awful pain she felt now from the loss of her lover. "Perhaps, Sylvia, but," she paused, and turned to look at her daughter, her soft grey eyes asking Sylvia, please, to believe her. "As long as we are here, on this earth, we will form attachments, dear, emotional attachments to others. And as long as we are here, we will experience death. Surely, Sylvia, no matter how much you may believe that the human condition is subject to change, you must acknowledge that death is not. Those we have grown attached to die, leave us . . ."

"But if we weren't so attached . . ."

"We cannot express ourselves fully, develop intimacy and deep connection with hundreds of millions of people, Sylvia. As long as humankind has been in existence, we have loved deeply best with just one, two, a few others, our families. And we have lost . . . lost those loved ones. It is a sorrow as old as time, Sylvia. Part of being human. We can't change it." Maureen took Sylvia's hand and held it in her own.

Sylvia looked again at the dark night sky, clearing now, a lone star shining through the shifting mists. She said quietly, "Can't we."

Chapter XI

The tides broke again and again upon themselves, the ocean pulling back into itself as swiftly as it lay its briny froth across the sandy beach. Grey, green, blue, brown, white, the feisty sea seemed formidable to even the most intrepid surfer, and nothing could be seen, not a single sail or ship, from the shore to the horizon. The newly risen sun found the beach uninhabited, and only the random beer can or twisted shape of plastic distinguished this dawn from any other dawn in the history of the Earth. Gulls flew low, dipping to the spray, as if to reclaim their ancient home in the depths of the sea, calling loudly to their fellows and ancestors beneath.

Just a half-mile away their calls could be heard in the stone-walled courtyard of St. Joan of Arc's, as the early morning light cast a long, deep shadow from the spired bell-tower above its eastern wall. Its northern wall stood solemn and stately, just its presence implying that a convent lay on the other side, and the sound of nuns' voices in the high, sweet song of Vespers wafting from the windows above served as its proof. The southern wall, nearly buried in ivy and ficus, held a heavy wooden door that opened to the newly remodeled gymnasium that, on its other side, opened to a vine-covered archway, walled on each side of its 90-yard length by classrooms, and ending at a three-story brick building—dormitories that housed as many as 300 students, and this morning, held 500 women. Even now, though it was just past 7:00, hundreds more were arriving at the front gate in the western wall of the flag-stoned courtyard.

Women. Women in every color and cloth, their dress startling, stunning to behold, the brilliant magentas, reds and golds, the serene blues and greens, centuries of ancestral knowledge in the magnificent weavings against the now silky, then full, vibrant black and sienna hair and brown, amber, black, gold complexions. The Allies. All but 40 whose flights had yet to arrive, gathering now in the courtyard, arriving from NEWS cadres' homes in cars pulling up to the western gate, or from the dormitories at the south end of the grounds, walking in threes, fours and fives down the chilly, vine-covered corridor, their voices rich and full in Spanish, Portuguese, Chinese, Togo, Burmese, Laotian, Thai, representatives from almost every country in East and Southeast Asia, Central and South America, the Caribbean, Pacific and Indonesian islands, and Black, Native, Latin and Asian communities in North America.

And among them were their hosts—NEWS cadres from San

Francisco, New York, Chicago, Montreal, Sydney, over 55 cities in the United States, Canada and Australia, as well as from NEWS chapters in Rome, Lisbon, Stockholm, every major European city, and Kiev and Moscow, Sofia and Bucharest, the cities of Eastern Europe and Russia—representatives from throughout the North gathering together with the Allies, each one keenly alive with the marvel of this moment, filled with an energy and hope for the work that lay ahead of them these next five days.

Standing in groups in the courtyard or sitting on benches against the convent and church walls, others taking seats in the gymnasium, serving now as an auditorium lined with 1,500 chairs, many were silent, studying their book-sized packets of information, while others engaged in lively discussion, a symphony of languages, laughter, and excitement.

Among the 700 NEWS cadres present, over 300 wore bright orange bands on their left arms, and a third of these women now stood silent and alert at their security posts about the grounds of St. Joan's, from every hall and door of the dormitories and classrooms to each walkway and garden in the walled grounds, as well as in the church and noncloistered rooms of the convent itself.

Rikki stood quietly at her post to the right of the stage in the auditorium. Her dark eyes were filled with tears as she surveyed the growing number of women moving in to take seats, most sitting quietly reading. The depth of their intent, the beauty of color and light in the room, the reality of this moment so long and monumental in its coming, moved her as she had never been moved, and a smile rising from deep within her, flooding her with an unknown pleasure, broke across her face as she looked back again at the stage. Stretching full across its 80-foot breadth was an elliptical map of the world, green continents sewn into a blue sea of fabric, a gift from the Sydney chapter. Hanging on the wall to the left of the stage was the Women's International for People's Sovereignty/North, East, West, South banner, the NEWS Declaration of Purpose, and throughout the auditorium hung posters and banners in every color and language, photographs of exquisite landscapes, maps and charts delineating cultural, economic and political trends, all gifts from the Allies Headquarters and European and North American Chapters.

JoAnn and Madeleine were still checking the sound on the stage, testing it with the interpreters seated at tables along each side of the hall as Vivian, Karen and the rest of the sound crew checked each set of earphones, clearing again each sound station, asking first a Burmese, then a Korean, a Filipina Ally to test their headsets, the interpreters practicing as JoAnn read from a text at the central microphone on the stage. Jill and Carol set up the slide and film projectors as Monica activated the motorized film screen, watching it descend from its suspended position above the stage, drop its full length and then return safely to its casing.

Other cadres busied themselves in the back of the auditorium, setting up tables filled with juices, coffees, teas, and a variety of foods of which the women would breakfast before the Conference Introduction and their first sessions. The Introduction was open to the public, including men, as was the forum on the Nonaligned Movement following it. Security would be doubled at the public forums, and presentations would be in English. Closed plenary sessions of the conference would be most frequently in Spanish or English, although many Allies would give presentations in their native tongues.

As the food preparation came to completion, the women began to move toward the back of the hall for breakfast, many walking slowly, studying the displays or still reading their conference materials.

At nine o'clock over 1,200 of the Women's International for People's Sovereignty/NEWS, cadres and Allies had assembled in the auditorium, women representing over 50 countries. NEWS security stood attentive at their posts throughout the hall. Members from the public still filtered in the rear doors of the auditorium as Security checked each person's bag and jacket. Though the Allies had not requested such procedure, they had acquiesced to the concerned urging of San Francisco NEWS for such precautions.

"What on earth?" Rhonda said, as a short young woman with red curly hair asked her to raise her arms and quickly patted her down, and a taller woman Rhonda's own age asked to see her purse, scanning its contents and handing it back to her with a warm smile.

"Sylvia didn't say this kind of thing would be going on!" Rhonda said in a quite audible, indignant tone. "Sylvia Bernetti, my niece," she added pointedly to the red-haired woman.

"Oh, hush, Mom," Linda said, smiling at the security cadres as they quickly and efficiently checked her, then Maureen, and Jack.

"Oh my," Rhonda said, her hand to her heart, as they moved beyond the foyer to the now almost-full auditorium and she was caught by the intense color, the stirring images in the posters and displays, the embracing expanse of world draped on the stage ahead, and the sense of animation, expectancy and purpose in the room that could not be seen, but which she fully felt present there. Linda and Maureen stood just beside her, they too lifted, carried by the moment, as Jack stood behind them, surveying the hall, nodding, definitely impressed. He moved ahead and quickly found them four seats in the back rows, standing aside as Rhonda, Maureen and Linda filed in past him.

"I've never seen such a mixed crowd," Rhonda whispered to Maureen as they sat down. "What on earth could all these people have in common?"

"Survival, Rhonda. Peace." Maureen folded her jacket in her lap.

"Well, I suppose, but . . ."

"Sshh, Mom," Linda quieted her as Ruth approached the microphone on stage, testing it quickly, and began to speak.

"Welcome. Sisters. Brothers." The audience settled to a respectful silence as she went on, speaking slowly, deliberately, pausing between phrases. "We, in the San Francisco Chapter of NEWS are . . . very moved, and honored, by the presence here today of truly courageous and dedicated women, from throughout the world. We meet here today in a historic unity, and purpose, that we most sincerely believe can move our world, toward peace. Peace, not between wars, but *beyond war*. Peace founded on the dignity, and power, of all peoples, all individuals, living in a united world system of justice, of economic equality among nations . . .

Rikki, standing quietly watching Ruth speak, turned abruptly as Marcia touched her arm. "Rikki," she whispered.

Rikki gave her a questioning look.

"Listen, I just saw this woman—don't look now—but," Marcia lowered her voice to a barely audible whisper as an Ally seated a few feet away glanced at her, "I swear she was at a meeting, last year. She just came to one, and just now she was acting really weird when she came in. Check her out, fifth row from the back, tenth seat in, I'll tell you later." With that Marcia turned and went back to her seat.

Rikki watched her walk away, feeling perplexed and annoyed. God, that Marcia. She's so fucking paranoid, Rikki thought, this not being the first time, by any means, that Marcia had found someone 'suspicious.' Still, Rikki slowly turned her head, surveying the rear of the auditorium, counting up from the back rows, and then over—oh, that's Linda, Sylvia's cousin. What? Wait a minute, what the hell? Ten seats . . . No, she counted again. That was the sixth row. But there, just behind Linda, a young woman was leaning to the side, her long, blonde hair half-hiding her tanned face. She did look kind of familiar. What an outfit, Rikki thought. A brand new ripped pink T-shirt. Macy's punk. Check her out, what? Rikki looked back to Marcia who was pouring over her notebook, taking down every word Ruth said. She's such a jerk though, if anyone's 'suspicious' . . . Rikki felt her palms begin to sweat. Why the fuck did she tell *me* about it, and besides, she's not even supposed to be looking for infiltrators, the Q Committee's supposed to be . . . Well we're all supposed to have an eye out . . . That never did get totally clear. She rubbed her hands against the sides of her cotton pants. We thought that upping the forces to 300 would be . . . Rikki turned her head sharply as from the corner of her eye she saw Cristina in the front rows with the Allies, straining her neck around, looking toward the back of the auditorium with a strange expression on her face. What was she looking at? Rikki tried to follow her gaze. That same woman? Or . . .

A thunderous applause broke from the audience and Rikki jumped an inch. Hey, OK, she calmed herself. Let's not start imagining things. She looked back at Cristina who was sitting, perfectly calm now, eyes on Ruth.

"And we wish our Allies in Amsterdam every success," Ruth said.

Another overwhelming round of applause filled the auditorium.

Marcia's nuts, Rikki decided. I'll tell Q Committee to deal with her at the break. She turned her eyes back to Ruth.

"In introduction to the work ahead of us," Ruth continued, "one of our Allies, from the People's Republic of China, will present us with a capsulized history of our human habitation of the Earth. This brief account of our development will give us a framework with which to understand our historic relationship to the Earth's resources. Then, after a short break, NEWS members and Allies will be meeting as scheduled. Those of you who are attending the forum on the Nonaligned Movement will be meeting again, in this hall, at ten o'clock." She looked to the side of the stage, smiled, and continued, "It is my honor to introduce to you, Ming-sheng Ka."

A long, warm applause followed Ruth from the stage and greeted Ming-sheng Ka, who, taking her position behind the podium, adjusted the microphone and prepared to speak in her superb English.

"Greetings, Allies, NEWS, Friends. I am filled with joy and pride to be here today. And I appreciate the honor of presenting introductory remarks to you.

"Our history, human life on Earth, began, in its first phase, approximately 100,000 years ago. Although we refer to our present age as the 20th century, in fact, it is the 1,000th century of human history on Earth. The '20th century,' like many of today's popular concepts of life, is a European one, a concept of time that originated with European Christianity.

"But if we are to understand our full, true history as a human species on the planet Earth, we must go back 100,000 years. At that time, as most paleontologists understand, the first human beings were born on the continent of Africa.

"These first humans moved in small clans, surviving by hunting and gathering, living a nomadic existence. And slowly, these small clans traveled from the tropics of Africa throughout all the major climatic zones of the Earth. Their migration was slow, their population very small, but the remarkable adaptability of humankind allowed them to move from the tropical rain forests to the highest mountains, to the arid deserts, and even to the ice tundra of the Arctic.

239

"For as long as 90,000 years, these isolated families, these clans of human beings, moved about the Earth, adapted to their particular environments, and survived. The clan served as the essential social and economic unit, hunting and gathering as the means of survival. Isolated. Primitive. We lived for 900 centuries in the hands of nature and managed to inhabit and adapt to every region of the Earth.

"The second phase of our human history began approximately 10,000 years ago. This phase is characterized by the development of agriculture. Although it is not known precisely where this development first occurred, most historians agree that the cultivation of wheat and barley in the Near East, and corn and maize in Mexico were the first introductions of agriculture to the Earth. With these developments, family and clan groupings began to form settlements. Populations dramatically increased, and skills such as pottery, crafts, tool manufacturing, and weaving were developed.

"Through the next several thousand years, eight major centers of development were established. Each center was a source of innovation in agriculture and produced sophisticated urban civilizations. These eight centers, or 'Southern Cradles' . . . " Ming-sheng turned around to the film screen, lowered now to reflect a map of the world with the eight centers marked. Pointing to each, she went on, "were located in Southwest Asia and the Mediterranean, South and Southeast Asia, Eastern South America, the Andean Highlands, Mexico and Central America, East Asia, Central Asia, and Northeast Africa. In each of these eight regions, a variety of crops and foods were developed and advanced civilizations evolved. Complex political structures, sophisticated art and remarkable architecture were typical characteristics of these societies.

"It is clear, and many of us may find ironic to note, that all of the eight centers of civilization lie to the south of what is now the United States, the Soviet Union, and northern Europe. These northern areas," she gestured at the empty outlines on the upper portion of the map, "had no major agricultural innovation nor significant civilization during this 10,000-year phase of our history. It was not until this last millenium, beginning approximately in the year 1,500 A.D., less than 500 years ago, that civilizations began to develop in the North. It was then that European colonization and domination of the world began."

Another map of the world appeared, this one with broad areas on each continent colored in shades of red and pink.

"By the way," Ming-sheng continued, "may I note that the source for this information, including these slides, is the RAND McNALLY WORLD ATLAS, published in the United States in 1983."

Rhonda sat forward in her chair, the doubtful, closed expression on her face giving way to concern.

"Initially, Europeans did not settle in their areas of conquest," Ming-sheng continued. "They preferred, as their motto—'God, gold, and glory!'—implied, only to loot the gold and silver from Central and South America, and the silks and spices from the East. In fact, if it had not been for the absence of military technology, that is, the absence of riding animals, iron and gunpowder in the Americas and Africa, the early civilizations may well have resisted the European plunderers, as certain of the Asian civilizations were initially able to do. However, as it was, the African and American centers of civilization were destroyed by the Northerners. Many of the Central and South American people were killed by forced labor in gold and silver mines, or committed mass suicide rather than live with the loss of their civilization. As we see, the centers in Mexico and Central America, the Andean Highlands, Eastern South America, Northeast Africa . . . all were overrun by Europeans.

"By the mid-17th century the European conquerors began to settle in their areas of conquest. These settlements took two forms. One was 'Farm Colonization.' By this means, European families established villages and towns in the new areas, killing most of the native population by force or disease. In this way, Europeans eventually inhabited the whole of North America, parts of South America," Ming-sheng pointed to the darker red regions of the map, "as well as parts of Australia, Asia, and Africa.

"The second form of European settlement was 'Plantation Colonization.' This was primarily confined to the tropics. By this means, small numbers of Europeans took the land by force, enslaved the local population or imported slaves by ship, and then proceeded to extract the fruits and resources of the land. The areas of plantation colonization were Africa, the southern United States, Central America, the Caribbean Islands, and parts of Asia.

"Beyond total European occupation such as in North America, vast areas of the world were subjugated to European mixed settlement, or to European economic and military control." She turned to the map again, pointing to the lighter red and pinkish regions. "This occurred throughout the remaining Americas, most of Africa, and a large part of Asia."

Ming-sheng faced the audience again. "That is to say, except for the civilization of East Asia, all of the world's eight centers of civilization were destroyed, dismantled, occupied, or controlled by European conquest within the last 500 years. If we superimpose a map delineating the habitable lands of the world," another slide appeared on the screen, "we will see that, by the 19th century, almost all of the habitable terrain of the earth was dominated by Europeans.

"Through colonization and control of the world's people and land, the Europeans established a global economic system. They accumulated the wealth of human labor and resources throughout the world, and imported it back into their own settled areas, that is, primarily Europe itself, and what is now the United States. Through this accumulation, European societies in the Northern Hemisphere were able to devote massive sums of time and resources to scientific innovation. This brings us to the third phase of our human history on Earth." Ming-sheng paused, taking a sip of water.

"The third phase of our human experience on Earth begins with this shift from 10,000 years of agricultural development in the South, to the era of scientific development in the North. The Industrial Age. Beginning just 150 years ago.

"I think all of us are aware of the radical transformation the Industrial Age has rendered to our human existence. After all, many of us here were asleep in our beds thousands of miles away just 24 hours ago. The Industrial Age has brought with it technological development that allows the human voice to be heard at once throughout the world, the human body to fly through space, to the moon and back, the human eye to see events that are transpiring on the other side of the planet, and the human heart to be removed, and replaced.

"Though the human creature presently seems to have evolved to a scope larger than the Earth itself, this third phase of our development sees us, as a species, occupying a *smaller* portion of the Earth's surface. Our population centers are now much more concentrated than they were in our agricultural phase." Another slide appeared on the screen, a map specked with dots, dense in Europe, the eastern United States, India, China, Japan, Southeast Asia and North Africa.

"Here we see," Ming-sheng continued, "where the majority of our planet's 4 billion people reside. In less than 15 percent of the land space! Major regions of the Earth are very sparsely populated or literally empty. And currently we find very large areas of habitable land becoming even *less* populated, that is, our *growing* population is inhabiting a *smaller* area of the Earth than was inhabited by human life in the agricultural period of development.

"This intense concentration of our species has various effects, including severe air and water pollution, and other both obvious and subtle effects on our physiology and psychology.

"However, the effect of this concentration that I would like to focus on, is its political implication.

"Recalling that our first two phases of human development on the Earth were periods of expansion: First, from our origin in Africa extending out to the far reaches of the climatic zones. And second, through agricultural development, the growth of our population throughout the world. During these periods of expansion, the family, the clan, the village, fief, town, city, the city-states, and the nation-states that evolved as the political and social units of human settlement were significantly isolated from one another, and allowed to develop within their own environment and context.

"The period of European occupation, especially in the last three centuries, shattered that isolation and shattered the privacy and self-sufficiency of individual social/political units.

"Now, in this century, 100,000 years since our birth, for the first time in our existence on Earth we are not expanding on the Earth's terrain, but rather we are concentrating into urban centers—centers of communication and transportation that link us around the globe. Yes. The world *is* getting smaller. Our human world. Radio, television, computers, electronic communication systems cut through the isolation of the past, unifying us all simply by the fact of our knowledge of each other's existence. In an instant we can know, hear, see what other members of our species are doing on the other side of the world. We can no longer ignore it. Now, the action of one affects us all.

"Here we seem to have, what dialecticians might call, 'a negation of a negation.' Remember that prior to the feudal societies of our agricultural phase, the family or clan—the social unit of our first phase of development—lived in total isolation, as if they were the sole inhabitants of the Earth, with only rare encounters with clans of another region. And within their isolated existence, each clan unit was wholly interdependent. All resources were shared. Each member of the clan labored, and had control of that labor, in equality with other members of the clan. That is, each labored according to her or his ability, and each received the fruits of the clan's total labor according to his or her need.

"However, in our second phase of development, with the arrival of agricultural settlement, surpluses of foods and goods could be accumulated. Private property came into existence. And with it came political/economic systems, such as patriarchy, feudalism and capitalism, to control and manage private property in the interests of the elites of those systems. Our second phase of development *negated* the equality, and individual control over one's own labor within the community, that existed in the pre-agricultural clan of our first phase of development.

"But now in the third phase of our human history, in this, our 1,000th century, we find ourselves linked one to another, interdependent, with a physical/technological reality of evolution we cannot escape. From the socialization of labor that emerged with mass production to the interconnection of communications and transportation, industrialization has presented us with the inevitable understanding that we are all one with, and part of, the whole. The scientific innovation characterizing our third phase of development makes this a very small world, indeed. We are all, all four billion of us, one clan inhabiting the Earth. This concentrated, interconnected physical reality of our existence here now *negates* the *negation* present in the agricultural phase, negates the privacy of the elites, negates the ignorance and isolation of diverse social strata. For now, with every act of greed and aggression, the whole world watches.

"Here we have the ultimate dialectic of our evolution. Here, now, at this time, we can synthesize the seemingly opposite social characters of our first and second phases of development, and this synthesis will take on the appearance of the old—the form of pre-agricultural interdependency, that is, *collective cooperation* and *individual control* of one's own labor, while *retaining the substance* of that which negated it, that is the scientific, technological advances brought about by the era of private property.

"The 21st century A.D., if, as a species, we are to live to see it, will be characterized by this dialectical synthesis. Interdependent cooperation and individual control of our own labor will once again be our social structure. While the substance of this advanced communal structure is nothing less than the accumulated wealth of the world. The brilliant technologies developed from the resources and labor of *all* of humanity during the agricultural and industrial phases of our development will belong to *all of us*. There will be a restructuring of trade relations. Redistribution of resources and production centers. Their transfer from military weaponry to communications, transportation, food production, service technology, research and development in the arts and sciences, all in compatibility and respect for the Earth of which we were born. Political and economic institutions will be redefined on an international scale, toward the elimination of national inequities and national boundaries—this will be the activity of our third phase of human experience, as *one clan*, we survive on our Earth, and set out for the heavens beyond."

As Ming-sheng paused a moment, a tremendous silence filled the room, and then a thunderous applause.

"Our work," she continued, "this week, as we have gathered from throughout the world, in San Francisco and Amsterdam, is to continue the development of ideas, the thought, the creativity that began with our species, in Africa, over 100,000 years ago. Our work is to share our knowledge, to assess our strength and weakness, and to develop an international strategy that will lead our clan, our one-world clan, to the activity and consciousness essential to the continuation of our existence.

"If we may take a moment of silence, to meditate and compose ourselves for our purpose here."

Ming-sheng was silent as were each of the NEWS cadres and Allies while only from the back rows of the auditorium could the sound of a cough or shuffling feet be heard. As two, then three minutes passed, Rhonda turned to Maureen, then stopped as she saw her sister visibly moved, though sitting motionless, her head bowed.

"Thank you," Ming-sheng concluded, turning and walking from the stage as the women in the audience, almost as one, stood from their chairs, applauding, calling out in rich, full voices their validation and approval. Maureen rose too, and then Linda and Jack and Rhonda, as the tumult of elation took several minutes to subside.

"Goodness!" Rhonda said, and then quickly picked up her bag and waited to file out of the row of chairs as people began to leave their seats. The four of them, silent, made their way through the mingling crowd to the courtyard outside.

They stood a moment, engulfed in the stunning melange of culture, language and color about them as the Allies and NEWS cadres crowded the courtyard, talking with excitement and checking their materials and programs as they prepared for the intensive meetings that lay ahead.

"Well, I had no idea," Rhonda began, "that there was no civilization in Europe until the last few centuries. What about Rome?" she said indignantly.

"Mom, Rome is in southern Europe—the Mediterranean. She was talking about *northern* Europe, the United States and the Soviet Union," Linda corrected.

"Yes, Rhonda, she said that the Mediterranean was one of the . . ."

"Well, then northern Europe. What about London! Shakespeare!" Rhonda argued.

"Shakespeare was in the 16th century, Mom. Part of the European 'Renaissance' that occurred at the same time as their colonial expansion," Linda reminded her mother. "Northern Europe was *not* a center of civilization until very, very recently. That's what the 'Dark Ages' was all about."

"But really, Linda, she made us sound like such *villains!*"

"Not as much as she could have, really," Jack mused. "Actually, I thought she did a very admirable job of exposing the myth of 'development' . . . "

"The what?" Rhonda looked at him.

"Well, you know, the myth that all human progress is due to white people, Northerners. When it's only in the past 500 years that the North has developed, and then because Europe took over the civilizations of everyone else on Earth. By means of gunpowder, which the Chinese invented, by the way."

"Oh, Jack, not you too." Rhonda waved him off.

"Rhonda, no," Jack touched her arm, "I'm not trying to discredit our ancestors, but I do think it's important that we are all aware of our history and get over this idea that we are the rightful owners of the Earth. Or that we, as a race, 'developed' while the rest of the people in the world sat around doing nothing." Jack paused as he saw Rhonda looking off impatiently. "I think her point, Rhonda, was that everything created by human labor has to be credited to all of humanity. And belongs to all of us."

"And that has to be reflected in our social systems, internationally," Linda added.

"Or our very survival is in question," Maureen said. "You know, Rhonda, that the world will no longer stand for so much of its power and wealth being kept in the hands of so few. That's where acts of terror come from. And we can't stop it with bombs. We simply can't allow greed and profiteering to govern our world any longer. We must acknowledge . . ." She stopped as she felt her daughter's arm link hers.

"Hi. Were you here for the Introduction?" Sylvia's eyes were shining, thrilled with the excitement of the morning.

"Yes, dear, we're just discussing it." Rhonda smiled.

"This is a remarkable event, Sylvia. Extremely important," Jack said to her sincerely.

"Oh it's great that you all could come." She smiled, glancing at her watch. "Can we meet for lunch? I have to go to my session but can we meet just here, at noon?" As they nodded in agreement, she gave Maureen a quick kiss and walked across the courtyard through the door in the ivied wall.

On its other side, Rikki stood deep in conversation with Cristina, barely smiling as Sylvia winked at her on her way across the hall.

"So you didn't even see her?" Rikki asked Cristina.

"No, no, I was just looking for my son," Cristina answered. "But Marcia—I don't think I know her—I can't say if she's imagining things or not. But I don't think we should take any chances. At all. If the woman comes to this next presentation tell the Q Committee to keep an eye on her. Otherwise, have them look for her around the grounds. But if she's just here at the forum, wait and have someone talk to her at the lunch break. There's not time now." She glanced around the auditorium as it filled again. "They'll be starting in a minute."

"All right. Thanks Cristina." Rikki turned just as Linda walked by on her way to her seat.

"Rikki! Hi! Isn't this exciting?"

Rikki grinned at her. "Really. Almost too exciting."

"Oh I guess they're starting. I'll talk to you later I hope," Linda said as Rhonda motioned to her to come along.

Several hundred people were already seated though a few still arrived through the security check in the rear. A table had been set on the stage, three chairs behind its length, a microphone at each place.

As Rhonda led her family to seats closer to the front of the hall, three women walked on to the stage and took their seats at the table. A few minutes passed as the audience settled, and the Ally from Sri Lanka, sitting at the table on the stage, asked, "Is there anyone who prefers translation from English? No English?"

Several people raised their hands and interpreters from the side tables went to them, locating the appropriate head sets as some changing of seats was necessary, and then the forum began.

The Ally from Sri Lanka continued. "We welcome all of you here today. We appreciate very much your interest and concern for these important topics that bring all of us together here. This morning, we will discuss the Nonaligned Movement of Nations.

"May I take the honor to introduce to you the dear friends and Allies who are speaking here now." She gestured to the women beside her, who smiled with a bow of the head as the audience applauded. "Anna-Maria Jimenez of Havana, Cuba, Elena Rios of Buenos Aires, Argentina, and I am Galle Hambantota of Colombo, Sri Lanka."

Galle paused, surveying the audience and then the NEWS Security, 40 women standing along the side walls of the hall and six on the stage behind her. Taking a sip of water, she went on.

"To begin. Nonalignment is a worldview that grew out of the Cold War. A view that became a movement of most of the world's nations as the only hope of survival. If we look at the international conditions of that period, we can understand the forces that shaped this movement. Let me quickly call to mind some of these conditions.

"Immediately after World War II, over 20 new nations were born in Africa and Asia. A spirit of freedom and self-determination took hold in the colonies as people enslaved by 500 years of European occupation rose up in rebellion. In the following decades, many more colonial territories in the South achieved national independence.

"At the same time, socialist policies were being adopted in many nations, especially in the East. This made socialism a political/economic reality in the world, and a viable option for the newly emerging nations in the South. And in turn, it created a greater polarity between socialist states and capitalist states internationally.

"In response, the Western capitalist states developed 'neocolonialism' as a means of maintaining their control over the South. This was achieved by keeping the old colonial elites within the new nations highly rewarded for servicing the interests of the West. Because the United States had become the center of Western capital after Europe was weakened in World War II, it also became the ruler of the neocolonial empire and dominated international trade.

"But imperialism, the system of maintaining and expanding the neocolonial empire, required a vast military-industrial complex. For in order to stop the rise of socialism and keep tight control over the neocolonized nations, the Western capitalist countries—with the United States in the lead—had to devote more and more of their resources to militarization. This included elaborate military pacts such as NATO, CENTO, SEATO and the RIO treaty.

"But then that sector of the socialist camp led by the U.S.S.R. also began to dedicate more and more of its resources to militarization, responding at first to international isolation after the 1917 Revolution, and then to its tremendous losses in World War II, as well as strained relations with the West. And they developed their own military pacts such as CMEA and the Warsaw Pact.

"Meanwhile, the profits of empire continued to pour into major cities of the West, increasing their concentration of wealth and giving rise to the multinational corporations. And these corporate centers, protected by world-wide military networks, grew bolder in manipulating the neocolonized nations. Corporate control of trade, exploitative investments, and Keynesian economic policies have all served to widen the economic gap between the centers of capital and the nations of the South. For example, the annual budget of General Motors equals the sum of 29 neocolonized national budgets put together.

"And finally, the invention of the atomic bomb and nuclear weaponry, by both the Western capitalists and the Eastern socialists, posed the ultimate threat to the unarmed nations of the South, which comprise over three-quarters of the world's population.

"These are, very sketchily," Galle smiled, "the conditions that gave rise to the ideology of Nonalignment."

"In 1955, in the city of Bandung, Indonesia, there occurred, as Sukarno described it, 'the first international conference of colored peoples in the history of mankind.' National leaders from both Africa and Asia were present. John Kotelawala, the prime minister of Ceylon, expressed the position of the Bandung conference delegates in comparison to the Northern powers:

> *We have no thermonuclear bombs in our pockets, no weapons of chemical or bacteriological warfare up our sleeves, no plans for armament factories or blueprints for ever more deadly methods of genocide in our briefcases . . . Today, the salvation of the world depends not on the great powers but on the lesser countries of the world.*

"Six years later, 20 of the world's national leaders met together in Cairo. Their objective was to 'analyze international peace and security and the possible means to strengthening them.'

"Three months later, in 1961, the first official summit of the

Nonaligned Movement of Nations took place in Belgrade, Yugoslavia. Twenty-five countries participated. Leaders such as Nasser, Sukarno, Nkrumah, Nehru and Tito were present. Criteria for membership in the Movement, as adopted at this summit, were support of national liberation movements, refusal to join military pacts or blocs, and refusal to concede land for military bases to foreign powers. Resolutions made at Belgrade were to: call upon the United Nations to hold a disarmament conference; urge greater economic and commercial cooperation among all nations; and call for coexistence and for mutual support in the fight against colonialism and racism.

"These common goals were based in the understanding that unity was the surest and the only path to their survival, and even, as Kotelawala had said in Bandung, 'the survival of the Earth.' And yet, as one might imagine, there were differing analyses and motivations within this historically diverse organization. But their common goal—cooperation for survival—transcended differences. Unity was the strength and hope of the Movement. And to protect that unity, it was agreed in Belgrade to make their decisions by consensus, for consensus prevents a fatal division. Decisions are shaped through exhaustive debate, in true democratic process, that gives voice to the genuine will of the majority of its members.

"Following Belgrade, the Movement continued to have summit meetings approximately every three years, each time its membership dramatically increasing. In 1964, 47 nations met in Cairo, Egypt. In 1970, 53 nations met in Lusaka, Zambia.

"At Lusaka, the growing protest against colonialism and the arms race also produced an emphasis on economic issues. A declaration was passed calling for cooperation among Third World countries on trade and monetary questions, food and agricultural problems, sovereignty over natural resources, and exchange of technology.

"In 1973, 75 nations met in Algiers. Here the Movement's economic agreements were advanced still further, as their position against imperialism also became more strident. Indeed, this fourth summit at Algiers marked a maturity and strengthening of the Nonaligned Nations, moving even a Western journalist writing for the magazine AMERICA in September, 1973, to declare:

If the developing nations that met there can swallow their differences and adopt a cohesive approach to their common problems, it is not inconceivable that they may yet one day affect the balance of power in the world.

"In 1976, the fifth summit of the Nonaligned Movement was held in my country, Sri Lanka. It was the largest international political gathering ever held in Asia. Eighty-six nations attended, including the Palestinian Liberation Organization. The emphasis at this summit was to demand that the wealthy nations of the North engage in cooperative dialogue regarding the severe economic depletion of the South.

"In her opening address, the Prime Minister of Sri Lanka, Sirimavo Bandarnaike, refuted the charge that the North has made regarding the South—that we are a 'tyranny of the majority.' To this she replied:

> *If anything, [the Movement] has been the most powerful weapon against other tyrannies which the world, especially the Third World, has been familiar with over the last five centuries: the tyranny of poverty, the tyranny of disease and premature death, and the tyranny above all, of complete absence of any prospect of hope . . .*

"Bandarnaike pointed out that more than 100 countries, housing over half the world's population, accounted for only 14 percent of the gross global product. And she foresaw that by 1980 the per capita annual income of the poorest billion of the world's population would be only $108 a year! While the average annual income of wage earners in the industrialized countries would have increased to $4,000.

"The focus of the Sri Lanka summit was the call for a 'New International Economic Order,' as defined in a document titled *Action Program for Economic Cooperation*. It proposed that international Third World producer associations be established to 'secure just and remunerable prices' in the world market.

"As Bandarnaike stated in her remarks on the *Action Program*:

> *Our movement has lent support to, and found inspiration from, the joint action of the OPEC countries in demanding a more realistic price . . . "*

As Galle spoke, Rhonda found her mind beginning to wander. OPEC, that was the thing Nick was always ranting about, she thought, suddenly caught back, away from this tale of a world she had no idea even existed. She saw Nick's face as he'd pulled out his Mobil credit card, cursing the price of gas and moving into a monologue on jet fuel and the deterioration of the airlines almost as complicated as what this woman said now. Of course she always tuned Nick out when he went on that way, just a few obligatory 'yes, dears.' But up to now, some of this had been making sense to her, at least, if it were true. All these meetings of so many countries. What would Nick say to . . . She tried to pick up Galle's words.

"The *Action Program* called upon the North to eliminate trade barriers, reschedule existing loans and cancel the debts of the poorest countries to compensate for depleting all those nations that have 'been subjected to foreign aggression and occupation, alien and colonial domination, racial discrimination and apartheid' . . ."

'*Apartheid.*' Rhonda's mind wandered again. Why do they use these foreign words? No, it was really too much. Too much rhetoric. 'Foreign aggression,' and this and that. She really couldn't follow it any longer. It couldn't really all be true. Not *all* the problems in the world are our fault. 'Cancel the debts.' What would Nick say? He'd just laugh. Or shout, probably, about the economy going to hell, and the banks . . . Oh, I don't know. She looked at Maureen. She's certainly taking it all in, Rhonda thought. Well. Sylvia is her daughter. But then she's always had some interest in this kind of thing. She seems to think it's going to save us somehow. From nuclear war. Though Nick would say we need more bombs, not less, if we're going to keep on top of it all. Nick. Rhonda frowned, then looked up suddenly as the audience burst into applause.

Applauding with them, Linda glanced at her mother, then back at the stage—it was unbelievable, this incredible movement of countries, places she hadn't known . . . She glanced at Jack as he studied the speakers, nodding his head in approval, his strong hands clapping in slow, rhythmic agreement and, catching Linda's glance, he smiled at her. Caught off guard, she quickly returned his smile and turned away. How had he known about all this? This was what Steven had taunted him about that night that—oh, Steven! She felt a surge of anger. Why wasn't he here? It all came back to her, the anger she had forgotten, so caught up in this world opening up before her, the *real* world as it exists beyond the hopeless news she saw on TV, she had forgotten, this past hour, her anger with Steven—his scene at dinner last night—and she felt it now again, a tightening in her throat and, worse, a sadness that Steven was not here now, sharing this with her.

As the applause quieted, Rhonda, seeing the unhappy expression on her daughter's face, leaned toward her. "I know," she whispered. "It's too strange, isn't it?"

Linda started to speak, but the audience was silent again as Galle turned to Anna-Maria, who sat forward toward the microphone. "Thank you, Galle." She smiled warmly at her Ally and then turned back to the audience. "I am Anna-Maria Jimenez of Havana, Cuba. I welcome the opportunity to speak with you today." Anna-Maria pushed her dark hair behind her shoulders as she glanced at her notes and then up again.

"Although, as I am told, you do not hear much news about the Nonaligned Movement in this country, it is now larger and stronger than ever. In 1979, the sixth summit of the Movement was held in Havana, Cuba. Ninety-five nations were present. That is to say, almost two-thirds of the nations of the world. Four of these were national liberation organizations, for example, Zimbabwe, which at that time was still under Rhodesian control.

"The 95 nations present were Afghanistan, Algeria, Angola, Argentina, Bahrain, Bangladesh, Benin, Bhutan, Bolivia, Botswana, Burundi, Cameroon, Cape Verde, Central African Republic, Chad, Comoros, Congo, Cuba, Cyprus, Djibouti, Egypt, Equatorial Guinea, Ethiopia, Gabon, Gambia, Ghana, Grenada, Guinea, Guinea-Bissau, Guyana, India, Indonesia, Iran, Iraq, Ivory Coast, Jamaica, Jordan, Kampuchea, Kenya, Korea (North), Kuwait, Laos, Lebanon, Lesotho, Liberia, Libya, Madagascar, Malawi, Malaysia, Maldives, Mali, Malta, Mauritania, Mauritius, Morocco, Mozambique, Nepal, Nicaragua, Niger, Nigeria, Oman, Pakistan, Panama, Peru, Qatar, Rwanda, Sao Tome and Principe, Saudi Arabia, Senegal, Seychelles, Sierra Leone, Singapore, Somalia, Sri Lanka, Sudan, Suriname, Swaziland, Syria, Tanzania, Togo, Trinidad and Tobago, Tunisia, Uganda, United Arab Emirates, Upper Volta, Vietnam, Yemen (Aden), Yemen (Sana), Yugoslavia, Zaire, Zambia, the African National Congress, the Palestine Liberation Organization, Zimbabwe, and the Southwest Africa Peoples Organization.

"Acknowledging that over 400 million people in the world are currently suffering from malnutrition, that is, starving to death in the most fertile agricultural areas of the world, the Havana summit proposed to 'eliminate injustice in the existing international economic system' and establish the *New International Economic Order*.

"The Movement proposed, in fact, that international economic cooperation is the only hope for world peace. As stated in the sixth summit's *Report to the United Nations*:

> *The sound of weapons, threatening language and arrogance in the international scene must cease. Enough of the illusion that the world's problems can be solved by means of nuclear weapons. Bombs may kill the hungry, the sick and the ignorant, but they cannot kill hunger, disease and ignorance. Nor can they kill the righteous rebellion of the peoples—and in the holocaust, the rich, who are the ones who have the most to lose in this world, will also die.*
>
> *If confrontation and struggle—the only road that seems to be open to the developing countries, a road that offers long and difficult battles whose proportions no one can predict—are to be avoided, we must all seek and find formulas of cooperation for solving the great problems which, while affecting our peoples, cannot be solved*

without also affecting the most developed countries, in one way or another.

. . . World military expenditures amount to more than $300 billion a year. This sum could build 600,000 schools with a capacity for 400 million children; or 60 million comfortable homes for 300 million people; 30,000 hospitals with 18 million beds; or 20,000 factories with jobs for more than 20 million workers; or an irrigation system for 150 million hectares of land—that, with the application of technology—could feed a billion people. Mankind wastes this much every year on military spending. Moreover, consider the enormous quantities of young human resources, technicians, fuel, raw materials and other items. This is the fabulous price of preventing a true climate of confidence and peace from existing in the world.

Let us say farewell to arms, and let us dedicate ourselves in a civilized manner to the most pressing problems of our times. This is the responsibility and the most sacred duty of all the world's statesmen. Moreover, it is the basic premise for human survival.

"With the sixth summit in 1979, the Nonaligned Movement's voice in the United Nations became even more powerful than earlier in the decade, further breaking down the mechanical majority previously held by the industrialized nations. Now it is the wealthy countries of the North who are shocked by the U.N. resolutions, and who are repeatedly in the unaccepted position in diplomatic agreements.

"But the seat of empire does not concede easily, even if its relentless grasp for control is at the expense of the Earth itself. Now the imperialist response is to try to isolate the nonaligned countries from one another, to sow dissension, division. It uses political and diplomatic threats and foreign assistance programs as blackmail. It threatens and carries out military invasions into sovereign nations. It finances covert operations against independent peoples seeking freedom. It formulates concepts designed to confuse political realities. Every day the imperialist press prints one or another falsehood or attack on nonaligned and socialist countries. As Antonio Blanco described it at a Howard University symposium in this country, 'This is the furious and irrational reaction of one unable to assimilate history's course.'

"For the centers of empire sense the tide, the rising up of the poor and enslaved peoples of the world. And they strike back against the inevitable evolution of humanity with their threats, their double-dealing, their mercenaries, their technology of terror and annihilation.

"The real struggle for power in the world is not between the capitalists of the West and the socialists of the East, led by the U.S. and the U.S.S.R. No. The real struggle is between the imperialists of the North and the majority of the world's population, the people of the South. But the demands of the South are not for empire and genocide. Their demands are for equality and cooperation. The demands of the people of the South have *everyone's* interests at heart.

"Yet the response of the imperial North is clear: to disrupt, divide and destroy the Movement. After the Havana summit, the Department of State of the United States reported, in February, 1980:

> *It is also incontestable that the Third World is much more important to U.S. security and welfare than it has ever been . . . They now command attention because collectively, they . . . have acquired the capacity to affect international events in significant ways.*
>
> *. . . We will judge its members as individual countries and will find we can work with some and must resist others. To do otherwise—either to reject the nonaligned countries in their entirety or to embrace them in their collectivity—would only damage U.S. interests.*

"Thus, U.S. State Department policy toward members of the Nonaligned Movement such as Vietnam, Cuba, Grenada, Nicaragua, is economic isolation and military assault. Toward Jamaica, Congo, Bolivia, it is economic manipulation coupled with covert destabilization. While toward members such as Saudi Arabia, Barbados, Argentina, Egypt, it is a self-interested alliance manifested by military favors.

"It is this policy of insidious . . ."

As Maureen listened to Anna-Maria and the edge of anger that seemed to grow in her words as she spoke, she couldn't help but think of Sylvia and the anger, bordering sometimes on hatred, that would creep into her daughter's voice as she seemed to want to rail against an enemy too large, too dark and monstrous. And still, Maureen thought, she could see it now, at least better than she had before. How many lives and hopes had been crushed by the cold, mindless power of the military, leaving whole nations so powerless and if one knew, or cared at all, as Sylvia had all these years . . . She saw her daughter's face, the curve of her mouth, sometimes so kind, and then set, in anger. But now—Maureen tried to picture Sylvia now—at this moment, sitting in a small room with these women, finally meeting together in a power that . . . Maureen almost shuddered. And what would they do? What would they plan in these closed sessions with all their passion for bringing this country . . . Suddenly a sense of danger so vivid filled Maureen with the desire to get up from her chair and find Sylvia, now, and . . . She looked quickly around the room, and then at Rhonda who was looking at her, curious. She settled back into her chair. Oh, I am getting old, she thought. And silly. These women want peace, and to end war, not start it. And what had the Chinese woman said? Their purpose is to 'share their knowledge.' This movement is about education, really, and that is very sorely needed. It's frightening how little we know in this country about . . . Well, yes, I'd better listen. She looked back at Anna-Maria, whose voice was gentler now.

"These developments bring us to the most recent, the seventh summit of the Nonaligned Movement held in March of this year, 1983. One hundred-one nations were in attendance at New Dehli, India. Although this summit received little coverage in the United States press, those journalists that did report it indicated that the Movement is now more 'genuinely' nonaligned. As proof they cited criticisms of the Soviet Union voiced by the Movement for the first time, and they declared that the Movement had become more 'moderate' in its view of the United States.

"There is both truth and misunderstanding in this assessment.

"Michael Manley, the former prime minister of Jamaica, in an article on the 1983 Summit, states it well:

> *When the Western press interprets 'nonalignment' to mean that vague state of suspension between the superpowers it calls 'neutrality', it misconstrues the purpose and the nature of the movement. Nonaligned countries cannot exist politically equidistant between Washington and Moscow because that would mean being oblivious to the positions the superpowers take on issues that affect them. For example, if Washington and Moscow refuse demands for a change in the world economic structure that would be beneficial to the underdeveloped countries, most members of the movement would oppose both of them. If, on the other hand, Washington supports the South African government while Moscow supports the African National Congress, most nonaligned nations would disagree violently with Washington and applaud Moscow.*

"The seventh summit reaffirmed its historic goals in many ways. Declarations were made condemning the policies of South Africa and Israel. Iran and Iraq were called upon to end their war. Support was offered to Mauritius in its effort to prevent the United States from leasing a neighboring island for a nuclear military base. And United

States policy in Central America, South Africa, and the Mideast was repeatedly denounced.

"In addition, during the period of the summit, Prime Minister Indira Gandhi and Prime Minister Mohammed Zia Ul-Haq signed a five-year agreement of economic, scientific and cultural cooperation, thus ending a 35-year war between India and Pakistan.

"As Gandhi stated in her opening remarks to the seventh summit, the Nonaligned Movement is *the biggest peace movement in history*,' for peace—beyond war—is the aspiration on which it was founded and which continues to build it today."

Anna-Maria stopped, folding her hands on her stack of notes as the audience applauded, respectfully and at length, and Elena prepared to present her remarks.

"Thank you, Anna-Maria." She smiled at her Ally and turned to the audience. "I am Elena Rios of Buenos Aires, Argentina." Her soft brown eyes surveyed the room. "I thank you for attending today to discuss with us our work and hopes, because as Anna-Maria has said, our hopes are for peace in the world.

"In my country, Argentina," Elena paused a moment, then looked out again at the room as if it were a distant horizon, "we are very far from peace. I imagine most of you cannot know what it is to be governed by a military junta whose army patrols the streets, or each night to wake trembling, wondering if your husband, your son or daughter will 'disappear' from your home, forever, because he has voiced an opinion at his job, or she has attended a meeting at school. I imagine most of you have not seen the face of a loved one who has miraculously returned from being 'detained,' or seen the scars of anguish deep in their skin, in their minds.

"This is what it is to live in a country—not at war—but in the grip of militaristic obsession, where mad generals and their eager troops have total control. For peace, like war, is not only a state of arms, it is a state of mind. I tell you this, not for pity, but as warning.

"In the Third World, Argentina is one of the major arms producers. Only Brazil, India, Israel and South Africa equal it. Yet throughout the Third World, military expenditures have increased *fifteen-fold* in the past 25 years. The Middle East accounts for half of that expenditure, with Iran at the lead.

"These are conventional weapons of which I speak now. Almost all of the wars fought since 1945 have been with conventional weapons and have taken place in the Third World.

"So where is this peace, then, that the Nonaligned Movement calls for in ever greater numbers at each of its summit meetings? Where has this shocking growth in militarization come from?

"Anna-Maria has told you of the U.S. State Department's policy of 'divide and conquer' among the Nonaligned Nations. But she did not tell you also that the United States accounts for 38 percent of the arms exports to the Third World. And in turn that the Soviet Union supplies 34 percent. And Europe the rest. It is the North that exports war to the Third World, for a total profit of $135 billion each year.

"And looking a moment at the nuclear arms market, from an article in *The Bulletin of Atomic Science* in 1978:

> *The (nuclear) market is controlled by the United States, France, West Germany, Canada, Sweden, Switzerland and the Soviet Union. The United States controls 70 percent of the world nuclear business . . .*

"It was in that same year, 1978, that the United Nations held their first 'Special Session on Disarmament' at the request of the Nonaligned Movement. Efforts for this Session had been in the making for 17 years. The People's Republic of China, for the first time in history, participated in disarmament talks with other nations at this Session. Thirty proposals were made, among them a call for the dismantling of foreign military bases and the withdrawal of troops from foreign territories.

"Yet despite this effort to bring a halt to the cancerous military growth in the world, weapons production continued to increase in the North as a whole, and within five Third World nations, primarily Israel and South Africa. For as the *Bulletin* also states:

> *The economic crisis, now affecting most countries in the Northern Hemisphere, is encouraging more aggressive arms selling [even though the] most likely way in which an all-out nuclear war will start is through the escalation of a Third World conflict.*

"In 1982 the world spent $550 billion on conventional, chemical and nuclear arms—2,300 times as much as it did for peacekeeping. Fifty thousand nuclear weapons with the equivalent explosive power of one million Hiroshima bombs exist now on our Earth. Most of this spending on weapons takes place in the Northern Hemisphere.

"If I may give you a few comments especially of interest to you who live in the United States, the May 1982 issue of *Nation* informs us that:

> *. . . subsidized dining by top military and civilian officials in the Pentagon cost U.S. taxpayers $14 per meal,*

while the Federal school lunch program for the poor spends only $1.20 per meal.

"These are the signs, of which I spoke, of a society gripped by obsession with militarism at the expense of its own people.

"But for those who are so deeply concerned that the Russians are becoming more powerful than the United States, it should be noted that if we look at the per capita gross national product of 141 of the world's nations, the United States ranks tenth while the Soviet Union ranks 31st. Even your venerable newsman, Walter Cronkite, had this to say in 1982:

> *You can get yourself pretty frightened looking at all of the Administration's maps and charts of Soviet aggression and military spending. But like so many of our perceptions of the Soviet Union, it tells you only half the story, the half the Administration uses to press its case for higher and higher defense budgets.*
>
> *This is the other half of the story. Since 1960, Soviet influence around the world actually declined. Their so-called gains, like Afghanistan and Angola, take on a different perspective, particularly when they're measured against losses, like Egypt and China. As for the military spending, the figures are also misleading. Our two systems, our two economies, are so different that to compare the costs of tanks and rocket launchers is just about as meaningful as comparing the costs of a college education.*
>
> *So we're back to our original question: Who are these Russians? What are their intentions? No one can say with certainty. But if their perception of America is as flawed as we believe it is, then our perceptions of the Soviet Union just could be flawed too.*

"In June of 1982, the United Nations held its Second Session on Disarmament. At this Session, Moscow's Foreign Minister Andrei Gromyko announced that the U.S.S.R. will *not* be the first to use nuclear weapons. It was an unexpected announcement, although the Soviets have long sought a no-first-strike commitment with Washington. Gromyko also stated that the 'Soviets are willing to limit or ban any weapon as long as the United States did as well.' In addition he submitted a draft treaty to ban all chemical weapons. These gestures were not met in kind by the United States. On the contrary, the Reagan Administration strongly indicated that they *are* willing to use nuclear weapons on first-strike. This posture strikes fear in all the world. Perhaps that is its intention.

"But at whose expense? At whose expense is this posture of aggression? This devotion to nuclear arms? Only the poor peoples of the South calling for peace? Or the more developed Third World nations who have been bought or coerced into joining the arms race and the military mania that amasses ever more complex weapons while their people starve? Or only the Russians who are compelled to devote ever greater portions of their mediocre economy to defense? Or only the Europeans who live terrifed, caught in the middle between thousands of nuclear warheads aimed at and across their lands? Do the citizens of the United States sleep well as their government continues to lead the world in production and export of weapons? And occupy and invade small countries, such as Grenada, around the world? And sell its weapons via Israel and South Africa to dictators and torturers in El Salvador, Chile, Brazil? Is it not at the expense of your people also?

"I was struck by just how much it is at your expense, the expense of your youth, when reading the remarks of Drew Middleton, the military affairs correspondent for the *New York Times*. He was responding to James Fallows who had said, in his book *National Defense*, that weapons have grown too complex and expensive to be useful in warfare now. This was Middleton's response:

> *Predictions that tomorrow's soldier, sailor or airman will be unable to maintain computerized weapons may overlook an emerging trend . . . the wide-spread popularity of computers and computerized games.*

He then quoted United States General Anson:

> *You've got high school boys doing computer programming, and you've got kids jamming amusement arcades to play complicated games. It's not going to be so difficult for them to handle the new machines as many think.*

"The 'new machines,' of course, are computerized nuclear weapons systems. Those young boys, so excited by blowing little dots off video screens, may never understand, as they sit at their video screens at military bases wearing the United States flag on their shoulder, that they have been trained, since their early youth, to become the most grotesque mass murderers in the history of civilization.

"At whose expense? Of course, it is at all of our expense! Military aggression, whether as for some, it keeps us in a state of constant fear, or as for others, it turns us into depraved murderers—it is at all of our expense.

"And in recent years there is a growing number of people in the North who understand this. The demonstration for disarmament in New York City in 1982 was said to be the largest in United States history. The Nuclear Freeze Movement has become a huge mass mobilization, one of international scope in cooperation between European and North American peace groups. 'International,' among Northerners that is.

"In fact, it is rather appalling to read the literature of this movement and find next to nothing in reference to the peoples of the South, the great majority of the world's population, the Nonaligned Movement, which, as Indira Gandhi said, is the 'biggest peace movement in history.' Could it be that the Northern peace movement suffers from the same racist mentality that their government leaders use as an excuse for military occupation of the world?"

Elena paused a moment, taking a drink of water, as an uneasy stirring crept through the audience, the shuffling of papers and feet, clearing of throats, and a handful of people left the hall. Elena took a deep breath, a glint of anger, and yet sorrow, in her warm dark eyes as she went on.

"We raise this difficult and delicate question in the interests of all of us. In the interest of unity and alliance. In the interest of the survival of the Earth. And in the name of genuine internationalism.

"There is no other way. No other way now but cooperation. And not simply cooperation in laying down our weapons as the Nuclear Freeze Movement calls for. It must be a cooperation that embraces *all* human needs. Not just the need to escape death in a nuclear holocaust. But the needs of life. Everyday life—food, health care, education—for *all* of our world community of peoples.

"And each of us, all of us, can make the conscious decisions that will lead us to international cooperation, resource redistribution and disarmament. We can shed our stifling prejudices and expand our understanding to engage all of who we are as human life on Earth. In the words of the man who is possibly the most venerated intellect of the West, Albert Einstein:

A human being is a part of the whole called by us 'Universe,' a part limited in time and space. He experiences himself, his thoughts and feelings as something separated from the rest—a kind of optical illusion of his consciousness. This delusion is a kind of prison for us, restricting us to our personal desires and to affection for a few persons nearest to us. Our task must be to free ourselves from this prison by widening our circle of

*compassion to embrace all living creatures and the whole
of nature and its beauty.*

"This is the knowledge that each of us has within us. And we can
make this knowledge a reality—through our human will. We can bring
our governments, our leaders, to bear. *We have the choice.*"

Elena stopped, shaking her head back, and then smiled as Anna-
Maria gave her a quick, assuring clasp of the hand, and the audience
applauded, at first as if reflecting, and then exuberant, filling the hall.
Several in the front rows stood, and soon most of the people in the
room, the Allies on the stage, too, stood, applauding, joy lighting their
faces as the calls and sounds of approval reached an even higher pitch.
And it seemed that then and there this roomful of people could change
the world, for certainly the will was there.

Gradually the wave of excitement receded, and the group began to
disperse as the Allies left the stage escorted by NEWS security. Amid
the aftermath of excited conversation and the motion of people leaving
their seats, Rhonda, waiting to file out from her row of chairs, stood
still, her eyes fixed on the stage, a look of wonder and doubt narrowing
her eyes beneath the raised brows. Maureen, too, looked at the now
empty stage, its vacant table and chairs so lifeless with the loss of
those three quite astounding women, only the great expanse of blue and
green world draped behind still giving meaning to their words.

"I'm going to go back and get a copy of their presentations," Linda
said as she followed Jack to the aisle, their line moving now.

"Oh, yes, I will too," Maureen said, turning to her niece. She
looked at her watch, it was close to noon.

"Well I'll go wait for Sylvia in the courtyard. I'll meet you there,"
Rhonda said, still preoccupied. She needed time to think, but Jack said
he would accompany her, giving Linda some bills and asking her to
pick up a copy of the text for him. Still Rhonda was silent as they
made their way through the mingling crowd to the corner of the
courtyard where they had agreed to meet Sylvia. Most of the audience
who had been at the forum were leaving through the gate in the west
wall, and the score of nuns who had attended moved through a small
passage at the rear of the church to the convent beyond. But just as
quickly the courtyard began to fill again as the Allies and NEWS cadres
finished their sessions and came out through the auditorium to get a
breath of the cool winter air. Again the color, the fusion of language
and culture, the startling contrasts and earnest yet delightful sense of the
women as they gathered in groups, still discussing their morning's
work, kept Rhonda's eyes still studying, questioning. All of this, all of
their speeches, the history and the theories were news to her, and she
really was not at all sure what to make of it.

"This is really something, isn't it?" Jack said finally, putting his hands in his pockets and turning to face Rhonda.

"Well, yes. It is that," Rhonda agreed as she watched a group of black women coming through the door in the ivy-covered wall. Now, were they from here or from Africa? And those Mexican-looking women with them, they could have been from East L.A., or maybe they were from Tobogo or something, one of those countries in that Movement. Maybe they all were. She'd really never even known such places existed. And there was Sylvia! Right behind them, talking to a woman in the most exquisitely embroidered, what was it, a shawl, or a . . . And Sylvia, carrying on, talking and laughing with these women as if she were one of them. She seemed, in fact, hardly to be Sylvia at all—but there she was in her black slacks and green sweater, Maureen's daughter, yes—her own family, her niece. It really was rather dizzying to see her there, as if she, Rhonda herself, were suddenly part of all this, this talk, these people, this whole North-East-West-South business. It was really too much. But then . . . here she was.

"Hi!" Sylvia greeted Rhonda and Jack. "How was the forum?"

"Oh, well. There was an amazing amount of information. I haven't really digested it all, I . . ." Rhonda laughed.

"Hi!" Linda appeared, putting an arm around Sylvia as Maureen stood beside her, a depth of respect in her eyes as she smiled at her daughter, who stood silent, her eyes rooted in her mother's gaze in a moment of purely unexpected fulfillment.

"Sylvia, the forum was excellent! I wish you could have heard it." Linda laughed.

"Oh, good," Sylvia answered, pulling herself away from her mother's eyes, though the sensation stayed with her, warming her still.

"But, you know. I really wonder how that woman, who was she?" Linda went on, "Elena Rios, the woman from Argentina. How is she ever going to be safe in her country again after the statements she . . ."

"Elena? She left Argentina, two years ago," Sylvia answered. "She was in prison there. They held her for three years without being tried. She was tortured . . ." Sylvia paused, looking off to the women still coming into the courtyard. She turned back to her family. "But they let her live. She was deported. She's been living in exile in Mexico."

"Ooooh. You mean she can never go back to her home?" Rhonda asked, horrified.

"Mom, you heard what she said about the military there," Linda said.

Rhonda nodded. "Yes. I see."

"Oh Rhonda, I found a brochure I wanted to show you," Sylvia said, looking through her notebook.

"You know, that woman looks so familiar to me," Linda murmured, gazing at a young blonde woman in a pink shirt standing a few yards behind Sylvia.

Jack followed her gaze. "Yeah, she does . . . Well, yeah," he laughed, "she was sitting behind us during the forum just now. I noticed her as we were leaving."

"Oh. Is that it." Linda turned away. But she was frowning now as suddenly Steven filled her mind again, a sorrow for him. Damn him though, she thought, angry now. She still couldn't forgive his drunken behaviour at dinner last night.

"What?" Sylvia asked, looking up from her notebook.

"We should have lunch, don't you think?" Maureen asked.

"Oh," Sylvia said, looking at her watch. "Well, they're serving lunch in the dining room at the dormitories. It could be crowded, but why don't we just go there. I have to do childcare, actually, at one o'clock. That's my shift."

"Childcare?" Linda asked her as they headed toward the auditorium door. "Couldn't you get people outside to do it so you could attend all the sessions?"

"Oh, it's just for an hour. Mainly we have volunteers—men, in fact, from other organizations," Sylvia answered as she linked her arm through Maureen's.

"Do you still need volunteers?" Jack asked. "I have plenty of time over the next few days."

"That would be great, Jack." Sylvia smiled at him as Linda turned to look at him with an admiration that Rhonda couldn't help but note.

Chapter XII

Steven sat alone in the cold living room. It was not yet dawn.
He grasped again at his thought, his eyes sweeping the room as if
the sense he had just made for himself, that he'd thought he'd made and
then lost to the haunting notion of his own inability to make any sense
at all, could be found somewhere outside of himself—in the corners of
the room, in the dark silhouettes of the cabinet, the chair, the
Christmas tree, now so stark and forlorn, a symbol not of cheer, but of
everything that was missing, that had gone wrong.
His cigarette, newly lit from the butt of the last, in a chain
of—how many? He'd been up for hours. Couldn't sleep, hadn't really
slept for days it seemed, except for the few hours every night it took
him to sleep off the whiskey he'd had before falling into bed. He took
another long draw, exhaling slowly, his restless eyes settling in the
upward drifts of smoke, as if some meaning might lie there. But it
failed. Sorely, sourly it failed to soothe the aching within him, not a
sharp, distinct pain, nothing so manageable, but a kind of airless
vacuum, binding his sorrow lest it flail to the outer edges, rending
asunder its gravityless mass. In the absence of matter, he could
disappear, lost, forever, in some uncontrollable chaos.
He stood abruptly, striding to the window, then back again to the
hall door. Smoking quickly he paced again, then back, to the window,
to the door as it all fell upon him again—the bits, the fragments, the
random comments, images, incidents—that had somehow, with some
incomprehensible significance in their own individual instance, come to
bear upon him in this desperate agony. It was Jack, his sighting that
tall frame standing out in the mirror at the Jury Room months ago.
Judge Whitmore ruling against him time and time again, the sagging
old jowls, sinister and sneering. His clients, sick and hopeless,
penniless and demanding, their faces flooding before him, frightened,
pleading. The D.A.'s staff, smug and contemptuous. The office
secretary laughing on the phone as she handed him his mail that never
included a payment. A few worn dollars laid on his desk by a welfare
mother. Linda, so tentative and pleading, too, that they ask Nick for
more money. Nick, clearing his throat as the football game broke for
half-time, to give Steven a lecture on supporting his family.
Humiliation, disgust. Jack, grinning at Linda on 24th Street as he
agreed to come for Christmas dinner. Linda, writing check after check
for presents, food, laughing at his fear—it would be all right. Linda.

The night she left him to go to Berkeley, so cold, distant, calling him a drunk, hating him. Her eyes lighting when she saw Jack—Jack—his easy liberal success as Steven lost case after case, blackballed by the judges. And Mark's face, full of pity as he bought round after round those nights in the Jury Room, egging him on to talk and talk about his problems, his losing cases, his dwindling finances, his arguments with Linda, his bad luck—first the car, his canceled credit, borrowing from Nick, unable to work for Mark and Drew, more pity because he couldn't stomach their leeching practice. Mark sneering at Jack, egging him on, and that sick, sick card he'd sent about Jack and Linda. Steven felt as if he might vomit. How had he let that snake so close under his skin, confided in him his most personal fears. And Jack, so healthy, that happy, grinning smile that sent Linda reeling every time until now she could barely stand the sight of her own husband—he, himself—who had worked and tried so hard, so hard to make their living and still be true to his sense of the law, to the right of defense for the poorest, most helpless in this fucked up world. And in two minutes she could turn all her affection to Jack—the superman, the radical lawyer superstar and all his lefty flash—it was easy for him, easy for him to be so righteous about his politics. They had made him rich. And if that wasn't enough, now he'd help himself to his old friend's wife, why not? His 'old friend' hadn't pulled it together in the big time. Somehow defending the helpless wasn't as lucrative as defending communists. Jack. Jack, ganging up on him with Sylvia in his own home, in front of his own family at Christmas dinner!

Steven slammed his fist against the window frame as he stood watching the early dawn light fill the sky. The motherfucker. He'd like to kill him. Smack that grin off his face. He lit another cigarette, inhaling deeply. His eyes narrowed as he watched a neighbor start his car in the street below, and the sound of Jack's voice when he came to pick up Linda, Rhonda and Maureen for the conference rang in his ears—so charming, gracious for the ladies. They were all just beside themselves, basking in the charisma of their escort. Linda hadn't yet spoken a word to him since the scene at the dinner table the night before, and there he'd been, left for the day with Nick, who was really a dullard of a man, sitting sullen all day on the couch, staring at the television, except, of course, for the time he took to give lectures on family responsibility. As if it had been Steven who wanted the old fart's money. No! It was his own extravagant, irresponsible daughter who was hitting him up, for god's sake. Why hadn't he raised her better? Why had he spoiled her rotten if he was so goddamned concerned about his money?

Ooh! Steven backed away from the window as if he'd seen a ghost—and that letter. He'd managed to completely put it out of his mind. Well, no, really, it had been in his mind for days, since Nick first handed it to him, after the game—but still it was too strange. Too strange to really even consider. He pushed it back again, out. It was too senseless. And still he relived the moment, taking it curiously from Nick and then—something about his name typed above Nick's address, he'd turned it over—no return address. He'd paused, and offering Nick another beer, walked back to the kitchen where his hand had actually shook, as if by premonition, when he tore open the envelope and pulling out the sheet of paper, read the one single-spaced paragraph centered in the middle of the page.

> *Family troubles? Can't make ends meet? Bad debts? Bad credit? Why rely on relatives? Or an estranged wife? Stand on your own two feet. Let us help you help yourself. For more information call 213-555-8329. Before it's too late.*

There was no threat, really, or menace in the words, but it had struck a note of terror in him that brought sweat to his forehead even now, as he remembered it. Who? Who in god's name had sent it? He would have thought possibly Mark again, for who else even knew of his dilemma, except Linda—and god no, maybe she was in love with Jack, even being unfaithful, who knew—but no, she couldn't do something like that, Christ in heaven, please! And Mark had no idea of Nick's existence, really, much less his address. It wasn't until after he'd turned down the job with Drew and stopped seeing Mark that he'd begun to borrow money from Nick. So who? Nick himself, he might have even considered, but then why had Nick so pained himself to give him that little lecture just an hour before remembering that he had this letter in his luggage. It wasn't, couldn't have been anyone he knew personally. It would just be too senseless. Yet who knew enough of his personal business—bad credit, estranged wife—to say . . . That was what struck the terror. After all, if his problems were public knowledge, then it could have been some church group—it sounded like it really—"Let us help you to help yourself." One of those evangelical fundamentalist Christian groups that had some TV station down in L.A. It was an L.A. phone number. But more likely, in fact the explanation he had allowed himself to believe just to get the fucking thing out of his mind, was that it was a credit bureau, nosing around in his business again, just like that 'neighbor' woman who had grilled Linda and then got their MasterCharge canceled. They'd probably traced him to Nick's through the bank transfer Nick had made to their account, and got confused about where he lived. But then why no return address? Or salutation or signature? No credit company had to be *that* secretive, though they did have some pretty underhanded techniques. But why the fucking snakes, whatever their operation, had to bring up his "estranged wife"—that was really low, really a cheap shot to try and rope him in to some financial snare—if that was even it. The thing made him feel creepy, invaded, somehow denuded by some ominous, impersonal big brother.

He walked back again across the living room, and then back to the window, pulling his robe tighter about him, the room was fully light now, and the sound of morning traffic made him conscious of the time. Linda would be getting up any minute. They were still barely speaking. She'd gone off again to that conference yesterday, taking Justin to their childcare center or something while he was at work, and for all he knew she was planning to go again today. Maybe Jack was meeting her there. Maybe they weren't really going to the conference at all. Jack had certainly hung around long enough with Linda and Rhonda Christmas night after that awful scene at the table. Whatever it was, it was hard to remember. He just knew Sylvia, or Jack, or both of them had been preaching at everyone, recruiting them all for this fucking conference. God, when the fuck would it end? It started Monday, one, two . . . This was the third day of it. Something had to break. Something had to give. Steven slumped back down into the couch. He couldn't go on like this. Slogging away at the office where he could hardly see, he was so damn tired. It wasn't just that. He couldn't face another client! Not another case! He just couldn't do it anymore! He buried his face in his hands, close to tears. The money, no money, debts to Nick, no credit. He thought he might suffocate. He couldn't do it. He couldn't do it anymore. He brought his head up sharply, wiping his eyes, and grabbed for his pack of cigarettes on the coffee table and, standing up again, he lit one and walked to the window. Why should he? Why should he be tortured while Linda ran off with Jack everyday to this crazy lesbian conference Sylvia had recruited them all for? Linda sitting around with her hero listening to communist speeches while I'm supposed to be plugging away at work to pay for her capitalist tastes! No thanks! No thanks, bitch!

Steven turned abruptly as he heard Justin in his room calling for Linda, and the rage in his face gave way to sickened sorrow. He bent his head to his hand. What would he have without them? His wife. His son. His "estranged" wife. Again the terror clenched his nerves, that sense of utter loss of privacy, of being watched, inspected, toyed with, by whom? He shook it off, a thick brush full of white paint making long broad strokes, covering over the letter, the images, the fear. He walked into the dining room, to the corner cabinet and, taking down a bottle, took a quick, deep drink of whiskey and, replacing the bottle, he walked to his room to dress for work.

Feeding Justin his breakfast in the kitchen, Linda heard Steven in the bedroom opening the bureau drawer for a fresh shirt, one she had ironed late last night while he had sat in the living room watching television, morosely sipping his endless drink, smoking his cigarettes. She frowned at the sound of the hangers scraping against the closet rack as he chose his suit. Would he speak to her this morning? They had barely exchanged two sentences since the family had left yesterday morning, and even Monday night after the conference, at dinner downtown, they had avoided each other as much as possible. He was drinking again, of course. What was the point. What was there to say that he could possibly hear? Please don't drink, Steven. Please be happy. Please love me, and your son, your life. Maybe she was being harsh, but honestly, he was really getting to her, his awful moods, insulting their friends, his lack of interest in anything but where his next drink was coming from. God, no. He wasn't *that* bad. What was the matter with her? But the fact was, she still hadn't forgiven him. She just couldn't seem to get over his horrible behavior at dinner on Christmas. The horrible things he said to Sylvia. And to Jack. What was the matter with him? And if only he had come to the conference, he could have seen what they were talking about! If he could just open his mind a crack. He used to be so interested in things, in people, and ideas, he used to be so . . .

"Mommy crying?" Justin asked, putting his spoon back down in his yogurt and looking plaintively up at his mother.

"Oh, Jus," Linda said, smiling through her tears, and pressing her cheek to his yogurty face. He was looking more and more like Steven all the time, that little dimple in his chin and the green of his eyes. "More yogurt?" she asked, smiling at him as she brushed the tears from her face.

"Yeah," Justin answered, "please."

She served Justin, and putting the yogurt back in the refrigerator, she stood staring at its contents, wondering what to do, what to say to Steven. They couldn't go on like this. Just not speaking, day after day. It had never been like this. This bad. She closed the refrigerator door and, as she turned around and leaned against it, looking on at Justin, she was careful now, not to cry. But if they were talking he would just ask her, viciously, probably, if she were going back to the conference today, and she would have to say yes, because she definitely was going. It was the most fascinating, illuminating thing she had ever done in her life, and his crazy jealousy about Jack was not going to stop her! And, of course, he would ask if Jack were going to be there, and just because he *was*—of course he was. He'd decided to go before she or Sylvia or anyone had ever even talked about it with him. Was she supposed to tell Jack he couldn't go? Or he couldn't talk to her if they saw each other there because her husband was jealous! Steven could have come to it too! It wasn't her fault he'd rather drink and watch football games. No, no! That wasn't Steven's way. That had never been his way. But it seemed . . . it seemed to be becoming his way. Hadn't he had the choice? Hadn't Sylvia told him about it a week before, and hadn't she herself told him that she would be going too? And he'd never shown any interest at all. He could have come, taken time off work . . . Maybe he would still like to come. And then he wouldn't feel so excluded. He could see what it was all about, and see that Jack was there because he was interested in the conference, not in her! Though to be honest. To be totally honest. She did look forward to seeing Jack. But, why not? She looked forward to seeing Sylvia, too. She looked forward to seeing a friend! Why was that so horrible? It was Steven who made it so horrible! But she had to talk to him. This had to stop. This deathly silence has to stop.

As she turned to the bedroom door, she heard Steven leave the room and walk down the hall. Was he leaving? She hurried through the bedroom to the hall.

"Steven!"

He stopped halfway to the front door, standing a moment, then turned around, looking at her. His eyes looked tired, dreadful, sad.

Her impulse was to run to him, hold him in her arms. But something held her back. No, she couldn't dispel the rancor she still felt from his scene at the family dinner. She looked on at him.

"Are you leaving?"

"I'm going to work." His voice was flat.

"Steven, we have to talk." She still stood at the bedroom doorway, 20 feet from him.

He shifted on his feet, impatient. They looked at each other, unwilling to move forward, unable to retreat.

"Later," he said finally, turning to go.

"Wait, Steven." Linda hurried toward him, stopping as Justin started to cry for her from the kitchen, wanting to be released from his highchair. She looked back toward the kitchen hurriedly, then at Steven, her face strained. "When?"

He started to speak, then shrugged. Justin had begun to shriek.

"Tonight. When you get home. At 6:00." Her voice rose above Justin's. "All right?"

He nodded as Linda continued to stare at him. "All right," he said finally.

Linda turned quickly toward the bedroom as Steven watched her run back through to the kitchen and Justin. He waited a moment, listening to her comfort their son as she lifted him to her. Then he turned and left the flat.

An hour later at 8:30 Linda had Justin dressed warmly, his diaper bag packed with his things, and was herself reaching for her coat. Jack had called just after Steven left, offering to pick her up for this morning's public forum at the conference. It would save her a long ride on two streetcars with Justin and all their things. Of course she had said yes. And now she saw from the window his little blue Datsun pulling up to the curb. She quickly picked up Justin and went to meet him.

At 9:00 they took their seats in the auditorium that was beginning to feel like home now, Linda thought, she had spent so many hours here in the past few days. Justin had been safely settled in the childcare room, which he had adjusted to amazingly well the day before. He actually seemed to love it. It was so rare that he was around other children, just an occasional sunny afternoon at the playground, and Linda had determined that after the holidays she was going to find a good day-care center for him, even if she had to get the money from Nick until she found a job to pay for it herself. She straightened her back as she promised herself again that, yes, she could and she would carry through with her plan, then glancing around the auditorium, she recognized many of the faces from the past two days of meetings. She hadn't seen Sylvia anywhere yet this morning, but they had planned to meet again for lunch after her session.

"There are really quite a few nuns and priests here," Jack commented and Linda noticed 70 to 80 clerics seated toward the back of the hall.

"I know, I haven't seen so many since I was in school."

"You were raised a Catholic?"

"Oh yeah. Sylvia and I went to the same Catholic school in Los Angeles for years. We're both Irish/Italian actually. Rhonda and Maureen both happened to marry Italian men."

"But wasn't Maureen's husband from up here, San Francisco? I thought that she had mentioned . . ."

"Yes, Uncle Louis was, and so were my mother and Maureen. But my father was from Los Angeles, or that area and . . . Oh! There's that woman again," Linda said, noticing a tanned, blonde woman a few seats behind her. "I'd swear I've seen her before. I mean before this conference."

"Not in this city. She looks like she's been living on a beach somewhere," Jack answered.

"Oh, that's Cristina Vargas," he said, watching the stage now as Cristina walked out and took a seat at the table facing the audience.

Where was it? Linda was still struggling with an image that tugged at her memory. For some reason MasterCharge, the word . . . Oh! The neighbor, the survey woman, of course! That one that Steven thought was a credit inspector—oh, god, Steven. Again she felt the anger, and fear. His drinking, and paranoid delusions . . .

"Good morning, and welcome to our fourth forum of the Women's International for People's Sovereignty Conference," Cristina greeted. "I am Cristina Vargas of AMES, and," she smiled at the Ally seated next to her, "my *compañera*, Rosario Alvarez of Puebla, Mexico. We are speaking this morning about Latin America and Liberation Theology.

"First I will present to you a look at Latin America, life there now, and especially conditions that relate to the United States. Then Rosario will discuss the response of the Catholic Church to those conditions and the rise of what is known as the Theology of Liberation.

"There will be a one-hour break after our presentation before returning for questions and discussion. Texts of this morning's presentation are available for a small donation. Also, for those of you unable to attend yesterday's forums, *Internationalism and the Mideast* and *African Liberation in the Americas*, texts of those presentations are also available in the back of the auditorium. Finally, tomorrow's forum, *Women as Internationalists: Women's Liberation* will begin at 10:00 a.m. and will last the entire day. And possibly the night." She smiled as the audience laughed. "And, it will be open to women only."

Glancing at her notes, and then leaning closer to the microphone, her voice deep and clear, Cristina began.

"It is with great concern that I speak, first, of North America and its activities in what the United States refers to as 'their backyard'—Latin America. Since the Monroe Doctrine in 1823 until today, U.S. rulers and corporations have regarded Latin America as their property—so much acreage to be planted, farmed or mined as best suits their interests—with, of course, only one rather difficult obstacle: the 320 million people living there.

"Over the years, this 'obstacle' has been used, manipulated, or eliminated by a variety of foreign policies, usually, in the end, involving military force.

"The United States has militarily invaded and occupied Latin American nations on 50 occasions since 1865. Argentina, Brazil, Chile, Guatemala, Puerto Rico and Uruguay have all been subject to U.S. armed invasion at least once. The Dominican Republic, five times. Haiti, five times. Columbia, five. Cuba, seven invasions. Honduras, seven. Panama, eight. Mexico, nine times. And Nicaragua also has been invaded nine times since 1865.

"With impunity, the United States military seizes sovereign nations whenever it deems it to be in its economic or political interests; the most recent occasion being three months ago when U.S. Marines invaded and occupied the island nation of Grenada.

"And with every assault the United States has brought a military presence to Latin America, training specialized troops, propping up dictator after dictator. In return for the favor, these dictators have allowed U.S. corporations to take over peasant lands and subject the people to slave-labor conditions in huge plantation systems—better known now as 'agribusiness'—for the development of crops such as sugar and coffee for export.

"The native agriculture of Latin America has been almost entirely destroyed. Crops such as maize, maioc, roots and grains have been plowed under for the development of luxury export crops and huge cattle ranches to export beef, while the native people are close to starving.

"What few of us realize, however, is that the conditions created by these practices, the conditions of abject poverty and repression in Latin America, are *worse* now, in the '80s, than they have *ever* been before. Various Northern economists may point to the rising gross national product of countries such as Brazil or Argentina, and, yes, it is true that Latin America is producing more food products than at any time in its history, but these are export foods—beef, sugar, coffee—products that are sent directly to the United States and Europe for consumption. Not only is the great majority of the Latin American population deprived of the benefits of their land and labor, they are denied even the basic living they were able to extract from their own native crops before the North began to 'develop' the area, and then are forced to pay high import prices for the barest essentials.

"It is important that we realize, yes, U. S. Armed Forces have been in and out of Latin America for over a century. But in this last decade, since 1970, there has been a dramatic *increase* in military dictatorships and repression. *Eleven* of the 18 countries in Central and South America are now under the rule of right-wing military regimes. And never, in its history, has the majority of the population been so impoverished as it is *now* in the 1980s.

"One third of the population of Latin America today, that is, over 100 million people, earn less than $2 a day. Less than $600 a year. And yet the price of a pair of shoes, in Brazil, for example—shoes that were *made* in Brazil—is four times what is charged for that same pair of shoes in England, where the average worker is much more affluent.

"In all of the countries of Central and South America, excepting Nicaragua now, an elite of one to four percent of the population owns almost all of the arable land.

"In the Dominican Republic, one out of every ten children dies in the first year of his or her life from malnutrition.

"In Nova Iguacu, Brazil, over one million people live in a slum that has no running water, no schools, and not one single hospital. Those who work in the city must board buses at 4:00 in the morning to arrive at work at 7:00. They do not return to their dwellings until after 10:00 at night. The average income for these workers is $50 a month per family.

"In Ecuador, the Andean Highlands—one of the eight centers of civilization before European colonialism—malnutrition among the Chimborazo Indians is so severe that 60 percent of the children die in their first year.

"In Mexico, unemployment is estimated at 40 percent. One-fifth of the adult population cannot read or write.

"In Paraguay, 60 percent of the population live without running water or electricity. Ninety percent of peasant deaths are caused by malnutrition."

Cristina paused, her head bowed as she took a breath, then looking up to the audience again, it seemed as if her eyes had caught fire. "What good is it to go on with these cold facts, numbers? The truth is in the living of it. This outrage, this bitter deprivation that is beyond our worst imagination. Unless people have watched their own children die of starvation, had their own homes, however simple, bulldozed before their eyes, been pushed and herded into miserable, filthy shanty towns within view of Hilton Hotels, what can they know of the horror and sorrow of life for most of the Latin American people? Paraguay, Honduras, El Salvador, Colombia, Peru. We can recite the facts, the statistics of poverty and death for each country. The truth is the same. The people's lives are being destroyed. More brutally now, in this decade, than ever.

"And why don't they protest? If there are so many people suffering, how can they let it happen? They're used to it, they don't know anything better, some might say. Of course, as history shows us, we *have* known better, far better. We have known what it is to live on our own lands without foreign occupation. And, as history also shows us, we *do* protest. With increasing success, as Nicaragua proves. But what is the price of protest in Latin America now? What is the price of demanding the right to food, health care, education, employment at a liveable wage?

"Perhaps we should ask Maria de Lorca, a nursery school teacher who was active in the charity work of her church in Argentina. She was 27 years old and four months pregnant when she and her husband were abducted by Argentinian police. As she sat in the police headquarters, she could hear her husband screaming, and then, in her own words:

> The police took me to their room where they kicked me and punched me in the head. Then they undressed me and beat me on the legs, buttocks, and shoulders with something made of rubber. This lasted a long time; I fell down several times and they made me get up and stand by supporting

myself on the table. The police continued to beat me. While this was going on they insulted me and asked me about people I didn't know and things I didn't understand. I pleaded with them to leave me alone, or else I would lose my baby. I hadn't the strength to speak, the pain was so bad.

They started to give me electric shock on my breasts, the side of my body, and under my arms, all the time asking me questions. I was given electric shocks in the vagina and a pillow was placed over my mouth to stop me screaming. Someone they called the 'colonel' came and said they were going to increase the voltage until I talked. They kept throwing water over my body and applying electric shocks all over.

"Of course, she lost her child." Cristina stopped, as if debating whether to go on, but with a look both sickened and resolved, she continued.

"What is the price of calling attention to the poverty and misery forced upon the Latin American people by foreign investors and military puppets? Perhaps we should ask Father Migel Corbazan, a Brazilian priest who spoke against the horror of poverty in Brazil and spent four months in a Brazilian prison. He describes just one of those days:

They kept giving me electric shocks, kicking and beating me in the chest with rods and their hands. Captain Albernaz then made me open my mouth 'to receive the Eucharist.' It was an electric wire. My mouth swelled so much I was unable to speak. They went on screaming and cursing the Church, saying that priests were homosexuals because they don't marry. This session ended up at 2:00 p.m.

At 4:00 p.m. some food was brought to me, but I couldn't swallow—my mouth was an open wound. A few minutes later I was taken to the interrogation room for an 'explanation' . . . again electric shocks, punches, and kicks on the stomach and genitals. I was beaten with hard little boards, cigarette butts were extinguished on my body. For five hours I was thus treated . . . Then I had to walk through the 'Polish Corridor.' I was made to run between two lines of soldiers who beat me until I fainted.

Then they wanted to keep me suspended the whole night on the pau de arara, 'the 'parrot's perch.' They would have hung me from a rod thrust under my knees. But Captain Albernaz said, 'No, that won't be necessary. He will stay with us a few days. If he doesn't speak, his insides will be destroyed, and we know how to do these things without leaving marks. If he survives, he will never forget the price of his insolence.'

I couldn't sleep in my cell. The pain kept getting worse. My head seemed three times larger than the rest of my body. I was haunted by the thought that my brothers would have to go through the same sufferings. It was absolutely necessary to end it all. I was in such a state that I didn't feel capable of suffering more. There was only one way out—to kill myself!

"Father Migel was not able to end his suffering, however. He was subjected to the depraved sadism of the Brazilian police at intervals throughout the remainder of his detention. Not long after his release from prison, he committed suicide."

Cristina paused again, waiting for the emotion that had risen in her to pass, and then in a voice, quiet yet clear, she went on. "These incidents are not isolated examples. They are the standard tactic of the Latin American military dictatorship. In Argentina alone, in September of 1977 there were over 12,000 political prisoners in concentration camps and prisons. You must understand, to be detained as a political prisoner, one need only have done some charity work, made a random comment, known someone who had criticized the regime, or, in some cases, merely have had no friends in the military. By July 1978 in Argentina, over 20,000 people had disappeared.

"Torture, and terror, as a means of crushing protest, as a means of keeping people nailed down to unbearable injustice and hunger . . . Torture and terror, as a strategy, is not unique to Argentina alone, far from it. This strategy is what keeps the military dictators from El Salvador to Paraguay, from Chile to Brazil, in power.

"A Brazilian priest explains it well:

It isn't just the fear of arrest that prevents people from protesting. It is the knowledge that their bodies and minds will be subjected to such excruciating pain that anything, including death, is preferable.

A Brazilian bishop explains it further:

Were it not for the guns, for the torture, and the terror, Brazil's military regime could not survive. And were it not for this regime, foreign corporations could not continue to make enormous profits at the expense of the people.

"Between 1950 and 1975, the United States trained 71,651 Latin American military personnel, including eight of the region's current dictators. Your taxes have been used by corporate industrialists to murder and torture tens of thousands of Latin Americans and keep millions of others in a state of constant suffering from deprivation of life's most basic needs.

"If it shocks or enrages you that as workers, as United States citizens, you are contributing to such debased human behavior, just as it must have shocked the people of Germany to discover the full truth of Nazi policy after the war—atrocities that one would never want to think of for themselves, their children, or anyone—let us look further at some of the uses of the U.S. foreign 'aid' budget and the military budget which is fed by 15 percent of every dollar you earn.

"The Agency for International Development, AID, is the major distributor of U.S. foreign aid. A study made in 1976, published by the U.S. General Accounting Office, stated that the AID 'public safety' program had encouraged the use of torture and assassination by Latin American police and para-police organizations.

"Police in Sao Paulo, Brazil, known for such things as torturing a three-month old baby to death in Tiradentes Prison, were trained by the United States in its ten-year 'public safety' program. Over 100,000 federal and state police, and 600 military officers were trained in the techniques of torture in Brazil alone. United States funding established Brazil's National Institute of Criminology and Identification so that now Brazil is able to share its techniques with other Latin American policemen, such as those in Chile. That is, they share technology they have received from the United States, such as sophisticated computer systems identifying thousands of citizens as targets for torture and imprisonment. Or they share torture paraphernalia such as the 'dragon chair' where victims have their teeth shattered by dentist drills while electric shock is applied to the rest of their body.

"The network of military dictators in Latin America is now able to create a climate of terror throughout the continent by the use of U.S.-funded computer systems and data pools. Anyone suspected of questioning or speaking out against the regime of any particular nation is known to the central computer bank. Coordination among the continent's secret police means that anyone who is targeted by those police has nowhere to hide. It becomes impossible to obtain a passport or visa, not to mention enough money to escape the entire region.

"But integral, central, to the coordination of torture and terror in Latin America, is the Central Intelligence Agency, the CIA. Through a variety of tactics, the CIA was instrumental in overthrowing the democratic presidencies of Arbenz in Guatemala in 1954, and Goulart in Brazil in 1964. In 1972, CIA agent William Cantrel provided financial aid and advice to the Uruguayan police to create their Department of Information and Intelligence—a Death Squad. In 1973 the CIA coordinated the violent overthrow of Chilean President Salvador Allende. In 1975 the CIA developed a master plan, known as the Banzer plan, for the persecution of Church liberals. The plan was adopted by ten Latin American regimes. Its major tactics were to provoke divisions within the Catholic Church, smear and harass progressive Church leaders, and arrest or expel foreign priests and nuns.

"The CIA also assists such right-wing organizations as 'Tradition, Family and Property,' a group that published a lengthy treatise denouncing the work of the liberal clergy for 'completely abandoning their duty and aiding the enemy of religion and country.' According to this treatise, the 'enemy' includes not only the Soviet Union, but the United States Democratic Party as well.

"The list of CIA activities—from manipulating the media to waging secret wars, and the literally billions of dollars that are spent on these activities—cannot be enumerated here, I'm sorry, we don't begin to have the time. But a list of the course subjects taught to Brazilian police in U.S. training classes, as revealed by a U.S. Senate Committee, may serve to summarize the extent of the CIA's operations in Latin America. These course subjects include:

> . . . *censorship, checkpoint systems, chemical and biological operations, briefings on the CIA, civic action and civil affairs, clandestine operations, counterguerrilla operations, cryptography, defoliation, dissent in the United States, electronic intelligence, electronic warfare and countermeasures, the use of informants, insurgency, intelligence, counter-intelligence, subversion, countersubversion, espionage, counterespionage, interrogation of prisoners and suspects, handling mass rallies and meetings, nuclear weapons effects, intelligence photography, polygraphs, populace and resource control, psychological operations, raids and searches, riots, special warfare, surveillance, terror, and undercover operations.*

"These are the kinds of activities that the United States teaches and promotes throughout Latin America, perverting and debasing the very fabric of human social interaction itself. At the bidding of the multinational corporations, they contaminate and dismember every human motion toward life and freedom, through one of the most highly funded U.S. government agencies, the CIA.

"What is the possible reason that Latin American police condone, much less participate in such extreme negation of their humanity, their own countries, and their own people? Are they so enamored of the 'spy' image, the James Bond mentality, that they romanticize their monstrous, sickened lives? Or is it some random freak of nature, as Theodore Brown, chief of the AID 'public safety' program said, when asked at a Senate hearing why there was so much torture in Brazil? Brown said he really couldn't explain, stating, 'Why do some people beat their wives, these things, why do they occur? It is difficult for me to answer.'

"Certainly, it is difficult for him to answer with any sense of truth, just as it would be difficult for him to answer truthfully why some people beat their wives. Because the true answer lies in the falseness of the system that keeps him in power, in the ideology of that system that poses racial and sexual inferiority as its reason for being. A system that claims as its mandate from nature, the right, the necessity to systematically oppress, exploit and humiliate the 'inferior' ones.

"Is it any surprise then, that the ruling elites of Latin America, trained and fed on this ideology, pride themselves on any ounce of European blood they may have or say they do—the lightness of their skin—and do their best to mimic European culture and tradition right down to murdering whole sectors of society in order to accumulate wealth. The Latin American military or policeman sees himself as emulating, embodying, the character of the European man.

"And the leaders of the United States? They are just another set of servants in the hierarchy, the hierarchy that includes the Pentagon, AID, the CIA, the hierarchy of servants to those who are really in control of our continent, and most of the world: the corporations, the agents of capital, the profit-seekers.

"Corporations such as Parke-Davis, which continues to market the drug Chloromycetin in Latin America despite the undisputed fact that it can have fatal side effects. Or Abbot Corporation, which continues to market the drug Cinchophen, taken off the market in the United States decades ago because it was found to cause fatal hepatitis.

"Of course the corporations are not interested in people's health. They are interested in one thing alone. Profit. Money. And it is not simply the people of the South who will be so adversely affected by their ruthless pursuit. In recent years, corporate interests have discovered a new frontier for exploitation and 'development,' the Amazon jungle. The Amazon is one of the last remaining regions of wilderness in the world. Its forestation produces as much as 50 percent of our atmosphere's oxygen. Ecologists refer to the Amazon as the 'lungs of the world.' But this seems to mean nothing to the industrialists. They are determined to clear away the Amazon forests to make more grazing area for cattle in order to produce more beef. Employees of David Ludwig's holdings are using Agent Orange to clear the land. Volkswagon burned seven and a half million trees on a 23,500-acre area. D. Harold Sioli of West Germany informs us that burning one single acre of Amazon forest gives off 120 tons of carbon dioxide. Sioli predicts that if most the Amazon were burned off there would be a ten percent increase in carbon dioxide in the Earth's atmosphere. Brazilian ecologist Vianna believes that the way things are currently going, the Amazon will be a desert in 40 years. This is to say nothing of the indigenous peoples that have already been killed and displaced by the encroaching cattle ranchers, such as the Apalai tribe who formerly lived where Ludwig has taken over, or the Araguaia Indians whose home is now owned by Volkswagon. This 'development' has also endangered 2,000 species of fish, and is destroying 80,000 species of plants that have not yet even been classified by botanists, 100 of which are believed to be medicinal.

"The mentality of the Northern developer, so evident in the destruction of the Amazon, the unconscionable mentality of men who, their minds set on empire, have lost touch with their very humanity, with life itself . . . this mentality is manifest in corporate activity throughout the world, and it is this mentality that underlies the torture, poverty, and suffering that we have seen running rampant in Latin America today.

"Corporations such as United Fruit, now known as United Brands, whose manager in Honduras had this to say:

We must produce a disembowelment of the incipient economy of the country in order to increase and help our aims. We have to prolong its tragic, tormented, and revolutionary life; the wind must blow only on our sails and water must only wet our keel.

Cristina paused a moment, her face expressionless. She took a sip of water and went on.

"Or Gulf & Western Industries which moved into the Dominican Republic when U.S. Marines occupied that country in 1965 to take over the sugar industry. As soon as it arrived, Gulf & Western proceeded to break the local union by denouncing it as Communist and murdering its leaders, then employed Haitians from across the border to cut cane for less than $30 a month. Now, 20 years later, Gulf & Western commands its own small empire in the Dominican Republic, producing one-third of the country's sugar, as well as having substantial holdings in the tourist and construction industries, and controlling interest in the Pablo Duarte Olympic Center, a sports complex which has ties with the Mafia. The U.S. Government has been involved in investigations of Gulf & Western's ties with organized crime for years.

"Finally, the profits produced by U.S. companies in Latin America do not stay there. The little that does is in the hands of the military elites. So what happens to these profits? Are they even taxed to provide revenue for the host nation? In fact, most of these profits are never even recorded as income but are funneled back to the United States by a mechanism known as 'transfer pricing.' For example, an automobile plant operating in Latin America will order parts from its parent company in the United States. The parent company will then bill the plant at ten times the actual cost of the parts. The plant will then pay the inflated price, booking the outflow of cash as an expense, and thus make its net profit—or taxable income—appear to be one tenth of what it actually was. The parent company will receive actual profits as 'payments for goods received'—tax-free.

"In Colombia, the transfer price on rubber is 40 percent; on chemicals, 25 percent; on pharmaceuticals, 155 percent. Transfer pricing by the pharmaceutical industry alone in Colombia cost that country $20 million in foreign exchange and $10 million in tax revenue.

"According to the Department of Commerce, for every dollar that the United States invests in Latin America, three dollars come back to the U.S. companies in profits. The Latin American economies were drained of $7.5 billion by U.S. companies between 1950 and 1965.

"Beyond this, through mechanisms such as 'price-freezes,' the United States is able to control the price at which it will purchase Latin American exports. For example, during World War II the U.S. Government froze the price of Chilean copper at the depression level cost of 12 cents a pound when the world market price was 21 cents. This cost Chile $500 million. At the same time the price of Bolivian tin was frozen at 42 cents a pound when the actual price was more than $3. Bolivia lost up to $900 million, much more than all of the U.S. aid given to Bolivia since that time. Yet now Bolivia is 'in debt' to U.S. banks.

"'Tax-free ports' in the Bahamas, Curacao, or Panama allow companies to ship goods throughout Latin America without paying import tariffs. And yet another form of market manipulation cost Brazil $100 million in 1974, this one instigated by the international commodity traders in the World Trade Center in Manhattan. After urging Brazilian farmers to plant major crops of soybeans, foreign monopolies worked a deal with the Brazilian dictator involving a ban on exports in order to lower the prices. Once the prices had dropped by 40 percent, the monopolies had the crops exported at 300,000 to 400,000 tons a day.

"As billions of dollars in tax revenues and profits are drained out of Latin America by the players of the free-enterprise game, U.S. banks scream for repayment of 'Third World debts' and the International Monetary Fund imposes ever more stringent 'austerity measures' on the impoverished economies of Southern nations. Is it any wonder that the Nonaligned Movement demands a New International Economic Order?

"For the current order gives the people of the South, the people who work the farms and produce the goods from which these billions of dollars are made, a *decreasing* standard of living, to the point of starvation. To protest, to organize, to form a union means inevitably prison, torture, or death at the hands of the U.S.-trained military regimes.

"Yet even against incredible odds, Latin Americans work to throw off the stranglehold of corporate and military dictatorship. Throughout the continent, there is resistance. And they can, and will, and do succeed. Nicaragua shines as a beacon of hope. Though many were tortured and killed, the Nicaraguans made their collective will for liberation and justice a reality.

"The will of humanity to live free from domination, for the love of ourselves and each other, cannot be stopped, it cannnot be crushed out of us, except by total annihilation. Though that may be the last insane act of the empire-builders, until that possibility occurs, the movement of people toward freedom cannot be stopped.

"In the words of Nicaraguan women . . . Dora Maria Tellez, a Sandinista, asks:

> What makes a man believe in his own potential as a man? What makes a woman believe that she is capable of anything? No one taught us. That is one of the great mysteries about the Revolution. They don't teach it to you at school. You don't learn to believe in humanity on the streets. Religion doesn't teach it. It teaches us to believe in God, not in men and women. So it's difficult to awaken that belief in yourself and others. But in spite of all that, many women and men did develop that commitment.

Or as Yaosca, a peasant woman who worked with the Sandinistas said:

> For the first six months I worked as a messenger between Esteli and Jinotega. Then I was sent to the mountains. I didn't find it hard. There was the cold, the mosquitoes . . . but when you looked at your comrades and

saw they were all suffering through the same things, that
you were all struggling together, you didn't mind it.
Actually, I was very happy there."

Cristina stopped. The audience hesitated, still caught in the motion of her voice. There was a feeling, for everyone there, that they had traveled a great distance, seen events they had never known to occur, that left them stirred, angered, outraged. The applause began slowly, then filled the room, a total, yet somber acknowledgement.

Linda sat nearly motionless, unaware of her own hands as she too applauded, feeling only the tears in her eyes, not just for the ugly truth she had heard, much of it she knew, had read in books Sylvia had given her. No, more she was moved by the courage of these women, the Nicaraguan women Cristina spoke of, and Cristina herself, so clear and compelling as she told a history of brutality that she herself had experienced in El Salvador, her own husband murdered . . . Linda studied Cristina's face, but still she saw there only the same composed expression with just the trace of defiance. Or was it power? The strength of her commitment, the kind of commitment she had described in the quote from the Nicaraguan woman. What must that feel . . . Suddenly Linda thought of Claire, in Nicaragua now herself. What must she be feeling? She tried to picture her there. It wasn't hard really. Somehow she could see Claire, her long legs striding along a dirt road through the area near the border, her hair damp against her skin in the sweltering heat as she looked ahead, assessing the situation. But god, what would she do, Linda thought, what would she do if she were captured by CIA Contra forces? Could she begin to endure the . . . No. No, it was too close to home, she couldn't picture it. She looked quickly back to the stage.

Rosario, exchanging a quick word with Cristina as the room quieted again, turned to face the audience. With a look both intent and gentle, she began.

"Dora Maria Tellez speaks to us of the mystery of faith in humanity. The love that guided the Nicaraguans in their struggle and their vision of human justice. She says that it is not something that is taught to us in school, on the streets, or by religion. And I would think for most of us here, if we recall our own past experience, we would have to agree this is true. But that does not mean that such a love and faith cannot become a part of the institutions of a society. Certainly, if a society is brought into being from the strength of such a vision, and it is allowed to develop without external attacks that consume its energies in defense, then that society can bring its vision to bear in all of its constructs, its activities. Faith and love in human life, human justice.

"I am a Catholic nun who has lived in Puebla, Mexico, for 32 years. As a child I attended church regularly with my family. In Puebla it is not difficult to do," she smiled, "there are 365 churches, one for every day of the year. My family was very poor, certainly very poor by the standards of life in this country, but not so poor as many people in the most impoverished provinces of Mexico, or others throughout Latin America.

"When Dora Maria tells us that religion does not teach us to believe in men and women, it only teaches us to believe in God, I know very well the truth of her words when I remember the many, many hours my family and I spent in the churches of Puebla when I was a child. There we would pray to God that we might find peace in heaven, after death. This was our only hope. We lived in fear that we would displease God somehow, and never see the light of heaven, where human sorrow, poverty, and despair would vanish and at last we could experience something of happiness, joy . . . an existence we had no hope at all to ever see on Earth. Any hope or faith we had was that God would redeem us in heaven, and for this we labored through the Catholic devotions with a gravity that made the rest of our lives seem meaningless. This well pleased our government, and the Church itself.

"From the time the *conquistadores* first stepped foot on Latin American soil in the 16th century, up until the very recent past, the Catholic Church has served as an instrument of colonialism. The conquering Europeans and their priests divided up the wealth of the civilizations they plundered, each as lustful of gold as the other. By the beginning of the 19th century, the Catholic Church was the largest landowner in Latin America.

"The Church taught the Indian and African slaves, and later the poor workers and peasants, to accept their fate of suffering because misery would guarantee them a place in heaven. It fostered the Spanish and Portuguese extremes of the mentality of male supremacy, or *machismo*. And it bargained with the upper classes, selling them prayers and Masses in return for the promise that God would forgive their plunder and slaughter of innocent people. Every Latin American dictator ruled hand in hand with a Catholic bishop.

"But then, after so many centuries of hypocrisy, in the 1960s, just as I was coming of age in Puebla, great changes began to stir within the Catholic Church. It all began with the Second Ecumenical Council, Vatican II, called by Pope John XXIII in Rome. Wide, sweeping reforms were carried out throughout the world's Church, but perhaps nowhere were they as significant as in Latin America. For the first time in the history of the Church, leading bishops spoke out of the need for social change—and this at a time when military dictatorships were proliferating. The military attempted to silence the bishops' concerns for the poor, and this further outraged the bishops, creating an ever wider gap between the once so interwoven church and state. Though not all of the Church's leaders were so progressive. No, unfortunately there are still many Catholic traditionalists who want to bring back the days when the Church was the not-so-silent partner of the ruling elites.

"In 1968 in Medellin, Colombia, for the second time in history, the bishops of the Latin American Church met together. And it was at Medellin that the voice of the new consciousness in the Church, the Theology of Liberation, was crystallized. For the first time the bishops authorized statements denouncing the horrors of dictatorship. They proclaimed that the mass of the Latin American people are oppressed by an 'institutionalized violence' that, 'seeking unbounded profits, foments an economic dictatorship and the international imperialism of money.'

"The bishops warned the 'developmentalists' that where there is no justice, there is no peace, and that those with the 'greater share of wealth, culture and power' who 'jealously retain their privileges . . . provoking explosive revolutions of despair' must face reality.

"Medellin promoted two key concepts: 'liberation' and 'participation.' It was proposed that the Church foster these concepts among the people by working toward two major goals. The first was to develop educational programs for the illiterate masses by the method of 'conscientization,' or consciousness-raising, as developed by the philosopher Paulo Freire.

"Conscientization is based on the conviction that people are 'co-creators with God.' That is, we can consciously affect physical reality and ourselves, thereby creating a new reality. This was used in teaching the poor to read and write by putting emphasis on words that describe the present reality—like 'hungry' or 'barefoot'—and encouraging the understanding of the meaning of these words. The teacher sees this process as a two-way activity, he or she learning about reality from the poor, just as the reverse is true. Both develop a greater awareness of existing reality and, in turn, see that it does not have to be so. It can change. Because changing our perception of ourselves and our purpose and potential inspires the social participation necessary to change physical reality.

"The second major goal set at Medellin was the establishment of Christian communities. These communities are composed of 12 to 15 members who participate as cooperative, almost familial groups, in developing their own Christian beliefs, again with an approach to learning by conscientization. Because this activity is a self-initiated and liberating process, these groups frequently go on to develop other cooperatives such as schools or health units. What is unique about these communities is that they come from and are developed by the poor themselves. They are *not* the temporary result of a charity-worker's visit to the impoverished masses. They emerge from and belong to the people.

"As of 1979, there were 100,000 Christian communities in Latin America. These communities are developing a new sense of kinship and cooperation that overcomes the despair of poverty and deprivation. When Santiago's Center for Urban and . . ."

As Rosario spoke, Cristina glanced to the side entrance of the stage where Rikki stood half-behind the curtain beckoning to her, a strained expression on her face. Cristina quietly rose from her chair and walked off the stage.

"Cristina, I'm sorry," Rikki whispered as they moved back stage. "Q Committee insisted I check with you . . ."

"That's all right. What is it?"

"The woman I told you about the other day, the one Marcia talked about . . ."

"Q Committee told me they were checking on her. They said they'd tell me if there was a problem . . ."

"I know, I know," Rikki said, "and they didn't until now. I mean, they didn't think she was a problem. They found out she was working with an anti-nuke group and was sent here as their representative. In fact, Terry kind of knows her . . ."

"But?"

"But this morning just before the forum, Gina—she's still been watching her—saw her come through the courtyard gate sort of pretending she was a NEWS member. She was talking to some of the European cadres. Apparently she didn't go through the security check in the auditorium, I don't know . . . Gina's out there now, keeping an eye on her. She told Kate to find me and come and ask you . . ."

"Show me," Cristina said, walking to the side door off-stage that opened out to the hall.

Rikki surveyed the audience as the two women looked out the half-open door. "There she is," Rikki said, counting, "Twelfth row, fourth seat in."

"Hmm." Cristina shrugged. "Have you seen her before?"

"No. At least I don't think so."

"Well we shouldn't take any chances. Tell Q Committee to send some cadres over here. Tell them to have Terry approach her with two Q cadres and ask to speak with her a minute. Get her outside in front of the auditorium to the street. Have some Q cadres posted there too. Find Ruth and tell her to mobilize a K team to question her further and, well, they know the procedure. It shouldn't be necessary but . . . Tell Q if there's any trouble in getting her to leave, to shake her down immediately and go into emergency position whether they find anything on her or not." Cristina stopped a moment, deliberating. "Yes. That's it. We can't take a chance." She looked at Rikki. "How long will it take you to do this?"

"Ten minutes?" Rikki said, taking her Telcom unit from her belt.

"All right. I'll alert security on the stage." With that Cristina turned and walked through the back stage and out to the table where Rosario continued to speak.

"Between 1964 and 1978, over 1,500 Catholic clergy were arrested in Latin America. Over 120 were tortured; 125 were murdered; 53 have disappeared; over 500 were deported. The countries where this terror against Liberation Theologians has been most severe are Uruguay, Paraguay, Mexico, Honduras, El Salvador, Ecuador, Colombia, Chile, Bolivia, and especially, Argentina and Brazil. Throughout all of Latin America, due to the work of the CIA, and in particular its infamous 'Banzer Plan,' the ruling military elites are attempting to crush the rise of Liberation Theology and the new hope it gives to the people.

"In just one case, in Mexico, in the northern city of Chihuahua, a young priest, Father Aguilar . . ." Rosario paused a moment, remembering her friend. She began again. "In 1974, just after his ordination, Father Aguilar arrived in Chihuahua, Mexico, to the community of Nombre de Dios, the 'Name of God,' where there lived about 20,000 people. There was no running water or electricity, no sewage system, no telephones, no mail service, no parks, and no high schools. There were none of these. But there was poverty, sickness, oppression, and despair. Within yards of this shanty town of Nombre de Dios were the major industries of Chihuahua, where many of the people worked. Also nearby was the residential area where the wealthy elite lived, its typical mansions and palatial estates in full view.

"Father Aguilar was a Liberation Theologian. Unlike priests of the past who never left their parish house, Father Aguilar celebrated Mass each day in a different part of the community. He met and talked with people throughout the shanty town, holding discussions that brought about the mutual learning of conscientization. Soon the community began to come together in a collective awareness of their problems and the desire to change them.

"When one of the families of Nombre de Dios was threatened with eviction from their one-room house, a house they had been living in for over 20 years and had been paying for all of that time, the community rose up in their defense, organizing themselves into the Committee for Social Rights. The Committee continued to grow after this issue was won and in 1975 sent 200 members to the governor of Chihuahua to ask for mail service, a sewage system, and land for housing. The governor's response was to wait a few days and then send police into the shanty town to beat up and abuse the people.

"But still the community movement grew. And then the government authorities demanded that Father Aguilar leave Chihuahua. Five thousand people from Nombre de Dios demonstrated against the demand. At this point in time, Sunday meetings were drawing over 500 people to plan programs to improve the community. Finally, the local government conceded to provide mail service, a high school, land for the construction of 400 houses, running water, and the beginning of a sewage system that would serve over 100,000 of Chihuahua's poor. When the government was slow to come through with work on the sewage system and was demanding an inflated price for the work, the people of Nombre de Dios decided to build it themselves.

"The response of the government to this was to send two agents to the home of Father Aguilar. The agents asked the priest to come with them, a friend of theirs was dying, they said, and needed to receive the last rites. They took him to another house. There they murdered him."

Rosario paused again, her eyes thoughtful, then she lifted her head. "But the people of Nombre de Dios continued ever stronger in their movement. This was what the government cannot understand. Father Aguilar was not their leader. The people lead themselves. The people of Nombre de Dios went on to form a cooperative, build a health center, continue work on the sewage system, found a parent-teachers association and extract from the government both running water and a system of parks.

"The Church's social and pastoral departments in Northern Mexico had this to say of Father Aguilar's murder:

> *We invite those who are glad of his death to open the pages of the New Testament and to ask themselves if they truly believe in Christ, for two thousand years ago another man was similarly criticized by those with economic and political power. His intentions were also misunderstood; he, too, was accused of popular agitation and of blasphemy for predicating a God who wanted equality and fraternity among men, and, because of this, he was condemned as a political leader opposed to the Roman Empire.*

"But perhaps Father Aguilar was fortunate. He was shot to death. He did not suffer the fate of, say, Father Bentancur of Honduras, whose work with the poor of Olancho had angered the wealthy cattle ranchers there. On June 25, 1975, he was abducted along with five peasants in his company to the home of one of the richest ranchers in the area. There, the five peasants were given the choice of being castrated or cooked alive in a bread oven. The peasants chose death. They were burnt alive in an oven. But the ranchers devised an even worse fate for

Father Bentancur. He was stripped, whipped and beaten. His eyes were gouged out. His fingernails, tongue and teeth were pulled out. His hands, feet, and testicles were slashed off. He was then dumped into a 150-foot well with the bodies of the peasants. Because of an investigation demanded by Father Bentancur's mother and the Church, the mutilated bodies were eventually discovered.

"But despite this . . ." Rosario paused again. "Despite the demonic attempts of the wealthy to crush the motion of the Latin American people, the faith, the knowledge of their own strength and power to create justice can never be crushed.

"And the Theology of Liberation cannot be crushed. Despite even the . . ." Rosario stopped as Cristina turned her head sharply.

"No no, go on," Cristina murmured to her, watching closely as three women approached the young blonde woman in the twelfth row of the audience and Rosario looked back to her notes, beginning again.

The three women stood close around the blonde woman's chair as Terry bent to speak to her, and Linda, a few seats away, turned her head at the sound of their hushed whispers. What's that about? Linda wondered as after a moment the woman rose and walked out of the auditorium with the NEWS cadres. Linda turned back to the stage, listening to Rosario.

"This for the fear of communism. 'Communism.' A word that most people in Latin America—and North America too, I am told—cannot even begin to accurately define. Yet in the name of 'anti-communism' three-month old babies are tortured to death. Men, women and children are murdered. Tens of thousands are imprisoned or 'disappear.' Masses of people are kept in conditions that barely sustain life—all this—horror and terror to protect the world from 'communism.'

"The military, the wealthy, the conservative bishops rush to call anyone who might question the injustice of their system a 'communist,' an object for torture and death. The words of a Oaxacan peasant woman express this very clearly:

> *The same thing always happens: anyone who complains that we peasants are the victims is immediately accused of being a communist, an enemy of God, and a subversive. He is tracked down, tortured, and murdered, and afterwards his corpse, totally mutilated, is dumped on some road.*

"A group of Mexican businessmen connected to the multinational corporations issued statements denouncing the bishops' conference claiming that 'Marxists in priests' dress were the cause of independent unions, economic instability, crazy strikes, and inflationary salaries.'

Inflationary salaries! They are referring to wages of 25 cents an hour. When the top corporate executive in Brazil receives $500,000 in *one week!*

"I believe that Archbishop Helder Camera of Brazil most clearly exposes the myth of 'anti-communism,' for he acknowledges that 'communism,' as a word, has *no* meaning. Too many individuals, groups, nations, have used the word to suit their own purposes, regardless of its original meaning.

"The voice of Liberation Theology in the Catholic Church does not promote any specific political ideology, system or organization. It does, however, demand an end to torture, starvation, and exploitation of the people of Latin America. As Dom Camera explains:

> *What we need to find for Latin America is a line of socialization adapted to Latin American needs. I am thinking of a conscious participation by more classes of the population in the control of power and the sharing of wealth and culture. The world trend is toward socialism. At this time, Christians offer to it the mystique of universal brotherhood and hope.*

"In conclusion," Rosario paused, reflecting a moment. "I believe that, for those of you who have not traveled in Latin America, or in Africa, or other parts of the Third World—you cannot imagine the depths of misery that exist there.

"And neither, perhaps, can you imagine the will of the people to break free of enslavement and degradation. Liberation Theology was born of the knowledge that this is the absolute right of all people, the right to be free of tyranny. The right of humanity to share, collectively, in the wealth of the world, with respect for life, and the beauty of creation. For this right, many are willing to give their lives. We nuns and priests are but a few of those. Yet, as Gustavo Gutierrez says:

> *Those who attribute violence to the Theology of Liberation do not know what they are talking about. The Theology's position on violence is the same as the Church's traditional teaching on 'just wars' that dates to St. Thomas Aquinas: that violence is possible as a lesser evil and last resort against a greater violence, such as tyranny, but that no Christian willingly accepts such a choice.*

"But when it is the only resort of the majority of people to free themselves from the likes of a Somoza, a Pinochet—a maniacal dictator who revels in terror to please the foreign investors—then we cannot denounce the act of the people to break free. We cannot denounce the Sandinistas of Nicaragua, or the FDR of El Salvador, or the URGP of Guatemala. We can only applaud their courage."

Rosario stopped and, as most of the audience burst into a resounding applause, Linda couldn't help but turn around to see the response of the 70 or so nuns and priests seated in the back of the hall. Some of them looked ashen, some hesitant, others jubilant. Certainly she herself had never heard a nun talk like this before.

Several people were standing now and, as Linda turned back around, she realized Jack, too, was standing and clapping, his strong hands somehow audible to her above the rest. She stood with him, carried up by the growing din of acclaim. Rosario and Cristina also stood, applauding with the audience, both emanating a strength—no, a power—that moved Linda again, as had every speaker that she had heard at this conference. Though each time, she was moved to a deeper level of respect for their movement, for this informed, dedicated, courageous movement of women as multifaceted, strong and sharp and embodied of light as a trove of jewels—jewels that were the world's treasure, that belong to all, that everyone could possess—no—could become.

As she left the auditorium with Jack out the heavy wooden door to the courtyard beyond, Linda was quiet, still feeling that motion within her, as if fundamental, rooted conceptions were shifting, opening. The courtyard was filling with NEWS Allies and cadres as various sessions were breaking for lunch. Again the image of glittering jewels, resplendent color, from deep in the earth took hold of her as at the same moment the sound of Cristina's voice detailing the brutality, suffering and torture inflicted on the people of these countries sounded in her mind—the filthy work of the Pentagon, the CIA, the United States corporations. And she understood, for the first time, what she had always known intellectually but felt now as a compelling, demanding reality. Yes, the empire-builders, the money-seekers are defiling and destroying the true treasure of the earth, a treasure they do not even see or comprehend: Life. They must be *stopped.*

"What are you thinking?" Jack asked gently as they stood by the wall of the church waiting for Sylvia.

"Oh, I . . ." Linda looked at him. "You know, I feel as if . . . this experience." She looked around the courtyard. "It's changed me in a way, that . . . I just feel, I'll never be the same." She looked at him again, a questioning smile on her lips.

Jack nodded silently and it seemed to Linda that he understood.

"Hi," Sylvia greeted, joining them as an almost imperceptible apprehension crossed her mind. She felt she was interrupting something, something quite intimate. But the feeling left her as Linda turned and, smiling broadly, gave her a hug, and Jack smiled warmly at her. It seemed they were both just energized, excited by the conference.

"Sylvia, I've been learning so much. I can't wait to talk with you about it, for hours, when it's over and you have the time," Linda said, her voice enthusiastic, yet slightly disconcerted.

Sylvia looked at her, then smiled. "I'd love to. We will." She looked around behind her. "Rikki's going to meet us here and then I thought we could walk up to that little park up the street. I got some sandwiches and fruit from the kitchen."

"That sounds great," Jack said, looking up at the sky. "It looks like the rain will hold off for awhile yet."

"There she is," Linda said, waving at Rikki as she came through the auditorium door and, making her way through the crowded courtyard, joined them at the church wall.

"Hi, how are you?" Rikki smiled at Jack, remembering him from the Berkeley demonstration. "Hi, Linda." She gave Sylvia's cousin a warm smile. "So, here we are, reunited."

Laughing, the four of them made their way to the gate in the west wall of the courtyard. Out on the street, Rikki said quietly to Sylvia as they fell back behind Linda and Jack, now involved in discussion, "Syl, there was some very weird shit going on this morning."

"What?"

"Well, Q Committee decided that that woman Marcia talked about wasn't OK after all and we had to pull her out of this morning's forum."

"Really? What happened?"

"Well, we just asked her to come with us, and she did, without any problem. I don't know. I can't tell . . ."

"Where is she now?"

"With the K team I guess. They'll figure it out. Cristina's with them. I went back to my session, actually. I'm not on the Q Committee, thank god." Rikki laughed.

"Hmm . . . Well I'm glad they're dealing with it," Sylvia said. "That's the first person they've had to deal with, as far as I've heard. What'd she do?"

"Snuck around the security check."

"Is that it?" Jack asked.

Sylvia looked up. "Oh, yeah." The four of them walked toward the little park where a picnic table stood in the middle of a grassy slope.

"Sylvia, did you read Cristina's and Rosario's presentations?" Linda asked.

"Oh yes, we've read all the presentations."

"And a few thousand pages of other materials," Rikki added.

"A few thousand!" Linda said.

"Well, no. But definitely hundreds," Sylvia said.

"When we're not meeting, we're reading. And when we're not reading, we're meeting," Rikki explained.

"What about sleeping?" Jack asked.

"That's what I'd like to know," Rikki answered.

Jack laughed. "Cristina's certainly a dynamic speaker though," he said.

"And so was Sister Rosario," Linda added. "You know, Sylvia, hearing her really did something serious to my image of a nun. Do you know what I mean? Don't you remember the nuns at St. Julian's? Some of them were nice, but. They were all so politically conservative, talking about praying for the 'pagan babies,' and how hateful the communists are."

"Well, I think probably there are still a lot of Catholics who think that way, in this country especially," Sylvia answered.

"Well, Syl, wouldn't you say, too," Rikki asked, "that Rosario is like . . . Well, if you took the political spectrum in the Catholic Church and said 'one' is the most conservative bishops—the ones who hang out with dictators—and 'ten' is the most revolutionary thinkers, then Rosario is definitely a ten?"

"Yeah," Jack remarked, "I was wondering how the Mexican government would take to her making some of the statements she did."

"I know," Sylvia agreed. "But actually she's not going back to Mexico. She decided a few months ago that when she came up here for the conference she would stay to work in the Mexican community in Los Angeles. More than a million Mexican people live in L.A."

"Really?" Linda asked. "I hadn't . . . But still, aren't the problems of the poor *in* Mexico more demanding, I mean . . ."

"But people of color have a completely different relationship to this country than we do, whether they live in it or not. In some ways, East L.A. isn't that different than Puebla," Rikki said as they seated themselves at the wooden table, she and Sylvia across from Linda and Jack.

"We certainly heard about how that's true for black people at yesterday's forum," Jack said.

"African Liberation in the Americas?" Sylvia asked, putting their sandwiches in the middle of the table.

"Oh, yes," Linda nodded with that disconcerted look in her eyes again. She gazed at the stark, bare branches of the elm tree hovering above them in the grey, winter light.

"I have to admit, I hadn't totally realized," Jack began. "I mean, the extent of it. That half of the black men in this country are dead by the age of 25! Or that the infant mortality rate is twice that of white people. And the unemployment, it's outrageous. In New York we were working with a . . ."

"What—there she is again," Rikki whispered, nudging Sylvia.

"Who?" Sylvia asked, following Rikki's gaze past Linda, who was listening closely to Jack. She looked out to the street 50 feet away.

"That woman I told you about," Rikki whispered.

Sylvia studied the young blonde woman walking, alone, quickly down the street. "Huh, I've never seen her before. Though you know, she looks a little like that woman at the airport. Remember? But it's not her. What was her name?"

"No, no. It's not her. I saw her close up. I wonder what she's doing? I guess K team let her go."

"What else could they do? Lock her up? Maybe she's OK. God, it's so hard to . . ."

"What are you two whispering about?" Linda asked, looking over at them now, laughing.

"I'm sorry, Linda." Sylvia looked up. "Just talking about security, actually."

"Speaking of security," Rikki said, standing up from the table. "I have to get back."

"Oh, that's right. Your squad's coordinating for the plenary." Sylvia glanced at her watch. "You didn't even have any lunch, Rikki. But yeah, you better go."

"It was nice to see you again." Rikki smiled at Linda and Jack. "Maybe we can get together sometime later." She turned to leave.

"Rikki, take an apple," Sylvia called after her. Rikki turned and held up her hands as Sylvia tossed her a bright, red apple. She caught it deftly, and with a grin, took a bite and headed out of the park.

"She's really cute," Linda said, "she seems so nice. And fun," she added, watching Rikki walk down the street.

"She is. She's a good friend," Sylvia agreed.

"Is she a lesbian?" Linda asked tentatively.

"Mmhmm," Sylvia answered, guessing what her cousin had in mind, though nothing could be further from the truth. She decided to put an end to Linda's speculation, adding, "Her lover, Carol, is in NEWS, too. They both joined about the same time. And they've started seeing a lot more of each other recently, too. Apparently they've decided it's going to work, and they don't have to keep all that 'safe' distance people do sometimes at the beginning of a relationship."

"Oh," Linda answered. She thought a moment. "And Ruth's a lesbian too, isn't she?"

"No, she's not. She's straight." Sylvia laughed. "Linda, just because I'm a lesbian doesn't mean everyone I know is. Most the women in NEWS are straight, you know. At least 90 percent. Though, yeah, anyone who wants to discredit us always calls us a mob of dykes, queers. You know. The usual. Even in this town, we get that label." She paused. "Though in the San Francisco chapter there are more lesbians, but that reflects the population. NEWS does—it's surprising how it does—represent the general population of women. All ages, religions, class backgrounds—and 'sexual orientations.'" She gave Linda a serious, teasing look.

"That really is impressive, though, Sylvia," Jack said sincerely. "I mean how diverse NEWS is, and still so clearly focused."

"Not only that, Jack," Sylvia smiled, "but as of Friday, it looks like we're going to have men as members, too."

Jack smiled. "Yes, I've heard."

"We should all get back, really," Linda said, checking her watch. "I want to spend a few minutes with Justin." She began to gather the remains of their lunch from the table as Jack and Sylvia helped her, and the three of them left the park.

At one o'clock the great stone church of St. Joan's, with its lofty gothic arches rising to an apex, enthroning the brilliant rose window high above the altar, housed over 1,200 women for the first plenary session since the opening of the conference. Though the session had not yet started, there was a silence within the vaulted walls, a silence humming with a sense of accomplishment and expectation. The Allies, seated in the long wooden pews at the front and sides of the cross-shaped church, sat in groupings by language, arranged by NEWS cadres who had worked much of the morning setting up the intricate electronics for the interpreters' translations. NEWS Security, out in full strength, stood alert at their positions. Sylvia saw Rikki, so serious now, at her post by the north side of the altar. And there was Olina, whispering something to Ruth at the end of the pew where Sylvia sat with JoAnn, Ellen, Laura, Catherine, the women she knew so well now, had worked with so intensely for so long. And somehow, it didn't seem to matter nearly so much that one woman, Claire, was not there. Sylvia was surprised herself by how deeply moved she felt at this moment, more even than that first morning of the conference that seemed so long ago now. But today she felt in these women a power she had never known she could feel. There, with all of them, after their days and nights of work, and late last night, the meeting of NEWS CLAN . . . they *were* making the difference, the critical difference. She knew now, sitting there in the quiet of the church. These women together, with all of their diversity in unprecedented communion and trust, would have an impact on the world that would be greater than, even in her most hopeful moments, she had begun to imagine.

She saw Olina stand and walk quickly to the front of the church. Olina. It was so wonderful to have her back. Olina understood her so well. When she had given her the letter she had brought from Claire, just the motion of her hand and, of course, her eyes, had somehow said it all. As if she knew everything Sylvia had been going through, and in that moment, without words, she had offered her the deepest comfort. And somehow, too, the inspiration to overcome her pain.

Olina stood now at the microphone on the steps of the altar, preparing to open the plenary. Behind her, at long tables stretching the width of the altar, sat Allies and NEWS cadres waiting to report on their sessions. Olina turned back a moment to check with them. Each would be presenting the proposals generated from their work groups, and the general body would then discuss and vote on resolutions. They hoped to be done by midnight. Much of the plenary was being videotaped for the Amsterdam conference and would be transmitted to them that night, if access to the appropriate facilities could be managed. In two days, on Friday night, there would be the final plenary where the NEWS strategy and 1984 program would be formally accepted. Most of the work on it, including achieving agreement, would take place in the next two day's work sessions, not to mention the months and months of preparatory work and the foundation that today's resolutions would provide. Direct communications with Amsterdam would be stepped up over the next two days to coordinate international strategic decisions by electronic systems set up in the administrative office of the convent.

Olina turned back to face the hundreds of women seated in the church. She began, "It is with great pride and joy that . . ."

A crash of shattering glass split through her words as a thousand fragments of colored glass and a howl of wind flew from the gaping, sharded rose window. The stage was vacated within the instant, NEWS Security surrounding the Allies through the sacristy door while as quickly as the wooden pews emptied, NEWS Security, lightning quick, filed the women through and out the side and rear doors of the church, forming cordons around them when, suddenly all stopped—deafened, bludgeoned by an explosion.

Flames leapt up the walls of the altar as fragments of wood, plaster, metal flew through the air. Without stopping to breathe, NEWS Security kept the flow of women moving out of the church as those in the front formed a human wall between the burning altar and the Allies still leaving the front pews, the heat and smoke suffocating, NEWS Security defying their own aching lungs as they stood firm, guiding the last women through the side doors of the church, and those outside surrounding the exiting Allies, guiding, escorting them quickly into the street to cars and vans that appeared, one after another, and kept appearing. While still in the church, the last of the women leaving in the rear, Sylvia couldn't help but look back and back again at the flaming altar, the NEWS Security barely visible now in the smoke, though she could see the dark red blood on a forehead, torn clothing, a gashed arm, and then, she saw . . .

She pushed past Gina, whose orange-banded arm stretched out to guide the last few women leaving by the rear door. "Sylvia. Go!" she commanded.

"Gina, let me go!" Sylvia said, pushing past her, running up the side aisle of the church into the thickening smoke and heat. Somehow, she had seen her, lying there, crumpled, so small, frail now, lying there in the corner at the foot of the altar behind the front Security cordon. She pushed through them. "Sylvia!" Lynn shouted at her angrily, her breathing heavy, weakened. Sylvia pushed past and, just behind the back of the cordon, she threw herself to the ground, to the woman lying there, a deep, ugly gash across her neck, her face and hair in a thick pool of dark, red blood. "Rikki! Rikki! Oh, god. Rikki." Sylvia bent low to her, struggling to lift her in her arms, as the blood still poured from her neck, her head half-sliced away from her body, her blood-drained face frozen in horror. "Oh, god, oh, god, oh, god." Sylvia laid her back again on the stone floor, laying her own face against Rikki's bloodied, stiff cheek as the heat of the flames grew closer, and Lynn, Jean and Karen left the cordon and came to her.

"Sylvia! Come! Now!" Lynn shouted at her. The flames had leapt the altar railing, burning the velvet carpet of the steps.

"Are the Allies out?" Sylvia shouted back. She couldn't see through the smoke, but most the women in the cordons were leaving now themselves.

"Yes!"

"Help me with her," Sylvia pleaded, still kneeling by Rikki, her hands and arms drenched in blood. Lynn ran from the altar, gagging, choking for air. Jean and Karen, with the last ounce of their strength, bent and lifted Rikki's legs and torso as Sylvia cradled her shoulders and head in her arms, the endless blood still streaming from the nearly severed neck. They walked slowly, choking, gasping for air, yet perfectly coordinated in their movement, they made their way to the side door of the church and outside.

They stood outside the church door, the three of them holding their dead friend, a macabre sight, as they strained for oxygen to quiet the agony of their lungs. The screech of sirens, so long in coming, now split their ears, and they became conscious of crowds of people down and across the street gaping at the leaping flames through the shattered rose window above the courtyard walls. The three of them, pushing themselves to move, walked again, slowly, to a lawn across the street away from the crowd, where in one gravely tender motion, they lay Rikki's body.

"You'd better go," Sylvia whispered to Jean and Karen, her voice hoarse, barely audible. "Go to Medical first," she added.

"The Allies have to be evacuated," Jean answered, mouthing more than speaking the words.

Sylvia shook her head. "Medical," she managed to repeat. Then they all sat down on the grass waiting for some semblance of breath to return to them. They watched, as if in a daze, as the firemen leapt from their trucks, roping off the area, uncoiling their massive hoses, some entering the church at the north side door that the four of them had just left moments ago, others charging through the courtyard gate beyond the convent, directing a flood of water through the gaping rose window in the church wall, destroying the last of its intricate stained-glass periphery. On this, the north side of the church where they sat, from which the grounds of St. Joan's extended to the south, nothing could be seen of the women of NEWS, Allies, cadres or members, although women's voices and the motors of cars could be heard around the corner near the main entrance to the church on its eastern front. Now at the northern and western walls, police cars roared up next to the fire engines, and pairs of policemen leapt from their cars, slamming the doors and striding forth, some walking back to the crowd still gathering around the north and west wings of the church, others approaching the firemen. Karen and Jean rose to go, alarm in their expressions, as Sylvia watched the scene before her through narrowed eyes.

She turned to Karen and Jean as they began to move toward the grounds. She tried to think. "Wait, but. Let Medical check you," she urged them again. "And send," she stopped, shaking her head, her voice choked by tears now. "Send some cadres for Rikki."

Jean nodded, the sorrow she felt deep in the lines of her face. The two women turned and left. Sylvia sat alone on the lawn just a hundred feet from the crowd of people fixated on the burning building and scene of rescue before them, Rikki's slashed and blood-drained body at her side. "No! Rikki. No. No." Shaking her head, no, and sobbing now, Sylvia laid herself across her friend, her face to hers, holding her still in her arms.

She didn't hear the policemen approaching, and only became aware of them when one roughly shook her shoulder. "What's the problem here?"

Her head rose quickly, her bloodied face looking up at them in shock as she turned herself abruptly, placing herself between them and Rikki.

"Jesus," one of them said, unnerved by the sight.

"Looks like they really nailed that one," the other muttered to his partner, sneering at the two women on the lawn.

For an instant Sylvia saw and heard nothing. Nothing but a hot, burning rage, hotter than the flames that had almost engulfed her at the altar of the church. Her hand gripped the telcom clipped to Rikki's waist and in another instant she was on him, kicking, pounding on the stunned officer, screaming at him as loudly as her singed lungs would bear. He was so taken aback at this bloody, wild woman's attack it was seconds before he had grabbed her arms and wrenched them around behind her back.

"We're taking this fucking she-bitch in!" he told his partner, still straining to confine her. "Give me a hand." They slammed her face down on the ground, the bigger one placing a knee in the small of her back as they clamped handcuffs around her twisted wrists, just as ten NEWS cadres were running up to the morbid scene.

"Here comes more of 'em," the smaller one warned as he stood by. "Bunch of bull-dykes." He grabbed his walkie-talkie to call for reinforcements as the big one got off Sylvia and pulled her to her feet. "Hold off. We'll just take this one. We can leave 'em that," he said, pointing to Rikki as he started to drag Sylvia, who'd had her last breath knocked out of her, back to the patrol car.

"What's going on!" Vivian shouted at the police as she neared them, Pamela, Lisa and Marcia close behind her. "What are you doing!" they called at them, following them.

"Just get Rikki. Rikki," Sylvia forced herself to call back to them. "Don't let them take Rikki!"

Chapter XIII

Sylvia opened her eyes. Everything was darkness. Ink black. She brought a hand to her eyes. Her arm felt as if it didn't belong to her body, as if it were an awesome weight that she could not begin to maneuver. She let it drop. Her eyes closed again, slipping back into nothingness. She started suddenly, opening her eyes again, utterly disoriented. Was she at Claire's? At home? She was on a floor. On her back on a cold cement floor. Her eyes closed, then fluttered, opened, struggling to stay open, as the pain in her shoulders and arms, the aching in her back, brought the crushing realization of consciousness. The explosion. Rikki. The end of the conference. She was in jail. In the hole. Broken glass and flames. Her eyes closed again. She was dreaming. This was a dream, a nightmare. Wake up, wake up! she commanded herself as her wakened, aching body forced the truth upon her, forced her eyes open, wide. It was not a dream. It had happened. The conference had been bombed. Rikki was dead. Rikki. Dead. No. Claire. Claire was gone. The conference bombed. The years, years of work smashed. Destroyed. NEWS defeated. Rikki. Dead. For that. It was true. This was death. Living death. She felt her life drained from her. Let me die, she pleaded, shutting her eyes again, shutting out the airless despair. The crushing sensation of total defeat.

Her face. Rikki's face, laughing. Cheeks glowing in the cold winter afternoon, the white lights in her black eyes dancing. *No.* No! Sylvia flung her hands to her face, covering her eyes, pressing hard against them, to shut it out, the cold, stiff, blood-drained face, the frozen look of horror. No! The look, in Rikki's eyes, as she smiled at her, "I'll see you later, Syl . . ." The sweetness in her eyes, her lips smiling. Never? It wouldn't ever happen again? Rikki? The drained, ashen face. Sylvia shook her head with a violence. Rikki! No. The laughter, her eyes, dancing. Gone. Where? *Why?* She can't! She . . . she was only 22! God, please. No. She . . . she'd just started to *believe in her life*. Sylvia felt the hot tears on her face as she pressed her hands hard against her closed eyes. She'd just started to believe. She'd worked so hard. So hard . . . they'd all worked so hard. Oh, god. No. It wasn't right. They'd worked so hard. For *what*? *What*? To be *killed*? Chased away, chased home by the monster? Fuck it! Fuck it all! Then let them blow up the earth! Kill us all. Again the wash of empty, deathly despair swallowed her in and she felt her mind go quiet, dark, as the dismal sound of her heart beating reminded her that she still lived.

Their voices. The Allies. Voices as they filled the church, a symphony, fluted color, she could hear it . . . The sound of hope, heightened, the way opening, they had found it. They had made the way, the mellifluous voices, slowing, a hushed expectancy. Now, the church filled, a pregnant joyful silence . . . "Oh god! *God!*" She clapped her hand to her mouth as her desperate words resounded in the dark cell and choked back, she heard the tense, dreadful silence of the Allies leaving, NEWS cadres rushing, all of them leaving the church in the terrible silence beneath the snapping flames, the belching smoke. Their rich voices gone. The Allies, gone! She gripped her mouth as the scream that tore through her mind stopped, kept back by the hand squeezing her lips shut. Where had they gone? What would happen to them? The stifled scream soured, seeping its terror back into her mind in a stagnant, murky wash of fear, and guilt.

She turned her body slowly onto her side, groaning aloud. There had to be some bones broken. Where were the Allies? NEWS? Had more been killed? How many hurt, maimed? Had they gotten out of the country? What had they done? Why hadn't she been there? Why hadn't she done her part in the evacuation? Why wasn't she with them now? A choking sob rose in her throat. Again, she relived the moment. There, in the suffocating smoke and heat, trying to lift Rikki to her and the head falling back, the face lit against the flames, horror on the young dead face as it hung from the slashed neck. She wept again for Rikki, her fists clenched against her eyes, even as she remembered forcing Jean and Karen, she cursed herself remembering how she had forced Jean and Karen to risk their lives for . . . for what. Rikki was dead. Why had she risked two women's lives? Why? What . . . Oh god, and the police. She'd been crazy. Why had she started a fight with the police? Against everything she had ever learned! She turned her battered body again, face down on the concrete floor, her fists still clenched to her face. Oh, god, where was her mind! Bringing the police down on them. Assaulting a goddamn cop. What would Olina ever think? Olina who had slipped through their hands so many times by her own sheer detachment, her commitment to NEWS . . . She heard Claire's voice, unable to believe it, 'Sylvia! What! For 'oo is this crazy act?' What had she been thinking? Rikki was dead. Yes *dead.* And she sobbed now, without thought. Her clenched fists falling open, she cried for Rikki. Rikki and all the love she felt for her. Her doleful weeping washing her mind quiet, hushing the angry questions, as a wordless pain within her rose up from unspoken depths, convulsing her shoulders, she sobbed aloud until there was nothing left.

She lay still, her face still in her hands. She felt them wet, sticky with mucus, a pool of it dripping through her fingers and onto the

floor. With a groan she turned herself over and sat up, holding her
hands away from her, she shook off the viscous mess and moved to
wipe her hand on the hem of her pants. They were gone. Her legs were
bare. She reached her hand to her chest, feeling slowly down. Oh yes,
she remembered the strange kind of gown they had made her wear. And
the injection, that's right! Just before they'd put her in here. She must
have slept immediately, she hardly remembered . . . What time is it?
The clock had said what, 4:00 something, yes, when they'd finished
booking her. It couldn't have been more than 4:30 in the afternoon
when they'd put her in here. Jesus. It must be the middle of the night.
How long are they going to keep me in here? Has anyone tried to get
me out? Maybe they're not letting them or, no, there was probably no
time at all. Maybe the cadres think I deserved what I got. Why waste
precious time on someone who's risked the lives of two security cadres
and almost got ten more into a fight with the cops? Oh, god. She
hugged herself. It was freezing. She wiped her hands carefully on the
bottom of her gown, then stood up. How big is this thing? She
reached out her arm. A wall. Her other arm. Another wall. Not very.
She fought off a trapping, damning sensation, hugging herself again.
She walked forward tentatively, one, two, three steps. A wall. She
turned and walked back. Six steps. Back again. And again. Then she
began to run in place. Her back and shoulders throbbed, but she felt
warmer. She focused only on the motion of her body, breathing deeply,
until she couldn't keep it up anymore. She sat down again, the warmth
she had generated turning to chill. All right. She steadied her mind,
steeling herself. This is just the beginning. Just the beginning. You
have one choice. To be strong. Stronger. And still stronger.
Whatever happens. Whatever happens. Besides. NEWS won't let you
rot in here. Despite your stupid, crazy errors. NEWS is about love.
The greater love. Rejecting no one. She cringed again, remembering
her assault on the police. It really was an act so unworthy of NEWS.
Self-defense, yes, but to attack. He hadn't killed Rikki. He hadn't
thrown the bomb. Though the CIA/FBI had, of course. Just like they
bombed the church in Birmingham in 1963 and killed four little black
girls, then blamed it on the Ku Klux Klan or whoever. Of course, the
police would put out, after whatever cursory investigation, that some
right-wing group, or some random freak had done it. God. It was so
hard not to hate them. But, that is the error. Hatred. That *is* the error,
that's why I attacked him! I *hated* him. No he's not the FBI but in my
mind he may as well be, some of them *are*, and all of them, the CIA,
FBI, the police and their sick cynical violence — I have hated them all.
I really have. That's why I attacked him. If I had been acting from love
. . . I never would have done it! If love for NEWS, and for Rikki, and
myself, for life, the Earth, if it were love I had let guide me, I *never*

would have done it. OK, self-defense, yes it can be from love. But a useless, violent attack—is only hatred. She bowed her head, at once ashamed and relieved. She understood it. Yes she could hate their sick, violent acts. But she could not hate *them.* For in the end, even the police, the military, the CIA itself were *people* and would have to be forgiven. Or the cycle would never be broken. The cycle of hatred, enemies, war, hatred, enemies, war. It would never be transcended unless . . . unless we learn, always, to be guided by love. Unless we make love the dominant force in the timeless contradiction of love/hate. But it isn't timeless. In fact, its time has come. The dialectic was reaching its synthesis. And it would be characterized by love and the continuance of life, or by hatred and the destruction of the Earth. Steven was right. Yes, Steven was right when he'd accused her of always talking about some 'they.' The 'they' she had always objectified, polarized, hated. She could condemn their acts, their violence, and do everything within her power to stop it—and there would be conflict, there would be death—but she could not carry around this *hatred* for them as *people.* This hatred that she had let guide her to that stupid act that, in its effect, its damaging effect, manifested hate for everyone—herself, NEWS. Everyone. She raised her eyes to the pitch darkness. Let love guide me, she entreated. Let me be strong. For a moment her mind was quiet as she stared, unseeing, into the empty night. Let love guide me, she repeated again, and again. She felt a meditative quiet. Entranced, motionless, she sat in silence.

Of an instant, 30 small squares of light in the shape of a rectangle appeared high on the wall before her. Her eyes widened as her mouth dropped open. Surely she was hallucinating. What had they given her? Or was this some kind of . . . a sign, or . . . She blinked, and blinked again. It was still there, more vivid than before, and then she saw the fine metal grate and, as her eyes adjusted to the change in the darkness, she saw the outline of the thick metal door that held the small barred window of light. They must have turned on the lights in the corridor. She started to get up when half a face appeared at the grate, two grey eyes staring at her.

"So you're awake."

Sylvia stared back, still seated against the rear wall of the cell. "Yes."

"Think you've slept it off?"

She didn't know what to say. Slept what off? "I guess."

The eyes disappeared. She waited a moment. Then, just as she began to stand, she heard the chink of a key in the lock, and the wide metal door swung open, letting in a flood of light that made her squint so that she barely saw the matron standing in the doorway as she flung a pile of clothes onto the floor.

"Get dressed. You're going to the Day Room. And if you're a good girl, you might not have to come back in here."

Suddenly she felt incredibly thirsty and a dire urge to urinate, but the heavy door had clanged shut and she was left in near darkness again. She stood up. Leaning over, she carefully scanned the floor of the cell, inch by inch, there it was, a small drain back in the corner. She picked up her clothes from the middle of the floor and placed them near the door. Then she went back to the corner and squatted over the drain, soothed by the relief she felt as the urine streamed from her. She wiped herself dry with the front of her gown, then returned to the metal door and peered through the open grid. A bleak, empty corridor lit by fluorescent light greeted her eyes. She turned back to the middle of her cell and quickly took off her gown, wiping her face and body with the still clean upper back. There was dried blood on her hands and face. She threw the gown into the corner. Focusing on the task at hand, she began to put on her clothes. How they comforted her—her black denim pants and soft, warm burgundy sweater, the thick grey wool socks. Only now she realized just how cold and miserable she'd felt. Even the aching stiffness of her back and shoulders was beginning to fade. And she was going to be getting out of here! Out of here! And water. Finally, some water. What time is it? The Day Room? It must be day, but . . . How long had she slept? What day? Dressed now, she stood by the door waiting, glancing every half a minute through the metal grate. She could hear sounds now, as if from far away, down the corridor, voices, some loud, angry.

Twenty minutes later she realized that, possibly, the matron wasn't coming back after all. She seated herself against the wall opposite the drain. At least she felt warmer. But so *thirsty*. She fought off the shadow of despair, the images that kept flooding her mind, the shattered glass, fire, Rikki, everyone gone, the scene with the cop, his wrenching her arms nearly out of her shoulders as he dragged her to his car and threw her in the back, calling her a bull-dyke commie, nigger-loving whore. She heard his sneering, vile words again as he sat there in the front seat of the car, deriding her all the way to the station as she lay helpless on the back seat. Finally they'd left her at the station, charging her with assaulting a peace officer, and then she'd been brought here. The county jail. She remembered it all again, her face expressionless. Something had changed in her. She did not feel the despair. No, she would not let it take hold of her again. Above all, she would not despair. It must have been an hour since the matron had been by. Let love guide me, she repeated again to herself, again, and again.

"Ready?" The grey eyes appeared through the grate.

"Mmhmm." Sylvia's own grey eyes met those looking down at

her.

"All right, then." The key turned in the lock and the heavy door swung open. "Let's go."

She stood up and followed the woman down the corridor, through more locked doors, through a small complex of cells to a large, barred chamber the size of a double garage. Under the high cement ceiling sat one metal picnic table in the middle of an expanse of concrete floor. A toilet jutted from the one solid wall at the back, half a screen beside it, and 25 to 30 women were standing or sitting about on the cold floor, a few at the metal table. The Day Room.

The high, barred door clanked open as the matron stood back to let Sylvia pass through. As the door shut behind her, Sylvia stood still, suddenly timid. It had been years since she had been arrested, in jail, in the early '70s, for drugs, cocaine. Even though she hadn't been seriously involved, had just been at the wrong place at the wrong time, she'd been convicted of a felony. But Steven, in law school at the time, had found her a skilled lawyer, and she'd ended up with a suspended sentence, just probation. In fact, she'd only spent a matter of minutes, it seemed, possibly a few hours in jail. She could hardly even remember it now. There had been five or six of them together and no one had seemed to take it too seriously.

But this was an entirely different situation. And today, she was alone. Her awkwardness had been perceived immediately by the rest of the women in the huge, brutal cell as some snickered at her and others turned away scornfully back to their conversations. She forced herself to move, uprooting herself from where she stood to blend in somehow with the harsh, naked environment. She walked casually over to an unoccupied corner a few yards from the toilet and sat down, leaning against the wall. Her heart was beating at twice its usual rate. She folded her arms and closed her eyes, steadying herself. She found one single sensation dominating her consciousness. Thirst. She opened her eyes and looked around the room. It was as if she had disappeared, the women had all gone back to their talking or reading magazines, others working laboriously at painting their nails and fixing their hair. Most of the women were black. Several were Latina, Indian, Asian. A few, four to be exact, counting herself, were white. Again the image haunted her—the Allies, their hope and power, everywhere the faith and spirit of liberation, then, the crash, a roaring explosion, the Allies, leaving.

She dragged herself to her feet, numb and disheartened, she walked to the toilet and around the half-screen. There was a small sink basin. She turned on the water and held her hands beneath it, the water running off them a pinkish red as the last of Rikki's blood washed away. She leaned to the sink and brought her cupped hands to her mouth, quenching the burning thirst, again and again, she drank. There were no towels and she leaned to wipe her hands against the sides of her pants, then froze as she stood, her eyes wide, transfixed on her burgundy sweater. The front and arms were stained, matted, covered with blood. She straightened herself, waiting for the grim nausea to pass.

"You kill somebody?" a voice asked her.

She turned to a woman standing beside her waiting to use the sink. "Not yet," she answered, her voice taut.

"What's all that blood?"

"A friend got killed."

"What you in for."

"Assaulting an officer."

"Hah!" The woman threw her head back. "You gonna be up for a *while.*" She paused, narrowing her eyes at Sylvia. "Less you got people."

Sylvia looked at the woman, the moment between them an acknowledgment of it all, everything that the conference was about, expressed in this instant, in the woman's words. The truth of how 'justice' here worked. Yes. She had people. She was white and her relatives had money. Deep within her she knew that NEWS or no NEWS, Linda, Maureen, Nick, their whiteness and their money would get her out of this. The woman she faced was black and she was poor. It didn't matter what she had or hadn't done. She would be in here, in and out of here, maybe for the rest of her life. But if the conference had . . . They could have changed this, they could have . . .

The woman turned and moved past her to the sink. Sylvia stood still. What could she possibly say? She looked around the stark, dehumanizing room, the utter absence of privacy or warmth, a cold, ugly, cruel room where 30 human lives were caged, for how long? For what?

"You better get yourself some fancy lawyer, girl," the woman remarked to Sylvia as she left the sink.

"Well, what . . ." Sylvia began. The woman stopped, looking at her with a mix of curiosity and disdain. "What are you in here for?" Sylvia asked, at a loss for how to get to know the woman.

"Bad checks," the woman answered, turning and walking away.

Sylvia walked back to her corner, sitting down again on the cold floor. She saw the woman she had met at the sink talking to her friends as they looked over toward her, some scoffing, others bored. Again she folded her arms, closing her eyes. If only she could sleep. But she must have slept for, how many hours? Twelve? Fifteen? Her eyes opened. It was day now, she could see the grey light through the narrow barred windows high in the concrete walls beyond the caged Day Room. When would someone come for her? How long would she have to stay here? Maybe she should try to call someone. Linda. Maybe Steven could tell her something. Wasn't she supposed to be able to make a phone call? She looked again around the cage. A young woman was sitting, not far from her, reading a magazine. Sylvia got up and walked over to her.

She squatted down next to her. "Hi, excuse me, uh . . ." The woman looked up, frowning, and Sylvia couldn't help but be startled by the youth in the woman's face, her vivid make-up and aloof expression not succeeding in hiding her touching vulnerability.

"Can you tell me how I can get to use the phone?" Sylvia asked hurriedly.

"Ask the screw," the young woman answered.

"Thanks," Sylvia said, looking around for the matron as she started to get up.

"But there's no calls till 10:00 today," the woman added, softening a little, though not looking up from her magazine.

"What time is it?" Sylvia turned back to her eagerly.

"It's not 10:00 yet. Coffee comes at 10:00." The woman looked up at her again, studying her now.

"Oh," Sylvia answered, looking at a loss.

"It's probably about 9:00," the young woman offered.

"Oh," Sylvia answered, grateful.

"When'd you get here?"

"Yesterday."

"I didn't see you."

"They put me in solitary."

"What'd you do?"

"Hit a cop."

"Hunh."

They were silent a moment.

Sylvia decided to try again. "How long've you been here?"

"Three days."

"Mmm."

"I been here before though," she said, almost defiantly, sensing that Sylvia had not.

Tentatively, Sylvia leaned back, sitting down and crossing her legs. "What for?"

"Hookin'."

"Mmm," Sylvia nodded.

"Why'd you hit on a cop?"

"I was pissed off."

"It's a felony."

"Yeah. I know."

"What's your name?"

"Sylvia."

"Lonnie."

They smiled at each other.

"You got blood all over your sweater. That from fighting with the cop?"

"No." She paused as Lonnie looked at her. "A friend was hurt. Cut." She couldn't say more.

"My boyfriend got cut bad last year."

"Yeah?"

"Yeah, my dad did it. Well, he's not my dad, I mean, he's my mom's boyfriend. He's a fucker." Lonnie looked angry, disgusted.

"Why'd he do it?"

"Oh, he's a fucker," Lonnie spat the word, even angrier now.

"I guess," Sylvia said.

"I *hate* him," Lonnie went on. "He's always beatin' on my mother. Used to beat on me too till I got the fuck outta there." She hesitated, looking at Sylvia's intent, concerned face. "He used to fuck with me too . . . all the time. Since I was ten."

Sylvia listened, stunned.

"I left there three years ago but he'd still come around, buggin' me, after me, fuckin' with me. He's so *sick*. I *hate* him." Lonnie paused, her pale blue eyes cold and bitter, her mouth drawn in a sorrow beyond her years.

Sylvia took a breath. "That's awful. He's really *fucked*. How'd you get rid of him?"

"Well, he hadn't been around for a long time, cuz I kept tellin' him I was gonna call the cops. But he kept tellin' me he'd kill me if I did. But he didn't come around for a long time. But then one day he did, last year. My boyfriend was there and when Stu saw him, he just went nuts, fuckin' crazy, started cuttin' Jim with his knife, real bad. It was ugly."

Sylvia listened, her eyes somber.

"Yeah," Lonnie looked away, "it was real ugly. But he got sent up for that. Five years. But he'll probably get out in two. If he does, Jim's gonna kill him," Lonnie finished with satisfaction.

"For sure?" Sylvia asked.

Lonnie's expression changed, doubtful, unhappy. "Well, I haven't seen him in awhile."

Sylvia was silent. What could be said? What could possibly help this woman? How long would this 'step-father' keep plaguing her? The rest of her life? How could she survive? Or break out of the only way she had learned to stay alive? She felt a helpless raging within her, dulling her mind as again the dark shadow crept over her. Despair. She fought it, pushing it back, now, for Lonnie's sake if nothing else.

"So you don't see Jim anymore?"

"No."

"Where do you live?"

"Nowhere right now." Lonnie shifted her legs, sitting up from the wall. "But I'm gonna call my mom today. She wants me to come and stay with her for awhile. She's got a new boyfriend now. She says he's not like Stu." Lonnie smiled happily. "I'm supposed to get outta here today." Then she looked at Sylvia sadly, as if she had been insensitive. "How about you, though?"

Sylvia laughed at herself, wanting to cry. Lonnie didn't need her pity or her despair. She needed respect. Like everyone.

"Hey, Lonnie!" a woman approached her. "What's happenin'?"

Lonnie turned to talk to her friend as Sylvia moved back, away from them, leaning heavily back against the wall, she sat. So what would all the theories, the position papers, the discussions, even the action, the February Action that would probably never happen now, do for Lonnie? What would it do? It wasn't that she didn't believe anymore, that she didn't still believe that NEWS would have—no—no, it still *could* make a difference. Still they could have a major impact on all the world's institutions, and some day bring a greater justice to women and men of every class and culture, a justice that would free both the Lonnies and the Stus of this world from this grotesque bondage of sexual domination. Yes, she had to believe it, it *is* possible to create . . .

The words fell, stale and tired. What did the words mean for Lonnie sitting next to her now? They meant nothing. She looked around the steel and concrete cage. What would all those words mean to these women, the lives of these women? Nothing. She knew that it didn't mean the words were false, that the vision was false. But somehow, sitting here, it all seemed as if it did, as if the power of oppression were . . . overwhelming.

She closed her eyes, the voices of Lonnie and her friend, their street-talking banter lulling her mind to a torpor as if, in fact, she might just sit here, right here, for the rest of her life. Did it matter? NEWS, the conference, all their work was shattered. And she didn't even have the comforting arms of a lover to go to, to hold her and share this awful sorrow. No. Claire was gone. And who could she blame for that? Not the State, or the cops, or the CIA. All the political and economic changes in the world wouldn't change that. Her lover had left her. She had no one to hold her now, to ease this awful pain. So what difference was it. The world was all fucked up. The only thing that made it even tolerable was some illusion of love we can have with a lover in some rare, tender moment when it seems like perfect love does exist. The rest is crap. She'd better face it. And she'd better face it that, now, she didn't even have the hope of a moment of illusory love. She was alone. Even the women here, at least maybe they had a lover's arms to turn to, somewhere. How else could they survive the horror of life? Without that comfort? And how would she without Claire? What was the point. What was all her dedication to NEWS. Just words. Words. Her back and shoulders throbbed as she sat slumped against the concrete wall, not bothering to move. It really didn't matter if anyone came for her or not. Claire was gone. Rikki was dead. NEWS defeated. What was there to go back to. Though she knew better. Or did she? Something in the sight of the big, ugly cage she sat in, the feel of concrete against her aching body, the sound of the matron screaming through the bars at the women at the table to shut up, the sound of a woman shitting in the toilet with only half a screen in front of her, the blood on her filthy clothes, the hunger in her growling stomach made her longing, longing for the comforting arms of love, into a weakness, a pathetic, hopeless cry. Despair.

"Sylvia." She heard her name called. It sounded in her ears, but still she didn't move, she couldn't. She wanted nothing but to be left alone, left here, slumped against the wall in her powerless misery.

"Hey, Sylvia." She heard her name again, more insistent. Opening her eyes, she sat forward. Who was calling her? She glanced around the cage. Lonnie was still talking to her friend, not even noticing her as she had sat there propped against the wall. Who had called her? None of the women in the room were even looking her way. She stood up slowly, the motion stirring her as she took a few steps toward the front of the cage and, suddenly, she found herself filled with gratitude. She could move. She felt an airy lightness, walking around the periphery of the cage. It was as if a tremendous weight had been lifted from her. She simply felt thankful that she could move. Breathe. The very knowledge of it strengthened her. As if she had stepped right through a filmy plane, she had broken through the illusion of her own powerlessness, the very motion of her body somehow breaking through the illusion of her despair—an illusion she had created herself in her moment of longing for the illusion of romantic love.

"Bernetti!" Sylvia turned her head slowly. It was another voice, a different voice, closer now. But held in the rediscovery of her own life power, unseeing, she stood, or no, it seemed she floated, gliding.

"Bernetti!" the matron shouted a second time. Sylvia's eyes focused. Seeing the angry woman standing impatiently outside the cage door, she walked toward her as still the tremendous relief she felt in the motion of her own body, the relief it gave as it challenged her state of mind, graced her lips with an odd, unearthly smile.

"You Bernetti?"

Sylvia nodded as her eyes glowed, radiant now with the sense of her own creative force, the phenomenal ability to make, however momentarily, illusion become reality.

"You ain't gettin' outta here," the matron informed her, disgusted by the joyous light in those grey eyes.

Sylvia nodded, as if in a dream, thick with sensation, each single cell in her mind finely tuned, taut, vibrating to the magic.

"You're going back to solitary," the matron sneered at her as she opened the cage door.

Sylvia nodded, unmoved, the exquisite freedom of this conscious moment carrying her in its power. The power to create her own state of mind, beyond the play of reality and illusion.

"Move it!" The matron jabbed her, thoroughly irritated. Sylvia walked through the door, moving silently in the direction of the dark cell she'd left not long before, feeling nothing but inexplicable delight.

"This way!" the matron commanded, walking off in the opposite direction as Sylvia followed her. She opened another locked door to a small set of offices and, unlocking another door to a room not much larger than a closet, she instructed Sylvia to sit in a chair that was placed behind a small table with two empty chairs at its side.

She sat alone in the room, laying her hands quietly on the table, the intensity of the moment slowly subsiding as still a warm glow of peace stayed with her. She looked about her. This wasn't the solitary cell. There were chairs to sit on here. And the light was so bright. Maybe they were coming to question her. She pushed her chair back against the wall, leaning back, and putting her feet up on another chair, she gazed at the far wall. Please, let love guide me, she heard herself saying silently again as images passed before her mind's eye—memories and images of her mother, her childhood, Claire, CECO, JoAnn, school, Rikki, David, NEWS, Miriam, Rena, Linda, occasionally the sounds of their voices, snatches of conversations—the images flowed one upon another, lost in a dream, yet she had lived them all, it seemed.

The sound of the door opening turned her head.

"Sylvia!" It was Olina, and Ruth behind her. Or was she dreaming? How had they gotten in here? But no, Olina's arms were around her, her warm cheek against hers, and tears, Olina's, yes, and her own. And Ruth, too, held her a long, caring moment. Speechless, Sylvia sat back in her chair as Olina and Ruth sat across from her. They both looked exhausted, more so than she had ever seen either of them to be.

"How are you, Sylvia?" Olina asked. The deep concern in her voice, hoarse from fatigue, moved Sylvia to an alert clarity.

"I'm all right. Honestly."

"They said you'd been in solitary," Ruth said. "Your cousin's friend, Jack, has been doing everything he can, though they wouldn't let anyone see you until now. They said they'd gone to get you 30 minutes ago. We've been waiting."

"Jack had an appointment this morning, but he's going to come and talk with you as soon as he can," Olina added.

Sylvia looked around the room restlessly and back at Olina, who shook her head. Taking out a pen and paper as Ruth continued to talk about Jack and his legal experience, Olina wrote, "All evacuated safely. Injuries but no one else killed. Most Allies left or leaving the country. But Amsterdam is still meeting!"

Sylvia took a pen. "What next for us?"

Olina wrote, "Several are still here, will meet in other location. The work continues."

Sylvia looked at Olina, hope lighting her face though she could see in the sorrow behind Olina's eyes that the setback was severe, that it was yet too soon to tell what could still be accomplished.

"Do you understand?" Ruth asked Sylvia, as Olina began carefully scratching out their written words.

"I'm not sure," Sylvia answered.

"Jack will go with you this afternoon to be arraigned. As soon as bail is posted, we should be able to get you out," Ruth repeated. "Although, there may be some complication. He's researching the options now."

Sylvia looked at Ruth, her eyes clouded now, remorseful. "What effect is this, my arrest, having on . . ."

"It's too soon to sort it out, Sylvia," Olina answered.

She flushed with shame. "How are Karen and Jean?"

"Medical was able to treat them. It wasn't as serious as it might have been," Ruth answered.

"Sylvia." Olina looked at her, waiting until Sylvia raised her head and looked back at her. "It's all right," Olina told her, that certain grace, truth in her eyes. "No one blames you."

"Rikki's parents came from New York this morning to take her body," Ruth said. "They expressed a deep gratitude to you."

Sylvia lowered her eyes. Rikki. Gone now. Forever. Then, looking back at them, she said, "Well. I'm sure Karen's and Jean's parents wouldn't have, if we hadn't been so lucky." She paused. "I realize," she looked at the bare wall beyond them, "I . . . It was a mistake, a . . . " she turned to Ruth, "a very seriously wrong mistake."

Ruth said nothing, a sad concern drawing her lips taut, her light brown eyes showing Sylvia the fullness of her sympathy.

"Sylvia," Olina said quietly, reaching to Sylvia's clasped hands as they lay on the table, and covering them gently with her own warm hand. "Karen and Jean are fine. No one blames you. Everyone sends their love to you."

Sylvia nodded, silent.

Olina stood up from her chair, reaching for her bag and setting it on the table. She looked at Sylvia another long moment. "We just want to get you out of here. And we will." Still her eyes held Sylvia's firm until, finally, Sylvia's lips parted in a smile of trust.

Olina smiled back at her, her hand gently smoothing Sylvia's hair, then, with a quick look at her watch, "I have to get back," she said. "Ruth will stay as long as they let her." She looked at the closed door with irritation. "They kept us waiting so long." She reached into the canvas bag on the table. "I've brought you some things." She laid a small pile of clean clothes on the table, saying, "Sylvia, take that sweater off and give it to me." She put three books, a notebook, some pens, a hairbrush and a few other articles next to the clothes as Sylvia stood and changed her sweater. "I'll be back," Olina told her as she embraced her again, holding her to her. "Don't forget how much we love you, Sylvia." Her voice was quiet, barely a whisper, "We are not defeated. We'll only become stronger." Sylvia nodded her head, feeling the truth of Olina's words and the courage in the look of her as she stepped back to the door soothe her own jagged nerves, giving her new strength.

"Patience, Sylvia." Olina's tired eyes smiled as she pushed the button near the door.

Sylvia sat back down as Olina was released from the room. "Twenty minutes," the matron snapped at Ruth.

"Sylvia," Ruth said. "Don't be too hard on yourself." The thin, graceful lines etched at the corners of her eyes deepened. "I know what a dear friend Rikki was to you."

Again the flames, Rikki, her head falling back, the blood streaming from her neck. Sylvia ran her long, narrow fingers back from her forehead, grasping at her dark tangle of hair. "I know, but . . ." She looked at Ruth. "I still don't understand what made me insist that Jean and Karen risk their lives. They were security, they'd seen what happened, they knew what they were doing." She looked back down at the table as Ruth listened silently.

"I just . . . couldn't leave her there." She felt tears on her cheek and brushed them away. "But to endanger Karen and Jean. There's something so . . . so selfish about it. Because it wouldn't do anything for Rikki. It was for me. I . . . I just couldn't face that she was dead." Sylvia covered her face, holding back the tears with her hands.

Ruth said quietly, "Sylvia, that's almost everyone's response to the death of someone they love. To deny it."

"I know, but . . ." She laid her hands in her lap, her head still bowed. "You know what I'm talking about."

Ruth took a deep breath, closing her eyes a second, then nodding her head, she acknowledged, "I don't think you used your best judgment, Sylvia. The kind of judgment that acts in the best interests of all concerned, to the extent that that is possible. A kind of judgment I have seen you exercise time and time again, with courage, Sylvia." She paused. "In this instance, though, I . . . It does seem that other feelings overrode . . ." She hesitated.

"Please say it, Ruth."

"Well. It's possible that, because also you've so recently had to accept the loss of Claire in your life." She paused again as Sylvia nodded, yes, that was part of it. "That you felt a terrible fear," Ruth went on, "that to lose Rikki, too, was so emotionally frightening that the physical danger of the situation was not clear to you. Your assessment of it was distorted." Ruth looked at Sylvia, questioning.

"I . . . hadn't thought of it as fear," Sylvia said quietly, thinking. After a moment, she went on, "But I guess it was. It is. I mean, I'd thought it was that I couldn't let go of my 'attachment' to Rikki. And that I was selfishly risking others' lives to preserve this attachment. And you're right, I know it's somehow mixed up with Claire leaving, and how hard I've tried to let go of her too. I couldn't, just couldn't face . . . It's like I went totally backwards. Holding on to attachment in this insane way." She paused a moment. "But that is what attachment is about, isn't it? Fear."

"It can be, I think. When it's extreme. When a person becomes so attached that her effort to preserve it overrides the welfare of those concerned. Oneself, or others. It's a terrible fear of . . . one's own inadequacy, or inability to . . . to find love."

Sylvia closed her eyes, silent.

"But, Sylvia," Ruth's voice continued, profoundly gentle, "fear is as basic to life as death itself. We feel it. All of us. We can't deny it. It is denial that is at the root of extreme attachment—denial of fear, refusal to feel it—because only by accepting our fear can we overcome it. Courage is not the denial of fear. It's the confronting and overcoming of the fact of our fear."

"But, Ruth, I've tried, I've tried to overcome the fear I've felt since Claire left." She was crying now.

"I know you have, Sylvia. Believe me, I don't think you should feel bad or ashamed of what happened with Rikki. It was so sudden, so terrible. You had no time. I think that, in that one awful instant, your fear of loss—especially given what you've been through—you just couldn't accept it. But, Sylvia, you know, we have all made such mistakes. None of us can make a claim to perfection."

Ruth paused, her eyes distant, as Sylvia looked up at her. "I remember when my son died," Ruth said after a moment. "He had just started high school. He was in a car accident. The driver who hit him was drunk." She shook her head, pain still in the memory. Then with a sad half-laugh she continued, "I bought a gun. I actually did. I was going to kill the man." Sylvia sat without a sound as Ruth, her voice terribly tired, distant, went on, "My husband realized what I was doing, or planning to do. I was crazed with grief, with the fear that I couldn't go on living with the rage I felt. When my husband tried to stop me, I almost shot him." Still in total silence, Sylvia watched Ruth. "I never would have really shot him. But just the moment of the impulse . . ." She stopped, saying nothing. "It was 20 years ago. I was your age."

Sylvia was quiet a moment. "But the loss of your son . . ."

"Yes, I had every right to feel grief. And rage. But it was the fear that I felt, that I couldn't bear the loss—it was the effort to deny that fear that drove me to such violent disregard of others' lives."

Sylvia thought a moment. "But how can we overcome the fear? If we accept that it's there, and we're afraid that the loss is unbearable . . ." She paused, the answer in her question. "Though if I accept it—admit it—it brings it back to me, within my power."

"Yes. And only then can you begin to summon the courage to bear it, and the courage to continue to love."

"But it takes a faith."

"Yes, it does. A faith that you will always find the love, if you seek it."

"You mean . . . you don't mean just personal love, romantic love."

"No. Though I'm sure you will find yourself in another relationship in your life, Sylvia, if you really want to."

Sylvia looked at the locked metal door, considering Ruth's words. "I'm not sure I do."

"No?"

Sylvia sighed. "I just seem to get too attached or . . . I am afraid. Afraid to lose someone I really love." Yes. She would admit it.

"But, Sylvia, I think there is a dialectic central to personal love—or 'romantic' love—just as there is to the broader unity of a greater love. There is a dialectic in relationships too, between independence and union. Both elements—individuality and collectivity—have to be nurtured to sustain love. Although one may be predominant at given times, as conditions warrant. Neither can be indefinitely sacrificed to the other, to the point of oppressing the other, or the love will be destroyed."

Ruth looked at Sylvia, who nodded, listening. "I suppose," Ruth said, "that it's our endless task to find a balance between the two. Politically, and personally. But in a relationship if one wants independence to the point of negating any unity, or one wants fusion to the point of negating individuality, no balance can be reached. For the most part though, we all treasure our individuality, and we all long for merging with others. Though both those feelings have accompanying fears. And the effort to deny them—fear of loneliness or fear of loss of self—may keep us from knowing in ourselves that we really do yearn for both fusion and independence. As much as we are discrete beings, we long for independence and, as much as we are part of a social species, we long for connection, union. Knowing that we need both, we can work to accommodate both needs in our relations with each other and not let them terrify us. If your lover wants more intimacy with you, it doesn't mean she wants to possess you. Or if she wants more independence, it doesn't mean she is abandoning you. The issue is in developing the balance within oneself and in the relationship. Though if fear of abandonment or loss of self are not acknowledged and overcome, if the fears are denied and therefore allowed to control, then it can be very difficult to achieve balance. Or impossible." Ruth stopped, waiting a moment.

"I guess," Sylvia began, "I guess I was denying my fears with Claire. Especially the last months." She looked at Ruth. "But she did, too. I think she had fears, too, that she wouldn't admit." Ruth nodded as Sylvia went on, "It just seems—I mean it seems that denial is such a part of how we're taught to deal with life. And I know sometimes I don't even see how I'm doing it. It's such a way of life. Especially in this society. Denying that there's anything important but individual success, that other people have rights and needs like we do, even denying that our government is torturing people for . . ."

The key sounded in the lock of the metal door. "Let's go," the matron commanded the two women. They stood and moved to the door as Ruth turned and put her arm around Sylvia. "I'll see you later."

Sylvia embraced her quickly. "Thank you, Ruth. So much."

Ruth left as Sylvia moved to pick up the things Olina had put on the table. Gathering them in her arm, she turned and gave a cautionary glance to the matron, waiting to be told to leave the things there, but the matron said nothing as Sylvia passed through the door and was taken back to the Day Room.

She found her place near the corner still unoccupied and, sitting down by the wall, she carefully arranged her things in a pile next to her, hungrily eyeing the books Olina had brought. She glanced around the room. No one was really paying any attention to her. She relaxed, leaning against the wall, reliving her moments with Olina and Ruth, their words and expressions, their presence like a fragrant, shimmering balm to the raw desolation she had felt since the first sound of shattered glass.

After a lunch of white bread and boiled hot dogs that she forced herself to eat, Sylvia sat reading in her cold cement corner. For the present, she felt reclusion from the women around her was all she was capable of. She was still too troubled, confused, to understand how to develop any trust with anyone here, or how she would or wouldn't respond to anything anyone had to say. Could she express her real feelings? Her beliefs about what was going on? Why she was here. Why Lonnie was here, why anyone of them was here. What was the best way for her to conduct herself, for NEWS, now that she had already put them into this useless, wasteful confrontation with the 'law' by her impulsive disregard . . . She looked back down at her book, trying to read.

Within this dream state, the symbology and action may be subordinate in significance to the succession of emotional sensations, and the transformation of feeling as it interacts with the symbology and action to a moment of illumination . . .

She reread the sentence for the fourth time, knowing that it had meaning for her, a very important meaning, if only she could focus. She looked up again. God, thank you Olina, she thought, her eyes resting on the small pile of things beside her, the collection of poetry written by Allies from 30 countries, a long novel by a Cuban author, this book on dream states she had been wanting for months to read, when she could finally find the time. Well. Yeah. She had the time now. How much time? When would she ever know what was really going on with NEWS, the Allies, the Amsterdam conference, but especially, NEWS CLAN. What had they decided about the Action? How could she ever discuss it with anyone, the details, and what about her reports? As long as she was locked up in here, the walls crawling with cops, no one could tell her anything. Maybe a few scribbled sentences as Olina had done this morning, but what about all the questions she had, and all that must be going on now, the changes. And what about the strategy? Was it being formulated now, somehow, in some other way? "The work continues." That's all Olina could write. How though? What? With who? As long as she was here she could only know a tiny fraction, next to nothing, only what whoever came to see her might risk to jot down, crossing it out before she'd hardly had the time to read it. Now, in the most critical moment NEWS ever faced, when decisions had to be made instantaneously and could make such a difference in the course they would take, and possibly, maybe still possibly, that the world would take, here she was, locked up, alone, knowing nothing, sitting here, for how long? She should be there with them. If *only* she could be there with them. If she hadn't done that stupid, goddamn, fucking thing with the cop, she would be with them still. But now, here she was in . . . "Patience, Sylvia," she heard Olina's voice, the loving smile in her tired, dark eyes.

Sylvia closed her eyes. Calming herself again, she turned and picked up the book of poetry, laying it in her lap as she put the other beside her. She opened it randomly and read,

fire raging still
roaring
of the engines
death hovering
with smell of burning
flesh
everywhere
the village dying

She let the book close on her hand, remembering their faces, their words, Elena, Lucia, Shui-Mak, Ming-sheng—women who had lived through a violence and sorrow she could never know, with a courage she could only hope to strive for. She let the memory of them flow through her, their presence those first days of the conference, the intensity of their knowledge, their power.

She looked back to the book, reading poem after poem, as it dwarfed her own private pain, their words, calm in horror, brilliant with hope in a love transcendent of personal fear, dedicated to liberation. She read on, each poem a statement of a truth she only now began to understand and, with the understanding her own personal sorrow slipped into perspective as really so very little to bear. Women whose children had been murdered, who had lost husbands, families, who had been tortured, raped. Women who could still speak out in heroic faith, *with love*, to the creation of a new age.

She held the book still a moment. This was about love as she had never really felt it, though she had begun to at the conference. Not the romantic idea of love she had learned in the movies, some chance chemical attraction that could lead to the union of two lone souls. Or that romantic aspiration for individualist power, because, yes—Ruth was right—love is about power too. But the notion of love *and* power in individualistic thinking is a random thing based on happenstance—a fluke, romanticized by bits and pieces of more genuine emotions, fragments, that become a fierce attachment to some accidental condition and elevated to a false sense of fated reality as the individual obsessively creates an illusional whole. This was the nature of that sensation she had tried to explain to her mother, of why that woman in the street who she'd thought was Claire was so infinitely more important to her than the actual woman herself, the woman who was really there. And this was the nature of the American Dream, the 'lucky' break that created business moguls and superstars at the tragic expense of all the people under their haphazard power. A total distortion of the real quality of love and its genuine power in concord among us *all*. But it was the illusion of romantic fate, "chance," that was the basis of Western culture and the motion of its entire politics and economy, from movie stars for presidents to the insane dice-game of the stock market that watches millions starve as it places its bets. And when it fails, for the millions for whom it fails—the failed marriage, the failed business, or the never-realized longing for the ideal lover or the millionaire's mansion—when it fails, the antithesis of romanticism infects the heart: cynicism.

Romanticism/cynicism—the lub-dub at the heart of the American Dream. This was the sense of love she had been born and bred to and, with a starkness she had never before experienced, here, now, it was exposed. By the words, but not words, no, the evocation of Rosario's, Yang Chia's, Sassan's, Juhila's poetry, bringing back to her the full empowering feeling she had experienced with them at the conference. So entrenched had she been in her own culture's ideology that only vaguely had she begun to embrace this understanding in her work with CECO and NEWS and her growing contact with the movement of human liberation throughout the world. And then, finally, at the conference, sharing the presence of this astonishing force, she had felt within her, for the first time, what this love could really be. It was beyond, so far beyond the chance of luck in love or "success," so far beyond the drugged fantasy of the new lover or the cynic's bitter depression. Beyond in a complete embrace of emotion, a totality of meaning—whole, genuine love, *purpose* in the reality of human life as one and the ever-expanding consciousness of that oneness, of our meaning here, as a force of life, to create life, a heightened quality of life in the shared experience of our being—hadn't Elena quoted someone, some scientist, Einstein! Yes, about, "Our task is to free ourselves . . . by widening the circle . . . to embrace all living creatures and the whole of nature in its beauty."

Sylvia sat motionless, gazing at the image in her mind. How had she lost that blessed understanding in just a day? How had she slipped so far from the freedom of this spirit, the consciousness of her part in the whole that had lifted and opened her so beyond herself those first days of the conference? Could it be so fleeting? No. No. She looked at the book of poetry again. Here it was, sustained, upheld, a way of life—the underlying motion of every protracted struggle for liberation.

A din of raised voices brought her head up sharply. Her breath stopped as her eyes took in a tall, angry woman, shrieking as she flew at the short, stocky woman across from her and for a full 60 seconds they grabbed, screaming, clawing at each other before the matron and two male guards slammed through the metal barred door, bellowing obscenities at them, jumping on them and pulling them apart, hauling them, dragging them across the concrete floor, a thin trail of blood following them out the cage door, locked again, and down the corridor outside.

Sylvia's heart was racing, the sudden, awful ruckus still sounding in her ears as a taut tension gripped the cage in silence. She stared at the empty place where the women had been, her lips parted, speechless. Again she heard the shattered glass. It was there, the smell of smoke, the feel of Rikki's warm blood streaming over her hands.

Slowly the women in the cage began to stir again, a nervous laugh, the harsh sound of a tense, daring voice, "Fuck you, bitch," and a hasty, quickly abandoned tussle over a ripped and ragged magazine. The matron returned to the barred gate. "Who's next?" A muttering quiet stifled the upsurge, a smoldering rage glowing in the eyes of the women at the center of the cage as the matron hovered at the door, then turned and strode back to her post.

Sylvia sat motionless, gazing at the scene. Then, setting her book down, she lay across the cold cement floor and tried to sleep. It couldn't have been more than 20 minutes, she had just begun to doze, when she heard her name called again. "Bernetti!"

She sat up quickly and seeing the matron standing at the door of the cage with her keys in the lock, she quickly gathered her things and tied them up in the shirt Olina had given her. Her bundle in hand, she approached the matron.

"Your lawyer's here," the matron snapped without looking at her, leading her back to the visiting room she'd sat in with Olina and Ruth that morning.

Jack was standing at the table, leafing through some notes in a file. He looked up as Sylvia was let in the room.

"Sylvia," he said, extending his hand, his voice grave, as he took her hand in his.

"Hello, Jack. Thank you for coming."

"Of course!" He sat down as she took a seat across from him.

"Linda and Justin are all right, aren't they?" she asked.

"Yes, they're fine. Linda sends her love. Luckily the childcare room was nowhere near the church. Only the church was damaged. There were no injuries to the public." He paused, his voice growing even deeper. "I'm very sorry."

Sylvia nodded, alarmed by the tears that his words stirred in her, she steadied herself, looking calmly into his somber hazel eyes. "Thank you."

"So," she began, as he seemed at a loss for words. "What did . . . I mean . . . I really appreciate your taking my case." She looked at him tentatively. "Ruth said you'd . . ."

"Yes, of course," he answered, then, his eyes questioning her, "I mean I. . . would like to defend you. If you agree, of course."

"Hell yes," Sylvia said with an assurance that made them both laugh, and Jack spread his files open on the table as she leaned forward to look at them.

"I've postponed your arraignment until tomorrow," he began. "I wanted to discuss the strategy of your defense with you first, and I had a little legwork to do this morning." He looked up at her. "Hopefully, bail will be set for you tomorrow morning and we can get you out of here." Sylvia's eyes lighted. "But if you plead guilty, with a request for a diminished sentence, which is another option here, I'll explain in a minute, then," he paused again, looking at her with concern, "you may be sentenced and made to serve a period of time."

"You mean, starting tomorrow?"

"Well, you would have to stay here until the hearing and then after that . . . It depends on what we decide here, though. Let me explain the options. If you plead not guilty to the charge, you can be released on bail. But, Sylvia," he hesitated again, "this is not a simple case, as I'm sure you realize. A not-guilty plea would have to be pursued to trial for any chance of preventing you from serving time. Assaulting an officer with a deadly weapon or instrument is a felony and, as absurd and disgusting as it is in your case, that is the charge. They're saying Rikki's walkie-talkie was a 'deadly instrument.' The maximum sentence is ten years. Of course, if you had no prior convictions and were not a 'communist' or a 'radical lesbian,' we could probably get you out of here with just probation."

"Because I'm white."

"Well," Jack nodded, "yes, that too, but the fact is, Sylvia," he looked at her with concern, "it's not going to be that simple for you. For one thing, you have a prior felony conviction. True, it was some years ago, but that fact is really going to work well for the prosecution in sticking it to you as much as they can, and, of course, you know, they'll want to make an example out of you, because of your politics."

"OK," she nodded, without expression.

"So we'll have to fight it. All the way. To trial. And the problem . . . the problem in that regard is that, if we do take it to trial, it will give the D.A. every opportunity in the world to investigate you, and NEWS, which, I'm sure you realize, could be harassing or even damaging to the organization."

"I see. I'll plead guilty," she said, her voice cold, certain.

"But, Sylvia, wait a second! I just wanted to be completely honest with you about what the risks are here, the worst and best possible on each side. There is still another side to this. A trial could be very helpful to NEWS. It could provide a platform for the organization to voice its own concerns. If it were handled skillfully, it could be completely turned around in your favor. Not only for you personally to be acquitted, but as an exposé of the injustice of the charge against you and the mistreatment of the organization. It could actually be an excellent way to publicize the goals and values of NEWS and your rights to political freedom. If we dealt with this strategically, it could actually promote the credibility and visibility of NEWS in . . ."

"No, Jack." She stopped him. His enthusiasm unnerved her. "We can't risk any investigation. We can't possibly have NEWS subject to harassment and probing by the D.A."

"But, Sylvia, NEWS isn't illegal! This is about your civil, political rights!"

"No. No. It's not worth it. This isn't a case for the press. The media manipulates anything the way they want. It's too much of a risk."

"But, Sylvia, it's been done by . . ."

"No, Jack. Please. I won't consider it."

Jack sat silent, perplexed as he looked at her. This sudden obstinacy seemed so unlike what he had known of her and, as he sat, Sylvia searched her mind for what she could tell him, how she could convince him that a trial, an investigation was impossible without giving him any indication that . . . that it would be utterly destructive. That if NEWS CLAN were . . . She shuddered, terrified by the thought of how her stupid, crazy act had brought NEWS to this terrible point of danger. She wanted to shriek and leap from the window but there was no window as she sat here with Jack, and she had to be so totally calm. Why was he here? Why hadn't Ruth told him to go away, just let her have a public defender, or . . .

"Well, Sylvia," Jack began again. "I don't want to talk you into something you don't want to do." He sensed her anxious, strained emotion. "Maybe you should think about it, we could talk again in the morning."

"No, Jack. I . . . I'm going to plead guilty and just have it over with. That's it. There's no other choice." She looked intently at him. What could she tell him? "You see, I . . . I really believe I would be much more effective in prison. There's no question in my mind. I just don't believe in all this hype about the media, and my First Amendment rights or whatever—all this legal rigamarole—it's a lot of crap. I don't mean to insult you, Jack, honestly, I don't, it's just . . . I can't stand the whole fucking scene. Honestly I can't. It would drive me crazy.

And it can't be trusted. At *all*. You know as well as I do that no matter what kind of brilliant liberal plea you can make for my whatever rights, I'm screwed. They want to get me, as an example, like you said. So, I go to prison now, tomorrow, or I go in six months, or a year, after a lot of crap. No thanks. I'd rather go now. Then I can do some real work, organize with the other prisoners, write about the conditions. It's just more real to me. Can you understand?" She sat back, looking at him coolly, distant.

Jack sat back himself, struggling with his irritation, or was it hurt? He looked down at his hands playing with his ballpoint pen.

Sylvia leaned forward again. "Jack." Her voice was earnest. "Please help me do this my way."

The smooth line of his straight, white teeth played with his lower lip as he reflected, looking away from her, still taken aback. She was so strange. He hadn't realized. But then, it was her right. She must have her reasons, her beliefs. How could he convince her to have faith in the law? He barely had it himself. And what did she know of law? Except her study of oppression and . . . Maybe he couldn't get her off. Maybe it would be hell for NEWS. Maybe it was all crap.

"Please, Jack," Sylvia repeated, worried that the matron would come for her before he would agree.

He sat forward. "All right, Sylvia. Of course."

"So." Her shoulders relaxed. She studied his file folder, unconsciously bending its top corner back and forth. "What is this thing . . . about a diminished sentence?"

"Well, actually," Jack thumbed through his notes, a professional again, "we can plead guilty, with request for a sentencing hearing. You'd be kept here." He looked at her. Her face was expressionless. "Until the hearing was held, possibly a few days, maybe a month. I'm not sure how tough they're going to be on you yet. You're not still in solitary, which is a good sign. Though on the other hand, they may be waiting to see what we do. If we were going the not-guilty defense/media route, they might be more careful about how they treat you at first, to avoid a big stink about your conditions. But with your pleading guilty, Sylvia, they just may decide to give you the shaft every possible way." He looked at her sadly. Did she really know what she was getting into by refusing a defense?

"So then what?"

"Well." He sat back again, resigned. "We'll ask for a suspended sentence based on exceptional conditions, not exactly temporary insanity, but . . . your distress over Rikki's death . . . I don't know." He seemed demoralized.

"I see. OK." Sylvia sat back again. "So what time is the arraignment tomorrow?"

"Ten o'clock."

"OK."

They were silent.

"You're sure, Sylvia?" Jack tried one more time, a bewildered sadness in his voice.

"Yes, yes. Thank you, Jack." She stood up. "Very much. I really do appreciate the work you've done, I really do."

"Well, Sylvia, I will do everything in my power to get the absolute minimum sentence possible," he said, standing slowly.

"Thank you, Jack. We . . . we can talk about the fee later, if that's OK," she glanced at the metal door, "I can . . ."

"Sylvia, please."

She turned back to him. "Did you talk to Ruth, or Olina, about this? About the options, and all?" She picked up her bundle from the table.

"Yes, I talked to them this morning."

"What did they say?"

"Well, they both said the same thing. That it was up to you."

"Mmm." She nodded, then looked at the metal door, desperate to be alone.

Jack stood watching her a moment, then turned and pressed the button by the door.

The matron released them as Sylvia turned and shook Jack's hand again. "Thank you."

"I'll see you tomorrow," he said. "Is there anything you need?"

"No, no. Good-bye. Thanks." She turned and walked back to the cage, the matron at her heels.

The door clanged shut behind her, the sound of the lock clanking, grinding in her ears. She walked slowly back to her corner. "Dear god. What have I done," she spoke the words aloud, leaning back against the cold wall and sliding down, sinking into her seat on the concrete floor. She gazed out at the ugly cage, the women clustered about, some angry, dejected, others bitter, defiant. She watched them. So. This is it. She closed her eyes. At least they trusted me. Ruth knew, they both knew I would plead guilty. How couldn't I! But had they known the choice before they came this morning? No, they couldn't have, it was too early. Anyhow, they did trust me. To be strong. Of course. She opened her eyes again. So this is it.

A fallow, stony sensation crept through her as she felt the earth open, longed for the earth to open beneath her and swallow her up. But no. There she sat. Her lithe, aching body crumpled against the rock-hard cement floor and wall. She leaned her head back against it, her eyes narrowed, scrutinizing the women before her. Where had they come from? Who were they? Some seemed to be friends, seemed to find comfort in each other. If they can live it, why can't I? she demanded of herself. Come on, little middle-class white girl, get with it. This is *home*. Abruptly she stood up and began to walk to them, time to *move*, but after a step she stopped, still, what could she say? Who could she be? She would have to talk first with Ruth or Olina, JoAnn—someone—maybe someone would visit her tomorrow, but they must be overwhelmed with work, picking up the pieces.

She turned back to her corner and lay down on the floor, resting her head on her lumpy bundle. She stared at the dirty grey ceiling. Of course they were overwhelmed with work and would be indefinitely. Who knows what direction things would take while she was locked up in here, alone. For how long? Years? God knows where NEWS would go while she was locked in here. Alone. She steeled her eyes. Staring above her, narrowing her eyes, she felt the sheer weight of her head, a thick weight like a cap on her brain, dull the sound of the voice within her relentlessly repeating, This is it, it's all over, it's all over. The light in the cage itself seemed to wane, the room about her growing dingier, a duller grey as the winter dusk obscured the little light that filtered through the barred windows. The sounds in the room, the voices themselves seemed sluggish, fading with the loss of day as the torpid dusk, its gloomy presence, settled upon them. With an effort that called upon her very last reserve of strength and determination, she turned on her side and tried to sleep.

Lying alone, in a dark, cold cave, she opened her eyes, woken by a sound of scraping, a harsh crackling, slowly, she sat up. She could see nothing. She reached out, groping in the darkness, she felt the rock wall of the cave, a damp, slimey mold swallowing her fingers. She recoiled, sitting back sharply, knocking her shoulder against the other wall of the cave, a panic seized her, frantic in the darkness, she scrambled up on all fours, somehow knowing not to stand, she crawled along the moist earth as if she were running. She stood. All was light now, a glaring, scorching light. With tremendous relief she felt she had escaped the cave, a hot, dry wind blowing, wafting through her hair, a dusty, arid heat. She felt crumpled paper, scraps and pieces, blowing about her feet, scurrying at her feet, torn wrappers, newspapers, sticks and cans buffeted by the hot, dry wind blowing about her, against her legs and arms. She could see the whole of the plain before her, an expanse of cracked, dry earth to the grey, undulating line of the horizon.

She stood at the horizon, looking back at the plain, a dump, the city dump, mounds of trash, garbage, abandoned cars crashed beyond recognition. Wandering through them, wading through the mounds she checked car after car, she knew that Claire was there somewhere, hiding from her. Angrily she pushed through stacks of stained, molded paper, searching, rummaging through a pile, she felt her arms steeped in wet garbage, rotting vegetables, somewhere Rikki had left her head, forgotten her head in here, she needed it urgently, she knew it was there, in there, but the deeper she steeped her arms still her hands only felt the rotted waste, at every turn her hands clasped only the wet slime in insurmountable frustration.

She stood at the outskirts of the dump. Claire was waiting for her in the office downtown and she was hopelessly late, her watch face said 1984. The meeting was planned for Christmas morning, she raced down Market Street, waiting for a bus, she looked down the tracks, the street was empty, barren. She sat on an empty bus, there was no one, though the motor ran, the driver was gone. Looking out the window she saw the trash and garbage blowing, still filling the streets, the hot, angry wind rocking the bus, even the buildings were gone, all of them gone. She ran down Market Street, searching for her office, for the buildings. Everywhere the wind blew trash across the hot, dry plane, mounds of trash, from horizon to horizon, of course, the bomb. Of course. The nuclear war. It had happened. There was no one. *No one.*

She opened her eyes, her body a molten weight hovering around her, a thick, glutinous weight surrounding the utter hollow within her, breathless with unbearable fear. It had happened. It had *happened.*

A crackling laugh and the sound of distant voices threaded through her waking mind, flickering distraction as her eyes blinked and she saw before her the sickly green cement wall of the Day Room, calming her throbbing heart. Oh, yes, yes, she was here, in the jail. In jail, with the others. The city still stood, the world still lived. Only Rikki was dead. There was time. There was still time. Even now they were meeting, they were alive, there was still hope. Hope. She let the tears slip from her eyes.

Chapter XIV

Steven lay still, his eyes wide open, facing the wall as Linda quietly slipped from the bed and went to answer Justin's call. He listened to her stepping softly, as if she might wake him, and the familiar flush of anger hardened in his mind. Of course she knew he was awake. How not, he'd hardly slept for days. But then they'd hardly spoken for days. She really just didn't seem to care at all.

The ring of the telephone seemed deafening in the early morning quiet. He listened to Linda murmuring to Justin as she stepped lightly, quickly down the hall, catching it in the middle of the second jarring ring. "Oh, Mom, hi," he heard her answer. "No, no they're going to court this morning at 10:00." Her voice was strained. "Yes, I know. How's Maureen?" The tense sadness of her muffled words, caught in a drama that really wasn't hers, that really had nothing to do with her, enraged him. He was sick of her self-importance, her vicarious succoring of this absurd situation, the persecuted revolutionary and, of course, Jack, Jack, Jack, the heroic Jack, jumping on the bandwagon, lapping up the worship of all the local Pollyannas.

" . . . plead guilty, but Jack's going to try to talk . . . I know . . . I know." Her voice trembled with emotion. Justin was whimpering, then crying. She couldn't even attend to her own son, this drama had become so aggrandizing to her. Ever since she'd started going to that conference, it was as if her family were nothing, a bother, a pain in the ass, something to be gotten rid of so she could pursue her egotistic fantasy of the dedicated leftist. It was pathetic. She didn't know a fucking thing about Marx, or politics. It was just her adolescent attraction to Jack ever since she'd gone to that fucking demonstration in Berkeley, and he and Sylvia, constantly spouting their simplistic slogans, she ate it up. Just let it completely take over her. Why not? It was a lot more fun than being responsible to her family, than taking care of her husband and son, than working for a living. He winced with the recollection of the morning, two days before, when she'd finally said they should talk, when she'd promised to meet him after work, and like a fool he'd thought, all day long, he'd thought about it, and he'd thought they could work it out, put things back together, get past all this craziness. He'd bought her flowers on the way home, and, of course, when he'd gotten here, she wasn't even home. She was still at that conference, with Jack, of course. But even still he'd put that aside, didn't let it bother him, he'd decided to do his best to make it up with her, no matter what. He turned restlessly in the bed as he remembered how hopeful, giving, he had felt. Like a fool, he'd waited an hour, and then he'd finally poured himself a drink and turned on the television. He hadn't really been paying attention, it was toward the end of the evening news. He'd just barely noticed a scene of firemen dousing some flames at the corner of an old stone church, and then he'd caught the name, St. Joan of Arc. It sounded familiar. He'd listened, " . . . the cause of the explosion is not known. Fire Department officials say they will investigate the possibility of a faulty boiler . . . A meeting of the Women's International Sovereignty Organization was being held at . . . everyone was evacuated safely . . . A spokesperson for the women's organization claimed that a bomb had been thrown into the church as a deliberate attack." The camera showed a slightly damaged area far in the back of the cathedral, then panned to a group of black women standing outside the front doors, some rushing into cars, and then the news shifted to the sports highlights, clips of football teams in training. He had watched dully, on his third drink, still not sure if the scene he had just witnessed was in fact the famous "conference" that had so enraptured Linda. It seemed more like a Southern prayer meeting. It was hard to tell what had happened. It hardly seemed real. But yes, that had to be the conference—St. Joan of Arc's, Women's International—where was Linda? And Justin? What time had they said? . . . But no one was hurt. "Everyone was evacuated safely." They seemed to all be leaving the place. And for a minute, he'd been glad, good. Maybe that would put a stop to all this bullshit. Maybe that was finally the end of it. But where was Linda? She probably had to rush to Jack's comforting arms after the trauma of it all, and they'd had to fuck for a few hours. Justin was probably wandering around alone among all those dykes who wouldn't know the first thing about what to do with him. He'd gotten up and slapped off the television and walked down to the bar on 24th Street. She couldn't even fucking call. Fuck her.

"Yes, OK, Mom. I'll talk to you later." Linda hung up the phone. He heard her starting back to the kitchen, talking to Justin, when the telephone rang again. She turned back and picked it up, pleading with Justin to wait just another minute. Steven listened. "Oh, Jack, hello." Her voice was low, relieved, intimate.

Steven jumped up from the bed and wrenched open the closet door, grabbing his worn blue suit. He slammed through the bureau drawers, dressing hurriedly, almost ripping out the elbow of his neatly pressed white shirt.

"Steven!" Linda stood in the bedroom door, holding Justin, who was crying again, squirming to get down.

"Don't even talk to me." His voice was little more than controlled rage.

"Steven, you have *got* to talk to me!" She sat Justin, crying still louder, on the bed, caressing his blonde curls. "Justin, please, please." She was crying herself.

"The hell I do!" Steven shot back as he reached for his suit coat.

"Steven, how can you! Don't you even *care*? Are you going to just keep going to work and the bar, and work and the bar? You know what is happening! I told you yesterday morning! How can, how . . ."

"You *bet* I know what's happening."

"Steven!" Linda screamed above Justin's crying. "What about Sylvia! Don't you even care? She's going to go to prison if we don't *do* something!" Linda slumped down on the bed beside her son, covering her face as she cried.

Steven stood still a moment, watching her, coldly. "Let your friend Jack take care of her."

Linda raised her head, her reddened eyes looking back at him, incredulous, stunned. Justin's sobbing had worn to a sporadic whimper.

Steven turned away as Linda sat, still gazing at him. Her voice was unbelieving, hopeless. "What has happened to you, Steven. What in god's name is wrong with you?"

"Me! What's happened to *me*? What's happened to *you*?" He was shouting now. "How the fuck would you even *know* what's happened to me? You're too goddamn busy running around to conferences and meetings, consulting with Jack every ten minutes."

"Steven!" Linda screamed at him as she stood up. "The most important women's conference in history was bombed! Sylvia's friend Rikki was *killed!* Sylvia is in jail and is probably going to end up in prison! Jack wants you to talk to her!" She stood closer to him, as if somehow to break through to him. "How can you ignore that! Don't you care?"

The dull, cold glaze in his eyes was her answer, as she stood silent, in shocked disbelief, watching her husband.

Steven turned to leave. Then abruptly he swung around. "Why don't you just quit pretending, Linda. Why don't you just get off this shit about history and importance," he hissed at her. "Why don't you just fucking admit it! You're in love with Jack!" he shouted. "It's Jack you want! And all this politics crap just feeds into it!" He felt the rage almost blind him as he saw her shocked expression, set to deny, deny it again.

"Admit it, goddamn you!" He lunged at her, grabbing her shoulders, gripping her shoulders between his hands, his raging eyes glaring at her, unrecognizable.

She stood stiff in an instant of fear, then tearing herself away, she pushed him off, still standing face to face. "All right, Steven." She was livid now. "All right! You want it so much! All right!" she screamed at him, "I love Jack!"

Steven fell back as if struck, his body limp now, his jaw slackened and his clouded eyes dark, dull.

"You pushed me! You pushed me, Steven!" Linda's hands trembled with anger as she covered her face again, sobbing. "You just keep pushing and pushing and drinking and drinking." But Steven had turned to leave, taking his briefcase from the chair by the bed.

"I'm leaving you, Linda."

"You just wouldn't let me be. I just wanted us all to be friends. At least he cares. He cares about Sylvia, about people," she sobbed, "You just keep drinking." The sound of the front door latch snapping shut stopped her. "Steven!" she cried after him, dropping her hands. "Steven!"

The flat was strangely silent. Even Justin seemed stunned, too frightened to make a sound. Linda stepped back, leaning back, she slumped to the bed, then flinging herself down across it, she grasped the worn blue spread in her hands, rending it through her hands as she wept.

So. Finally. The truth was out. Good. Steven almost laughed with relief as he maneuvered his Toyota through the morning traffic. His mind felt clearer than it had in months. Hah! He wasn't so crazy after all, not the least bit crazy, no, goddamit, though she'd tried to drive him crazy, that was sure. Thank *god* he'd escaped! That he'd forced it out of her. He should have done it weeks ago, but no, she was so into denying it then. She probably hadn't slept with him yet. Then. God! The lying bitch! Incredible! It was all clear now. Crystal clear. Out in the open. They can have each other, goddamn fucking . . . Maybe *they* had sent him those sick little letters, that card, and then that letter to Nick's house. Try to make him crazy so he'd just get out of the picture. Sick assholes, couldn't even treat him with common decency. They can fucking have each other—their secrets, and lies—supposed to be so high-minded. Hah! As slimey as they come. Couldn't even admit it! Be *honest* about it. Had to resort to sneaking around and all this hiding out at that conference, their whole insidious little passion harbored by all those dykes, spouting all their utopian crap. They're all motherfucking *nuts*. What had happened to *him*? Hah! *She's* the one who had lost it, flipped out on this leftist shit, gone off about Jack, so motherfucking hung up on him. Good riddance! Lying bitch. Trying to drive him crazy. Maybe it *was* them who'd sent that card, not Mark. Of course, and that letter to Nick and Rhonda's. Who else knows their address? Nobody but her. And now him too, sure, that slimey . . . Maybe he would just call that number and . . . What, though. What the hell? The truth was out now. That's all that mattered. It was all perfectly clear.

He swung around a corner nearing his office and turned into the lot to park the car. Turning off the engine, he sat a moment. So he would leave her. Good. Finished. He was *free*. Maybe now he could start making sense of life again. Who needs her! Goddamit! He shoved open the door of the car, slamming it behind him, and strode across the lot to his office building. Oh, Christ. He'd forgotten. He had a hearing at 9:00 at the Hall. He hurried back to his car, checking his briefcase for his notes.

He drove quickly the mile to the Hall of Justice, he wanted a cup of coffee badly and it was already 8:30. Those pretentious motherfuckers. The most "important" thing in history. Sylvia in prison. Boohoo. What about the other hundreds of thousands of people in prison? Why wasn't she all worked up about that? All the people he worked his butt off for every goddamn day while she and Jack were listening to rhetoric in a church, holding hands. What about the people he sweated blood over 50 hours a week? "How can you ignore that! Don't you even *care*?" his mind screamed back at her. I pushed her. I pushed her by drinking. Bull*shit!* Who pushed *who*? "At least Jack cares about Sylvia." Hah! He knows how to weasel his way to another man's wife. *That's* what *Jack* cares about. Fuck them both. Just fuck them both. Noble, nimble Jack, jumping on Sylvia's bandwagon, just thriving on all the hype. And *me*, I'm supposed to be such a slug, such a nowhere slug because *my* clients aren't famous rich brats who become revolutionaries when they can't find any other hobby, or a bunch of women who don't even know how to relate to men. Sylvia. He could defend her better than old Jack-ass ever could, but no, he didn't pretend to think she was more important than everyone else in jail. They can have each other. They can all fucking have each other! He swerved into the Hall of Justice lot and parked his car. Slamming the door shut behind him, he stood in the cold, grey winter morning surveying the building before him. Lighting a cigarette, he headed for the basement cafeteria.

Eight floors above, Sylvia sat in her corner of the Day Room, the sickly smell of the morning's breakfast still heavy in the air. She hadn't slept well, fragments of dreams, vivid and frightening, had wakened her throughout the night. She sat, quiet now, trying to doze, hoping that a friend would visit to help her understand, to know how she could be here, how she could act, who she was here, and most important, if there were any way possible, to give her news, to somehow let her know what was happening in Amsterdam, and what was being salvaged here. But of course nothing about NEWS CLAN could be said here in any way. It was too great of a risk just to satisfy her burning curiosity. And at the same time, she hoped no one would come. What, really, could be said. "We're sorry, Sylvia, that you made

such a mistake, that you'll be going to prison. We'll remember you."
Yes, actually. She would like to hear even that. Or would she? The
sorrow in their eyes, wouldn't it just be more painful? More
excruciatingly frustrating? But if someone, if someone could just help
her understand how to be here. How in god's name could she do it
alone? After so many years of working so closely with all of them,
discussing, analyzing every decision, every act of their lives seen in a
strategic context. How could she do this all *alone*?

She saw the other women around her, their presence a denial of the
word. No. She was not alone. There were over 20 women here, in
this cage with her. She would just have to take her cues from them.
This was her life now. She was not a cadre of NEWS alone in jail.
She was Sylvia Bernetti, one of 20 women in a jail cell. Maybe she
should forget her politics, her need for strategy. Maybe she should play
this the way of the people who knew it best. She started to stand,
eyeing the women, trying to decide who was the least intimidating.

"Bernetti!" A different matron was on duty today, her voice much
less hostile than her predecessor's.

Sylvia turned and saw the woman standing at the gate to the cage
with her keys ready. The beat of her heart quickened as she picked up
her bundle and approached the matron.

"Your lawyer's here." She swung the metal barred door open.

Sylvia's heart sank as she followed the matron into the corridor.
He'd said he wouldn't come until right before the arraignment. He'd
probably come to try and talk her into a trial again, and again she'd have
to make excuses, evade the real issue, convincing him to let her plead
guilty.

The matron opened the heavy door of the visiting room.

"Steven!" Sylvia was taken by surprise.

"Hello, Sylvia," Steven answered cautiously, standing awkwardly
behind the table. Her large grey eyes, so much more vulnerable than
he'd remembered, touched him a moment, even through the shield of his
own pain.

They stood a moment, Sylvia wanting to reach out and embrace
him, to hold a friend in her arms for just a minute, but his manner was
so guarded, strange, he seemed not himself at all, and he looked like
he'd been through hell. Not just the unhealthy flush of alcohol, the
stale odor of tobacco and whiskey, but like . . . as if he were . . .
broken, breaking down.

"How are you, Steven?" Sylvia asked with concern as she sat down
at the table, hoping he would join her there as if that, at least, would be
some kind of coming together.

"I've been better. How about yourself?" he responded, still
standing, avoiding her eyes.

"Steven." Sylvia watched him as he played with the change in his pocket, rocking back on his heels as his eyes searched the thick metal door of the room. "What brings you here?" she asked.

"I thought I'd check on you. Sorrenson wanted me to talk to you." Still his eyes avoided hers.

"He did. Why?"

Not knowing why Steven flushed slightly, then looked at her, finally, his eyes defiant, accusing. "I'm leaving Linda."

Sylvia sat back abruptly in her chair as if he had thrown her a massive weight to catch, her eyes wide. For less than an instant the apprehension she had felt that moment in the courtyard at St. Joan's, when she had walked up to Jack and Linda, returned, but no, impossible, it faded.

"What? Steven! Please sit down," she urged him, leaning forward again.

He stood, looking down at his hands on the back of the chair opposite her, deep in thought.

"Steven. Please talk to me."

Slowly he pulled out the chair, leaning back as he sat down, studying her coldly.

Sylvia lowered her eyes, her mind racing. Would it make a difference? Would it make a difference to tell him now? How could she find out what was really doing this to him? His drinking? The covert harassment? Jack? Would telling him make the difference? What would it mean? What would he do with it? She looked up at him, her head cocked as her eyes sought some sense of him, something deep within him that might guide her to the truth.

Steven shifted in his chair, her intensity disturbing him, catching him up from himself. What was she thinking? What was she feeling, sitting here, as so many of his clients had sat? But this was Sylvia, not his client. Somehow the situation seemed suddenly reversed. Her familiar face, in this room, and her manner now, questioning him, oddly inverting his traditional position here. Who was counsel? Who was he here?

"What happened, Steven? Is it about your drinking?" The question was sincere, without judgment.

Steven turned his head, watching the bare wall. He shrugged with a short, hard laugh. "She'll say so. Sure." He turned suddenly back. "It's about Jack. Jack Sorrenson." He felt the rage rising in him again. "She's been in love with him for months, denying it the whole time." His eyes narrowed, accusing. "Fuck you, Sylvia. You know it. You've known it the whole goddamn time. You must have seen what's going on with them at that conference. If they were even there."

"Steven, I don't know! I didn't know. Linda hasn't said anything about it at all to me. I've hardly seen her for weeks. Did she tell you that?"

"Yes."

She closed her eyes. "I see."

Steven sat forward, watching her closely. "You mean to tell me, Sylvia, that you knew nothing whatsoever about this?"

She looked back at him, her eyes wide now, honest. "No, Steven, really. I mean, I knew you and she were having problems that, you know, the last time we all had dinner. I mean, last month, before Christmas. And you'd had problems with your car, and money. All the pressure of that." She was searching. How much of it was that?

"Yeah, yeah. My luck's been bad." He sat back, waving it off, and then forward again. "But I didn't think, I never thought," his face looked ashen, ill, "that Linda was the kind of woman who would desert her husband because . . ."

"Steven, wait, what did she say?" Sylvia couldn't believe it either.

"Sylvia, look, you *know* they've been at that conference together every single day—OK, I'll believe you weren't around, or they weren't, whatever—Linda has not even been speaking to me, she, she . . . I just can't believe it!" He slammed himself back in his chair, against the wall. "She's such a fucking *coward!* She won't, she hasn't even talked to me for days, since that fucking Christmas dinner, and she, I can't *believe* what they've *resorted to!* Sending me sick little letters, anonymous letters about, fuck, I don't know, like they're trying to drive me crazy!"

"What letters? What kind of letters?"

"Oh some sick card, like a *Christmas card*, last week, with that sick, stupid nursery rhyme—Jack be nimble—Dgghgh!" The sensitive curve of his mouth was contorted with disgust. "And then to Nick, to Nick and Rhonda!" He looked at her in hurt and disbelief, a wildness in his eyes. "They had him give me . . . They sent a letter for *me* to *them*, about if I had so many problems, about money, to call some number. They're fucking goddamn crazy! Trying to do any goddamn thing so they can get rid of me, they've got such a passion."

"Steven." Again her intensity arrested him. "Steven, I have to tell you something." Her urgency unnerved him. What did she know? She did know. She . . .

"Steven, listen, I . . ." She reached for his briefcase as he watched her, astonished, and taking a legal pad, she held out her hand for a pen. Nothing was too absurd now. He handed her a pen from his pocket.

"I know as fact," she wrote hurriedly as he watched her, reading, "you are under surveillance. Government intelligence harassing you—vandalized your car, canceled credit, questioned Linda. They're watching you, trying to break you. They sent the letters—trying to destroy your marriage. Typical tactics. It's because of letter for Claire you got in September—they think you're with NEWS. Believe me. I know. Couldn't tell you before. You must not tell anyone! Extremely important. Tell NO ONE. Dangerous to many. But you must know. They sent the letters." Even as she wrote she felt the clamor of fear. Could she trust him? And yet the necessity, he had to know. And when would she ever see him again? Quickly she scratched out every word carefully as Steven looked on aghast. This was truly insane.

She looked up at him, her eyes demanding belief as they pleaded for his silence. Steven sat another moment, then dropped his head back, laughing, and looking back at her, shaking his head, laughing in genuine amusement, he said, "Sylvia. You really are too much."

Now Sylvia looked aghast. He didn't believe her! She looked on at him, incredulous herself, her clean, dark brows arched as her eyes glared at him, her hand crushing the yellow sheet of paper into a tighter, and tighter wad. "Steven!" she said.

"Nice try, Sylvia. But *really*," he said, pity in his voice. He shook his head at her, with kindness, he thought. The poor girl, she was really losing it in here. It must be hard on her really, this wasn't her league. No speeches and theories here. He laughed again. And Linda called *him* paranoid. Well, too, it must be hard for her, being homosexual, never really accepted anywhere. Of course, she could distort things. And her rabid radicalism, ending her up in the slammer.

Sylvia sat quietly, watching Steven's amused pity as it seemed to relax him, give him comfort, his power momentarily restored. She could see, yes, he saw her as crazy now. And that made him sane. She pressed her minuscule wad of paper between her thumb and forefinger, and with a quiet, angry dignity measuring her words, she said, "Steven, I know we're very different, you and I. Our life-styles. And our beliefs about the world. We both know that, if you weren't married to my cousin, we would never have befriended one another." She paused as Steven shifted in his chair, frowning, though listening to her. "And because of our differences you may be tempted to dismiss my perceptions, or my understanding of reality, and of what is true. Our experiences are very different." She looked carefully at him as her eyes held his. "But I promise you. What I'm telling you is the truth. You will do such a disservice to yourself, and to me, if you don't accept it." She closed her eyes a moment, struggling for the words, then, looking back at him, said, "Steven, if you don't take me seriously now—believe me and take this confidence I'm sharing with you as deeply significant, and commit yourself to silence, to tell no one at this time, but to act accordingly—you will be making a very serious mistake. You have got to trust me now." Again her eyes sought some sense, a recognition within him.

He looked away. In fact, it was true. They were very different. She did, when it came down to it, belie his very sense of . . . of what life is about. Of family, and love. What else was there? And what on earth did she think she could do for the world if that was not central? No, he never really had understood her. About that she was right.

He gazed at the bare walls of the room. How many hundreds of times had he sat in here, listening to story after story? And why? It seemed so dim now, the reason. But wasn't, hadn't he believed so strongly? About rights. To defend the rights. Everyone's human right to a legal defense. Something in what she said, it was about that. That right. To be believed. Understood. Despite the difference. Despite the differences of class and race and . . . even Sylvia's. To be able to believe others' perceptions as valid. My god, had he lost that? Had all these years, haggling with this judge and that D.A., the constant battle over just how many lies to accept, while his own clients pimped him and . . . Did he believe any of them anymore? The people he saw in this room day after day, in the courts, in the . . . any of it. Did he even believe that the law . . . No. No, he didn't. There was no truth in it. In this room, in these walls. In this legal farce. The truth had gone out of it. "The rights of everyone." The truth. It had never really been here at all.

Sylvia felt herself tremble as she watched Steven's blue-green eyes, keen now, gazing at the wall beside her. What in god's name is he going to do? She glanced at the clock. Nine o'clock.

No. He didn't believe Sylvia. How? Her whole thing, everything was so crazily distorted. No he didn't believe her spy stories, but what's more, he didn't believe *anyone*. There was no truth here. None. There never had been. It was simple. He had to get out.

"Sylvia." He stood up abruptly as Sylvia started. Oh god, what could she do now? "I have to get back," he said.

"Steven, *wait*. What, what are you going . . ."

"No, no. I won't tell anyone." He looked at her with a certainty she'd never really seen in him, a resolve that assured her. "You can trust me, I will never repeat our conversation." It was the least he could say.

She was visibly relieved, and still she looked at him with concern. She knew he still didn't believe her. "But Steven, for you. For you. If you could understand . . ."

"Yes, I know. I understand what I have to do." His smile was strangely sad, and sweet. "Good-bye, Sylvia." He reached out his hand, taking hers a quick moment, that same smile, so distant, and then he turned and pushed the buzzer by the door as Sylvia scrambled up from her chair, as if she could stop him, but the matron was there. "Take care, Steven," he heard her anxious concern as he walked quickly down the corridor.

What had just gone on? What was going on? So she had told him. She had told him and he didn't believe her. In all the times she'd thought of, imagined telling him, she'd never thought he wouldn't *believe* her, *at all*. She'd thought she would have to explain it carefully and that—that had been the problem—how to disclose it without saying too much, and yet insure his confidence, but this, this . . . But then she'd never imagined that she would be here, in this way now . . . She sat back down in her cold cement corner, as familiar to her now as her own bed at home. She leaned her head back against the wall. What was going on? Should she even have told him? But, yes, it had been right for her to tell him, she felt that. Though, objectively, it was really the worst circumstance. If she'd had time, if she'd known before, thought about it, she'd never have done it. But still, yes, it just felt like the right, the necessary thing to do. It wouldn't endanger NEWS. She knew, somehow, even though they hadn't been able to discuss it, all that it meant, she knew it was all right. He wouldn't tell anyone. Though he didn't believe her, and he would still drink, and he was in terrible pain, it seemed like he had already dismissed her words before he'd even left, and that he would dismiss the letters, he would not call that number. Her heart stopped in her chest. Or would he? Would he call? And play right into their hands? But what did he know? What could they have him do? And, no. No, he wouldn't call. Something in that distant smile, his strange resolve, convinced her that . . . that what? That he was going to do something else. Something completely different, completely unrelated to all of this, unrelated to NEWS, or her, or even Linda. But what? What was it about him . . . She jumped up from the floor. She had to call Linda. Scanning the corridors surrounding the cage, she looked for the matron. It must be well after 9:00, Jack would be here any minute, then the arraignment. She had to call Linda *now*.

She saw the matron at the cell door calling the names of two women, waiting for them to come forward. Sylvia walked quickly toward her as an officer approached and consulted briefly with the matron. She frowned, and then, as Sylvia walked up to her, she looked at her. "Another lawyer's here for you."

"For me?" Sylvia asked.

"Yeah. Come on," the matron answered, gruff now, as she opened the barred gate and the two women crowded by.

"But I need to make a phone call."

The matron ignored her as she directed the two women toward the officer.

"I have to make a phone call," Sylvia repeated, half pleading.

"Get moving." The matron directed her back to the visiting room.

Sylvia gave it up, maybe Jack would help her call. But Jack . . .
What *was* going on? Were he and Linda really . . .

The metal door swung open and Jack stood, just as he had the day
before, a pleasant, easy vitality gracing his tall frame. An overcoat was
slung over the chair, the shoulders damp with rain, and his curly dark
hair glistened with moisture. He smelled of the cool, fresh winter air,
and despite her urgent need to call Linda, Sylvia felt a sudden longing to
be outside, to breathe the air of the wide outdoors, alive, as the moment
of what was to come, of the pronouncement to be made upon her stilled
her heart, catching at her in an instant of dire apprehension. She shook
it off, calming herself, and looking back at him she said, "Hello, Jack,"
as she took his outstretched hand.

"Sylvia." Jack smiled at her, a happy excitement in his eyes that
seemed oddly inappropriate.

"Listen, Jack, I have to make a phone call before the arraignment.
I have to call Linda immediately."

"But, Sylvia, wait, listen." He was really elated. "I have a note
for you from Ruth." He handed her a slip of paper.

"But, Jack, I'm telling you . . ."

"Sylvia. Read this first."

She looked down at the paper. "Sylvia. Jack is going to enter a
not-guilty plea for you. He will post bail and you will be released. Do
not question this. Call Thomas at two o'clock today. Love, Ruth."

Sylvia studied the sheet of paper in her hand. Was it true? Could
it really, no . . . But this was Ruth's hand, Jack couldn't possibly . . .
Though if he were so manipulative as to encourage Linda, Steven had
said . . . But Steven was so, disturbed, he . . . Jack couldn't know
Thomas, this must be . . . yes. It was Ruth. It *was* Ruth, but why?

"Sylvia?" Jack questioned her.

She looked up at him, her eyes wide with hope, though still she
held back.

"Is it clear?" he asked, adding, "I didn't read it."

Still she was silent.

"Ruth called me this morning, I've just come from a meeting with
her," Jack explained. "She insisted that the not-guilty plea is
appropriate. I told her your concerns as you stated them to me. I did
not argue my own position. But she had determined that this was the
best course, and I assured her, that with your consent . . ."

Sylvia was rereading the note. Yes. It was true. Her smile gave
Jack his answer.

"Your bail was set for $10,000. I've already been to the bondsman,
this shouldn't take long at all. And I promised Linda I'd bring you by
her place as soon as you're released. You can see her, probably before
noon. Let's get down to the courtroom." He grinned at her.

Yes. She could talk to Linda privately, then she could explain. What could she really say to her over the phone anyway? Yes. She would talk to Linda in private. She was getting out of here! Getting out! She could find out what was going on, with *everyone*, everything! She would straighten it all out. She was getting the hell out!

Jack had pushed the buzzer by the door and stood with his briefcase and coat in hand as the matron opened the lock, and Sylvia quickly crumpled Ruth's note, shoving it in her pants pocket. Yes she would talk to Linda alone today, this morning! She'd explain Steven's visit and together they could decide what was best, what needed to be done about Steven. She had until two o'clock, and then, then! She would be back with NEWS, thank god! The future looked wonderfully free, open, beautiful. It would be all right. Everything would be all right. Steven would be all right and she would be back with NEWS!

She followed Jack through the offices, waiting silently as he exchanged a word with the matron, and, still exhilarated by the sensation of escape, she followed him to the elevator. They rode down in silence. She felt Jack's warm glow beside her, as if he shared her elation. Or did he feel . . . Was it the sense of his own power, pride that he had gotten his way and that he would take her to trial, that so buoyed him? She looked at him. He smiled warmly, pleased, his gladness for her, simply and genuinely for her. She smiled back at him, and at the same moment she felt a sharp sadness for Linda, for Steven, for the three of them.

The elevator doors opened and they walked to Municipal Court. Checking the docket, her name was there, they entered the courtroom, taking a seat near the back. Sylvia looked around her. Of course, next to the lawyers in their suits and ties and expensive dresses, sat the poor, black, Latin, Indian, those without privacy or privilege. She watched as the judge entered and all were made to stand as he barely took the time to glance them over, his face a mask, a sham of wisdom. They sat, as first one and then another human being was called to the bench, the charges read to them in grave hypocrisy, their rights to defense muttered dully as they stood, some trembling with anxiety, others brazenly cold, resigned. She imagined herself as them, without Jack, without the privilege of her family and her color, without the force and protection of NEWS, but in complete absence of power, helpless at the whim of these cardboard characters calling themselves lawyers and judges who cared as little for these people as they cared for so many bags of trash, the only question being how to dispose of them with as little effort as possible. This was the scale on which the lives of the people before her were weighed and the presence of it overwhelmed her, sickened her. Had she forgotten in her short isolation from the world, that it was everywhere in this society? The injustice, the cheapness of human life that was not of the world's privileged few. And what sickened her here was nothing compared to the courts in the imperialist colonies where death squads and torture chambers replaced the mindless apathy that simply wasted lives in this stale, bitter pretense at democracy.

She started as her name was called and Jack stepped from the wooden pew. Waiting for her to pass in front of him, he followed her to the podium before the judge. She stood still, feigning respect at the sound of the judge's voice reading the charges and her rights, and then Jack's entering her plea—the two of them discussing the conditions of her release, distant, removed, as if she were not really present at all, as if this were really a private affair between the two of them—two men quietly discussing her fate, assured, of course, that they, by dint of their superior perception, had the right. She smiled respectfully as the judge finally glanced at her. Did she understand? Yes, I do, your honor. Best not to risk arrogance with a simple yes. But what had they said?

She followed Jack to the bailiff's desk and watched him take out a checkbook as he prepared to pay the court. She was getting out. This was it. She was out. Her things. She had left her things in the Day Room. Oh, leave them. Just get out of here. She would probably be back soon enough as it was. She glanced back behind her at the people still sitting in the courtroom, caught by the powerless sense of the travesty that awaited them. Her eyes teared as she studied the room. There *will* be justice, she pledged to them silently. Her mind lifted to the first days of the conference. Women throughout the world, liberation movements across the Southern Hemisphere, NEWS in every major city in the North, together they were millions, mobilized. They would stop the violent injustice. Her eyes scanned the judge's stately bench. We will destabilize the empire. And transform it. We will free the spirit of trust to build new societies, beyond wars of greed and privilege. There will be justice on this Earth, whether she lived or died, she knew it now, as inevitable truth—the evolution of human hope and liberation. And yes she was free now, for awhile, but she would be back, here, in their hands. But soon, sooner than anyone might think, there would be change. Profound change.

"Sylvia," Jack whispered again. She turned quickly, looking back at him. "Let's go." He gave her a quizzical look, then grinned as she smiled and they left the courtroom.

Riding in the car down Harrison Street, Sylvia felt as if she were returning home after years away, half expecting to see different buildings, different streets—but what—it was just five days ago that the conference had started, only two since she'd been in jail, and still the tinsel of Christmas ornaments glittered from passing windows. Christmas. She'd forgotten. Though the air was cold, she had the car window wide open, letting the frosty wind blow through her hair. She would have to call Maureen as soon as she talked to Linda.

"Is this too cold, Jack?" She turned to him, laughing, then rolling up the window.

"It's a bit of a chill," he answered, smiling.

"God, it's good to be out of there. Just for awhile," she said, relaxing back into the vinyl seat.

"You might not have to go back, Sylvia. Trust me a little."

"Mmm."

Jack laughed. "I know you don't have any faith in the law, Sylvia, but it's precisely the contradictions in it that we're going to use to get you off."

"Is that so?" She matched his teasing tone.

"You know," he was serious now, "I've decided to join NEWS. An ad hoc men's committee is forming. We'll be attending the general meeting next week."

"Really?" She sat up, looking at him.

"Yes. And your cousin . . . Linda's joined, too. She'll be meeting with the orientation committee tomorrow."

"*Really?*"

"Yes." He looked at her, then back at the road as they turned up Army Street. "I think that, regardless of the bombing, a lot of the people who attended the public forums would have joined. But remarkably I think even more women, and men, were moved by the attack, and the courage and efficiency of NEWS' response to it. It's put everything at another level. People, at least the people I've been in contact with, the Guild, for example, have been moved to come to terms with the gravity of conditions now, and the significance of NEWS. I mean, the significance of an international mobilization of women and its allegiance to national liberation movements. But it's not just the liberal left that's coming around. I even overheard a conversation in a coffee shop on Market Street—some young women who work downtown were having lunch—they'd heard about the conference and NEWS, and that you protest nuclear war, that there were 1,000 women in that church, and that it was bombed. They were angry. And curious."

Sylvia drank in his words, so, so—it was building. Still it was building. Jack in NEWS. And Linda! Again she felt the sharp sadness. Where was Steven in all this? What could they be thinking of Steven? And yet, Linda joining NEWS, it. . . it was wonderful.

"I'm really happy to hear that." She smiled warmly at Jack. "I guess we'll have to change our name," she teased again.

"Wasn't it Worker's International for People's Sovereignty originally?"

"Yes, it was."

They pulled up in front of Linda's flat. Sylvia got out of the car, grimacing as she looked up at the front window and saw the shiny balls of the Christmas tree reflecting in the winter sun as it made a brief appearance through the clouds. Where was Steven? She turned back as Jack still sat in the car and leaned over to the open door. "You're not coming in?"

"No. But call me later." He rummaged in his shirt pockets and handed her his card. "We should meet soon."

She looked at him. He was smiling, at ease. Was Steven wrong? Well. She would find out. "Jack. Thank you." Her eyes held his a moment. "I'll see you later." She closed the car door and turned to the house.

Ringing the bell she had rung a hundred times before, she marveled at the strangeness of it now. When would she feel herself again? Or was this the self that was her now?

The door opened and Linda stood, her eyes red and swollen, Justin just behind her. "Oh, Sylvia! Thank god." They held each other a long moment. Sylvia felt the tension, a desperation in Linda's embrace. "How *are* you?" Linda asked, standing back, her hands on Sylvia's shoulders as she studied her face.

"I'm fine. Really." She laced her arm around Linda's waist.

"Hi, Justin. How are you?" He let her take his hand as the three of them walked into the living room.

The two women sat on the couch, Justin between them. "Sylvia, I'm so sorry about Rikki." Tears came to Linda's eyes again. Sylvia turned away as Rikki's face, her smile that day in the park with Linda and Jack reappeared yet again in her mind. She nodded her head slowly, silent.

Justin scrambled off the couch, running out of the living room, down the hall. "Oh." Linda clasped Sylvia's hand quickly. "Let me just set him up with something to play with."

"Sure."

In a minute Linda was back. "He's really fascinated by Play-Doh these days, thank god." Linda laughed, though the strain in her voice was evident.

"Linda." Sylvia looked carefully at her cousin as she sat back down on the couch. "Steven came to the jail this morning, he visited me there."

"What! When?" Linda fairly jumped at the words.

"I think, it was before 9:00. He'd left by 9:00."

"What did he say?"

"Well, he . . . he said he was leaving you."

"Is that all?"

"Well. I asked him why. I mean, if it was because of his drinking, or other problems. And he said that you would say the problem was his drinking, but that . . . that the reason he was leaving was because you're in love with Jack. That you'd told him that." Sylvia looked at her, her eyes gently questioning.

"Oh, god, I don't know what . . ." Linda's hands covered her face as she strained to silence her weeping and Sylvia put her arm around her.

"Is it true?" Sylvia asked her.

"Oh we had a horrible fight this morning." Linda bit her lip, biting back the tears. "We, we'd hardly spoken since that scene he made at dinner on Christmas. And then, I don't know, I was so involved in the conference . . . and then the bombing, the fire . . ." She looked at Sylvia, a confused rage in her eyes. "He didn't even seem to *care*. All week when he wasn't at work, he was at some bar drinking and, when I told him yesterday finally what had happened, he just shrugged his shoulders! And I told him about Rikki, and that you were in jail, and it was just *nothing*, nothing to him. He just shrugged and left for work. And then this morning he kept insisting that I tell him that I love Jack, I love Jack, and so finally I just said *yes*, yes I do." Her eyes searched Sylvia's. "I just wanted him to *stop* it, to stop harping on Jack. For months he's been so, like he's *obsessed* about Jack. He's so threatened by him."

"So, you just said yes, because you were tired of denying it?"

Linda looked away, then bowed her head to her hand. "I don't know, Sylvia," she said quietly.

Sylvia leaned back into the couch, silent, deliberating.

"I just wanted to be friends with Jack," Linda began again. "I just wanted the three of us to be friends! Steven knew Jack in law school, they'd been friends then. Steven . . . Steven and I needed more friends. We've been so isolated, especially since Justin was born. And I knew Steven liked Jack, he'd talked about him in the past, and when we met—that night in Berkeley—I really liked him too. I was just happy that we would have a new friend. That's *all* I felt. I *love* Steven. He's my *husband*." She looked at Sylvia, demanding belief, as Sylvia nodded, yes, and she continued, "But then when Jack came to dinner, Steven was so . . . awful! Insulting him . . . He just acted like an asshole! Well, he was drunk. And then he started in, or he'd started before even, about 'my' friend Jack this, and 'my' friend Jack that, as if he were someone I'd picked up on the street. As if Steven hadn't known him for years! So I just dropped it. I never suggested we get together with Jack again, and I didn't see him anymore myself either. We'd had lunch once. It was so innocent you could laugh. I thought we were all going to be friends. But then, the way Steven was, we cut it off. Until

we ran into him a couple weeks ago. Steven had stopped drinking, I
thought we'd cleared it up about Jack and we invited him to dinner . . .
and . . . Well, you were here for Christmas dinner, you know the rest."

"Well, no, I don't exactly."

Linda was silent.

"I don't either, really, Sylvia," she said finally. "I don't know what
I feel."

"Well, what does Jack think about all this? Have you . . ."

"Oh, he's been very gracious, very . . . respectful. I mean, I know
he's guessed that Steven is threatened by him or, jealous of him. But it
was so obvious that I was just interested in friendship, and he too. But
then, in the last few days, I . . . It seems something stronger, though
nothing . . . nothing's been said yet."

"Mmm."

"But, Sylvia, I really feel that if Steven and I could just
communicate. Something has really broken down. And his drinking! I
was so happy, it was so wonderful when he stopped those two weeks
before Christmas. I felt our marriage, our love was so revived. But
then, he just started again, almost worse than before! I know it was the
holidays. But I also knew he wouldn't stop. It was just starting up all
over again and I just, I just didn't want to *deal* with it. I just wanted to
attend the conference in peace. When would I ever have such a chance
again? And I was learning *so* much. Oh, Sylvia. I'm so sorry about
what happened."

"I know, I know, Linda." Sylvia laid her hand on her cousin's as
they sat quietly a moment.

Then taking back her hand, Sylvia ran her fingers back through her
strayed hair. "Linda," she began. "I want to tell you something, in
confidence. And I hope you'll forgive me. That you'll understand why
I couldn't tell you before." She looked at Linda with sorrow, remorse
in her eyes.

"Sylvia. What is it?" Linda smiled at her, unable to imagine what
she could be so rueful about.

"Well, Steven. I mean, it's not just drinking that . . . He's being
harassed by the FBI. He's under surveillance. They vandalized your car,
canceled your credit and sent that supposed neighbor woman to question
you, and also this morning, he told me he'd received some strange
letters, one about Jack. He'd actually thought you and Jack had sent it
to him." Sylvia bit her lip, watching Linda's eyes grow wider,
astounded, then angry. "It's the FBI, I know it for a fact," she finished
hurriedly.

Linda stood up from the couch. "*Sylvia*. What are you *saying*?"

"I'm sure of it, Linda, those are their tactics. And it began when
that letter for Claire was sent to his office."

"Why didn't you *tell him*?" Linda was enraged.

"I wanted to, believe me, Linda, I wanted to." Sylvia's eyes, full of tears, pleaded with her cousin to understand. "I only realized it just last month when I talked to you, when you called me and told me about your credit being canceled, and that woman coming over. But his drinking. I just felt, Claire and I felt, that Steven . . . It was too great of a risk to let him know, to have to tell him, because who knows what he might say about NEWS and, with the conference coming and, and . . . other things, we really just could *not* risk rumors about covert activity of any kind, or confrontation with the State, you have to understand, I . . . I just felt that—Claire was insistent that—until he stopped drinking, and could be trusted, or until NEWS had accomplished certain things, there was too great a risk to too many people, and I didn't know about these letters about you and Jack. I was going to tell him, as *soon* as it was possible. You *have* to understand what's at stake here, I shouldn't even be saying as much as I am." Sylvia rested her head in her hand. "I did tell him. I told him this morning," she finished.

Linda looked on at her, less furious now, frowning as she tried to grasp Sylvia's logic, recalling the image of the woman, that "neighbor" woman being escorted out of the conference by NEWS security, though why . . . But she sensed it, that there was something, something very important that Sylvia was not telling her, could not tell her, and in that was her reasoning. But, letters about her and Jack! It was so invasive! Disgusting! She shuddered. Poor Steven, oh Steven, dear god!

"What about these letters? How many were there?" she asked, and Sylvia felt the urgent anger in her voice was no longer so much for her. It seemed that she really might understand.

"He just mentioned two he'd got in the last week or so. One was a card, with that nursery rhyme, 'Jack be nimble, Jack be quick,' you know," her lips twisted in disgust, "they're so demonic. And then something they sent to Nick and Rhonda's about his financial problems or . . . He didn't really tell me any more, he, he was really agitated, strange, Linda, I wanted to call you right after he left, but then Jack was there. And then I realized I'd be released, and I'd be seeing you, and I felt it was much better to try and tell you all this in person. This morning when I told Steven, after he'd told me about those letters and you and Jack and I realized I *had* to tell him, and too, since the conference was attacked the relationship between the State and NEWS has changed . . ."

"What did he say?"

"Well, I had to write it, you know."

Linda nodded.

"I told him the letters, the car, all of it was FBI harassment because of Claire's letter. Just what I told you. But that's all . . ."

"But what did he *say*?"

"Well." Sylvia bit her lip again, remembering. "He laughed. He didn't believe me at all. He seemed like he thought I was crazy." Linda closed her eyes. Yes. Yes, she could see it. He'd said as much before when he was angry, "your crazy cousin," and the state he was in now . . . Though he may as well have believed it, it's no crazier than anything else that's been going on with him. "Really? He didn't believe you at all?"

"No. He really didn't. I tried, I really asked him to try to understand and put our differences aside — I mean just the fact of how different we are as people — and believe me and trust that I was telling him the truth. But I could see that he couldn't. He just didn't believe me."

"So, he thinks that *I*, or *Jack* sent him those letters?" Linda asked, shaking her head incredulously as she sat back down on the couch.

"Well . . . he said that. And then he didn't believe what I told him. I guess he still does think that. I don't know. I really did try to convince him to trust me, Linda. But I could see that he really didn't. He just stood up and said he had to leave. Though he said he wouldn't repeat what I'd told him."

"Oh, Steven, Steven." Linda shook her head again as she gazed out the window beyond them. She had to talk to him, dear Steven, no wonder.

"I'm really concerned about him, Linda," Sylvia went on. "He had such a strange look. He suddenly seemed like, like he'd made a decision. Some kind of major decision, and I asked him what he was going to do—I wanted him to believe me for *himself* so he could sort out what was going on—and I said, 'Steven, please understand,' and he said, 'Oh yes, I understand what I have to do,' or something like that. He just seemed really determined. And then he left."

"I have to call him." Linda leapt up from the couch. "Can you check on Justin?" she called back to Sylvia.

"Yes." As she walked down the hall to Justin's room Sylvia looked at her watch. It was just after 1:00. Justin sat playing quietly with little shapes of colored dough, looking up at her as she came in, his eyes sad, lonely. It must be hard for him, she thought, alone with Linda in this flat all day, and the tension now, for months really, between Steven and Linda. Despite Claire's words, she felt guilt. Justin smiled shyly at her as she sat down on the floor with him, her mind recalling, suddenly, her own work, her job, wondering if she would be fired from Hansen, Rykoff & Shaw, and if they knew she'd been arrested.

"What are you making?" she asked him. Maybe she would try to help Linda find a good day care program for him and a job for herself. Now that the conference was over, and certainly if she got fired from her own job, she would have more time, unless, of course, the court proceedings . . .

He held up a yellow-blue blob for her to examine. "Wow, let's see. What is it?" she asked him, laughing, as he laughed back at her. He really was sweet.

"Sylvia!" Linda rushed into the room. "He's quit his practice! He's left!"

"What? What do you mean?"

"The secretary said—I asked for him and, she was embarrassed, she knew it was me—she said he'd skipped his hearing this morning. He came in around 9:30 and said he was leaving. Then he took a few things from his desk and left!"

"He didn't say . . ."

"No. Nothing."

Sylvia looked around. "But he doesn't have any of his clothes, his things, does he?"

"No."

"He'll come here, don't you think?"

"I don't know, I . . ." Linda looked intently at her. "He's serious. He's leaving. If he left his practice. Just like that."

Sylvia sat still, thinking, her eyes still on Linda's as she saw Steven's odd smile, his sudden resolve.

"We've got to find him." She jumped up.

"I'm going to call the Jury Room," Linda said, leaving the room. She picked up the phone in the hall and dialed the number.

"Jury Room," an abrupt male voice answered.

"Is Steven Walden there?"

"Oh, Steve? No, not here yet. He doesn't usually come in 'til about 5:00 or so."

"Thank you."

She dialed the bar near his office. Then the neighborhood bar.

Sylvia left Justin sitting with his Play-Doh and found Linda at the phone. "Linda. I don't think he's drinking. He seemed—this morning, when he left—he seemed like he had a plan or . . . I don't know." How could she say it? Her fear. That same urgency that had compelled her to try to call Linda the moment Steven had left the jail. No, she didn't, she really didn't think he would . . . But what? Something final. He was going to do something final, complete.

"What, Sylvia! What do you mean?" Linda asked, sensing Sylvia's trepidation as her own began to escalate.

Sylvia stood looking at her cousin. How could they find him? And at 2:00 she had to call NEWS. Where could they even begin?

They had no car, and Justin . . .

"I'm going to call the police."

"Linda!"

"What can I *do*, Sylvia? I feel like you think he's going to *kill* himself or something!" She was becoming terribly frightened. "And the way he's been—he hasn't been sleeping, and our fight this morning, *leaving me,* leaving his *practice,* he has *nothing* with him." She turned to dial the phone.

"Linda, Linda! Wait! Please!"

Linda looked at her, the receiver in her hand.

"Don't you see? Steven is under surveillance. The FBI, the police. It's the same! They're the ones trying to *destroy* him. They're *not* going to help. We'll just be playing into their hands. They'll ask you a million questions. They can only hurt us, all of us. We *have* to remember *who* we are here. What they represent."

Linda hung up the phone. Resting her clenched fists on the table, she leaned forward, her head bowed. Sylvia laid her hand softly on Linda's shoulder. What could she say to her? But she had to understand, even as desparate as the situation . . . In fact she did understand. Hadn't she made the choice? She was a member of NEWS herself now. And she had to accept the consequences of both her understanding and her choice. It was absurd to call the police for help now.

Linda straightened her back, slowly turning around, her face exhausted, though resolved. She looked at her cousin. "What will we do?"

Sylvia looked away from the fear in Linda's eyes, her mind searching. Where? Where is he? She couldn't believe he would actually kill himself. It wasn't that. It was something . . . more. Or he wouldn't have gone to the office, told them he was leaving . . . Leaving. He was leaving. Leaving the city. Disappearing. That was it. It had to be.

"Linda. Do you have any money in the bank? The two of you?"

"Yes, but?"

"How much, do you know?"

"I don't know, Sylvia. Less than $3,000. What . . ."

"Wait, but exactly, Linda."

She shrugged. "Around $2,700."

"Let's call the bank. See what the balance is now. I think Steven's leaving. Traveling. He'll need money."

"But where?"

"I don't know. But at least we'll know, if he's taken money, he's not going to kill himself."

Justin was calling for Linda. "I'll see to him. Please, call the bank." Sylvia hurried down the hall.

"Justin. Do you want some lunch?" she asked him as she sat back down on the floor with him. "Did you have any lunch?"

"I want juice."

"Oh OK. Let's go. Let's go in the kitchen." She stood up, taking his hand. She sat Justin in his booster seat at the table then looked in the refrigerator and found the apple juice. "Here we go." She smiled at him. "How about some apple juice?" As she set his cup in front of him, Linda came in the room.

"He withdrew a thousand dollars this morning." She was markedly relieved. Sylvia felt her own tension dissipate as she slipped into a chair next to Justin at the table. Linda joined them. They were quiet as Justin slurped at his juice.

"Now what?" Linda finally asked. "You think he left the city?" A hopeless sadness seemed to be replacing her fear.

"Yeah. I do."

Linda turned to the kitchen window, gazing out to the street.

"But I can't believe he would take the car," Sylvia said. "I mean, I know he's preoccupied with himself, and he's furious at you, but . . . We could call the airlines."

Linda laid her head in her arms on the table, terribly quiet, beyond tears.

Sylvia looked at her in silence, then at her watch, she had to be at a phone booth at exactly 2:00 and then who knew what she'd have to do. She couldn't leave Linda like this.

"Linda, I'm going to call Mom. I'm going to ask her to come up here." She jumped up from the table as Linda remained motionless.

Sylvia ran to the hall phone and dialed her mother's number. No answer. Now what? She picked up the phone and dialed again.

"Redondo. Could you give me the number of Nick Delgatto? 1027 Ocean Palms. Thank you."

She dialed the phone again.

"Aunt Rhonda? Hi. Yes. Yes. Yeah, I'm at Linda's. She is? Oh, great! OK. Hi, Mom! How are you? No, no, I'm fine, really. Just fine. Everything's all right. Yes. Yes, he is. Yeah, I'm really glad he's going to defend me. Oh, I know. Are you OK? Oh, good. You *are*? Oh, great, I was just going to ask you. Listen, Mom, there's a problem. I'll tell you more when you get here, but, apparently Steven's left his practice. Yeah. Well it seems like he's leaving Linda. I know. Yeah. She's really upset. No, she just found out. Well I thought . . . Well when would you arrive? Yeah, that would probably be good. Ask her. Yes, I'll wait." Sylvia glanced back toward the kitchen, then back to the phone.

"Yes? Oh, good. I think it would really be good. Oh the sooner the better. But, listen, there's no car here, and she's got Justin. Can you get a cab from the airport? OK, good. That's perfect. I'll tell her you'll be here around 5:00 or—but it's Friday after—oh, Nick can take care of it? So five o'clock for sure? OK. Good. Thanks, Mom. I can't wait to see you! Yes. We have *lots* to talk about. Yes. I love you. Bye."

She went back to the kitchen. Linda was sitting up now holding Justin in her lap as he slept against her, her eyes gazing out the window. Thank god Rhonda and Maureen were coming, Sylvia thought. She had never seen Linda so . . . lifeless. It was 1:45. She had to go. She walked over to Linda and gently put her arms around her shoulders as Linda still sat motionless, then leaned her head against Sylvia, letting her cousin's cool hands stroke her hair, her forehead.

"Linda," Sylvia said after a moment. She moved back a step to look at her. "I'm sure we'll find Steven. Please, forgive me."

"It's all right, Sylvia." Linda looked up at her. "I understand."

She really did. She could see it in her eyes and, even beneath the depressed exhaustion, the new commitment from where her understanding came. Linda looked back to the window, her gaze lost again as Sylvia pulled a chair close to her and sat down. "Linda, I called Rhonda. She and Maureen are flying up here this afternoon. They'll be here about 5:00. They've got a ride from the airport."

Linda nodded, her slight smile telling Sylvia it was good that she'd encouraged them to come. Sylvia glanced at her watch again. She *had* to leave.

"Linda. I have to go out. There's something I have to . . ."

Linda nodded, unquestioning.

Sylvia stood up. "I'll be back as soon as I can, I promise. Take care, Linda." She embraced her. "We'll find him, I know we will."

Linda took Sylvia's hand, holding it tightly, and looked at her intently now. "You be careful, Sylvia."

Sylvia hugged her again, then turned and left the flat.

She ran to the corner store, checking the five dollar bill in her pocket that Jack had given her in the jail. Quickly she bought some gum and, taking the change, ran on up to 24th Street looking for a telephone with some privacy. The sky had clouded back over, its whites and greys buffeted by the reckless gusts that foretold storms, the cold, snappy air whipping through her sweater. Still, she fairly leapt as she ran to the thrill of the winter wind.

Her cheeks a bright rosy glow and her thick tousled hair blown back, she stopped at an empty restaurant just opening and asked for a telephone. Yes, there was one in the back by the restrooms. She hurried back, looking at her watch. Two minutes to 2:00. She held the receiver in her hand, studying her watch, waiting one more minute.

She dialed the number.

The phone was picked up immediately.

"Hello, Thomas?" she asked.

"Sylvia." It was JoAnn.

"Hi!"

"You're out?"

"Yes."

"Good, good." Her voice was pleased, despite the evident fatigue. "Can you get to BART?"

"Yes, I'm really close."

"Take the Richmond train to El Cerrito and get off at the Plaza. Go to the shopping center, to the east mall, #307, Tully's, and order something to drink. How long do you think it will take you?"

"An hour and a half, at the most."

"Good. Good. Someone will be there for you."

"But, JoAnn, will I . . . Linda's . . ."

"We have to move quickly, Sylvia."

"I'm leaving now."

"Good."

They hung up. Sylvia walked quickly back through the restaurant as a young fashionable couple at the posh bar for an afternoon drink caught her eye and somehow their world felt lost to her, gone from her life.

She hurried down the street. The wind growing still colder, she laughed, raising her arms out as if she might fly. She felt she was flying. Holding back the urge to skip, she stepped quickly, composed, as the hustle of people about her gearing up for the holiday weekend seemed so strangely distant. She had nothing, nothing but herself flying with the wind.

She ran down the steps to the BART station, reaching in her pocket for more change and, buying her ticket, she ran toward the trains.

At 3:20 she sat alone in Tully's Cocktail Lounge, a glass of wine before her at the little table in the dark, stale room. A few people were at the bar with their backs to her as she sat, silent. She had one dollar left in her pocket and the clothes that she wore. She felt wonderfully exhilarated as if the whole world were open to her, as if she were embarking on an endless voyage. Discreetly, she watched the door.

Within a few moments a young woman, very tan, in a smart woolen jacket, the upturned collar catching her long blonde hair at the neck, walked into the bar, stopping a second as her eyes adjusted to the darkness. She seemed remarkably familiar, yet . . . Shelly! It was that woman, Olina's friend, again. Sylvia's expansive frame of mind shifted, tensed. Was this a coincidence? She couldn't possibly . . . But in the next instant Shelly saw her and smiled warmly, approaching the table.

"Hi! How are you?"

"Oh, fine." Sylvia felt ridiculous with her glass of wine in the suburban bar.

"Ready to go?"

Sylvia sat, looking at her. What?

"They're waiting," Shelly added, not impatiently but slightly unnerved by Sylvia's reluctance.

It had been less than a week since she'd met Shelly that day at the airport, though it seemed years past, and still the apprehension she'd felt . . . She really did look like that woman in the park too, Sylvia thought as she silently stared at Shelly, the one the Q Committee . . . But Rikki had said it definitely wasn't her, no. No, she was Olina's friend. What was she thinking? Hadn't her suspicions at the airport all been proved wrong, completely false? Yes, come on. She smiled casually at Shelly and got up from the table, walking with her out of the bar in silence.

The sky threatened rain as they got in the small green Fiat. "You must be freezing," Shelly said sympathetically as she started the engine. "The heat'll come on in just a minute."

"Oh, that's fine," Sylvia answered.

"I didn't see you at the conference," Shelly began purposefully. "I was at all of the public forums, except the last morning when I went to the session on peace camps. Olina knew I would be joining NEWS at the next orientation and cleared it with the session representative."

"Oh. No. I guess I didn't see you."

"I've been asked to act as courier for NEWS. That's why I've come for you. They felt it was safest."

"Oh." Sylvia was taken aback, hearing the term that so few even knew, "courier for NEWS," from this woman. It shocked her, and yet, at the same time it relieved her. She was obviously *not* the same woman the Q Committee had isolated, and too, she had proven herself as a courier before. But still. Sylvia glanced quickly at Shelly as she maneuvered her little car along the suburban boulevard. Why did she have such a hard time accepting this woman as a part of NEWS?

Shelly pulled off the busy street and, with a quick look behind her, she headed east. "I am very new to the organization and very unlikely to be in anyone's files or arouse suspicion." She paused. "And Olina knows I can be trusted." Her tone implied "even if you don't."

Sylvia sat back into the vinyl seat as the warm air from the heater vents began to thaw her feet. OK, yes, really. It was true, Olina did trust this woman. She had that day at the airport anyway, and . . . That must be what it is, that day at the airport and how nerve-wracking it had been. And this car, Shelly's car, the last time she had sat in it . . . Sylvia shifted in her seat. That must be what made her still feel so . . . uneasy with this woman.

Large drops of rain spattered against the windshield, first one, then another. Then a downpour seemed to engulf them. Sylvia strained to see through the misting window. She had no idea where they were.

"So, we're going to?"

"Just up the road. They told me to bring you to a construction site up ahead."

"What?" She didn't like this at all. Why hadn't JoAnn told her on the phone? What were they all thinking? It seemed like everything had changed, with this Shelly woman driving her around in the middle of nowhere, and nobody telling her what was going on, it didn't seem, it didn't feel like NEWS at all. Was it possible? Could this be the trap that finally . . .

"Here we are," Shelly said, turning into a gravel drive at the base of a barren hill and smiling at Ellen who sat in an old cream-colored Volvo just in front of them.

Sylvia couldn't help a deep sigh of relief at the sight of Ellen, sitting there, grinning at her as they pulled up beside her. Her own smile must have seemed ecstatic as she looked at Ellen, waiting for Shelly to stop the car.

Shelly opened her door and, getting some things from her trunk, brought them to Ellen's car as Sylvia walked quickly to the old Volvo and got in the front seat.

"Thanks very much, Shelly. We'll talk at 7:00, OK?" Ellen asked as Shelly nodded, "Sure," and walked back to her car. With a wave to Sylvia who, collecting herself, called out, "Thanks Shelly," she got back in her Fiat and drove away.

"Sylvia." Ellen hugged her. "How are you!" she asked as she turned to start the car.

"Oh, good, Ellen, but what's happening? Where are we going?"

Ellen pulled onto the road, looking over her shoulder. "To Jean's grandparents' house. They're in Europe for the holidays, for another two weeks at least, and she's been taking care of it. It's a huge old place, it used to be a dairy farm, so it's been perfect for us so far."

"But who? Who's there?"

"Ruth, JoAnn, Jean, Laura, Susan . . . Well all of local NEWS CLAN. All of us now. With you." She smiled at Sylvia. "And then Elena, Anna-Maria, Olina, Teresa, Kareem, Chan-pheng, Cristina, Lourdes, Alaya, and Rosario."

"Those are all the Allies?"

"Yes," Ellen answered, thoughtfully, without emotion, as if the conference were a distant memory now. "Everyone else has left, most via Mexico. And it wasn't easy to do, believe me. But thank god it's the holidays, you know? It's delayed the State in clamping down. Some of the Allies were able to fly out of San Francisco directly on Wednesday, just after the bombing. Those who didn't get out then were taken by car and train to Mexico. Some of our cadres just left with the last groups this morning. We didn't want to take any chances of getting detained at U.S. airports."

Sylvia nodded, thoughtful as she looked out the side window at the rain, still falling heavily. They had turned from the two-lane highway to a winding country road.

"Did you hear that the police are saying we're responsible for the bombing ourselves?"

"What?" Sylvia turned back, looking at Ellen. "Are you serious?"

Ellen nodded, eyes on the road in the darkening sky. "The District Attorney's Office just issued a formal statement this afternoon. After you were released. Ruth spoke with your lawyer, Jack. He said they're claiming that a homemade incendiary device has been discovered to be the cause of the explosion, and that a 'dissident faction of the Women's International for Peoples' Sovereignty' was responsible for it." She paused as they pulled into a puddled dirt drive leading to an old wooden farmhouse standing stark against the winter dusk.

"What! Oh, *god*. And who the hell are they going to say this faction is?" Sylvia asked as they bounced and swerved up the rutted, muddy drive.

Ellen stopped the car. "Well, Ruth can explain it. I thought you might have talked to Jack about it." She opened the car door as Sylvia sat frowning. Then opening her door, she followed Ellen through the swampy yard to the front porch.

They ran up the front steps and Ellen banged on the door rhythmically, four-two-three, four-two-three.

Ruth opened the door. Smiling at Ellen as she passed through, Ruth turned and embraced Sylvia, then standing back, she chafed Sylvia's arms with her hands. "You must be freezing." She shut the door behind them as Sylvia looked around the huge living room. Most of the furniture was carefully stacked to one side and tables on the other side held their computer systems from the Market and Oakland offices. Maps were spread across the floor over the worn hook rugs, and a wood stove glowed in the far corner where Olina, Rosario, JoAnn, Susan, Elena, and Chan-pheng were deep in discussion. They looked up.

"Sylvia!" Olina rose and came over to her, embracing her, and putting her arm around her, she walked her back to the group. Sylvia embraced each of them, feeling the beautiful heat of the wood stove, the warm faces, the gentle arms of the women as the fear that Ellen's words had stirred in her evaporated with the steam from the kettle sitting on the top of the iron stove. She felt a thick, wool sweater draped over her shoulders and, turning her head she saw Olina smile at her with a wink. Their spirits were high. The force of spirit in the room was stunning. Smells of fresh vegetables cooking, wafting through the door from the kitchen, gripped her stomach. She had never been so hungry.

"We're meeting at 5:00?" Ruth checked with Elena.

"Yes. All of us. I'll wake Anna-Maria." Elena stood up. Sylvia looked at her watch. It was 4:30.

"Would you like to have some 'real' food, Sylvia?" Ruth asked, turning to her with a smile.

"I really would," she nodded.

"Good. Let's get something and go have a talk before the meeting." They turned toward the kitchen, Ruth stopping to give Sylvia a quick, warm hug. "Thank god we've got you back."

Sylvia felt the tears coming to her eyes as she smiled, unable to speak. She followed Ruth to the back of the house. The kitchen was as big as the living room, a massive wood cutting-block at its center. Jean and Laura stood at the wide old range preparing the steaming pots of vegetables, beans, rice. Ruth and Sylvia took plates from the counter and helped themselves as the other women, still deep in discussion, came into the kitchen and began to serve themselves.

"Why don't we go in here," Ruth said as Sylvia followed her through a pantry to a little nook of a room with a small table. A broad window looked out upon a deep green curve of hill against the sky, a running stream just at its base. Sylvia set her plate on the table, standing a moment, resting in the peace of the scene before her.

"It's lovely, isn't it?" Ruth smiled.

Ruth sat at the table as Sylvia joined her. "Sylvia," she began. "I spoke with Jack this afternoon."

"I know, Ellen was telling me, about the D.A. blaming the bombing on a 'dissident faction' of NEWS. Though she didn't tell me who that faction is supposed to be, or what exactly the charges . . ."

"The charge is murder, for Rikki's death."

"Oh god."

"It's a common tactic. It was used against the Black Panthers several times. Police informers attack an organization and then the State charges the organization itself with the crime. It was used many times by the FBI's COINTELPRO to assault the Black Liberation Movement, and the American Indian . . ."

"But *who* are they charging? Who is this 'dissident faction'?"

"You and JoAnn, as the leaders."

"*What?*"

"Because you live together. It will be easier for them to invent the story."

"Oh, *Christ!* And because I hit the cop, they can say a fanatic . . ."

"Sylvia, Sylvia, I told you, it's a common tactic. We suspected this would occur, in *any* case. The Q Committee suspected the woman they'd isolated the morning of the bombing as the agent responsible for it, and, when the K team questioned her, she claimed to know you. She did seem to have a lot of information about you. The K team was going to consult with you but, they didn't have the chance. She'd probably had you under surveillance for months. In any case, she can claim ties with you and then be granted impunity on the charge herself for testifying against you."

Sylvia listened to Ruth in silence, the cold chill returning to her.

"But actually, Sylvia, we're lucky that it is you that they've decided to charge. It made it easier for us to get you out today. They'll want to let the incident with Rikki blow over, minimize it, before attempting to claim that you were responsible for her death. Of course we can't prove that it was you who actually brought her out of the church or even that she was there next to you when . . . But Sylvia, you know I'm not saying that it's 'lucky' you will be charged with murder. The fact is," Ruth paused, waiting for the tumult in Sylvia's eyes to settle somewhat, to focus on her. "Sylvia. NEWS CLAN came to a decision last night. We've gone underground."

Sylvia's eyes widened now, her lips parted as she looked behind her to the sound of the voices in the kitchen, and back to Ruth, questioning.

"We can stay here for another ten or 12 days. Another house is being located for us by the leadership in NEWS MASS. NEWS MASS elected another steering committee today. JoAnn met with Karen, Estelle, Candice and all of the committee coordinators in Oakland, just before you spoke with her. And New York, Chicago, L.A., Houston, Madison, Seattle, Atlanta—all of the U.S. NEWS CLAN cadres—are going underground. We agreed to it at the meeting last night. They're all on their way home now. Some have already returned. Amsterdam was still in conference until this morning, evening their time. We've been in constant communication."

Sylvia tried to clear her mind, to focus on the specifics. "Then, they did appropriate the satellite dish?"

"Yes, two days ago. And just this afternoon we've heard that European, Soviet and Oceanic NEWS CLAN are going underground as well—572 of us in all. All of us. And there'll be more."

Sylvia sat in silence. Though somehow she'd known. Or had she? Had she really thought, when she'd left Linda, when she'd talked to Maureen . . . Maureen.

"But we didn't make this decision for you, Sylvia. It's still yours to make. Of course we assumed you would want the option, which is why we had Jack get you out this morning. But no one will question if you choose to stay above ground and have Jack defend you . . ."

"Ruth, don't," Sylvia interrupted her. "For one thing, that would feed right into their plan, setting me off from the rest of you, the 'dissident faction.'"

"Not necessarily, Jack was full of ideas on how to handle the case. He even thinks he could turn it into the interests of NEWS, as well as get you off. He has no idea of NEWS CLAN's decision, or even our existence, but his strategy sounds conceivably . . ."

Sylvia wasn't listening. Of course, there was no choice. Her place was here! With NEWS CLAN. There was no where else she wanted more to be. There was no question. But Maureen, arriving in the city in, what? Less than an hour. Expecting to see her. Oh god. She pushed her plate of cold food away and, putting her elbow on the table, she rested her head in her hand.

"Sylvia, you don't have to feel pressured by a decision we've made without you. None of the rest of us are jumping bail on a felony. We just felt that you should have the option and we wanted to see you. You can still return."

"No, no!" Sylvia answered, impatient now. "It's just . . . my mother." She stood up from the table abruptly, unconsciously, moving to the window. "I know it sounds absurd," she went on, "given everything." She paused, turning back to face Ruth who watched her quietly. "Of *course* I'm just grateful for your getting me here, to be able to be here. There's *no* question, of course there's no question in my mind, and the courage you've all shown. It's magnificent! Please, understand, it's just . . . my family, my mother. She's alone."

Ruth sat back in her chair, a gentle smile gracing her lips. "Sylvia. You are such a loyal woman. To those you love."

"But to NEWS. To NEWS first, Ruth!" Sylvia insisted. Then, remembering her reaction to Rikki's death, "I mean, I *want* to be, always, I do. There's no question."

"I know. I know, Sylvia."

"I mean, I know all of us have families, all of us have . . . This is going to be painful, in many ways, for all of us." She thought of Maureen, never hearing from her, arriving at Linda's, expecting to see her. If she could just talk to her once.

"It is, possibly, the most difficult question we face in this work," Ruth agreed. She looked out at the light rain in the evening sky. "Because despite our vision, the family—of humanity, to whom we have chosen to give our deepest loyalty—is for most of our blood families, only an abstract concept, at best. 'Family' to most means mother, husband, children and, in the structures of our societies, it is still, just that." She looked back at Sylvia who stood, listening carefully to her now.

"But Sylvia, even though only the seeds for developing the world family exist now—and the emotional forces behind social relations are still rooted in the traditional blood family—as I recall, your mother attended the conference and is even involved in her own work with the United Nations. Surely, she, if anyone, will understand. You are not abandoning her. This is not an act of rejection. It's a motion toward creating structures that will *minimize* rejection and carry us *all* beyond the isolated, limiting 'family' to the emotional liberation of a wider embrace—an identity with the interests of all life, with creation itself."

Of course, yes, she knew this. Hadn't she expressed this same understanding to her mother that time they'd talked, Christmas night? Hadn't Maureen seen this spirit at the conference? She would understand. She would have to.

"Yes. Yes, I know, Ruth. I'm sorry."

"Don't be, Sylvia. There is a beauty in your feeling for those close to you, its intensity. Though at times, you can make it your greatest weakness. But you're learning, as we all are, to feel that passion as compassion, for all of life. But don't apologize for your emotion, Sylvia. Free it."

Sylvia stood at the window, watching the gentle fall of rain, the gift of the open sky to the earth beneath. Yes. She could feel it now, its grace—freedom. Not the wild flight as she'd run through the wind hours ago, but centered, within her. Her passion, her emotion, her love, her feelings of themselves were *true*. The truth of herself. And she let herself *feel* them. Not caught up in attachment—to Claire, or anyone—not distorted by fear of being alone. But free to feel her love fully, flowing through her, for once not straining against it as her fear caught her up against herself, against her vision, driving her mad with questioning how she could love this one so, and that one not at all, as if her feelings themselves were crazed, unjust. No, she felt the passion in her freed now, from the illusion of isolation and its prison of fearful attachment. And in the very emotion of that freedom, she forgave herself her fear, and her love filled her with the gift of her being—pure self in existence. For the first time in her life she rejoiced, forgiving herself as she silently watched the gentle rain. She rejoiced in the beauty of her own intense love, freed, freed at last.

Ruth had stood, soundlessly, clearing the plates from the table. Turning to the door, she said, "We'll be meeting in just a minute," and left the room.

At 5:00, 33 women had gathered in the living room of the old farmhouse. Ellen was quickly coding a response to Amsterdam as their latest communication appeared on the screen. She stayed at the terminal as the rest of the women gathered in a circle around the room.

They sat in quiet attention as Anna-Maria began to speak.

"We are still receiving responses from Allies, all of them positive so far. Everyone is prepared. We should have finalized agreement by—midnight?" She turned to Ellen.

"Possibly a little later. Everyone at Amsterdam has agreed, but we're still waiting for Allies at our conference who have just returned, or are returning. We've heard from Manila, Seoul, Tokyo, Bangkok, Bandung, Malay, Bogotá, Quito, Caracas, most of Latin America. I would say by 3:00 or 4:00 a.m. we should have complete response."

"So, we have, what—80 percent response as of now?"

"At least, yes."

"So. We are going ahead then. As soon as total response is complete, shall we say by 6:00 tomorrow morning?" Anna-Maria glanced again at Ellen, who nodded, and then back to the group. "At 6:00 a.m. we will synchronize the final plan. Amsterdam is at this moment completing the master. Of course, because we are moving the Action ahead, we cannot have the total refinement we would be able to have if we still had one more month to . . ."

The February Action. They were talking about the Action. Sylvia sat forward in her chair as she looked at Ellen, Olina, JoAnn, their faces calm, determined.

Anna-Maria glanced at Sylvia, then at Ruth, who answered her, "Sylvia's joining us, but we didn't have time to complete our discussion." She turned to Sylvia. "The Action will take place this Sunday. New Year's Day."

"Yes, I see." Sylvia's eyes shone as she smiled at the women.

Anna-Maria nodded, her eyes returning the moment of power and realization in Sylvia's own. "They think they have struck us down, defeated us by their attack," she said. "That is the historic flaw of empire. For they never understand that by their violence, they bring about their own downfall. It has been a setback for us. But we will turn it into triumph."

"Yes. Yes." Sylvia's heart raced as Anna-Maria's eyes held hers in the knowledge, the knowledge they all shared, of their own infinite power of love.

Chapter XV

Sunday, January 1, 1984
LONDON, ENGLAND 12:00 A.M.

For five centuries the bell tower of Haworth Manor had embraced the toll of its great brass bell, vibrating to the hourly knell of reckoning, the very granite stone of its walls rich with the keeping of centuries' time, as if the luxurious wealth displayed beneath its domain were the source of its endlessly precise fidelity. And now, as the streets of London were filled with revelers, thronging in the intoxicated merriment of an ancient ritual, rollicking in hasty embraces, or the impassioned kisses of bare acquaintances taking this one moment of the year to fly in the face of traditional British reserve, the great bell tower fairly shook with the tremendous sound of the coming of the New Year.

Less than 100 yards away, in the offices of the American Embassy, a stately gathering in black-tie and dress, having drunk of the best of champagnes and dined on the finest continental cuisine, exchanged the usual empty affections and weak witticisms, only the known wags of the party daring to allude to Orwellian prophecy as they toasted the dawning of yet another year of empire.

On the second floor of the Embassy's east wing, referred to as the "new addition", it having been constructed only four decades ago, the offices of the Chief of Intelligence stood empty. Only the black security guard at his desk sat drumming his fingers in angry boredom to the sounds of his tapedeck. As any other night, the metal desks and vinyl chairs, the panel of video monitors and their terminals, and the massive CompuSystem 16/32 with its storage capacity of 10,000K sat motionless, stark, alien before him. The last beat of the song faded to its end. He flipped the tape.

Three miles away in central London four women sat in intense concentration, their faces hooded in stocking masks, their hands glistening in thin transparent plastic gloves as they spoke in hushed, urgent tones on the 16th floor of the Townsend Building, a uniformed security guard bound and blindfolded on the floor ten feet away, his mouth taped shut.

"Yes, yes, that's their baud rate. I set the modem Friday lunchtime."

"It's not coming through!"

"It will. It will. It starts slow."

"Do you have the other disks?"

"Of course."
"Here! It's coming. Here's the first. Gloria. Can you get it on the Facs? Is it printing? Yes. Copy it."
"Will we have time to do the Yard's?"
"Yes, I'm sure. I did a simulation last weekend. We'll be done in four hours."
"The program for the Yard is complete?"
"Complete enough. We can get most of it."
"Yes, we can totally blank theirs and we have the codes to delete their key. They'll never have access to those files again. But, hurry now, let's get all of the Embassy's here first."
"We have to get the copies, especially the faces, to Virginia no later than 4:15. They'll be at Trafalgar for only 20 minutes."
"Yes, yes. I know. We will."

FEZ, MOROCCO
1:00 A.M.

The strains of a very poorly rendered "Marseillaise" still drifted from the President's Suite of the Hilton Hotel, followed by a raucous effort at "America the Beautiful" as the Europeans and Americans continued a party that had begun at 4:00 that afternoon. The manager of the hotel himself had just commanded yet another case of champagne to be brought up from the cellar.

The administrative offices were locked and dark, the entire hotel staff in attendance to the needs of the revelers eight floors above, and only the desk clerk sat sleepily at her post, paying less than attention when her co-worker, Tanée, walked past the desk with a smile, *"Je te vois à la soirée tout-à-l'heure?"*

"J'sais pas. Ils m'énervent," she replied, looking back at her magazine.

Tanée rounded the corner of the desk and, with a glance back at the clerk, silently unlocked the door in the rear wall and turned to give a snap of her head to Gabrielle who waited at the far corner and now quickly, soundlessly joined her. They slipped into the office, locking the door behind them. Gabrielle opened her bag, producing a high-powered flashlight and thin plastic gloves. They sat at the computer terminal.

"Tu as les disques?"
"Oui, bien sûr."
"Bon, donne-les moi."
"Elles ne peuvent pas le faire à Marraquech. Il faut que nous fassions Casablanca et Rabat aussi. Crois-tu que nous avons le

temps?"
"Aie! Vraiment? J'sais pas. Il faut essayer. Si nous pouvons,
elles peuvent envoyer les photos avec leur équipement?"
"Oui, elles ont dit que oui, mais il faut les leur donner bientôt. De
toutes façons, c'est sûr que nous pouvons effacer les donnés et la clé à
Rabat, hein?"
"Bon, oui, allons-y."

CARACAS, VENEZUELA
3:00 A.M.

Still the city did not sleep, though the euphoria of welcoming in
the New Year had long since dissipated into heated debates on
hopelessly opaque abstractions, raging arguments, or the stupor of
played-out emotions for those who still haunted the night clubs, the
parties, the streets.

In the Plaza de Ponce de León, three women in evening dress
chattered gaily as they sat in the back of a cab. *"Allá. Allá,"* one
directed the driver as he pulled over to the curb in front of the Hotel de
Oro.

"Muchas grácias. ¡Felíz Año Nuevo!" They smiled at him as they
handed him a generous tip and he pulled back out into the night. The
women entered the glass doors of the lobby and walked to the bar,
laughing, as they passed on through the still noisy crowd to the corridor
behind, and through the service entry to the dark, empty dining room.
In seconds, at the rear of the expansive, high-ceilinged room, they had
changed their shoes and whisked off their long skirts, revealing the
jeans beneath as they stuffed the discarded clothes in their overnight
cases and, donning ski masks, slipped out the delivery entrance at the
kitchen corridor and into the alley beyond.

"¿Está abierto?"
"¡Sí, vamos!"

Katia aimed the blow gun carefully, shooting the hooked metal
claw securely into the wooden ledge, the knotted rope undulating as it
hung 30 feet to their waists. Within an instant, Isabelle was up at the
ledge forcing the old wooden-framed window up higher. She
disappeared inside as Magda followed her and, in less than half a
minute, Katia joined them on the tiled floor of the Office of Social
Security. She snapped in the rope, closing the window as Magda
hurried soundlessly to her desk and unlocked the top drawer, producing a
manila envelope and a small metal box.

"Vamos. Por aquí." They followed her through the pitch dark
office as if guided by light, pausing at the glass-doored entrance as
Magda removed an electronic key from the box, coding it quickly, and

the doors opened. They turned at the corridor. Again the key was coded, and they slipped through a heavy metal door as it closed behind them to a windowless room walled with electronic surveillance systems. Slipping the thin plastic gloves on their hands, they approached the central terminal and Magda sat at the keyboard, logging into the data base. She studied the monitor, waiting a moment. Then quickly producing a second, and then a third and fourth display, she whispered, "¡Sí! ¡Todo está aquí!"

"¿Todo?"

"Bién, suficiente. No necesitamos más que esto. Con los datos que tenamos aquí, es mejor hacer lo más posible sin usar DECNET. Las otras compañeras estaran tratando de usarlo en este mismo momento. Chela dijo que sería mejor si pudiesemos usar los más archivos posibles sin conectar. Hay suficiente aqui. ¡Realmente, es perfecto!"

"¿Cuántos agentes?"

"Setenta, ochenta, más de los que podemos usar. Podemos borrar miles y miles de archivos secretos individuales."

"Primero tenemos que buscar por los desaparacidos."

"Sí, por supuesto."

"¡Hágamoslo!"

"¡Immediatamente!"

TEGUCIGALPA, HONDURAS
5:00 A.M.

A warm gentle rain, unusual for the season, fell softly to the empty city streets. Only the priest at La Iglesia de Christo Santo stirred as he prepared for the first Mass of the morning, and of the year, in Barrio Moraga. He turned slightly, annoyed by the jarring sound of a car engine starting, disturbing his quiet prayers. He didn't bother to look as two women drove by his bedroom window, the delapidated Volkswagon belching its black smoke as it rounded the dusty curve of the road heading to the center of the small city.

The two women drove quickly, exchanging a brief glance and a laugh as a U.S. military jeep passed them, weaving down the road as it headed south out of town. "Pendejos," Lucia said quietly. They drove on to paved streets, glistening now with the fresh, sweet rain as the lush expanse of meticulously landscaped estates sloping up to the palacial residences of the region's affluent families marked the perimeter of the vast expanse of lands developed by Standard Brands, formerly the United Fruit Corporation of America. Barrio Moraga was on Standard Brands' land as well, but it had yet to have access to even a sewage system, a generator for electricity being the greatest luxury recently conceded to the area, through efforts both Lucia and Carmen had participated in.

Patricia met them on foot in the predawn dark at the western gate of the Standard Brand regional offices. The rain had stopped, leaving the air cool and clear. Without hesitation Lucia and Carmen jumped from the car, Carmen fitting the silencer to her .45 as they ran 50 feet from the car toward the gates, Carmen turning and shooting three quick silent blasts to the gas tank, the explosion nearly deafening them as the hysterical barking of dogs vied for the shattering of the morning silence. The gates flung open as armed uniformed guards rushed out, their faces lit by the roaring flames, their swollen eyes blinking, their arms flung up, shading their eyes against the heated glare of the fire in the pitch dark, the dogs frothing and yapping in front of them, straining at their leashes in aborted lunges toward the raw bleeding pounds of beef Lucia had flung to the east of the car, the guards fumbling about each other, *"¿Que pasa? ¿Que está?"* the stale smell of late-night's drinking still reeking in their flesh as they struggled to focus their bleary senses.

The three women had long gone, slipping through the gates the instant they had opened, they raced through the side yard of the low-slung complex of buildings. Approaching the central office entrance and shooting open the lock, soundlessly, they ran into the plush offices and at once were at the computer terminals joined by Lisa and Anabel who had entered at the northern gate after detonating their own car. Without a word the women worked, loading the terminals, monitors, drawers of disks and mag tapes into a motorized metal cart, Lucia turning her silenced automatic to the massive central computer, drilling its control panel and the guts of the mammoth machine itself. The women raced out of the offices guiding the heavy metal locker of equipment as they heard the ominous roar of a helicopter above them, hovering over them as they rushed out to the broad brick terrace just outside the executive suites at the northwest corner of the complex and Anabel flashed a high-powered beam, one-two-one. The women ducked, moving away from the roar, their locker at a safe distance, as a mad rush of wind whipped their hair to their faces, threatening to suck up their clothes from their bodies and the helicopter landed, a United States flag on its rear. Maria leapt from the cockpit as Lucia wheeled their broad metal locker forward and Anabel and Patricia fixed the tentacles of the winch grapple about its base. The six of them crowded back in the cockpit and in an instant they were aloft, racing as well as their weight would allow, the flames of the burning cars still lighting the dark earth behind them as they neared the Nicaraguan border.

SAN FRANCISCO, CALIFORNIA
8:00 A.M.

"The system's crawling. I can't," Ellen fairly hissed, the sweat beading on her hands beneath the plastic gloves.

"We'll have to wait," Olina answered, determined, looking at her watch with an eye on Sylvia as she sat at the second terminal.

"Who's on it?"

"Manila, Bangkok, Tehran . . . Oh, fantastic! Johannesburg!"

"It's 10:00 in Johannesburg, right?"

"Yes, yes. 10:00 last night—now."

Olina checked her notes. "They'll only be on for 45 minutes." She glanced at the locked doors behind her, then at her notes again.

"Is Caracas on?"

"No."

"Good. Then they must have enough locally. What about TELNET? At least we could delete . . ."

"All the nodes are active," Ellen waited a moment, "San Juan . . . Waipahu . . . Mexico City . . . Chicago! What the hell?"

"They're supposed to be on RADNET."

"They probably couldn't get on."

"Ellen are you *sure* the security guard's shift is until noon?"

"Unless they've changed their shifts in the last 48 hours."

"That's very possible."

"Diana talked to Jim late Friday night. He was sure then."

"All right. We have until noon."

"I can't believe she had to sleep with him."

"Juneau's on DECNET! Great!"

"What about the Aleutians?"

"Juneau's doing the Aleutians. They're going to delete the files in memory and the access key. The back-ups will be useless. Though they're not transferring anything, still, that's enough," Olina answered, turning through her thick sheaf of notes. "It must be almost noon there."

"Manila's off!"

"Then they started before 4:00 p.m. even."

"Their offices close at noon Saturdays."

"Well, they can't be in the streets until dark."

"It will take at least a few hours to print the posters, I'd think."

"God, I wish we could get on."

"Patience, patience. It's more important that the South finish."

"Then let's tell Chicago to get off."

"Not yet. They must have their reasons."

"Paris is on TELNET too, now!"

364

"Are Gwen and Laura monitoring both RADNET and DYNANET at the Alcoa Building?" Ellen asked.

"Yes, yes. Stay on DECNET. That's what we really want." Olina looked at her watch again. 8:30.

The absence of sound in the office suite and in the lifeless streets 14 floors below quieted their nerves, as at the same time it put them on edge, waiting, waiting as they studied their monitors, intermittently entering commands to reveal who occupied which nodes of the international government and corporate computer networks as Olina checked their own expected use times. Around the 24-hour clock of the world in over 200 cities, NEWS CLAN and ALLIES at this same moment sat at computer terminals tapping into the networks, intruding on computer storage systems in American and European embassies and CIA headquarters around the globe. In one synchronized motion, they were invading CIA surveillance systems in every major city and town throughout the seven continents; copying CIA agent profiles as well as the profiles of secret police agents such as the DINA's in Chile, the KGB in the Soviet Union, the MOSSAD in Israel, the BOSS in South Africa, the FBI in the United States; collecting the facsimile print-outs of the agents' identity photographs as they appeared, to be reproduced by the thousands in a matter of hours. In the same moments, they were intruding on the files of the millions and millions of individuals identified as "subversive" by secret police agencies and CIA agents from Buenos Aires to Berlin, from Juneau to Leningrad, from Manila to Tehran, Tokyo to Warsaw, Tel Aviv, New Dehli, Melbourne, Kabul. The electronic surveillance systems developed and supplied by U.S. and European intelligence operatives as well as those of the Soviet Bloc, the secret data banks of "security" files on hundreds and hundreds of thousands of individuals throughout the world were invaded and, one by one, in an instant, deleted and destroyed as the secret access codes to the files were also deleted or distorted so that even the back-up disk files would be useless, forever lost, impenetrable on their tiny, illegible electronic diskettes.

In Eastern Asia, working in the still light hours of Saturday evening, December 31, on through the growing darkness in Central Asia, the approaching New Year in the Mideast and South Africa, the stroke of midnight in Western Europe and West Africa, the early hours of the morning in Latin America, just before dawn in Central America and the midwestern United States, to the bright morning sunlight of New Years' Day in San Francisco, hundreds of women worked at that exact same moment of time, crowding, jamming the international electronic networks, sabotaging, neutralizing, utterly destroying the very brain of the Empire—taking the time only to save the names, faces, profiles of the few—the agents, the double agents, the secret "security" servants of the Empire's diseased, now dying electronic mind.

"There's a node free! Can we go on?" Ellen broke the silence.

"Not yet. Let the South finish. We're totally safe here compared to the access they've got. Most of them can only stay for a very short time. God knows how they've all managed access. It's incredible."

"I really didn't expect it," Sylvia agreed. "I thought there'd be a lot fewer of us, that we'd have to do as much as we could from here. TELNET's probably totally blanked now. We're even going to have time to delete their financial data banks!" She was elated.

"I'm sure that's what Chicago's doing, though they should get off."

"They've probably found out that all TELNET's security systems have been done."

"Is Standard Brands on TELNET?"

Olina checked her notes. "Yes. Honduras is supposed to be taking care of them, though."

"I want Standard Oil. I hope Chicago's taking care of them."

"They must be, because New York hasn't even been on yet."

"Well, they're waiting for the South like we're supposed to be."

"Well, I just hope Chicago gets IT&T if they're going ahead with the financial files."

"Maybe they just have an interminable number of local agents."

"God, I wish we could get on. I want to see their faces."

"Let's hope to god we don't find anyone we know."

"Don't even joke."

"We're bound to."

They were silent a moment, nearly wild with tension and the ominous fear the turn of the conversation had triggered within them all.

"Patience," Olina said quietly again. "It's almost 9:00. We should be able to get on soon."

"Two nodes are clear on DECNET! Three!"

"Just another minute."

"Five now."

"All right."

Olina read the codes slowly, clearly, as Ellen's fingers raced over the terminal's keys. They waited. Sylvia looked away from her display a moment to study the one above Ellen's terminal.

"Never heard of him," Ellen said as the first agent's profile appeared on the screen from the Northern California Regional Offices of the Federal Bureau of Investigation.

"Facs it out. Let's print them all," Olina said. "We have until noon. Or just before."

"Let's not cut it too close, Olina. We have to get out of here with the stuff," Sylvia warned.

"We can print for two hours then," Olina answered. "We'll start deleting at 11:00. London's going to be on the entire four hours."

"Yeah, but it's the middle of the night there."

They sat silently, studying the screen, Sylvia occasionally returning to her display to monitor TELNET.

"It's really up to the North to do all the financial data banks. The South will barely have time to deal with intelligence," Olina reminded Sylvia, who was waiting longer and longer intervals to return to her display, preferring to watch face after face slowly appear on Ellen's screen, then quickly print out as Olina collected each one, stacking them neatly on the desk beside her.

Thirty minutes into the printing, Ellen gasped, "Oh, I knew it!"

"Who is she?" Sylvia looked up from her terminal, studying the face on the display in front of Ellen.

"Don't you remember? Well, no, you wouldn't have seen her. She came to a general meeting, three or four of them, in Oakland last fall. Actually, I didn't know. I just thought she was kind of a bitch, a snob."

"That's not much to go on." Olina frowned. Would she see Shelly's face? Something still told her, promised her, no, she wouldn't. But had she trusted too soon? That morning on the plane a week ago, her instinct had served her right, yes, give Shelly the tapes. But then, in fact, she may have gotten through with them herself after all. But yet, she may not have, and then she wouldn't have had them at the conference, wouldn't have been able to give them to the Latin American Allies, those tapes that were so central to their action now, in Panama, Honduras . . . She studied the display, slowly taking each printout as it emerged from the Facs.

At 10:30 the telephone rang. The three of them started, looking at one another. It did not ring again. Only the sound of the Facs machine printing, printing, filled the small room.

"It's Diana."

The telephone rang again. Sylvia picked it up.

"Michael?" a voice asked.

"Yes."

"Happy New Year."

"Thanks."

Sylvia hung up the phone. "Let's go. We've got to go."

Ellen and Olina quickly packed up the printouts, shutting off the terminals after Sylvia had checked the last file code printed. She dialed the phone, gripping the receiver in her gloved hand. "David? Is the party over? No? Well let me tell you my New Year's resolutions."

"Hurry, Sylvia."

She glanced at Olina, who nodded, and then said quickly, "Pick it up at RP7-843-598." She hung up. "They'll get the rest at Alcoa."

Sylvia glanced back at the room as they were leaving. Everything was exactly as they had found it. They hurried to the stairwell just outside the office suite, the three of them running down the steps as Sylvia couldn't help but think of the day she had raced down these same stairs, alone, terrified. It was odd—today they were doing it, had done it, the ACTION, and she felt, really, she had never felt calmer in her life.

In the lobby, the guard still sat in his chair, his head leaning back against the wall, his eyes closed. They had had to drug him when they had first arrived, Olina jabbing the needle into his thigh the instant he had opened the glass door in response to their pleading and motioning outside as, recognizing Sylvia, he had come to see what on earth all the commotion was about. It had taken less than a minute. Now they took his electronic key from his pocket, opened the door and, throwing the key on the sidewalk, they ran quickly around the corner and up California Street to Montgomery. Susan sat in a black Datsun at the corner, the engine running. They jumped into the car and headed north.

"I hope to god Laura and Gwen got all the 'subversive' files and access keys deleted, even if they can't get the rest of the agent profiles for us," Sylvia said, pealing off her surgical gloves.

"They must've by now, it's 10:45," Ellen answered.

"What happened?" Olina asked Susan.

"I'm not sure. Diana just buzzed me on the TelCom and told me to pick you up. I think she's with Jim again. She must have found out they'd changed shifts. Did you have any problems?"

"No. It was fine. Though we did have to wait an hour to get on, we didn't finish. But hopefully Gwen and Laura can do the rest. They just have to keep on DECNET. There were several nodes free and, by now especially, most of the Allies will have finished."

"Did Shelly and Karen get the offset press?"

"Yes, this morning. We're all ready."

"Great!"

They were quiet as they wove through the stark, empty streets of the financial district, the tall, looming buildings like silent tombs without the pulse of thronging workers that Sylvia, Ellen, all of them, were so familiar with. Susan turned off Stockton onto Broadway, and within minutes they were on the Bay Bridge. Yes, for them, this part, was almost complete.

The beep of Susan's TelCom gave them a start. Ellen laughed as Susan answered. It was Ruth. What? Her voice was fuzzy. Something about Chela, a report. Tegucigalpa, San Salvador, Guatemala City, Panama City, all were complete. One hundred percent success. Even beyond to military data banks. Absolutely no incidents or injuries. Similar reports from the East. Congratulations! Hurry home! The voice was gone.

The four women, suddenly as one, let out a jubilant cry, whooping as they sped across the nearly empty bridge, the bright morning sun shining on the blues and greens of the choppy bay beneath.

Within 15 hours of the moment the Action had started over ten million posters were displayed on the walls, in the streets, of over 700 cities and towns throughout the world. The faces, names, addresses of thousands of CIA agents and informers, DINA, MOSSAD, BOSS, KGB, FBI, every secret police agency's leadership, middle command and supporting network of agents had their faces splashed, life-size, throughout the cities that had hidden them for so many years. On the Avenida Reduicas of Sao Paulo and Makhsus Road in Tehran, on Chuo Kosoku Doro in Tokyo and Heidelberg Road in Johannesburg, in Poto Mpila in Brazzaville and on Taft Avenida in Manila, in Wangsim-ni in Seoul and Baranagar in Calcutta, on Moskovskijin in Leningrad and Fifth Avenue in New York, on the Champs-Elysées in Paris and on Leichardt in Sydney, in Djakarta, Hong Kong, Jerusalem, Lima, Stockholm, Athens, Reykjavik, Los Angeles, Cairo, Vienna, Bombay—every urban center of the world woke to new faces in the news, as the Empire, unmasked, isolated, knew nothing.

Epilogue

Snow still lay thick in the west Georgia hills, and though it had been cleared from the parking lot of the General Motors Plant, all but the most carefully maintained cars carried two or three inches of the dense white powder on their roofs, hoods and trunks from the late-night storm. In the administrative offices of the production complex, Steven sat at his desk on this, his first morning as Assistant Manager to the Second Vice-President of Production. His function, as he had begun to understand it or as Martin Lobes, his old roommate from college who sat less than 50 feet away at his own desk now, had vaguely explained it, was to advise the production management staff on the feasibility of increased production methods within the context of pushing regulations to whatever the limits of the law would bear. At the same time he was to develop "a rapport" with the assembly workers in order to field their complaints and analyze the legalities before they came to the attention of the union or, when they did come to the union's attention, to provide the appropriate inside information to the corporation's attorneys. It was a muddied, murky role, the extent of which he had yet to fully comprehend. But when he had run into Martin in an Atlanta bar New Year's Eve and said he was looking for work—well, yes, he'd said it, he was desperate for work—and Martin had given him his card, he'd waited only a day, then called, and, within the week, he'd been hired.

He strained his eyes, still slightly swollen, tired. He'd been up half the night watching the flurries of snow from the aluminum-framed window of his studio apartment, and now the charts and graphs of the production report before him blurred, fairly swam, as he wondered if he might not need glasses, his stomach churning with its usual morning tension, and he fought off the impulse to leap up from his desk and run, flee, race from the building, the complex to . . . Where? His company car in the parking lot?

He stood up from the desk, straightening the grey jacket of his new suit, and mumbling something about checking the line to the secretary on the other side of the Plexiglass partition, he headed toward the plant cafeteria.

The morning break had just begun and over a hundred workers were plugging change into the vending machines or standing in line with steaming cups of coffee, donuts, sweet rolls, as the cashier processed them with an amazing rapidity. Steven loosened his tie at his throat, unbuttoning the top button of his shirt. He felt ridiculous as he rammed two quarters into the slot of the plastic paneled machine and waited for a can of Coke to thud down the chute. With a glance around at the rows of long formica tables and the scowls, jibes and banter of the workers, he sauntered to a nearby table and, pulling out an orange plastic chair, he sat down, alone.

A group of seven or eight men, scraping steel chair legs across the linoleum floor, noisily seated themselves a few feet from him.

"No, I swear, I saw it on TV," a young bearded man insisted.

"Naw. That's shit."

"No, man, listen. They said that's how come the war's over in Salvador, and the Communists won. They're winnin' all over the place."

"Yeah, it's fuckin' weird, man," a short, stocky man nodded. "In Nicaragua all our troops are comin' back, man, my brother got sent home two days ago. He said the CIA's pullin' out, too. They're actin' all fucked up."

"Well, Nicaragua's been Communist for a long time," an older man informed them.

"They say they're not," a dark young man began.

"Hey South Africa, too, man," a tall black man added. "It ain't Communist—SWAPO—but they winnin' now, big."

"Yeah hey, I saw that. It's in the paper. About a million or somethin' whites leavin' there. Goin' back to Europe where they come from," a shorter black man next to him agreed.

"Or comin' here."

"No, listen," a pale blonde man leaned forward, "it's Poland where it's at, man. Solidarity's on the move again, I saw it on the news last night. There's millions of 'em in the streets. They're just about to fuckin' take over, man. Kick those fuckin' Russians out. They've got *power*, brother."

"Yeah, but South Africa, they goin' to get rid of those racists, now," the taller black man answered. "Mozambique, Namibia, they all together now, Zimbabwe—talkin' about a socialist union."

"Socialists! That's who they want to get the fuck *out* of Poland, man!"

"No, man, it's the *Russians* they tryin' to get rid of."

"I don't know," the older man interjected, his face drawn in a morose frown that belied the jaunty cap set high on his forehead. "I think things are goin' crazy all of a sudden. All the news these last days, just since New Years all of a sudden—the world's gone crazy. I've never seen it like this. Even WW II, it wasn't . . ."

"That's what I'm tryin' to tell you!" the young bearded man finally broke in again. "My girlfriend, she was watchin' TV last night, somethin' on cable, some program about how computers—computers

Mother Courage Press

In addition to *NEWS* by Heather Conrad, Mother Courage Press also publishes

Why Me? Help for victims of child sexual abuse (even if they are adults now) by Lynn B. Daugherty. This book was written to be read by survivors of child sexual abuse who are now teenagers or adults. It is also intended for counselors or other people who want to understand and help these survivors. It was chosen for the Editors Choice Award for Young Adults in 1986 by the American Library Association's publication, *booklist*. Its reviewer wrote, "Emphasizing the responsibility of the abuser, the fact that abuse is a widespread experience, and the dynamics of an abusive situation, Daugherty begins the process of healing psychological wounds."
Paperback, (112 pages) $7.95

Something Happened to Me by Phyllis Sweet. This is a sensitive, straightforward book designed to help children victimized by incest or other sexual abuse. A reviewer for *Young Children,* the Official Journal of the National Association for the Education of Young Children, wrote, "The marvelous introduction and epilogue are written for adults and reveal the extraordinary care that the author, a school psychologist, has taken to assure the dignity and self-worth of children from troubled families."
Paperback, Illustrated, 8-1/2 by 11, (36 pages) $4.95

Fear or Freedom, a Woman's Options in Social Survival and Physical Defense, by Susan E. Smith. The Library Journal called this book "an important new approach to self-defense for women . . . (Smith) points out, for instance, that acquaintance rape is by far the most prevalent kind; it operates under different assumptions than stranger rape, and should be the easiest type of assault to combat. However, women are too often prevented from resisting strongly (although many do resist successfully) because of conditioning that makes them feel responsible for men's behaviour in social situations. . . A reassuring work, refreshingly lacking the emphasis on technical expertise. Highly

recommended." *Fear or Freedom* is an empowering, personal growth and life-expanding book. The author's dynamic style and careful scholarship and research make the book not merely a self-defense manual but a social and psychological study of the dynamics of violence, rape and attack.
Paperback, Illustrated, 8-1/2 by 11, (224 pages) $11.95

Coming in late 1987, *Rebirth of Power, Overcoming the Effects of Sexual Abuse Through the Experiences of Others* edited by Michele Gorcey, Pamela Portwood and Peggy Sanders. This book seeks to shatter the silence which preserves and condones sexual violence in our society and break the stereotypes and illusions surrounding sexual assault. Those most qualified to address the issue share the knowledge they have gained at painful prices. The survivors are the ones who know what it means to be raped by a relative, friend or stranger. They know what a lifetime of silence about incest can do to a person's psyche. Theirs are the voices which can compel us to understand, to care and to do something about sexual violence.
Paperback

Also from Mother Courage Press

Rowdy and Laughing by B. L. Holmes. These poems encompassing the joy of life and being in love were written during the initial turbulence of the author's love affair with another woman.
Paperback, (99 pages) $4.95

Watch for more bibliotherapeutic books for healing and helping, novels, biographies and poetry with a feminist perspective from Mother Courage Press.

If you don't find them in your local book store, you may order books directly from Mother Courage Press at 1533 Illinois Street, Racine, WI 53405. Please add $1.50 for postage and handling for the first book and $.50 for each additional book.

at, like, the FBI, and KGB, and CIA—and all these police computers all over the world had got messed up, and those posters all over . . ."

"A big short circuit, huh? Come on, kid, their stuff don't mess up like that," the stocky man sneered.

"No! That's the thing, they're sayin' a lot of women did it."

"Hah! Hahha!" The men burst into laughter, slapping their thighs, that's a good one. It made their day.

"Hey! Listen. It was on TV!"

"Fuckin' A, so's Disney World, kid."

"No, listen, some of 'em got caught, in Germany or somewhere, a bunch of women. Right on New Year's Day. They had these masks and gloves on, and they snuck into this big bank or some building with a great big old computer, and they were messin' around with it, pluggin' it into all these other computers . . ."

"Listen to this guy!"

"No, hey, man, listen. They said all these companies got their computers messed up and they won't admit it and they paid off all these newspapers to keep it quiet, but it's starting to leak out. Secretaries or something are starting to . . ."

"Horseshit!"

"No, and they said there's this big organization of women, all over the world! Yeah! Really! The Women's International something."

"Hahah!" The laughter started again as the pale blonde man leaned forward. "No, wait a minute," he began. "Forget this shit about the broads — but maybe there is somethin' wrong with all the computers, you know? Didn't they tell us the computer was down Monday, on pay day? They had this whole fuckin' crew of accountants or whatever in there makin' up our checks, remember? We had to fill out those forms."

"Yeah."

"And my old lady had the same thing happen at the phone company, she works over to the phone company."

"Well, yeah, my bank really fucked up my stuff bad the other day when I was down there."

"Yeah? Mine too."

"Anh, those computers are always fuckin' up."

"No, man, listen though. If we all had some fuck-up cuz of the bank's or the company's computer or somethin', just in the last week—I've heard other guys talkin' about it too—haven't you guys?"

"Well, yeah, I have," the older man conceded as one by one, each of the men nodded, agreeing. It was strange, weird.

"See!" The young bearded man grinned, validated. "That's what they were sayin', and all these computers all over the world are messed up and Wall Street's goin' crazy and everything. You wait and see, it'll be in the papers, if they let it. All the banks in the fuckin' world are completely fucked up! And a *bunch of women* did it!"

"Naw!"

"Yeah! And they don't know where any of 'em are, either. Just these ones in Munich or somewhere, and somewhere else, Japan or somewhere. And that's why all this stuff's happenin' in South America and Africa and everywhere else, cuz the police, and the military and secret police and all, are all fucked up, cuz all those posters all over town were their secret agents."

"Hunh? That's fuckin' nuts."

"Yeah, but if they don't know where all the broads are, they can't nuke 'em, huh?" The stocky man laughed, not believing a word of it.

"Yeah, but that's bullcrap. It's not a bunch a chicks."

"Naw. It's the fuckin' Commies!" There was a fierce tension in the pale, blonde man's voice.

"No, listen. It happened in Russia too. *Everywhere.* The whole goddamn world," the young bearded man insisted.

"I don't buy it, kid." The short stocky man stood up from the table crumpling his Coke can in his hand. The others followed, scraping their chairs back across the linoleum, still laughing, though some were quiet, taking the story half-seriously now as they headed out of the cafeteria.

Steven sat motionless, bent forward in his chair, his hand gripping his can of Coke on the table. Women's International. All over the world. Christ. It couldn't be. He saw Sylvia's face, that last morning in San Francisco, that desperate, earnest look. "You are under surveillance . . . the letter to Claire . . . can't tell you more." Jesus Christ! He took a gulp of his Coke, then held it still in his hand. Maybe she wasn't crazy. Hysterical. Maybe it was true. Maybe it was the goddamn, fucking truth. What was this TV show? How could he see it? He looked up at where the men had sat. Christ. What's going on! He hadn't seen a newspaper in a fucking week. Maybe the world was going crazy. Maybe those letters *were* from the FBI. Maybe Sylvia was telling him the goddamn truth! Linda would know, she . . . Linda.

He let himself think of her. Finally, he let his mind dwell on her, without the stroke of the white brush, he let the image of Linda fill his mind, hearing the sound of her crying, sobbing as he'd left the flat that morning, the day he'd left her. Linda. The beautiful smile on her face, the black hair waving back from her face as she'd looked at him that day, the day he'd stopped drinking. Linda, holding Justin, his son who he hardly knew now. His family. He stood up from the table and walked out of the cafeteria, through the complex, to his company car in the lot.